# "ALL EMBRACE
# WITH ME. NOW!"

Colors dimmed to sepia and then darker. The air thickened, muffling all sound.

From behind, something struck Luke a solid, massive blow. In growing dimness, shapes wavered and vanished until only hints of movement remained, shifting and passing, slowly at first but then streaming past at a rate too fleet for recognition. Breathing became an ever-greater effort, like trying to take in and expel some strange, bland, heavily viscous fluid. Consciousness wavered, then held at less than fullness.

What this felt like, Luke decided, was swimming down a big river of breathable molasses.

*To where?*

# ISLANDS
# OF
# TOMORROW

# F.M. BUSBY

AVON BOOKS • NEW YORK

**In memory of my mother and dad,
who taught me early to love a good story.**

ISLANDS OF TOMORROW is an original publication of Avon Books. This work has never before appeared in book form. This work is a novel. Any similarity to actual persons or events is purely coincidental.

AVON BOOKS
A division of
The Hearst Corporation
1350 Avenue of the Americas
New York, New York 10019

Copyright © 1994 by F.M. Busby
Cover art by J. K. Potter
Published by arrangement with the author
Library of Congress Catalog Card Number: 93-91661
ISBN: 0-380-77231-0

First AvoNova Printing: February 1994

AVONOVA TRADEMARK REG. U.S. PAT. OFF. AND IN OTHER COUNTRIES, MARCA REGISTRADA, HECHO EN U.S.A.

Printed in the U.S.A.

RA 10 9 8 7 6 5 4 3 2 1

# ONE

**C**asey hadn't been gone five minutes, rushing to her next class, when Rozak barged into Lucian Tabor's small apartment. Mostly dressed, Luke was tying his second shoe.

From the living room Rozak yelled, "Hey! Where the hell are you?" And as Tabor came out of the bedroom, "You sleeping afternoons now? Or do you have company?"

"I did have. Can't you ever knock?"

"The door isn't locked." The lean intruder gave his best innocent grin. Locks didn't stop Jay Rozak; if a credit card wouldn't slip him past one, he'd use something else. "Who was it? Little ol' K.C.? I like her."

Maybe so, but Karen Cecile wouldn't have appreciated being caught in Luke's bed. Tabor shrugged; no point in fretting over what hadn't happened. "All right, Jay; what is it?"

"The demonstration tonight. Are you in?"

"I said I was. Though I'm not sure why." Luke Tabor was here at Washington State University working toward his doctorate in physics—well, first the master's degree—with a part-time teaching assistant job to pay the rent; student protests weren't his kind of thing. Nor was Ol' Wazoo, an enclave of Academe in the farming country of the Palouse hills, much of a place for such doings. Even though the school's enrollment nearly matched the full-time resident population of Pullman, WA 99163.

But one Friday night, he and Casey unwinding over a couple of pitchers, Rusty's Tavern downtown got too crowded for normal semiprivacy. And among the four extra people who came to sit at their table was Jay Rozak, older and articulate and persuasive.

Tabor didn't know which of Jay's stories—if any—bore much resemblance to fact. The army service, probably; Luke had been subjected to a few months of that himself, called up with the reserves at the time of the Caracas Incident. And the combat duty; Tabor hadn't been posted to any action zone but he'd heard enough to spot pure bull, and on that topic Rozak sounded factual. The secret agent stuff, though (NatSecAgency, the army's CID, or whatever), he rated doubtful.

No doubt, though, that Rozak had put some time in, down LatAm way. Nor that the leathertanned redhead knew how to move and shake things. At Rusty's that night it was obvious that he and his three companions formed the core cadre of a *sub rosa* campus group none of them actually named. By the time Luke and Casey left, brewed-up enough to need the long walk up College Hill to burn the load off, they had somehow, wordlessly, been enlisted as spearbearers in a cause never clearly stated. Rozak wasn't a political science major for nothing.

Over the past weeks they had attended four loud, somewhat confusing meetings. But until now, until this plan to raise halftime hell with national holovid coverage of Wazoo's season-ending Apple Cup game, its traditional cross-state gridiron rivalry with the larger University of Washington, Luke hadn't been asked to put anything on the line. Now, though . . .

Irritably he said, "Yes, I'm in. Was that all you wanted?"

Taking Luke's own favorite chair, Rozak sat. "You have any beer in the fridge?"

"One." The syllable closed that subject. "I was going to make coffee. Want some?"

"If that's your best offer."

Tabor busied himself until dark brown fluid seeped from the cone-shaped filter into an old fruit jar. "Cream or anything?"

"Sidearms? No, thanks." Accepting the cup, Jay said, "What do you think of this Derion guy?"

"I don't know." Derion—first name, or last?—had shown up only a couple of days ago, representing a U. of W. group similar to Rozak's and offering cooperation. A quiet type for the most part; when he did say something, people seemed to pay attention. Maybe that's what was bothering Rozak now. Luke said, "What do you mean?"

"The way he goes around, giving advice like a volunteer scoutmaster."

"What kind of advice?"

"Beats me." Rozak shook his head. "But he always has a hand on somebody's shoulder, him talking and them nodding, and they come away looking like they've decided something."

"Have you asked? Derion? Anyone?"

"Hell no. What's to ask? Pardon me, but is this guy trying to sell you something in the line of Brand X?" At Tabor's frown, he added, "Brand X? The competition. Before your time, maybe."

"I've heard of it." Rozak's disquiet wasn't getting anything done. Luke said, "Look; he says he's the advance man for a U-Dub contingent, wanting to help out. What else *would* he be selling?"

"Damifino." Jay shrugged. "The main thing is, if the cops move to break us up tonight, everybody just lie down and stay put."

Rozak grinned. "It'll play great on the eleven o'clock news."

The demonstration's targets were the governor and state legislature. As Luke's uncle Burnie liked to put it, that gang could really frost your potato.

Just now it was the Misery Taxes. Some bloc or other was always trying to hang a levy on people's distress: medical bills including prescription drugs, legal fees, insurance premiums and/or claims, tuition costs, *funeral* expenses for Chris'sake, as well as services in general—if you tipped a waiter, you'd pay sales tax on the same tip the recipient reported as taxable income. And a new law gave the state access to all electronic fund-transfer records, to collect tax on out-of-state purchases.

The principle was simple enough: any time a dollar shows its face, grab some of it. Washington's state sales tax, highest in the nation, was periodically legislated onto basic food sales and then removed via the referendum process by outraged citizens.

The trouble was that most politicians were lawyers and most voters weren't. It was like a pickup team going against the Lakers.

This time, encouraged by newly elected Governor Roger Axelson, the legislature was putting together the worst Misery Tax package yet, slapping an emergency clause onto it, and surrounding it with nitpicking restrictions to block or hinder voter repeal. Their excuse was that with the state's economy slumping, the revenue base had to be extended. When Mitsuboeing lost the BOAC scramjet order to Airbus Industrie, and fifteen thousand jobs along with it, Axelson sent up flares. On both sides of the aisle, taxminded legislators rallied to him.

Not many average citizens did, though. And at Wash State U there existed a fervent, though minor, center of organized resentment against this particular indignity. For one thing, the buggers were going to tax tuition.

So what made tonight the time to speak up? This year the Apple Cup carried a major prize: whoever won, WSU Cougars or UW Huskies, the winner had a clear lock on the Rose Bowl.

So the game had been rescheduled from afternoon to evening for the benefit of network holovid, and Governor Axelson would be on hand to speak at halftime.

As Jay Rozak said, if they hand it to you on a platter, don't drop it.

Being low boy on the Department totem pole, Lucian had drawn the Saturday afternoon lab section. So he had to shoo Rozak out and then make tracks, to get across campus on time. Students appreciated the Saturday schedule no more than he did; his section held only eighteen: eleven male, seven female. Luckily the Department paid by the hour, not per head.

Proceeding more or less on automatic, Tabor fell into his habitual self-scrutinizing reverie: "Get your head out of your navel!" was a frequent admonition of Casey's.

But he couldn't help it. Living as an only child on a small farm (too hilly and diverse for agribusiness methods), seeing other children only rarely throughout his preschool years, socially he'd always felt several jumps behind his classmates. Being sick in bed for most of the summer he was nine hadn't helped. Even now, some (though not all) of his early loner tendencies still persisted.

One was the habit of analyzing everything he did: trying to compare, to see if his actions made sense in other people's terms. His conclusions seldom reassured him, but like a tongue to a chipped tooth, his mind couldn't leave such things alone.

Just now, he puzzled over Casey. Was he really adequate with her on a mature social level, or would her attachment to him fade when the novelty went? While in the back of his thoughts, the coming demonstration stirred anxieties.

When he reached and entered the building, the dash up two flights of stairs pretty well cleared his mind for business.

Sixteen of his eighteen were present in the lab. Harbin, he supposed, was still out with the flu, and Krieg was chronically late. So, "Afternoon, class. We'll get right to it." He tried to show more confidence than he felt, because he knew he didn't give much of a professional impression. His voice, though probably pleasant enough, was too light to carry any great authority. His brush-resistant cowlick, large ears, and roundish face made him look younger than some of his students.

*Oh, well* ... Today's experiment concerned measurement of electrical impedances using a modified Wheatstone Bridge method. Accordingly, he began plugging up four setups and divided the group into working teams. Lee Krieg arrived just in time to be fifth wheel at table C.

This class wasn't Physics One, the stiff five-credit regimen designed for science and engineering majors; Physics Seven carried only four credits and required no use of the calculus. Basically, Tabor knew, it was a slightly souped-up high school course, for liberal arts majors who needed a few science credits. He was lucky enough to have two, maybe three, bright lights in this section, but the majority glowed at about five watts.

And five-watters were given to dry-labbing, to comparing results between teams, to avoiding real work at all costs. So after telling the class to read the instructions in the Lab Workbook, Luke blithely set up his four Bridges with totally different values, and each with unequal arms. Likewise, every "unknown" was different—and, of course, quite innocent of label or color coding. When he was done he had no idea what the "right answers" were. After the teams were finished, he'd do quick balance checks on each setup and make his own calculations. For every one of the five rounds he was putting them through.

"All right, class. Experiment Seventeen—it's all yours." And Luke sat back to finish a lab report of his own while he waited for the inevitable uninformed questions.

First to approach him was Alycia Frazier. Silently, Tabor groaned. It wasn't that Alycia was stupid; as near as he could tell, she simply felt that cuddly-looking blondes shouldn't have to study, so she would come around and lay erotic hints on him instead. Nonverbally, of course. He didn't give thought to whether she would actually deliver, because he wasn't interested. Aside from the marginal ethics of student-teacher dating at the lab assistant level, Casey Collins was as much puzzle as he was up to.

As Alycia began, "Mr. Tabor, I don't understand how any of this can balance when everything seems to be different," he noticed something odd. From a little distance he'd assumed that she had for some reason arranged her hair lopsidedly; now he saw that on the left side it was drastically shortened, not at all artfully. The term "scraggly" came to mind.

His automatic response, "If you'll read page twenty-two again—" faltered. Without thinking, he said, "What—?"

She colored. Behind her, waiting to ask what would probably be an equally mindless question, Bruce Garner giggled. "Chem lab, this morning. She was heating her sample with two gas burners, and pulled one hose loose without turning it off first."

He gestured. *"Whoosh!"*

Alycia glared. "Everybody's been doing it that way! I—"

"But not with two burners sitting close together," Luke said. By main effort he kept his face straight. "Bad luck." And then, "Page twenty-two, Frazier."

He wasn't worried about her temporary disfigurement. By tomorrow at the latest, he guessed, she would have the ravaged area trimmed to look purposefully stylish, and within the week a number of other girls would be imitating her "look."

Bruce Garner's question had a real point; his team's galvanometer barely moved, no matter what. Luke found that someone had left the shunt-selector switch on a high-voltage position. Any serious student would have found the problem and taken care of it. But what would a serious student be doing taking Physics Seven?

Tabor was glad when Lab was over. Of the four teams, he found that two had done reasonably well. The one he thought of as Alycia's had obviously dry-labbed, copying parts of their readings from each of the groups making an honest effort; even his sketchy checkup made the subterfuge glaringly obvious. After a brief spurt of anger, Luke shrugged. He could give the team members a D, which he'd probably have to justify when they complained to Fitzhugh, the lab prof.

On the other hand, why bother?

The group that included Bruce Garner had taken their readings honestly, then somehow screwed up royally on the calculations. Tabor was surprised. Most of this team were lightweights, but Garner himself majored in genetic engineering and had a fairly systematic turn of mind.

On a quick look, Luke didn't spot where they'd gone wrong, but their answer was off by nearly two decimal places. The initial measurements looked reasonable, though, so he gave them a break. "Garner, you folks take your workbooks home with you. Sometime during the weekend, start from your experimental data and recalculate the results."

One of Garner's lab partners wanted to know why they should have to do all that extra work. Tabor gave him the Parade Ground Stare. "Because somewhere between your galvo readings and your final results, you made a mistake that will give you an F for this week if you don't."

At least Alycia Frazier hadn't made a second run at him. As the class left, Lucian locked the lab behind him and headed for home. Mentally he was in a hurry, but his blood sugar level wouldn't cooperate.

Luckily the walk was mostly downhill.

As he'd hoped, Casey was there to greet him. But instead of a lounging robe she wore going-out garb, with her hair coiled in party mode, and showed no sign of romance in the offing. She stood, though, five-six stretched against his five-ten, and gave a thoroughly satisfactory kiss. Then, pushing light copper curls back off her forehead, she said, "Jay's throwing a chili feed; I've made a bale of salad to take. Big powwow with some of Derion's U-Dub people." She looked at her watch. "You have time for a shower."

His expression must have told her something; she said, "You feel up to it, don't you?"

How Luke felt about it was "Oh, shit!" but he didn't say that sort of thing in mixed company. "I'll get ready."

In New York, Jay Rozak's place would most likely have been called a loft. On the western slope of College Hill, above the steep drop to the valley that held railroad tracks, a creek, and the Palouse highway, a onetime fraternity house had been converted to rental units. Above two floors of more usual apartments, Jay's area included what had been the major sleeping dorm; adjacent, a toilet-with-lav and two small study rooms had become a real bathroom and a kitchenette.

Entrance was at the rear, sharing a flight of stairs with the second-floor apartments. At the foot of a second flight, its doors standing open on this late afternoon, Rozak's Afran roomie Carla Duvai handed the newcomers each a flyer and flashed them a friendly grin. "Go on up. I see you brought the greens."

Hefting the large clear plastic bag of tossed salad, Casey smiled back. "Enough to feed a rabbit farm."

They walked up to the landing at the rear of the third floor and turned to enter Jay's main room. A long space with its ceiling angling down at either side, it was not well-lighted; the only windows were a couple of dormers at the far end, the front of the house, and aside from a pair of fluorescent fixtures mounted along the ceiling's long axis, only a few floor and wall lamps lit the large space. Smudged, nondescript grey-brown paint failed to add any cheering note, and three vivid holoposters were clearly outvoted by the rest of the place.

The thirty or so students present didn't seem especially subdued by the decor; to the contrary, the room felt charged with nervous excitement Tabor could neither ignore nor resist. Aside from a quartet sitting on the huge futon at the far right corner, they stood talking in groups, quite ignoring the dozen or so miscellaneous chairs. Traffic centered around a table flanked by two desks, all of which held food and drink. There Casey deposited her bag of salad. Saying "I'll look in the kitchen for a bowl or something," she left Luke to his own devices.

First he rooted in the tub of ice until he found a beer. Not just any beer, but a product of one of the state's own microbreweries. Unlike most of the nationally advertised brands, local beers and ales had real flavor. He peeled away the plastic top and took a long, satisfying swallow.

Then he looked for his host. Sure enough, in the middle of the largest group of talkers he spotted Jay, hands and jaw all moving in discussion mode. Tabor moved over to say hello.

Rozak saw him coming. "Hey. Chili in a little while. For now, plenty of horses' d'ovaries on the table. Come over and meet—" So Luke said hello to some he'd already met and was introduced to the rest, hoping he could remember the names five minutes from now but knowing he probably wouldn't.

He was saying something profoundly trite to a serious young woman who seemed to be paying real attention, when the overall sound level dropped near to quiet while the air of excitement somehow calmed to a more comfortable level. Stopping in midsentence, Luke saw that everyone was looking past, to the door behind him.

He turned to see for himself. Six persons had entered. Two of them were of striking appearance. One of these was Derion from the U.W. contingent, and the other wasn't.

He'd seen Derion before, of course; the fellow was about Luke's height but built more strongly, maybe twenty pounds over his own lanky one-sixty, and much of it obviously muscle. And besides the uncanny *presence* that became the automatic focus of any group's attention, plus a way of moving like a lazy cat, he had the kind of dark, lean handsomeness which, unless tempered by a disarming personality, could easily be resented by plain-looking folks like Luke Tabor. So far, Luke was on the fence. But no doubt about it, the guy was a natural takeover type; he didn't even have to *do* anything.

The woman, now. She seemed vaguely familiar but he was sure they hadn't met; if they had, he'd know it. Top to bottom he scanned: oval face framed by abundant black hair falling well below her shoulders, bosom a bit emphatic for the slim body, long elegant legs, the whole package perhaps two inches less than his own height. No, he couldn't have seen her before. But still . . .

He knew he was staring, began to look away. But Derion beckoned, and called to him. "Lucian Tabor, isn't it? Come here, would you please? Vivi wants to say hello."

When he didn't move, Derion's brows raised. "You remember Vivi, don't you? Vivi LaFleur?"

After a moment the name clicked; of *course* he'd seen her face. On magazine covers touting the new holo star of vid and cineplex. But they'd never met; how could they? So why—?

Undirected, his feet took him to face her and Derion. She reached out a hand and he took it. "Uh—pleased—"

She laughed. "You don't remember, do you?" He shook his head, and watched her widemouthed smile twist. "I guess your memory has no room for leftovers."

"Leftovers?" *Ohmigod!* Back at Lewis Gap High, that had been the clandestine, derisive nickname for plain, awkward Vivian Lefebre. Luke had never used it himself; feeling sorry for the girl, he'd always tried to be courteous to her. It was a distant courtesy, though; no adolescent could afford schoolmates' jeers linking him to the School Bowwow. But—could this woman be—?

Just then Casey joined the three; Luke stumbled through introductions and then, confused, let Derion steer all of them to chairs alongside the desk with the drinks, where the U.W. emissary offered him a tall glass of fluid with ice in it. One look told him it was Jay's idea of "punch"—lab alcohol thinned down by cheap mix—and that he wanted no part of it. "I'll stick with beer; thanks."

Wanting to tell Casey what was happening, but realizing the briefing would have to wait, he looked again at Vivi LaFleur.

Could she really be Vivian Lefebre? Given a dental bridge replacing the worst buck teeth he'd ever seen, a nose job and chin augmentation, some kind of depilation to raise the hairline and widen the forehead now shaded by fashionable cobweb bangs, collagen injections to give fullness to thin lips—maybe she could. Now that he thought back, the dark eyes and arched eyebrows and slanted cheekbones had been fine all along—but as part of the original face they'd been overmatched.

Setting her own glass down while maintaining a non-committal expression, Vivi leaned forward. Low neckline and all. Lefebre women, as Luke recalled, seldom showed bustlines except when pregnant or nursing; he was facing Silicone Valley.

Embarrassed, he looked up to meet her eyes. After thirty silent seconds that felt like an hour, what to say? "You're, uh, *looking* well." Dumb, dumb, dumb! "Uh—what are you doing, these days?" Even dumber. *"Here,* I mean."

"Adding a little hoopla to halftime tonight." Pleasure showed in her face. "I'm a local success story, you see. I put in two quarters here at Wazoo—you were doing something dismal with the army, I think—and finished up in drama at the U-Dub, before I went through factory recall." She gestured toward her face. "I'm toward the end of a promo tour, personal appearances pushing my newest feature holo, and Derion wangled me into doing a brief spot this evening at halftime, alongside the governor."

Derion's face showed nothing but bland. Vivi's smile would have shamed an angel; she said, "He wants to sugarcoat his tax package, sell it to the public. But I'll be introducing him. And I'm going to shoot the bastard right out of the water."

Vivian Lefebre's personality had been understandably dour; Vivi LaFleur's was quite, quite different. After everyone lined up for chili call, she and Derion and Luke and Casey regained their original table. Vivi said, "Do you ever want to go back to Lewis Gap, Tabor, and kick sand in somebody's face?"

"Er—no. Do you?" *Like mine, for instance?*

"Not in yours." She hadn't really read his mind; the inference had been obvious. She said, "I always felt you treated me as well as you dared. Though of course you weren't around when I caught all the crap for getting pregnant, and my own family threw me out. But the people I really hated—" She shrugged. "For revenge, how could I top simply being *me?*"

Luke nodded. "Strikes me as a winner." He thought back: the pregnancy must have occurred after he left Lewis Gap. Yes, some scandal rag had hinted at a miscarriage in Vivi LaFleur's past. But that was routine hatchet on female celebrities. . . .

Jay had supercharged Carla's chili to at least four-star rating; Luke exhausted his first beer and went for a replacement. Casey tagged along, giving him the opportunity to say, "I was in high school with that woman, but she's changed totally."

"Why, she seems nice enough."

"That's not what I meant. Back then, we're talking Gladys Gunchbutt; now she's world-class. *And* big on holo."

They got back to the table. Vivi was speaking. "—so then I say that now he's going to tax the only thing the legislature left out of the package: his own credibility." She laughed. "You like it?"

Jay certainly did. Frowning, Luke said, "Don't think I'm not appreciative of what you're doing—but couldn't this hurt your career?"

Brows rising, she paused. "Bedamned; Tabor, you've stayed human, of all things. You're concerned about *me?*"

"Well, I just—" Why did he feel foolish?

She put a hand on his, then belatedly looked to Casey's reaction. Apparently reassured, she left the hand where it was. "That's good of you. But dinna fash thaself, laddie—" The brogue, quickly affected, was dropped as easily. "I'd do this if it *did* get me in trouble. But it won't. These days a performer needs more than professional notice; we need hooks into the real world, my agent says. And this one—I haven't checked with him but I know he'll love it. Hey, I'm standing up against Big Greedy Gov'ment, on behalf of the Littul Peepul."

She shrugged. "How can it lose?"

Finished with serving chili, Jay Rozak pulled a chair over and joined the group. "Everybody get enough to eat?" Without waiting for answers, he said, "Derion—Luke—there's a slight change in procedure. So I don't have to pick the tunnel gate lock and flimflam Security, I've arranged to substitute a program leaflet that officially *lists* the Flag Brigade as the guv's honor guard during his speech. The band marches around until he's driven in on his speaker's float; we wait and go out on the field while the band's coming off. Through the same gate." He looked around the table. "Everybody got it?"

Luke nodded; Derion said, "But have we time to inform all concerned?"

Rozak grinned. "It starts out the same; we all get there early and sandbag Section C, the front rows. *Then* we pass the word, that at the start of halftime we ease down front and go out the left end, not the right. Everything else goes just like we had it before. Any problems with that?"

No one spoke, until Jay said, "Just don't anybody get so wrapped up, worrying whether Hurlin' Hal breaks some more Pac-Twelve passing records, that we forget we have to prime all the cadres. Each and every."

Tabor needed a break; he and Casey began to make their best polite, appreciative good-byes. Carla had a final word: "Why don't you drop back here after the game? Jay and I are going to unwind with some old Marx Brothers movies." As Luke sought to decline with courtesy, she said, "I found a disc made from the original versions, before the Turner people messed with them. Black-and-white, flatscreen view, *and* unhumorized."

"No laugh tracks?" Casey sounded interested.

"Right."

"Sounds good," Luke put in. "If we're up to it by then."

Finally they escaped to his apartment. There were still two hours before game time, and Casey agreed it would be a shame to waste them.

# TWO

**O**ver in Seattle the U-Dub's Husky Stadium had grown a dome, but Martin Stadium at Wazoo rated only a plastic bubble held up by air pressure. Originally called Rogers Field, some decades ago the facility had been renamed in honor of the state governor who first introduced Washington's sales tax. It figured.

That levy, Lucian recalled from History 14, had been imposed as a temporary measure, with ironclad limitations to hold it at its initial value of two percent. Now the state alone took ten; its openhanded delegation of the taxing prerogative allowed counties, municipalities, school districts, etc., to tack on another two. When it came to oxymorons, "temporary tax" was one of your basic winners.

Walking up the hill to Colorado Street, then over that street's summit and down past the gyms and field house, Luke and Casey reached the gates to the student section before much of a crowd had gathered. So far the group included a fair sampling of the Flag Brigade. Luke knew only a few by sight, but like him, all were stopping just inside the gate to pick up from Jay's man their furled, two-ply plastic flags, which would first be shown as such, then reverse-folded and hooked together in pairs to display the demonstration signs.

Two of the cadre leaders were on hand; Tabor briefed them quickly, then kept watch for the others. By the time the gates opened, Rozak and Carla had arrived. Jay would take over now, so Luke relaxed, he and Casey moving with the rest of Rozak's oddly assorted troops, first inside and then to the lower left of Section C.

Well before game time Derion came in—breathless, saying he'd been delayed getting Vivi LaFleur to the gov-

15

ernor's box on the far side of the field. For once the man's presence didn't automatically focus everyone's attention on him. *How about that, huh?*

Hail, hail, the gang was here, all right. Luke sat back, waiting for play to start.

These days he wasn't much interested in football. He had been; all through childhood and adolescence he'd followed the fortunes of college and pro teams avidly, and in high school had been a fair-to-good wide receiver until a knee injury and medical advice took him out of the game. When he was fourteen he'd ridden a bus down to Portland to see the Ducks knock the Honolulu Raiders out of the NFL playoffs. Louis "Loose" Cannon had completed thirty-seven passes for the Raiders but also threw thirteen interceptions, five of them to Jim Hooker, Jimmy the Hook. It was one of the best days of Luke's young life.

During his army hitch he'd lost touch, mostly. But returning, enrolling at Wazoo, he looked forward to sitting in the student section and cheering the Cougars to victory. Until, under well-meant pressure from a family friend, he'd pledged that man's fraternity, the house Tabor still thought of as Rho Dammit Rho. And the Rho Delts were heavy on jocks.

Jocks, he found, were a pisser to live with. In high school it hadn't been that way; being on the team gave you a little extra prestige, but athletes weren't a caste apart. At Rho Dammit, though, those paid amateurs acted as if they owned the place; nonjocks, even upperclassmen, were inferior beings. As a lowly pledge, Lucian Tabor was one of those catching the worst of it. And when, one evening, the members called an illegal, hazing-type Paddle Party, he told them where to stuff their pledge pin, and moved out.

"Even in the army," he managed to say, sweating with a sort of panic, "I didn't have to take this kind of shit. I sure as hell won't take it from you."

Apparently fearing exposure, some of the frat members tried to intimidate him to keep him from reporting their offense. Two of them cornered him one day, on his way between classes, and made veiled threats. Well, not all *that* veiled. When he figured out the situation Luke said, "I wasn't planning on telling anybody anything. But if you don't leave me alone, starting right now, I could change my mind."

Staring Crusher Craig right in his slaty eyes, denying himself the relief of blinking, finally he saw the Crusher nod. "All right. Just make sure you do."

Articulation was never the Crusher's strong suit.

The band played. The rooting section sang:

> *"Fight fight fight for Washington State,*
> *"Win the victoree...."*

Even Luke's disillusion with the mystique of gridiron warriors as such couldn't suppress the old thrill. Casey squeezed his hand; he took a deep breath and sat back to enjoy himself.

Onto the field the teams came running: first white, trimmed with Husky purple-and-gold, then the crimson-and-grey Cougars. For the holo viewers' benefit, team captains and referee acted out the ritual of the coin toss, just as if it hadn't been decided beforehand; the Cougars "won" and chose to receive.

The band played the national anthem—and praise be, the singer was no "song stylist." She sang it straight.

The Huskies kicked off. The crimson-jerseyed kick returner took the ball on its first bounce, bobbled it, dropped it, dived at it, missed it, and along with fifty thousand immediate spectators plus a few million via holovid, watched a Husky pick it up and run it in for a touchdown.

Luke looked at Casey and shook his head. First play of the game, and already they were shooting themselves in the foot.

"The way it looks, this is going to be a long evening."

* * *

Twenty-four playing minutes later, he began to allow himself some grudging optimism. The man who'd fumbled the first kickoff ran the next one back past midfield. Three tries up the middle got nowhere, but a fake punt went all the way: the up man made a throw of over sixty yards, and Ombuto, the Nigerian converted pole-vaulter, had five steps on everyone and leaped high to snare a ball that was on its way to the end bleachers. Seven-all.

There were good series and bad. Hurlin' Hal was pretty well on target when he had time to get set, but at least twice a Husky cornerback jarred the ball loose. Penalties hurt both sides: the Ref giveth, and the Ref taketh away. Wazoo scored a TD, the Huskies got one and missed a field goal. With six minutes to go in the half, U.W. was held at the two yard line. A Cougar blocked the kick attempt; another ran it the length of the field. A touchdown in the pros, but only two points by NCAA rules.

Against his inclination, Luke Tabor was again caught up in the game. The last six minutes before halftime, he yelled his fool head off. When the gun sounded, Cougars up sixteen-fourteen, he felt a distinct jolt.

The fun was over. It was time to do what they'd come for.


As the marching band left the stands, Rozak and Derion moved their people down to that same exit gate. How it had been arranged for U-Dub students to sit in the Cougar rooting section, Lucian had no idea. Borrowed student cards, maybe? Not really caring, he gave a mental shrug.

The band played and marched, marched and played. After a time the west gate opened to allow the governor's float, mounted on a flatbed truck, to come onto the playing field. Actually it took two gates, one at each end of the airdome extension, to act as an airlock and avoid loss of dome pressure. Beside the goalposts the float paused, waiting for the band to finish its last presentation.

Tabor looked. Yes, Governor Axelson was there, and Wazoo's president, each accompanied by satellite groups.

And alongside the governor, smiling and apparently making lively conversation, sat Vivi LaFleur.

The float bore no speakers, and to it no cables ran across the field. So the guv would be using a remote mike to the PA system. Did Rozak have one, too?

Luke shook his head. There was, he thought, a great lot he didn't know about this caper.

Spreading its formation, the band formed a single line, a circle that opened to allow the speakers' float to reach the center of the field. Then, still playing, the marchers spiraled outward and single-filed toward their exit.

Before they arrived, Rozak was leading his Flag Brigade out that same gate. Derion, Tabor noticed, brought up the rear initially but then moved forward, saying to Jay, "Remember to reassure the crowd, immediately, that our demonstration is to be brief, not protracted."

Rozak grinned. "Don't I know it? You don't get people on your side by raining on their picnic." He spoke up, to the entire group. "All right; it's newsbreak time."

Once on the field, the flags were unfurled and shaken out; then Luke and the other cadre leaders herded the overall group into something resembling a platoon formation.

Precision marching it wasn't—but on balance, not bad for amateurs. Approaching the float truck, the formation arced into a crescent shape around the major attraction. As Rozak yelled, "Halt! Present flags!" each person held a staff forward at an angle, letting the banners droop in the governor's direction. Briefly Jay dipped his in salute, then nodded.

Alongside Luke, Derion caught his gaze and winked. One way or another, the show was on the road.

A university official introduced a state official, who introduced the university president, who introduced Vivi LaFleur, who drew more applause than all her predecessors combined. They were using a remote mike, all right, each speaker in turn handing the cordless unit on to the next. Standing, Vivi began her speech; at first it was so banal that Luke could barely follow it. But then—

"... to introduce Governor Roger *Tax*elson, who is here to sell you the Agony Tax package he has put together with the aid of your House of *Reprobates* and Department of *Senation*. He—"

Separating the folded layers of each plastic flag, Rozak's Brigade spread them to reveal the slogans printed large on the hidden sides, then fastened pairs together, to hoist each between two flagstaffs and display to the crowd.


Axe TAXelson!
Down with the LegisLOOTure!
Tax Profit, Not Pain!
If You're Out of Money, Do They Take Blood?


And more ... but now Vivi was saying, "—you'd think there was nothing left untaxed, but you're wrong. I give you our beloved governor, who will now tax his own credibility out of existence!"

She'd said it all so loud and fast and fiercely that she was nearly done before any of the startled fatcats moved to stop her. Holding his breath, for a moment Tabor saw Derion fixed in an intent, yet somehow *passive* gaze toward the group; then he exhaled and relaxed, just as one of the men reached for the mike. But LaFleur stepped back, eluding him, and tossed the thing out and away—to land almost at the feet of Jay Rozak.

Rozak scooped it up. Looking toward the stands, to the gates where security men were beginning to emerge, he spoke quickly. "We are *not* here to disrupt this game. After I say a very few words on *your* behalf, on behalf of all taxpayers in this state, we will disperse back to the stands. There is no need for any unpleasantness; hear me a moment, that's all. We—"

He began a brief, cogent summary of the blatant injustices of the new tax package. Looking to the sides,

Luke saw the security troops slow and stop. *It was going to work.*

Halfway up the stands to his left—not the students' rooting section, but the other side—a very tall blond man stood, and threw a small canister, about the size of a beer can. It wasn't his first throw; while that one was in the air another hit the turf about halfway between the signholders and the security forces, and a cloud of brownish vapor erupted.

That was a longer peg than anyone should have been able to make; unbelieving, Luke saw the second missile jerk and *accelerate,* landing squarely in the midst of the security group. Now a third came straight toward him—but somehow swerved to strike about ten feet away. *How*—? No wind in here; maybe some freak of the ventilating currents?

He heard Derion mutter something that sounded like "Lord Fray!" Then the gas cloud reached them; the burnt, bitter tang stung his nostrils and he felt a wild surge of recklessness.

"Hibit!" Rozak shouted. "Stand still!" Hibit? Luke had read of the stuff; a relative of PCP, it temporarily destroyed all normal inhibitions. The "high" from a whiff of Hibit didn't last long—but with so much of the stuff, here in an enclosed volume, it would be just one snort after another. And from what he'd heard of the *price* of the drug, this prank was costing somebody a real bundle.

Now, for what it was worth, at least he knew why he felt urges to—to do *any* crazy damn thing. But the knowledge did him no good at all. Panting in the turbid air he looked for something, anything—some target for these vague, unformed lusts.

More gas bombs spewed, while the dome's air intake quickly spread the vapor. In the stands, spectators began to stand and move; it wouldn't take much to spark a stampede. And the security men, no longer unmoving, had their guns out.

Derion grabbed Luke's arm. "When this quiets down, lead me out of here. To your rooms."

*What*—?

* * *

"Lead you out?" Past the drug-induced surges of intent he tried to think. "Did it get you in the eyes? Are you—"

"Be silent and listen." Derion's quiet tone somehow held Luke in place. "Stay until I tell you it is time, then escort me to safety. *Do you understand?*"

Luke's mind wouldn't hold still, but he gasped out, "I'll try." Derion didn't seem to hear him; the man's eyes closed and he sagged against Tabor's supporting arm.

With his own thought going strangely calm, Luke looked around him. In the stands, the frantic motion slowed and stopped. The security men, vengeful Storm Troopers only moments before, also slowed to a halt, guns lowered.

Luke turned to meet Jay Rozak's puzzled stare. In uncharacteristic, quiet tones, Jay said, "I think we'd better leave." Unhurriedly he motioned to his cadre leaders; refurling banners as they went, the Brigade began to move back toward the student section. Some left the sign sides facing out, others the flag sides; no one seemed to care which.

Casey was near the middle of the departing group; Luke called to her, but although the place was unnaturally quiet, she didn't seem to hear. Well, all right . . . however the riotous mob had been calmed, it seemed to be passive enough now, and by this time the steady air intake had to be diluting and dissipating the Hibit. Casey should be okay.

Tugging at his arm, Derion mumbled, "It is time."

Time? Oh yes—get the man out of here. He'd said he would, so now he'd better.

He looked around. Making their exit through the stands, crowded with stunned-looking people, seemed impossible. Which left the west end gates, where the guv's car had entered. Derion stood unsupported now, though blank-faced and not appearing to comprehend much. *What's wrong with him?* With a hand on the man's upper arm, Tabor led him past the goalposts to the gate. The guard said something and Luke said something back; none of it seemed to matter as doors alongside the inner and then the outer gate opened to let him and Derion emerge outdoors.

Now what? Oh yes—*back to my place.*

Luke took a deep breath. For a pooped man with a zombie in tow, it was going to be a long walk.

Tabor's apartment was second-floor rear in one of a connected series of old brick buildings. The first floor held a small grocery, Sarge's Select Foods. Not that Sarge carried much of a selection, but the place was handy when Luke ran low on anything in the line of staples.

Now he urged Derion up the stairway between Sarge's and the next-door photographic studio. At the top he unlocked his door, flipped on the overhead light, and sat Derion on the couch.

"You want anything?" In no hurry for an answer, Luke looked out his living room's rear window. The building sat at the top of a steep hillside—too steep for cost-effective construction, so the rock-scabbed slope stayed vacant—facing more or less toward Pullman's downtown area at the right of Luke's view, with a small park below at the left. The vista may not have been much, but it beat having close neighbors; certainly he never had need to pull his shades for privacy.

He looked back to Derion. The man was slumped sideways along the couch; Luke went to him. "Are you all right?" No answer. He tried to pull his guest upright, but the man grasped his wrist and said, hoarsely, "It drains one. Must lie down."

"Sure." But the couch was short and narrow and lumpy. "Here, come on, get up. Let me help you," pulling as he spoke, and Derion did half rise and hold on. "We'll get you in here where you can stretch out."

It was like trying to lug a half-empty water bed, but they reached the bedroom with enough momentum for Tabor to propel the other man fully onto the bed. He rolled him over onto his back, removed the shoes, and tucked a pillow under Derion's head. Seeing nothing more to be done he said, "Get some sleep, then," and went back to the living room.

Before he took his last beer out of the refrigerator he put in the six-pack that had been sitting in a paper bag alongside it. He hadn't exactly lied to Rozak earlier; there *was* only one in the fridge. And with the demonstration still ahead, not to mention the party or rally at Jay and Carla's, it had been too early in the day for beer anyway.

Belatedly he thought to find out what had happened at the stadium, and turned on the holo to find the Cougars leading by five points and making a goal line stand with forty seconds left in the game. Interested in spite of himself he watched the Wazoo defense stuff the fullback on a draw play. Huskies' time out, their second; then a reverse that covered thirty yards laterally but barely regained the line of scrimmage. An offside penalty put the ball on the one: still second down, twenty seconds on the clock. A blitz forced the U.W. quarterback to dump the ball into the end seats, and on the next play their tight end dropped the ball.

Fourth down, and wouldn't you know it? Everything riding on the one play. The halfback pass fooled everyone except Crusher Craig; he batted the ball straight up, to be caught by the nose tackle who lumbered nearly twenty yards before Washington's quarterback saved the insult of a gift touchdown with a shoestring tackle. For only the third time in the school's history, Washington State was in the Rose Bowl!

Only then, seeing the student section empty onto the field to tear down the lightweight breakaway goalposts, did Luke Tabor find time to sit down.

He waited through the spate of commercials interspersed with game highlights and profound-seeming analysis by the network commentators, noting that Hurlin' Hal had indeed set a new Pac-Twelve single-season record for completions but came up a bit short for career yardage.

There *had* to be some kind of report on what had happened at halftime, and Luke wanted to see it.

Vivi's and Jay's words would have gone out nationwide, no doubt of that. For a regional broadcast, local announcers might well have cut the feed at Vivi LaFleur's first departure from orthodoxy. But network people? They wouldn't care diddly about the embarrassment of state politicians; to them, this surprise was *news*, and would damn well be aired. And now, rerun.

After a State Lottery commercial, which trumpeted the joyful message that three million to one were truly great playing odds, the sportscaster began "Today at halftime . . ."

Tabor sat back to watch.

Except for the shift to seeing from the camera angle, events were as he remembered them. The band left the field, Rozak's Brigade came to salute the governor's float, introductions were made. Then LaFleur volleyed her verbal bombshells and tossed the mike to Rozak. His propitiatory words slowed the security troops. Knowing where to look, Luke spotted the tall blond man at the edge of the holoscreen: standing, unslinging a rucksack, and from it taking, one after another, *six* Hibit canisters to hurl out onto the field. And sure enough, by no means did those things follow the normal laws of ballistics.

The camera turned to show pandemonium beginning in the stands, security men drawing and aiming their guns, the announcer on the original tape sounding like a replay of the *Hindenburg* disaster.

Then, beginning somewhere in Rozak's group, you could *see* activity die down, a wave of quiet spreading across the field as even the announcer's voice slowed and calmed. Up into the crowded stands the effect made its way, until fifty thousand people stood or sat or milled slowly around, all looking dazed.

Focusing on the major crowd, the camera showed little of Jay's group rejoining the spectators, let alone Luke and Derion exiting via the end gate. Present-time commentary took over: "No theory has been offered to explain this unprecedented phenomenon. The person who bombarded the playing field with canisters of an incitatory drug escaped and has not been identified. Whatever neutralized the drug's effects, we can all be thankful that it did so. And now, right after these important messages, we take you to New York for further analysis and some expert testimony."

*Click.* Expert, huh? They wouldn't know any more than he did. Less, probably, because they'd never heard of Derion.

It was time to ask that enigmatic person a few questions.

Propped up on a couple of pillows, half-sitting, Derion still looked like a case of terminal fatigue; his drawn face displayed a sallow paleness. To Tabor he would say only "I must eat first." So Luke fixed food for two. After a can of chili with hunks of cheese, two slices of wheat-berry bread and most of a quart of milk (Two Percent was all Luke had), Derion wiped his mouth with a paper towel. "Thank you. I feel much better. I had been—nulled, almost."

Nulled? Screw the terminology; get down to cases. "What happened back there—the zonked-out crowd going quiet—*you* did that? And messing with those cans' trajectories?" No answer. "How?" Silence. "What the hell are you, anyway? Where do you come from?" Passport signed by one of Steven Spielberg's disciples? Or would it be Stephen King's?

Renewed vigor showed in Derion's face; his color improved visibly. "You must tell no one."

"Tell *what?* Look, I'm not interested in spilling anybody's secrets to the tabloids. But goddammit I did get you out of there, and took care of you. I have a right to know a few things." Well, it sounded good. . . .

Surprising him, Derion nodded. "Of course you do. It is only that—what is *correct* to tell you, I must decide."

"Correct? What's that mean?"

"Permitted? Yes, permitted is more accurate."

The guy hadn't talked oddly, like this, before. And what had happened to the strange *force* of him? He had to be really in phase lag. So, "You did cool the crowd down; all by yourself you did that. How?"

The wave of Derion's hand was minimal. "By *will*, of course. Imposition of emotion or movement or temperature change or—it is all the same. Only by *will* may these things be done." His eyes widened. "Does this carry any meaning for you?"

Did it? Luke wasn't sure; he said, "How do you do it?" No, that wasn't the right question. "Who taught you?"

"Persons of skill, adeptness." Derion waved away another question. "That answer misleads you. More truly, I was taught skills possible to me but not to you."

"Why not?"

The combination of scowl and grin carried a devilish charm. *This guy belongs on holo.* "Because our origins differ."

Origins. What *was* this? "Sure. You're just a refugee from Shangri-La. All right; where *do* you come from?"

Now it was pure frown, no grin at all. "It is not on your maps. And will not be, for—" Derion shook his head. "I hail from the Far Islands.

"And until tonight, when I saw Lord Fray, I had not thought any other of us to have reached here."

# THREE

To that, Luke Tabor found nothing to say. Not that he was the least bit satisfied, but he couldn't think straight enough to decide what questions to ask.

And now *he* felt pooped. "Okay, I'll let it drop. For now. Move over, would you? I need to flat out for a little while myself."

Comfortable, Luke dozed. And dreamed of Casey. They were in some unspecified place with nowhere near enough privacy, but ignoring that factor she was touching him and trying to get his pants off.

The feeling became real enough to wake him. But it wasn't Casey's hand at his fly; it was Derion's.

Abruptly Luke rolled away, fell to the floor, and scrambled to his feet. "What the hell do you think you're up to?"

"In gratitude for your invaluable assistance, earlier, I was paying you the compliment of an erotic overture."

"I don't do that stuff!"

"You are celibate?"

"Not so you'd notice." Not recently, anyway . . .

"Autoerotic, then. Surely not a bestialist."

"I like *women.*"

"Ah. You select your partners purely on the basis of gender? An interesting deviation, though quite limiting. Widespread in this place and time, it would seem." Smiling, Derion shrugged; once again his sheer *presence* made itself felt. "It seems I have added to my debt by embarrassing you. Perhaps I should go now."

"You don't have to—I'll make some coffee—" But even to himself his protest sounded halfhearted, and within minutes his visitor had gone.

Leaving Luke feeling, quite irrationally, in the wrong.

\* \* \*

The facts were: Intellectually, Tabor accepted bisexuality as one of several normal conditions. For *other* people. Socially far behind schedule throughout his early school years, he'd run up against the usual pack of competitive trickster kids and discovered his gullibility the hard way. So while he knew from around age twelve that sex play was going on among his fellows, and was curious about it, he wouldn't trust a one of those angleshooters with *any* kind of word or deed that could be used against him.

To some extent the same factors applied to his *de facto* exclusion from the school's minor epidemic of early pubertal coitus. By the time he realized it existed and nerved himself to have a try, one girl had "gotten in trouble" and the rest swiftly folded the action.

Lewis Gap didn't speak of gays or homosexuals or sexual orientations. "Perverts," yes—but young Lucian had no clear idea what those despicable, somehow dangerous creatures actually did. In the army there were still those who maintained that if a queer braced you, you should bash him—but he himself never actually did so. A simple "No" was all it took; later, in the milder ideological climate at Wazoo, he might even say, "No, thanks." It was the suddenness, the jar of surprise, that had made him so abrupt with Derion.

Current medical/psychiatric thought had it that sexual proclivities were innate, not learned. Maybe so, maybe not. One idea he'd read lately did seem to make sense: that an increase in homosexuality was nature's response to overpopulation, much like the unexplained mechanism that tipped male/female birth ratios during wartime. In preindustrial times, this hypothesis asserted, fluctuations were slow enough for the phenomenon to hold the balance—and that a *massive* change in orientation ratios might well be overdue and possibly underway.

All Luke really knew was which way he himself swung. And that he was glad of it.

The nap had left him logy but unrested; he soaked out in a hot shower and went to bed.

First thing next morning Tabor tried to call Casey but could get no answer. He put coffee and eggs and toast into preparation, poured juice, and brought in the Sunday paper, the *Spokesman-Review* from Spokane.

Wazoo's victory, clinching a Rose Bowl berth, fronted the Sports section, but halftime made Page One. The headline read "Apple Cup Riot Aborts." As with any newspaper story Luke had ever seen, of which he had personal knowledge, the reporter had several things totally backward.

For a start, in his version the Flag Brigade had thrown the gas canisters. How this was supposed to jibe with "no charges have been filed" was anybody's guess. Certain hints indicated that Governor Axelson wanted Jay Rozak and Company charged with *something,* but that the authorities were not inclined to oblige him. (As Luke recalled it, the chief of campus police had two sons in university and a daughter due to enter within the year—and the Agony Tax package did apply to tuition.)

The cessation of incipient riot madness was credited solely to efficient air renewal by the airdome's ventilating system—a claim not credible to anyone who had experienced three hours in the place with fifty thousand other people. Two spectators' reports of thrown canisters swooping or swerving in midair were dismissed as hallucinatory effects of the gas—although to Luke's knowledge, Hibit possessed no psychedelic qualities whatsoever.

But that was a Free Press for you.

After reading the comics and working the puzzles, Tabor skimmed the rest of the paper; since he had long since trained his mind to skip advertising without noting its content, the task didn't take long. The only other item relating to Wazoo was a speculative piece on Whither the Genetic Engineering Program; two fundamentalists on the Board of Regents labeled it blasphemy and wanted it killed stone cold dead.

He tried Casey's number again; this time she answered. "I'd like to see you, Luke, but I'm ironed too flat to get dressed, even. Much less go over there. If you'd like to come here . . ." She paused. "Maylene's going off to a picnic. Someplace over in Idaho, the hills east of Viola."

So her roomie wouldn't be home until evening. "I'll see you in a little while."

Outside in the building's cramped parking area he unplugged his five-year-old Chevy Tesla from the metered charging post which was one of the advantages of living here, and drove up and over the ridge of College Hill to the rooming house he couldn't talk Casey into leaving. He could have walked it and often did, but today he felt logy. And the car had been sitting too long.

The house Casey lived in, formerly a department head's home, was fairly large, sided with white shingles not quite in need of repainting. Old Prof Durkin would have steamed, Tabor thought, to see most of his lawn converted to parking.

Maylene's space was handy, so Luke used it.

This time of day the front door was unlocked; he walked in and headed for the stairs, saying "Hi" to a couple of students watching holo in the former living room, now used as a communal dayroom.

The second floor boasted only one full bathroom for its four dwelling units, but the room-and-a-half Casey shared with Maylene Norris had its own basic plumbing, and for cooking they managed with countertop appliances: minirange and so forth.

Casey answered his knock within seconds; today her bright coppery hair, nearly waist length, hung loose and wavy. Hardly seeming all that tired, she gave him a long, slow kiss hello before he had to turn and face the room itself. Everyone said Maylene had a real touch with color, but nobody ever said it was subtle. Never mind; Luke was used to it.

He passed the offer of an Almost Original dietcoke. "Every new sweetener is God's gift to the human race;

then a year later the FDA says it causes elephantiasis in mice." Enough of that. "Casey—yesterday, after I hauled Derion out, what went on?"

Well, nothing much, she said, sliding down to lie with her head in his lap. Everyone simply appeared to forget or ignore the strange interlude, and watched the rest of the game. "I don't know; we all seemed to be slowed down—a little *numb.*"

The two teams, Cougars and Huskies, certainly hadn't been! Of course they'd been out of the stadium, safely in their own locker rooms, when the Hibit hit the fans. Not to mention Derion . . .

"And you got home okay."

"Sure. All the Brigade came away together, people dropping off to where they lived; Jay and Carla walked me home specially."

"Nice of them." He thought of something else. "Did the guy ever give his speech?"

She sat up, leaning against him with an arm around his shoulders. "Sort of. After things calmed down, I guess somebody found his mike for him. We were still getting back to our seats, so I didn't hear too well. But mostly he said thank you all for showing up and he was glad to be here, and sat down."

So Derion's *will,* however it worked, had zapped Axelson, too. Maybe the Taxpayers' League should hire the guy to kibitz legislative sessions. Or let's think big: how about the new Balkan "peace" talks? PaxTerra would pay him a real load. . . .

Thoughts freewheeling, Tabor said, "There's something, I don't know if I should tell you. I—"

But Casey was going into caress mode. When she retrieved her tongue, she said, "Did you come over here to spill your guts, Luke, or to donate some rare and precious bodily fluids?"

It wasn't the right time to get picky about anything.

Lucian had come late to sex. Having missed his opportunity at age thirteen when he was still unseeded with

Basic Guilt, he went through high school practically date-less, except when he was dragooned into escorting some-one's sister to a school dance. Even if he'd had any idea how to go about a seduction, he knew better than to try it. And the overall atmosphere of the small, isolated town was one of deterrence.

Lewis Gap held four churches, but the True Worders sat topmost on the totem pole. As recently as his own par-ents' teen years the congregation's young people were not allowed to dance or play cards, nor the girls to wear makeup.

To some degree those strictures had eased, but still if someone said "morals" you knew it meant S*E*X, not stealing or telling lies or cheating on your income tax; with or without cause you felt guilty. Especially when you didn't really know much of anything about the forbidden topic.

When he graduated from high school, Lucian Tabor still had ignorance he hadn't even used yet. All four min-isters sat on the town council and three on the Library Board; the courts kept throwing out the town's obscenity laws but the council enforced them anyway. Since Lewis Gap's one and only satellite dish and cable distribution system were municipally owned, minions of the Reverend Dr. Nathan Hornsby exercised *de facto* censorship over the community's holo viewing. Prime time soaps, for example, were routinely deadended at the control panel.

So Luke and a couple of his classmates, entering the Armed Forces at eighteen, were likely the greenest hands the recruiters had found in quite some years.

He wasn't at all taken with the whorehouse he went to with a few of his squadmates on completion of Basic; the slides shown along with the STD lectures cooled any desires his load of beer might have raised. To avoid being called chicken he went into the room with the woman, and paid her, but that was all.

The grade of literacy considered normal in Lewis Gap's isolated, outdated school system seemed to startle the army's testers; Luke was shunted away from the Infantry into a hush-hush Signals unit. At first he thought he'd lucked out, but he drew outpost duty at a crypto intercept station on a remote Alaskan peninsula. As he wrote to his parents, "There aren't any people here, just army."

Eventually he came home and took his GI Bill money to Wazoo, where he still didn't date heavily but did learn to kiss and feel around with reasonable proficiency.

One young woman's initiative and persistence came close to relieving him of his virginity. Her effort was interrupted by the end of his junior year, and in September she didn't return. But that was when he met Casey, and unbelievably she took a loving to him; despite his involuntary reluctance she plied patience and tolerance until he let her give in.

Over the past two months, a little more, Lucian had learned more about women than in his previous twenty-three-plus years. Compared to other men his age he was still in kindergarten and knew it. Casey never complained, but he could tell when his residual timidities disappointed her. It didn't help that only gradually was he getting free of instant guilt for simply Doing It; when it came to innovative measures he tended to freeze up. Maybe he needed a little Hibit.

He tried, though. What he was doing right now, for instance, would have seemed unthinkable a few short weeks ago. Not to say he felt quite comfortable about it, as yet.

But he was getting there. And so, sounds and movements indicated, was Karen Cecile.

They napped for a time, getting up when hunger announced time for dinner. Chicken with spaghetti sauce was a new one on Luke, but that's what Casey threw together, along with a mix of unidentified vegetation, and he found it good.

He'd forgotten she was out of wine, that he was supposed to bring some. Maylene's jug-Chablis wasn't very palatable at room temperature, but chilling their poured glasses helped a lot.

As they ate, first Casey tendered a couple of reserved, nonexplicit compliments on his recent performance and he sweat bullets trying to reply in kind. Then she grinned. "I should know better by now, trying to *discuss* it with you." She shook her hair back. "When you got here—something you wanted to talk about . . ."

Huh? Oh yes; Derion. But wait a minute. The *will* business: "You must tell no one," the man had said. No one?

He shouldn't have promised on those terms; he tried to recall his exact words but they eluded him. Seeing her looking at him, waiting, he thought *Oh the hell with it; I trust Casey,* and said, "It's about Derion. Only it's two separate things. And one of them, he made me promise not to tell anyone. But—"

A one-sided smile. "But you're going to, anyway?"

"I have to. It's too crazy; I can't handle it by myself." So, slowly and carefully he told her what he'd seen, what he'd guessed, and what Derion had admitted. "By *will,* he said he shut that mob down. And joggled those cans around, flying through the air." He felt the muscle tension in his face and wondered how it looked from the outside. "What is he, Casey?"

Her eyes were wide. "What does he say he is? Or has he?"

"Not exactly." Luke thought back. "He said he comes from the Far Islands, and that they're not on any map."

"And—and that there's another here. Another like himself, I mean."

Casey cocked her head. "That wouldn't, by any chance, be the big jaybird who *threw* the gas bombs?"

"Now how did you figure that out? Yes, it is. Derion called him Lord Fray, or something like that."

"Frey? The Norse god of fertility and crops, one of the Aesir? Sounds like some kind of cult thing." She chuckled. "Derion looks devilish enough to play Loki, don't you think?"

Luke didn't know too much about the mythology, but in his mind the blond man's name changed its spelling. He let out a deep breath. "We don't have any answers at all, really, do we? Just telling you, though, takes a load off my mind."

"Right. Same time next Thursday, and pay the nurse on your way out." Then her smile stopped, and she said, "There were two things. What's the other?"

So he told her about Derion making a pass, and his own reactions. Soberly she shook her head. "Ol' Tight Collar Luke."

Casey had never burdened him with her sexual history in detail, but he knew she'd had a lesbian affair one summer, and that she viewed it as an adventure she probably wouldn't repeat but by no means regretted. "For one thing, you might say it loosened my attitudes. So they fit more comfortably."

Without her saying so, he knew that's what she meant now, about *him*. He nodded. "Tight collar, yeah. And staying that way, too, it looks like."

But not so tight that a little later they couldn't go back to bed for a time.

Practice might not make perfect, but it was fun trying.

If it hadn't been for the unmistakable shrillness of Maylene's laugh, audible all the way from the first floor, she and Cliff would have caught the lovers still in bed. As it was, Casey made do with a robe while Tabor hauled his clothes into the lav closet and dressed there. Coming out, he said his hellos and hoped he didn't look as flustered as he felt.

"Are you parked okay, Maylene? I could move my car."

Short blond hair barely ruffled with her headshake. "I'm in Martin's space. He won't be back until late, and then he can use mine overnight. Everybody here, we all do that a lot."

She went to the fridge. Still standing near the door, Cliff Perkins said, "Wild game, huh?"

Cliff played football but didn't wear the jock attitude. As a flanker his good moves kept him on the squad; his lack of speed placed him third-string. But he was a clutch player; according to the sports pages, in yesterday's second half he'd made catches for two third down conversions and drawn an interference penalty for another first-and-ten. Since Luke hadn't been there, he said only, "I like *your* stats. Nice going."

Cliff grinned and sat down, as Maylene brought him a glass of internationally advertised brown sweetened soda water. Luke shook his head. "Rot yer guts, son." And to the others, "Time I headed home. 'night, Maylene."

Casey joined him in the hall for a good-night kiss. "Get some sleep, Lucian. And don't worry so much. You don't need to know everything about everything."

"Sure. What's the point of having ignorance if you don't use it?"

Home again, he was making a cup of decaf when his phone rang. It was Rozak, all fired up again. "Channel Four in Spokane wants a bunch of us on their political talk show. 'State of the State,' you must've seen it. What they have in mind, we talk about our protest, why we did it, kick back and forth how the Misery Taxes impact different kinds of people."

With barely time to take a breath, he went on: "They'll send a crew down early tomorrow morning and disc it here. About six of us, I thought, and I want you in on it. We can—"

Tired, Luke cut in. "Exactly when is this, what you're setting up? Tomorrow starts the heavy end of my week."

"What's so heavy?"

"Classes, Jay. You remember classes? And either tomorrow or Tuesday night I have to take Franson's tutorial section; I owe him from last month. So this had better fit in, or I can't—"

"Oh come *on*, Luke!" Jay wouldn't give up easily; he

never did. So: how long would it take? An hour; not over two, I swear it! All right, "I have fourth period clear, but my Extended-spectrum Optics lab starts with fifth, so in case this talk thing runs past an hour, I'd better *bring* a lunch."

"And eat with the camera on us?"

Tabor laughed. "Ethnic realism: the student condition."

He didn't ask who else was being tapped; he didn't care. It was sleepy time and Luke was a tired tot.

Everything else could go hang.

Monday morning was Quantum Mechanics, Theoretical Fusion Procedures, and Astrophysical Theory. At least those were this term's course titles; the assistant department head liked to change things. Well, it gave him papers to put his name to.

Weekend events had set Luke behind schedule and this Monday was loaded, so after breakfast he called Gerald Franson and arranged to take the man's tutorial section on Tuesday evening instead.

Before first period he had to hustle, to rough out the parameters for Prof Eldridge's assignment. He had no idea whether his arbitrarily specified device had, in theory, any possible chance of working; all he did was develop the given equations and plug in numbers until he found some that fit.

The 168-hour week didn't stretch well to include classwork, necessary employment, political activity, and romance. When it came down to cases, Tabor could most easily spare the politics.

But after he'd plowed through the end of third period, the "State of the State" talk show was next up. Barely remembering to bring along his lunch bag, Luke headed for Wazoo's holo studios.

The setup was in Studio B, where Channel Four's crew had pushed the university's equipment off to one side and were now busy arranging their own gear.

With increased camera sensitivity and digital disc recording, high intensity lighting and compensatory makeup wouldn't be needed. Having done a lab lecture series using Wazoo's older paraphernalia, Tabor appreciated the difference.

From the talk-panel table past the heads-on camera position, Rozak let out a hail. "Hey Luke, come on over." Stepping among cables and dodging a crewman who seemed determined to back into him sight unseen, Luke got there. Neither early nor late, it seemed: Jay and Carla were the only ones here before him.

Jay was chattering on; we say this, we say that, don't forget to, blah-blah-blah. Luke tuned it out; he hadn't wanted to be here, and by now he truly didn't give a damn how the show went. He would try to say something effective if he got the chance; rehashing ahead of time wasn't going to help. Only when Jay said, "I wanted to get Casey, but her fourth period always gives pop quizzes on Monday," did Luke pay heed again.

"Too bad. Who else *is* coming?" Because time wasn't standing still; if these troops didn't get the show on the road soon, Tabor might have to bail out short of its final curtain.

Rozak didn't need to answer. As the noise level dropped suddenly, Tabor looked around and was not surprised to see Derion entering with Vivi LaFleur. "Just the five of us," Jay muttered. "I think we can handle it."

Vivi wore a tailored suit; her hair was pulled back as in the schoolmarm role from her last-year's feature holo. She greeted Luke with an unexpected kiss that began with surprising fervor, then teased off chastely. Backing away with a quick grin, she murmured, "Are your batteries up for this?"

Then she turned to Jay. "Can you get it moving? I have to catch the one-oh-five to Seattle." According to Tabor's watch, and allowing twenty minutes to the airport, Vivi had a point.

Showing no particular feelings behind a measured smile, Derion said his hellos before Channel Four's moderator breezed in, bright dress and brighter hair fluttering, with her own greetings. Then, across the table from the cameras, the six of them settled into a seating arrangement.

The crew chief spoke his ritual words and countdown; the moderator began. "Good evening. I'm Sybil Shumway and this is 'State of the State.' Tonight we have with us a group of concerned persons who two days ago brought their concern to the notice of the public with a demonstration at the Apple Cup's halftime break. But someone else, as yet unidentified, had other plans, and events from that point have not been explained.

"When we come back my guests here will tell you, as best they can, what really happened last Saturday at halftime."

So she didn't give doodly about the Cause; all she wanted was the sensational stuff. *We'll see about that.*

The camera-on light darkened. Sybil Shumway looked at Vivi to her immediate left and at Derion on her other side. "Now don't freeze up, folks. I think we have us a good one here."

Maybe it was good, maybe not; to Luke Tabor the ordeal went on interminably. All in all the panelists did fairly well in focusing on the tax package; only a few times did Shumway drag them into speculation about the disruption. Jay and Vivi gave the most and best responses, with Carla adding a few choice fill-in lines to Rozak's prepared-sounding spiels. Derion provided calm, deliberate commentary; another fitting adjective, Tabor thought, was "evasive."

Luke spoke only three times. At first he stopped short of his conclusions because he felt he was hogging the floor; next time he was interrupted in midpoint, and he blew his third chance by getting off on a side tangent and forgetting his way back. When the session came to an end he was close to being late for lab, so he gave brief scattered good-byes and left.

He'd forgotten to eat his sandwich, so he munched it on the way to Physics Annex Number Two.

Lab was okay. He and his partner worked well together, and the experimental procedure, though indirect, was straightforward in the logical sense of the term. Putting the equipment to bed, painstakingly so as to maintain its alignment, kept them later than usual. Walking home, Tabor felt he'd had as full a day as anyone could really want. He was pooped.

Checking his shirt pocket, he found he'd remembered to bring his grocery list. Nothing fancy; he managed to fill it all at Sarge's, and—after taking a thin batch of miscellany from his mailbox—made slow work of climbing the stairs to his door.

Inserting the key, suddenly he had the feeling that someone was inside. He hadn't heard anything; he just felt it. He shrugged; not likely it would be anyone to worry about. Maybe Jay barging in again, with his usual disregard for locks—or, for that matter, privacy.

He opened the door and found he was only partly right. Sitting in Luke's own favorite chair, leaning back, feet on a footstool, looking as if he owned the place ...

Lord Frey.

# FOUR

Luke moistened dry lips. "Did you bring your six-pack?"

"Six-pack? I do not understand." Deep and at the same time nasal, the intruder's voice was distinctive—and Luke recognized the same kind of innate clout projected by Derion.

"Like at the ball game Saturday; you threw out six cans." Walking over to set the mail on his desk, Tabor tried to think. When in doubt, bluff; payday poker had taught him that much. "Frey, isn't it?" Damned if he'd give the man a title. "So where's Thor? You could have used him, there at halftime."

"Thor?" Heavy eyebrows, so blond as to appear almost white, drew down and then relaxed. Under sunstreaked hair, not much darker, Frey's mildly sunburned face was dominated by jaw and cheekbones, the nose a harsh blade between pale eyes set wide and deeply. His broad, thin-lipped mouth twitched into a faint grin. "Ah. The Norsepeoples' thunder god, armed with the hammer Mjollnir which returns to his hand. But I am no part of those myths. Nor is my esteemed cuz-cousin Derion."

He wasn't stuttering; the term meant something to him, some cousinly relationship which might or might not have a different name in Luke's vocabulary. "Then what are you? How did you put body English on your beer cans? By *will*, I suppose?"

Frey stood: at least six-six, and no beanpole. Don't push a bluff too hard: "Well, that's what I was given to understand."

"Derion speaks more than is suitable. But—" A look of effort came to the man's face, and suddenly the bottoms of Luke's feet felt strange. It took him more than moments to identify the feeling as a lack of pressure. He looked down to see his feet hanging in midair, an inch or so above the floor. Then, not in haste, he sank to stand in normal fashion.

Derion's paranormal doings had scared Tabor a little, but only in an abstract way; this was closer to home. Trying to hold his voice steady, Luke said, "I don't believe in magic. Where does the energy come from?"

Frey's sudden smile looked wholly genuine. "From myself. As though I had used my hands to lift you. How could it be otherwise?"

Whoever, whatever this man was, scary as he might be, Luke wanted to know more. What to ask? He began a question but Frey, suddenly looking toward the door, lifted a hand. "Derion. He is coming." The man stood. "How may I leave?"

"That's the only door. Are you afraid of Derion?"

He thought he'd gone too far; briefly something jerked him toward Frey. Then he was released. "Afraid, no. But my need to face him is not yet." He strode to the rear windows and swung one open. Deftly he unhooked the screen and set it down inside. "This will do."

"But we're—" Four stories up, he was going to say. The building had a basement level, and below that, at least another floor's height of foundation on its downhill side. Frey didn't wait to hear; he stepped out as though onto solidity and sank slowly out of sight. Rushing to the window, Luke saw him drift down and land, bending his knees slightly to take whatever jar there was. Frey looked up, gave a brief wave, and began walking along the path next to the foundation. When he reached the east end of the building he turned; leaning forward as anyone would for the steep climb to the street, he went out of sight.

Without having heard a thing, behind him Luke felt a presence. Turning, he faced Derion.

\* \* \*

"Do come in." Sarcasm was childish, but after all!

"Thank you." Perfectly straight-faced. "Frey was here."

"How do you guys—" He shrugged. "Oh, never mind." After all, if *he* could sense them . . . Gesturing toward the window, "He went thataway." Derion, of course, wouldn't be at all surprised.

"What did he want?" The voice was calm, not demanding.

What *had* he wanted? "I don't know; he didn't say."

If Derion recognized the old gag line, he gave no sign. "Frey did not harm you, nor threaten?"

"No. No, he didn't. Why should he?"

"I do not know. But my cuz-cousin is a dangerous man."

Cuz-cousin again. Oh well. Any time now, presumably, Derion would tell what *he* wanted. Luke said, "Would you like a beer? I could use one." And moved toward the fridge.

"Something of savor, yes. If not—" He made a gesture. "I do not thirst."

So Derion shared Luke's aversion to beer brewed for people who don't like the taste of beer. "Try this." On sampling it, Derion's face showed pleasure.

Seated, Tabor leaned forward. "Tell me something. *How* do you people put your energy into—through—your *will,* to do all those things?"

Scowling mildly, Derion shrugged. "Since those abilities are not yours, the details would hardly interest you. The only valid generality is that we cannot exert greater force by *will* than would be possible by ordinary bodily effort—and that the physical effects, such as fatigue, are comparable."

"But exerting force at a *distance*: those canisters were well away from the stands, almost to the middle of the field when they accelerated—or swerved, like the one that was coming straight for us. How about the inverse square law? Doesn't that cause you a lot of wasted effort?"

Derion's hand signaled negation. "In this case that law is not applicable. *Will* is focused, not radiated in all directions. Distance is a factor, yes. But not in such proportion."

He paused a moment. "Enough of these matters. If you need to learn more, which seems doubtful, this can be accomplished at some later time."

"Then why did you tell me any of it? You or Frey, either one? And I still can't figure how he found me, or why he bothered. Anyway, isn't it all supposed to be a big secret?"

Derion's look implied that only innate courtesy kept his patience intact. "I, because you alone both saw that something unusual had happened, and asked questions. Frey—" He shrugged. "How he found you: possibly he noticed you helping me leave the stadium, and followed us. Or later traced you here. Though what he may have wished from you is still a puzzle. As for secrecy—who would believe you if you told? Among your people here, nothing is known of the Changed."

Stymied. "All right then; how about the Far Islands? What kind of a place are they?"

Derion seemed to look into distance. "They are, in essence, the domain of the Changed—yet with a place, an important place, for the Unchanged also."

Genius IQ wasn't required; context said it all. Changed meant people like Derion and Frey, wearing titles and throwing their *wills* around; Unchanged presumably minded their manners and sat to eat below the salt. It figured.

Still, Tabor listened. Almost chanting, Derion's voice carried a hypnotic quality as he spoke of strangely named places: Hykeran Outjut, the Node of Terlihan, Dietjen's Hiatus—but never quite saying what they were, let alone where. His descriptions smacked more of allegory than travelogue.

"One finds depth there," he said of the Hiatus. "When the court assembles, that awareness cannot be ignored."

The court. Not judicial, Tabor hazarded; royal, most likely. Lord Frey, yes. He ventured, "What makes Frey a lord? Is he your superior—in rank, I mean?"

Derion shook his head. "We are roughly equals. At home I would be called Count Derion. We do not use such titles . . . here."

"But you have royalty in your country—nobility, all that? Doesn't it seem a little anachronistic, in this day and age?"

Having closed to slits as his voice droned, Derion's eyes now opened. "Days and ages. And social systems. These things follow cycles. It is a conceit of ours to enjoy pageantry and trappings. Also, we have determined that for psychological reasons the ordering of societal matters is best conducted under a system based, in a flexible manner, on the principles of aristocracy, which seem to fulfill some basic human drive." His mouth quirked. "Our institutions, however, do not necessarily correspond to your own traditional modes."

Evocative though Derion's words might be, informative they were not. Even direct questions failed to help; the man wouldn't say what continent the Islands were near, nor in which ocean. He didn't refuse to answer; he simply evaded, or opened a new subject. Obviously aware of Tabor's frustration, finally he said, "There is no point in giving data that is useless to you. I should not have said so much as I have done." He stood. "I will go now. I thank you for the beer; it has excellent flavor."

Luke rose, too. "Sure; you're welcome. But you never did say what you came here for."

Derion's smile showed a kind of impish glee. "That task was accomplished before I entered."

Huh? Oh. "Chasing Frey off, you mean?"

"Indeed."

So Derion had known his "cuz-cousin" was on the premises *before* he arrived. No matter; Luke said, "Why? Do you really think he's a danger to me?"

"I—" A pause. "Not a good influence, let us say."

Derion left. *Good influence?* Luke thought about it. *Derion makes the pass at me, but Frey's the one to watch?* Well, maybe so. . .

As yet Luke's beer was nearly intact; taking a sip, he wondered what to do next. Might was well look through the mail; maybe his overdue GI Bill check was in there. He sat and sorted, but no such luck. A batch of junkbulk joined the accumulated pile in File Thirteen. An army buddy who had re-upped wrote from Caracas, where he'd drawn duty as an Embassy guard: "Rebuilding here goes slow, but the bars and whorehouses got open again right away. After what happened when we had leave in Anchorage I take it cautious." Yeah; ol' Slim had been lucky to get out of that one without a court-martial, let alone keeping his stripes. . . .

Luke's cousin Josie Marie, who lived with her husband and two kids across the Cascades in the Skagit valley: ". . . not sure if we can stay on here, the way things are going. Developers buying up big tracts, knocking down the existing houses and putting up new ones. Two bedrooms for half a mil and up from there. Nobody can get a permit to just build a house around here; the conglomerates put them up in quarter-section installments. So *our* property tax is going out of sight, and . . ."

Tabor sighed. Local planning commissions ate from the developers' hands; development built up the tax base, and what else was new? He'd have to answer Josie Marie soon, try to cheer her up. She was right, though; people like her and her family were being Yuppie-gentrified out of the valley, and no help for it.

An odd item caught his attention: a loose piece of paper, a sheet torn from a pocket notebook and folded in half.

*Luke:*
*Couldn't reach you by phone. Watch out for yourself off campus; the guv couldn't get action locally so he's sicced state troopers on us. If they get you,*

*make your phone call to ME (Carla will be here if
I'm not). Or did I tell you we have a lawyer on hold
to take care of this kind of crap? Ray Higgins, just
in case it gets TOO deep.*
*Keep your zipper up, buddy.*

*Jay*

Well. Rozak was becoming positively civilized, leaving his communication in the mailbox rather than slipping
the lock to bring it inside. Absently Tabor looked through
the remaining items, found they didn't suit his current
needs, and dumped them.

Jay's note itched at him. State cops, huh? The Washington State Patrol, as its name implied, traditionally roamed the
state's highways in search of speeders and the like. Over the
years its duties had broadened to include such things as bird-
dogging for drug and arms smuggling—or indeed, for people
bringing *anything* into the state to avoid Washington's cham-
pionship sales tax.

But the Patrol had no jurisdiction inside incorporated
municipalities. Nor, of course, on Wazoo's campus or any
other.

So Roger Supertax was stretching his authority. Luke
shrugged; they had nothing on him. He'd participated in
the demonstration, which had been orderly until Frey cut
loose with the Hibit canisters. And that was all he'd done.
No one could prove anything more, because nothing more
had happened.

Still, as he finished his beer and commenced putting
enough odds and ends together to pretend to be dinner,
Luke felt unease.

Setting his few dishes to soak, he was glad he'd put
Franson's tutorial section off a day. Now he could sit back
and watch "Monday Night Football," an indulgence he'd
enjoyed since he was about six, the Reverend Dr. Hornsby
having deemed the spectacle wholesome enough for youth
and age alike in Lewis Gap.

Tonight's game continued the bitter feud between Seattle's Seahawks and the Vancouver Broncos. The U-Dub/Wazoo rivalry extended to Luke's attitude toward any Seattle team, so naturally he favored the Broncs. The odds didn't, though; the B.C. team was four-four against the Seahawks' seven-one.

This one might be a cliff-hanger.

But midway through the second quarter, holo coverage returning to the game after a string of commercials, Luke realized he'd lost track of down and yardage; he wasn't even sure of the score. When a knock sounded he almost welcomed the interruption. Turning down the audio, he went to the door.

He wasn't sure who he was expecting. Derion or Frey again? Jay Rozak? Police? Not Casey; she'd have called first. But at the door, lab folder in hand, stood Bruce Garner.

"Come on in. Would you like—" Woops; the kid was probably under age and Luke was, marginally, faculty. And he didn't stock soda pop. "—a cuppa decaf?"

"No, thanks. Mr. Tabor, I don't know how we screwed the data up so badly; thanks again, for giving us the chance to fix our mistake. We—"

Luke knew where the error probably lay. Undergrads tended to do everything by keypad and blithely ignore the possibility of numerical typos; it took a few solid bloopers to convince them that a quick approximation check, mentally or even using (heaven forbid!) a real live pencil, was good insurance. No point in giving a lecture; he said only, "I could see that you'd done the actual work correctly; seemed a shame to give you a week's flunk because somebody hit the wrong key." Well, a small nudge: "I like to run a quick check, myself: round numbers. It helps."

"I can see how it would." Edging over toward the holo set, Garner said, "Hey, the Seahawks may score!"

So Luke cranked the sound back up. And now Bruce Garner did accept the offer of a cuppa. With someone else watching the game and making comments, Tabor had better luck keeping his mind on it.

The outcome did not push his joy button. Tied twenty-all at the end of four quarters, neither team could score during the overtime period: two missed field goals, and in between, a Bronco TD called back for a holding penalty. Where was John Elway now that they needed him? A retired legend, was where.

Oh well. A moral victory for the Broncs. But moral victories never put anybody in the Super Bowl.

Garner didn't care; he left happy. What else could you expect from a Raiders fan?

Tuesday was easier: two morning classes and an afternoon lab. In between, Tabor met Casey for lunch at the CUB. The old student union lounge, redecorated during the previous summer, was handy for her but a fair uphill trek for Luke; at least the walk back to lab, while his lunch settled, would be no strain.

Casey liked big salads but turkey breast struck Luke's fancy; he went for the TLT. The two hadn't talked since their parting Sunday night; now over decaf he told of Frey's visit, and Derion's. "I don't know who or what the Changed are, but those guys could make a lot of money doing Special Effects." He wasn't sure Casey really believed his story; she looked as if she suspected some kind of spoof. "I'm not kidding," he insisted. "Frey did step out my window and drift down to a soft landing."

Casey shook her head, not negating but cutting free of any serious consideration. "Maybe it's some kind of trick gadget, like the atmospheric potential toys two-three years ago." Could be; he nodded. She said, "We had visitors, too. One, anyway. A state trooper last night, looking for *me*, no less."

She'd also had warning from Jay—or rather, from Carla. "So when Martin saw the car pull in, he yelled up the stairs. Maylene and I went down the hall and locked ourselves in the bathroom." She grinned. "Not to waste my time, I ran the tub full and got in."

She took a time telling it, but it boiled down to: (1) the trooper wanted to know who was in the bathroom, and Maylene answered; (2) nobody else knew Casey was home, so no one could spoil the ploy; (3) Casey did not own a car, to be spotted outside and give her away. So the trooper asked questions of all present, including Maylene, who yelled through the bathroom door and made a point of not hearing too well with the water running.

"And eventually he left. Just as well; I was turning into a prune."

Afternoon lab, using very old-fashioned optical devices, was a little tricky; the one Luke drew had a loose vernier. But patience always wins, supposedly; he took his time and entered pairs of readings, coming in from each side of the mark to average out the effects. And what was the name of the old M/Sgt who taught him that trick, on some kind of primitive surveying instrument the week after Basic? The army wasn't all bad. . . .

With Franson's tutorial coming up at seven, it was hardly worthwhile going home. Tabor spent an hour studying at his small workdesk in the assistants' area, then walked over to a nearby ReburgerTaters for the gooiest salad-stuffed burger in town, plus a side of unsalted fries.

Several paper towels later he decided he had all the goop off his face and walked to Physics Annex One. Franson's group, Physics One students, were a pleasure to work with; the ninety minutes of problem solving went fast.

Walking home afterward did not. This time of year, eight-thirty was dark and cold and wet. Approaching Sarge's Select Foods, Tabor almost failed to notice the State Patrol car parked down the block.

Now what? They'd know who he was; he couldn't get away with walking past, pretending he didn't live here. He hoped he hadn't paused or shown any other sign of reacting to the car's presence.

All right, follow right on through. He didn't need

anything from Sarge's but he would think of something. He turned and went inside. Behind him, a distance away, he heard a car door close.

So the trooper was coming. Of course. More or less at random, Luke picked out bread, buttermilk, and a wedge of Swiss cheese. While he paid Sarge's evening clerk he took a sidelong glance outside. The cop was walking past, moving out of sight.

There was absolutely no point in hurrying; outside, Luke walked the few paces to his entrance and trudged up the stairs. Past the midpoint landing, he heard the street door open and close. Damned if he would look back!

Just for the hell of it, once he was out of view he moved rapidly, and had the satisfaction of hearing feet take the stairs two at a time. He had his key in the lock and was turning it when the clumping footsteps came up behind him.

Short of breath, the man said, "Lucian West Tabor? Sergeant Manning, state police. I have a few questions for you, budsie."

Inside or here? The hell with it; Luke wanted to set down his groceries so he opened the door and went inside. He neither invited the cop in nor tried to slam the door in his face; he turned to see the trooper standing just inside the open door. Unwilling to feed him any straight lines, Tabor waited.

The Patrol officer stood about six-three, all of it bone. Closing the door he impersonated a friendly smile and stepped forward. "We want to talk about what happened at Martin Stadium. While you're thinking it over, I'll have a look around."

The man moved to Tabor's desk and pulled a drawer open. Before Luke got past "What the—?" the trooper punched a switch on the gadget hanging at his belt and said, "You invited me in, so I don't need a warrant."

"Like bloody hell you don't!" *Oh-oh!* That was a recorder the guy switched on, so hold it down to a dull roar. "I mean, I made no invitation. Said nothing of the sort, and you know it."

A skunky grin. "You made a welcoming gesture. Your intent was obvious." And kept pawing through Luke's papers.

There was, Luke considered, nothing incriminating among them—or for that matter, in the whole place. Adrenaline had him shaky; he fought for steadiness. "All right, I'll pass that. Please don't disarrange my stuff, okay? Look at whatever you want, but try to keep it in the same order you find it."

Surprisingly, the man nodded. "See? I knew we could get along." Luke sat, waiting; in less than twenty minutes Manning was done, and stood holding only one item: a piece of junk mail from the wastebasket. "Now what would this be?"

Luke didn't recognize it. "I have no idea."

"It's addressed to you."

"So's a lot of other stuff I throw away without reading." Curious, he asked, "What does it say it is?"

"Just a subscription issue of the Aryan Protection Society magazine. I didn't figure you for one of those."

"I'm not. I don't know how I got on their list. I deep-six that kind of crap on sight." *As you can see for yourself.*

Manning frowned. "I'd like to have that statement under oath. And I think it's time to start videocapping your testimony." Out of his shoulder pouch came—no, not a holocam, but the simpler and cheaper flatvid model. "Now then. Do you swear to—"

"I do not. I don't have to testify under oath unless I'm charged with something."

How skunky could the grin get? "You do now. Don't you read the papers, budsie? Alabama isn't the only state that knows a good thing. Axelson signed the new law yesterday, and it comes with an emergency clause, to take effect immediately."

Shit oh dear! The Alabama statute was under heavy ACLU attack and not expected to survive, but the battle was sure to go all the way to the Supreme Court, still heavily influenced by three dinosaurs from the Reagan-Bush era. The question was, did Tabor want to get himself into this kind of hassle over an abstract issue, when he had nothing incriminating to say?

"Let's get on with it, budsie; I don't have all night!"

On some level, apparently, Luke did want a piece of that legal fight. With more surprise than purpose he heard himself say, "Why don't you go piss up a rope?"

Ten minutes later, downtown, Manning took the handcuffs off and shoved him into the holding pen.

At least he wasn't in there with no one but strangers.

The prebooking area was coed. Standing aloof from the drunks and miscellaneous scrunges, Casey wore her fighting face. When Tabor went to her, her lips stood stiff against his: stiff, and trembling. "The bastards!" she said through clenched teeth, cutting off his attempts at comfort. On second look he saw she wore only a light robe over bra and panties; they hadn't even allowed her time to dress.

A hand touched his shoulder; he turned to face Jay Rozak's sheepish grin. "They foxed me, Luke. Higgins— the lawyer, remember?—he's off to some cockaroonie meeting I never heard of, and his answering machine says he won't be back 'til Friday." Alongside Jay, Carla Duvai nodded, saying it was one real cute frame, dammitall.

Tabor looked around. "Are we all the Brigade that got nailed?" Behind Jay he noticed Bruce Garner and Alycia Frazier. "Hey, *they* weren't any part of it."

Soft-voiced now, Carla said, "Jay was after recruits. We were all having dinner when the cossacks charged in."

Luke shook his head. "This is pure bullbrick; we have to—"

"We have to keep our heads down," Rozak said. "I don't know where the heat came from, but I heard a trooper tell one of the town clowns we're all going up on felony counts."

"Felony? Where do they get *that?*"

"I'll tell ya where, bubba." A heavy hand turned Luke around; he looked up at a beefy face he'd never

liked. Junior Yancey was a Rho Delt jock who had trans-
ferred to Wazoo when his original school caught two
years' probation. But during his mandatory redshirt season, Junior hadn't kept his grades up; WSU profs, it
seemed, wouldn't pad grades to give the coach a hand.

Instead of studying harder, Junior was basically ma-
joring in booze and bimbos. Plus, judging from the look of
him right now, an elective in controlled substances. He
said, snarling, "You bastids tried to break up the game; we
don't like that. You—"

Rozak pulled at Junior's arm. "No such thing,
Yancey. We had something to say, that's all; then we were
going to trot right back into the stands and yell 'Yea,
Team' with the best of 'em. It wasn't our fault some
joyboy started throwing stuff out on the field. Hey—!"

The backhand cuff sent Jay spinning against the wall,
and down. Released, Luke backed away to see a number
of the other, miscellaneous prisoners getting up, looking
entirely too interested in a share of the action.

He slipped past one to get to Jay. "You hurt?"

Teeth bared, Rozak came off the floor. "Outa my
way!" He moved on Junior Yancey. "Watch who you're
shoving, paunch haunch!" He swung a looping right that
Yancey easily deflected, but it was a feint; stiff-fingered,
Jay's left hand sank into the big man's belly. Suddenly
bent double, Yancey threw up.

Half the tank was well into a threatening scuffle.
Rozak turned to Luke. "Oh, shit! That stupid son of a
bitch's set off a fight. And we've got *ladies* in here."

Without warning the noise level dropped; prisoners
turned to face the door. As a pair of troopers pushed
Derion into the tank. Derion, and Vivi LaFleur.

*How—?* Moving quickly, Tabor got to Derion's side,
where Vivi clung, speechless. "How could they take *you?*
Why—?"

Derion gripped his arm. "It is necessary. I tried other
measures, but Frey was able to negate them." He shook
his head, saying, "Your authorities plan to subject all Jay's

cohorts to a machine testing—polygraph was, I believe, the device named."

He motioned to Jay. "Bring our group together; gather everyone here!" Then, addressing Luke, "To me the thing is a toy. But from you and perhaps these others, it could elicit information that must not be disseminated at this time."

Rozak came bringing Carla and Casey, Alycia Frazier and Bruce Garner. "Hey, Derion. What do you have in mind, here?" He looked around, toward prisoners reviving their belligerence. "Whatever it is, I'd recommend you get at it!"

Derion spread his arms. "All embrace with me. Now!"

Derion to one side and Casey at the other, Tabor waited while Jay and Carla and Bruce and Alycia came to clasp together as one mass. Vivi was in here some-place. . . . As the other prisoners milled around, staring in threat but apparently too confused to mount an attack.

Colors dimmed to sepia and then darker; muffling all sound, the air thickened. From behind, something struck Luke a solid, massive blow. In growing dimness, shapes wavered and vanished until only hints of movement remained, shifting and passing—slowly at first but then streaming past at a rate too fleet for recognition. Breathing became an ever-greater effort, like trying to take in and expel some strange, bland, heavily viscous fluid.

Consciousness wavered, then held at less than fullness.

What this felt like, Luke decided, was swimming down a big river of breathable molasses.

*To where?*

# FIVE

The river analogy wasn't entirely figurative; in a way Luke couldn't define, he found himself rushed forward, sidetracked into eddies, buffeted by onrushing obstacles. Laboring to breathe, he clung to the companions his arms no longer felt.

Yet he knew they were there with him, and when he sensed the loss of one and then another, that knowledge held certainty.

Who was gone? Jay, he thought, and Carla; some essence from each, palpably felt, had now vanished. Were they dead? He had no idea, no way of knowing.

And then the river spewed him out.

Spent, feeling only a sort of dazed wonder, he lay alone in twilight. After a time Luke Tabor brought himself up sitting. To look at a place he'd never seen before, nor heard of.

He found himself on the bushgrown bank of a real, visible river, winding its eighty yards or so of width along the central part of a wide, flat valley with wooded foothills to either side.

Warm breeze, filled with hints of growing things, indicated that the sun, hidden below the horizon but putting a vermilion tinge to high cirrus formations, was setting rather than rising. Of animal life, including human, he saw no sign except tiny flickers of motion by the distant trees: birds, perhaps, and not large. From nearer-by came sounds of insects. But nowhere any hint of man: building, road, power poles, cultivated land, or fence. Nothing. Wherever he might be, it wasn't the Palouse country, the breadbasket of eastern Washington.

Coming here, though, he hadn't been alone. Where *was* everybody? He'd felt at least two drop away before his own exit from whatever strange continuum Derion had brought them through. Where had they gone? As hard as he peered, scanning to the horizon in one direction and then another, he saw no movement, or other indication of anyone else's presence.

Well, if that was the situation, so be it; there must be something constructive he could do. How about some orientation? Until darkness came, and stars, he could have no exact idea of directions. But the combination of temperature and twilight spoke of Temperate Zone latitudes, and against all logic his senses told him he had somehow left winter for summer. And not too far either way, his hunch said, from summer solstice.

Which meant that the fading sun-glow came from— well, maybe twenty degrees north of west, give or take a little. Unless, of course, he was in the southern hemisphere, which would put it *south* of west.

*. . . assuming you're still on Earth! . . .* But he had to assume *something,* so until proven otherwise, Earth it was. Therefore: on the sand beside the water he drew a line pointing to the brightest part of fading sunset, guesstimated twenty degrees to its left and seventy to its right and drew those lines. His stipulated north was, he saw, just off the leftmost spread of a great tree standing sentinel where the river bent, perhaps a half mile downstream. If it turned out to be south he was looking for, seventy degrees to the *left* of where the sun had vanished, he'd need better light to spot a landmark.

When the stars appeared, he'd know. One way or the other.

Suddenly it struck him: why was he being so unreasonably *calm* about all this? Surely any *will*-imposed serenity would have worn off by now. The only answer that came to mind was that ever since learning something of Derion's powers he'd been more or less waiting, on some level or other, for something truly bughouse to happen.

Now it had. So here and now his only option was to explore his situation, try to understand it. Because that's the way to survive and always has been.

His mind took a sidetrack: back home, what would happen? Who would teach his lab classes? Who else might miss him? His parents maybe, though since their sudden out-of-the-blue divorce and subsequent remarriages he hadn't felt exactly welcome in either household. Luke shook his head; he had to think in *now;* whatever he'd left behind would have to take care of itself.

His next step, then; take inventory. Item: no food, not even the bread and cheese and buttermilk he'd bought at Sarge's, all of which still sat in his kitchen, unrefrigerated. Well, it's hard to carry anything with your hands cuffed behind you, even if he'd thought of it and the trooper had agreed.

But this was fruit tree country if he'd ever seen any, and at least some of the bushes along the bank should have berries ripening. Enough to hold him, with luck, until he found some *people.*

Water. At the river's edge he knelt and sniffed. It smelled clean; the hint of plant and possibly animal life was mild enough to be more pleasant than not. He dipped his cupped hands to bring up a drink. Something brushed against his fingers, its touch too solid for the two-inch minnows he might expect here in the shallows this time of year. Memory clicked in; he decided it must have been a crawdad, the convulsive flip of its tail sending it backward to safe cover. What with leaks between his fingers, he managed one scanty swallow per dip until his thirst satisfied itself.

He walked up the sloping bank, past the sand and rocks to grassland fringed with bushes, and sat. What else did he have? Well, his clothes: basic shirt and pants and shoes (canvas, rubber soled) and socks and underwear, plus the jacket and light overcoat the trooper's harassment had distracted him from removing. He felt in a coat pocket and found his rain hat folded there. Good.

Pockets, then. The coat's also held a pair of driving

gloves, small flat packet of tissues, crumpled handkerchief, a roll of electrician's tape about half its original size, wad of knotted plastic string from some forgotten bundle, and several books of matches, some partly used. Not much else.

Inside jacket pocket: sunglasses in a clip-on case, and several folded sheets of blank notepaper. Side pockets: one candy bar from heaven only knew how long ago, and a packet of antihistamines dating back to pollen season.

His shirt had only one pocket; he preferred two, but the manufacturers didn't seem to care what he liked. Clipped onto it were three pens: black, red, and green; inside was his pocket calculator, a little jewel which did logs, trig in three systems of angular measurement, exponentials, binary, octal, hexidecimal, Boolean algebra, and options he hadn't explored yet. Solar powered with battery backup, and all for $29.95 plus the nation's premiere sales tax.

Which left the trousers. Wallet, change pouch, loose pennies, handkerchief, nail clipper, his keys, and an old bone-handled three-blade pocket knife. One blade was a leather awl; the knife had belonged to Luke's grandfather. By now, the smallest blade had nearly a quarter of its original bulk honed away.

Oh, yes. He did have his wristwatch. After the battery died in his digital, at the crypto intercept outpost where it had taken three weeks to get a replacement through army channels, Tabor had bought himself a quasi antique, a windup job with hands and a dial. Right now it read a little after midnight which was obviously untrue in this place, but what the hoot.

Also from his army days he wore a silver ring bearing the crest of his Signals outfit rendered in bright enamel.

And that did complete the list. Not much of a camping outfit, but it would have to do.

Darkness had become almost total. To the east a faint lightening foresaw the imminence of what should be, rising so early, nearly a full moon. But it wasn't here yet. Be-lately, Tabor thought to inspect the stars. Sure enough, there was the Dipper—and thus, Polaris.

Mentally locating his landmark tree between the barely seen silhouettes of foothill shoulders, he decided that his guess at north wasn't too badly off. Close enough for Physics Seven. But before he settled in for the night, Luke went back to the bare soil of the bank and drew a new, emphatic line, aimed where the Pole Star hung.

Tabor hadn't slept outdoors without a sleeping bag since he was ten or so, but it was no great trick. He spread his coat on the ground, settled a hip into a shallow natural hollow, rolled hat and jacket into a pillow and lay back, breathing deeply and trying to quiet the questions in his mind.

It didn't take him long.

Morning came chilly, with dew on leaves and grassblades, and a low-hanging mist to haze his view and limit vision. He didn't remember waking during the night, but he must have done, enough to pull his coat around him as cover of a sort.

He stood, pulled on his jacket and looked at the coat; he didn't want to wear it or carry it over his arm, either one.

That could wait. Automatically he stepped behind a bush, then realized that first, here in the open there *was* no behind to it, and second, no one was around, anyway.

Down at the river he doused cold water on his face, drank some, and peered to see if last evening's crawfish had any friends. No luck; when he decided which way to go from here, he'd keep his eyes open for fruit and berries.

Checking the two sets of lines he'd drawn in the sand, he was irrationally pleased to see that his sun guess was less than five degrees off his star sighting. *Nice to know you've got it.*

Back to the coat. Folded, it was still awkward to tote. Finally he rolled it into a bundle which he fastened, after considerable experimenting, by buttoning things together which weren't intended to fit that way. He slung it from his shoulder by its own belt and scanned the valley again.

There was absolutely no clue to the imminence of humans in any direction. But history gave Luke a bias. People tend to settle and build cities along rivers, and especially at river mouths.

Walking on sod alongside the sloping bare bank he headed downstream, toward a distant point where the bracketing foothills almost met. From this angle of view, at least.

The river, he noticed, flowed in a generally northward direction. He tried to think of any he knew in these latitudes that followed such a path, but came up empty.

As dew evaporated and the air warmed, Tabor found his jacket uncomfortably warm. He had to undo the bundled coat and repackage it together with the jacket, arranging one coat pocket to be accessible and stuffing into it all the contents from both garments. He wished he had an extra belt; he'd improvise a shoulder pack rig. He couldn't use the one from his slacks; without it they had a stubborn tendency to work their way south.

There had to be another answer. As he walked, Luke looked for something useful. In accordance with the principle that in order to find something you look for something else, what he spotted first was a stand of berry bushes. Tiny black raspberries—"blackcaps," where he grew up—tasted delightful, but in the quantities available did little for his hunger. Nor did green currants—gooseberries—or the barely ripe blueberries do much more. Over a time, though, this sparse but steady input took the edge off his stomach's protests.

A flattened tuft of long, coarse grass nearly tripped him; as he caught his balance, Tabor laughed. Right in front of his eyes—! He set to pulling up handfuls of the stuff; when he had a plenty, he sat down to work with it.

If a grass rope was good enough for Tarzan of the Apes . . .

\* \* \*

It wasn't all that easy. Twist strands together, their lengths overlapping, and try to braid three such skeins into a binding mass before one or more components raveled apart. Several times he lost ground and had to commence again, but after he began to secure each twisted hank every few inches with a cinch of two or three blades tied around it, gradually a solid length built.

When he had it long enough and several inches over, his problem was how to secure the ends. The grass itself was past ripe and starting to dry, tensilely tough and still holding enough moisture to obviate brittleness—but it wouldn't hold a knot worth damn-all. Compression expelled just enough fluid to make it slippery.

Wait a minute. From the coat's catchall pocket he grubbed out the wad of plastic string and began working the knots loose. There were, it turned out, three lengths ranging from two feet to six. After deliberation he cut the shorter piece into two. He worked the grass rope's ends, one from either direction, through one of his coat's belt loops, then used the two short lengths of string to wrap and lash the rope strands solidly together on each side of that loop.

His resulting straps weren't entirely symmetrical, nor was their placement. But the pack rode well enough.

Judging by the sun, when Tabor reached the big rock the time was past midmorning. Thinner now, the mist hadn't yet dissipated completely. Up from the riverbank the huge boulder thrust, half its circumference rising from land and the rest from water, to a height of perhaps eighty feet. And on the land side that rise was steep, nearly vertical.

But the stone was rough, scarred by cracks and wrinkles, knobs and hollows. In short, it didn't look like a bad climb. And up top, the view might tell him a lot more about this place.

No point in seeking unnecessary difficulty. Luke set his pack down, brought out the driving gloves and put them on; rock of this texture could be tough on hands.

Aerating with a few deep breaths, he addressed himself to the climb.

Heights were not Tabor's best thing, but keeping his gaze on the rock face itself he could ignore the drop below. After an initial burst of overeffort that ran him short of breath, he eased off to a feasible pace, slow and deliberate; the only real symptom of exertion was increasing perspiration.

Footholds and handholds were easy to find, and after one projection broke off in his hand—luckily before he'd put much pressure on it—he tested each before giving it full weight. And just as he began to think he'd bitten off more than made comfortable chewing, the next move brought his gaze level with the monolith's nearly flat top.

Tabor clambered up over the rim, looked across the rock's mossy, grass-tufted upper surface, and lay back for a good breather. A few minutes later he stood up; after all, he'd made the climb to have a better look around. Up here above the mist's remnants.

Okay; like the fillyloo bird which flies backward because it doesn't care where it's going, it just wants to see where it's been, he faced south.

He'd looked in that direction earlier, but through brush and mist, so without much result. On either side a range of hills stretched into distance. Between them, so far-off as to be hazed with purple, stood a cliff demarking this area from a higher tableland. A vertical glint of silver wavered in and out of visual definition; it could, he thought, be a waterfall feeding this river.

Well. Interesting, but that wasn't where he was going. His higher viewpoint gave him no better view of the hills to either side than he'd had before; he turned his attention north.

The way the hills pinched in, not too much farther along, only a narrow segment of horizon showed between. What there was, though, lay flat and very distant. Or so Tabor first thought. Then, squinting, he saw that part of what first seemed haze was actually snow on mountains.

So far away, they were, as to bear no relevance. If he

didn't find some people before he got *there,* it would be because there weren't any.

And there had to be. A few, at least: those who had come here with him, on the same strange swim.

Climbing down the rock was scarier than going up; he had to find footholds without seeing them first. But aside from one breath-stopping slip, quickly recovered, he got down all right.

Hunger had become serious discomfort; Luke hand-dipped enough river water to take the edge off. Here he did see some crawdads and probably could have caught one if he'd taken the time, but they were awfully small. Besides, he had nothing to cook in, and was not yet famished enough to try them raw.

Since he didn't know where he was going, he wasn't in any real hurry to get there; why not head over toward the hills and see what he could find? Across the river, their rise began only about half a mile from the bank; on this side, though, they lay perhaps three times as far away. Never mind; he set out.

The plain was definitely alluvial and given to occasional floods; the ground lay flattish to the edge of the hills, then sprouted thicker brush, spotted with trees, and rose abruptly. The trees were mainly deciduous, with only the occasional darker-foliaged conifer.

As he neared the edge of the brush Luke spotted signs of ground animals: holes surrounded by mounds of loose earth. The smaller ones, he supposed, were dug by ground squirrels; others might be home to anything from woodchucks to badgers—not to mention that a variety of species, including foxes and coyotes and bullsnakes, liked to usurp the diggings of others.

He sincerely hoped this wasn't rattlesnake country.

Tabor had string, and a knife for cutting sticks; he could set snares. With matches and plenty of dry tinder he could make fire. A woodchuck or even a ground squirrel would be worth it, for roasting on a stick. Purely on impulse he rummaged two books of matches from his coat and put them in his shirt pocket instead—in front of the calculator, to shield them from the sweat-dampened cloth. Then he walked toward the nearest stand of trees. None of which, unfortunately, seemed to bear fruit.

He was almost there when off to his left, twenty or so feet away, the air began to darken, thicken, and swirl.

Like a murky, viscous cloud the nebulous mass convulsed. Then it steadied, commenced to thin and lose opacity, wisping away until a human figure could be discerned, standing half-crouched and wholly still.

Obscurity dispersed; the figure moved. Karen Cecile Collins looked around her, straightened, and said, "You do have crazy friends, don't you?" She took another panoramic scan, then shook her head. "It's a good trick. Two minutes ago—"

Two minutes? Carefully, Tabor said, "You mean you're fresh from Pullman?"

Her lower lip jutted. "How else? Are you saying you're not?"

"Casey, I've been here—let's see—" He thought. "A little after sunset last night. And now it's close to noon." Which reminded him, his watch read four-seventeen. Noon being his best guess, he reset the timepiece to that position.

Also, he realized suddenly, noon gave him a chance to learn another fact. He held up a hand. "Hold it a mo. Latitude check." Say it *was* very near summer solstice. Tearing a reasonably straight branch off a bush, he stripped it and crouched to push one end into the loose soil, aiming the other directly at the sun. At a quick glance, the ground was level as made no difference. He could think of no simple way to measure the angle without instruments; he'd have to estimate, and did so. Straightening up, he spoke his guess aloud: "I'd say we're at about forty-eight degrees latitude. North, as it happens."

Face flushed, Casey spoke with bravado. "How much is that in dollars?"

"About like Spokane," he said. "But longitude—I

have no idea. And as far as I know, there's no place like this, in a decent climate but with absolutely no evidence of human existence, anywhere on this planet."

Casey moved over to a fallen tree and sat. "This planet? Now look, Tabor. Anybody who can take us from winter to summer—and without changing hemispheres, you say?—maybe we're *not* on Earth." She began to tremble; tears came, and Luke Tabor moved to sit beside, to hold her.

She wiped her eyes. "Sorry. It all just got to me."

"I know. But don't worry about which planet. The stars say we haven't left home." He explained.

When he was finished, she nodded. "You know what this means, Lucien." He knew, all right, but he waited. To see if she knew, too.

She did. "I don't know how it's possible, and maybe I never will. But wherever we are, we can't be in our own time."

Luke couldn't argue with that; he said, "So that's what Derion meant, saying the Far Islands weren't on our maps." He thought back. "And *wouldn't be*, is what he said before he shut up fast. So I guess it's clear enough: he's from our future, and that has to be where we are now."

After her initial outburst Karen Cecile was calm; her gaze held level. "How far, do you suppose?"

Luke shrugged. "No idea. No clues. And what I'm wondering is, why he dumped us off one or two at a time, spreading us out *in* time." Now her arms were around him, too. "Did you feel it when Jay and Carla left? And when *I* left?"

Casey frowned. "I'm not sure. There was something— but I was too confused—" Now she grinned. "Confused is what you call it when you can't spell scared-spitless."

Under the circumstances Luke's reaction made no sense at all. What they needed was to get moving, find food, discover and learn more about their situation.

Instead he began peeling her out of her robe. As soon as she realized what he was doing, she helped.

Pleasurably spent, Tabor lay with Casey's shoulder under his chin, mumbling vague endearments around the earlobe he'd been nibbling to good effect. He didn't expect to be pushed sharply to the side, as Casey sat up, yelling, "Look the other way, dammit! How'd you get here, anyway?"

Rolling aside, looking up and back, Luke saw Lord Frey standing maybe ten feet away, grinning in an interested fashion. Oh, hell. How the guy got here was less important, in Tabor's estimation, than what did he *want?* Trying to keep all expression from his face Luke took his sweet time getting up, collecting his clothes and getting into them. Casey, he saw, had shucked frantically into the bra and panties and now wrapped the robe around herself, cinching the flimsy belt tight. As she advanced on Frey, her lower lip held promise of a fat one for the tall man. "What are you here for?"

Frey spread his hands. "Why, only to succor those of you who are marooned, abandoned, by my impetuous cuz-cousin. But I do see I might better have been less prompt. I did not expect . . . Yet what could I do?"

Unappeased, Casey said, "Take a walk around the friggin' block and come back later, that's what!"

As Frey's prominent brows began to slant, Luke cut in. "Okay, so you like to watch. She still has a good question. Now you've found us, what happens next?"

Hoisting a knapsack off his shoulder and setting it down, Frey said, "I shall summon transport for us all. And while we await it, offer food, and answer such questions as you may have."

Maybe Casey wasn't hungry yet, but Luke was. He said, "That sounds fair enough; we accept, with thanks." He gave Casey a warning look and mumbled to her, "I'd kill for this lunch; don't untrack it."

Eyes widening, she nodded. Then, getting into the

spirit, she said to Frey, "While you're calling the taxi, d'you suppose you could round me up some *clothes?*"

The best grade of daggers he could summon up, Tabor looked at her. *Don't push it.* Casey smiled. "It can't hurt to ask, can it?"

"No harm whatsoever," said Frey. From the knapsack he drew what looked to be a polished piece of grained wood, thumb-thick and curved like a telephone handset. Sure enough, when he held it, almost hidden in his unnecessarily large hand, to his face, the ends were at the right places.

He spoke. "Lord Frey requesting services. Transport for three persons including myself. One usage of clothing, topical to the day's ambience, for a female person of the dimensions—" Apparently Frey was confident that his estimates, in units unfamiliar to Luke, were entirely credible. He paused, apparently hearing a reply though Tabor detected no sound at all, then said, "Register the coordinates of this transmission. I anticipate that when transport arrives here we will be within visual range of the locus indicated. But since the case may be otherwise, program the transport vehicle with option to call me and request reassignment of destination. Lord Frey concludes."

Well. When *this* guy called the AAA for a tow truck, he expected everyone to snap-to. *We'll see. . . .* And Tabor reminded himself: Derion had called Frey a dangerous man.

Opening the knapsack down one side, Frey unfolded that part flat on the ground, disclosing an array of containers which he proceeded to open. "Shall we take nourishment?"

*I thought you'd never ask,* as all three seated themselves.

Sampling, Luke tasted breadstuffs light and crisp and chewy, their flavors hovering just past the edge of familiarity. Rich spreads of meats and cheeses, subtly spiced. Fresh, chilled vegetables—the celery stuffing looked like ordinary cream cheese but carried a smoky undertaste. A tangy grape-sized fruit like a miniature tangerine, with a skin so thin and delicate as to make peeling quite unnecessary.

From a knapsack pocket Frey brought a large, ovoid flask of wine and a set of nested glasses. Pale yellow, the fluid held no hint of sweetness: slightly tart, a bit fruity, the flavor always seemed to demand another sip to realize fully. It effected only a mild stimulation which reached a pleasant level and went no further. Whatever its chemical basis, it wasn't alcohol as Lucian Tabor knew alcohol.

At Frey's gesture, he held his glass out for refill.

They were nearly finished when the egg arrived, appearing over the western range of hills and dropping rapidly, though silently, to touch down a few yards away. It wasn't exactly egg-shaped; that had been only Luke's first impression, seeing it front-on. Even then he noted that the silhouette was compressed laterally and flattened at the bottom. When it swung to land he saw that the stern cut off squarely, a plane surface studded, as was the underpart, with a pattern of glow-pulsing nodes.

While Frey reclosed his knapsack, properly stowing away all used containers and implements, Tabor eyed the egg more thoroughly. Less than five feet wide and not much taller, perhaps eight feet long. Most of its outer surface carried a dull grey-bronze finish, but the front half of its upper third showed transparent. Reflection dimmed Luke's view of the interior, but seatbacks could be seen, and segments of wholly unfamiliar apparatus.

"Our carrier," said Frey, approaching the egg. At his touch a hull segment, part metallic and part clear, contracted rearward in a way Tabor could not fathom, to create an opening.

Now, belatedly, he felt alarm. Here was the man who'd tried to turn Martin Stadium into a fifty-thousand-person free-for-all, and they were accepting a ride from him? Food was one thing, but this? He started to draw back, then shrugged; suddenly his alarm seemed foolish. He realized Frey was calming him by *will* but couldn't bring himself to care. Casey had also paused, but now moved ahead to the egg's entrance.

Giving her a hand up and inside, Frey reached to make Luke the same offer, but Tabor was already climbing in. Casey occupied one of the two rear seats; Luke took the other, leaving both front positions empty until Frey boarded and sat in the left-hand one. As the hull closed itself he turned and said, "If you are ready, we will proceed."

Automatically Tabor looked for seat belts, but found none. In total silence the egg lifted, turned southward, and gained forward speed; not even wind noise entered the capsule. Without looking around, Frey said, "We will take a fairly direct route; still, there is much to be seen."

A true statement. Calm or no calm, though, Luke asked, "Where are we going?"

"To a place where I have friends. Its name would mean nothing to you."

Snubbed, Tabor turned his attention to the view. From an altitude of perhaps three hundred feet he saw the valley end as the egg moved to soar above the vast plain which stretched toward distant mountains. Then the vehicle swung west and climbed. As Frey leveled off, he reached and handed a bundle back over the seat to Casey. "The clothing you requested."

There were several items. What she unfolded first was a sort of tunic, taupe with silver-green edgings. In the limited space she shucked the robe and worked her way into the new garment. Knee length and sleeveless, with a squarecut neckline, it fit quite snugly; Frey's estimates had been good indeed.

Next came a capelet, colored much like the tunic but with a greener tinge and darker edging, falling to cover Casey's shoulders and upper arms but loose enough for free movement. Then she unfolded an olive green headpiece, like a baseball cap with a somewhat convoluted visor turned up out of the way. Settling it on her head she moved to bring the visor down, but rather than stopping at proper visor position it snapped down to cover forehead, nose, and cheekbones. Ample eyeholes, however, allowed for visibility. After a moment she took it off and replaced it in the bundle. "Not my style."

Finally she slipped on a pair of sturdy-looking sandals.

Frey turned his head. "Do you find my offerings satisfactory?"

Looking down at herself, Casey said, "Yes, they're fine. Thank you."

"I am pleased. Now—" A chimelike sound interrupted; Frey pulled out what Luke thought of as his phonestick. "Lord Frey."

Whatever he heard appeared to concern him; several times he nodded, asked monosyllabic questions, and said "Yes" again. When he put the thing away he turned and said, "I must leave you. For that reason, your immediate destination is changed." He gestured. "Do not be anxious; the guidance system is thoroughly dependable. When you arrive you may cite me as your guarantor; if you are not met, request that you be taken to the Lady Aliira."

Frey smiled. "Now if you will excuse me, please do not speak until I am away. Speech would disturb my concentration, necessary for precise assigning of destination." He smiled. "My appreciation to you."

Frey stretched, leaned back in his seat and breathed deeply; Tabor guessed the man's eyes were shut. Bewildered, holding Casey's hand tightly and wondering what new strange event was forthcoming, Luke waited, but for long moments nothing happened.

He expected the air to curdle and darken and writhe, for Frey to be carried away in a pall like dirty smoke. And the curdling part did begin. But at the same time the man began to *shimmer* and to glint; only a brief flare of light, not at all dazzling, momentarily hid him from view.

Then he was gone.

# SIX

**C**asey stirred. "Hadn't you better get in the front seat?"

He looked at her. "What on earth for?"

"*Somebody* has to drive."

For a moment, laughter bent him over. "I hope to hell not!" Then, just as suddenly, anxiety flooded through him—misgivings, and resentment. "Christ on a crutch! Casey—we just let that damn Frey walk in and take us over!"

He saw realization strike her. "Luke. How—?" But then she nodded. "Yes. If Derion could quiet the whole stadium—"

"Sure." Now he acted on her suggestion, climbing over into the seat Frey had left. "Child's play, with only the two of us." Omnipotence, he decided, could get very tiresome—especially someone else's.

"And then he just teleports off," she complained, "without a by-your-leave." She frowned. "Teleport? Is that the word?"

"Yes. But he couldn't." Because, he explained, according to both Frey and Derion, *will* used the body's own physical energies. "And nobody has the energy to move anything any real distance instantaneously, let alone their own bods."

"So how—?"

He thought about it, then said, "The river of time; when they're in it they can move geographically, too; I mean, this isn't the Palouse hills. No knowing what their limits are; for all I know, maybe he can swim just a few seconds and go halfway around the world."

"Humph." Casey snorted. "Well, *we* can't. So why don't you figure out how to work this flying pillbox?"

A good question. He looked at devices incomprehensible to him; how the egg might be controlled remained a complete mystery. No wheel, no foot pedals, no joystick. A sort of dashboard, speckled with colored lights: some blinking, some not. Outcurving from it a foot-wide projection, like a keyboard but marked in no recognizable characters, and above that, a small oval grill.

Communicator outlet? To where? Maybe just the egg itself. In any case, why not try it? Clearing his throat, he said, "Pilot to ship. Where are we going?"

A pause, and then, "Proceeding to assigned destination." The soft voice sounded perfectly human, not mechanical at all.

Assimilating the new development, Luke paused a moment, then said, "Where is assigned destination?"

"At location specified by Lord Frey."

Let's see about that. . . . "Lord Frey has changed his mind. Land now, at—" He looked down; ahead lay a small lake ringed by trees. Casey put a hand on his arm but he shook his head; he had to test this thing out. "Land alongside that lake below us."

"Change of destination recorded."

But course and speed continued unchanged. Tabor said, sharply, "Why aren't you landing?"

"Awaiting confirmation of change, from Lord Frey."

"He isn't here! He left."

"Until confirmed, change cannot be implemented."

"Oh, fuck!" The indelicacy was out before he knew it.

"Communication unclear. Clarify?"

Climbing up front herself, Casey said, "We won't be able to change Frey's orders, it looks like. But maybe we can get some information."

Luke spread his hands. "*You* try."

She nodded. In a self-consciously loud voice she said, "What is our present speed?"

"One-point-six rambs per second."

"Well, bully for us." A little wild-eyed, she grinned at Luke. "Just one good ramb after another. But—hey, the damn thing did say *seconds.*" Then, "How much time will elapse before we reach—uh, assigned destination?"

"From—*now*—approximately one-zero-four-seven seconds."

Luke thought round numbers. "A little under eighteen minutes. If you want to ask much more, Casey . . ."

"What is the name of our assigned destination?"

"That disclosure is not authorized."

Casey threw up her hands. "Oh, the hell with it." She glared, not at Tabor but only in his direction. "Why couldn't we have drawn a nice obedient egg? As if Frey himself wasn't bossy enough—he even has bossy *machines*."

Luke shrugged. "I never met a computer that wasn't."

Much sooner than the machine's prediction—or so it seemed—an item of interest came into view. They had lost track of the river, so when Luke saw one ahead he had no idea whether it was the same or another. Either way it was wider here: two hundred yards, maybe more. And at a fairly abrupt bend, from whatever cause in this near-flat plain, spread a veritable forest, a tree-covered area stretching perhaps five miles along the river's flow and nearly two at either side.

Almost immediately Luke realized his first impression was wrong; this was no pastoral scene. Among the trees showed buildings, some with spires rising above treetop level. And along the river's edges, when the egg's path brought those into view, appeared a complex of docks and strangely designed boats or perhaps ships, the whole backed by structures every bit as drab as warehouses in Luke's own time.

Fast-seeming to the eye but decelerating gently enough, the egg descended. It passed the forest's edge, gliding at treetop level until a small gap appeared. Abruptly then, it dropped twenty feet or more to skim barely above the ground along a corridor overhung with branched foliage. At the sudden drop, Casey gasped; Luke exhaled explosively. "Watch out for that first step; it's a honey!"

As the egg slowed he began to get a better grasp of their surroundings. Among the trees and sheltered by them were situated numerous buildings, mostly of only one visible level. Some were half-sunken, only a few feet of height showing above ground level; several of the latter had earth mounded above them, itself bearing trees and bushes.

Was this camouflage purely for esthetic purposes? Or could there be a less peaceful reason?

In a courtyard of sorts, shaded all round its edge but with a central patch showing clear sky, the egg came gently to ground. Time to get out. But Tabor found no sign of a door handle, nor outline of the opening itself. "What the—?" Outside, human figures approached, pausing to look; somehow until he could get outside this thing he wasn't ready to stare back.

"*Ask* it, why don't you?"

Well, sure! "Open up; okay?"

"What is it, that should be opened?"

"The door! Exit. The way out of here . . ."

As before, a section of the left side slid backward without any clue as to where it went. It wasn't a panel sliding into a groove; the slit simply appeared, then widened. Making sure they both had all their gear, Tabor preceded Casey out of the egg. He turned, remembering that to open the door Frey had touched something, but he saw nothing to indicate where. Finally he leaned near the opening and said, "Close the door."

The opening narrowed and disappeared. All right; taking a deep breath, Luke turned to see what he was up against.

Among the fifty or so persons near or distant in his field of view, the variety of clothing was confusing. One popular outfit consisted of Bermuda-length shorts with a shortsleeved blouse; another was something that looked like leather (but on this warm day probably wasn't), skintight from chin to ankles. At least one person, walking away into a building, appeared to be nude until Tabor spotted thin blue lines indicating this era's version of a string bikini.

That woman also wore a long braided scalplock bleached white, surrounded by dark hair at little more than stubble length. A quick glance showed him several other getups unlike anything he was used to.

As he and Casey stood, only a few steps from the egg, Luke hadn't much time to muse over these vagaries. Almost immediately a woman flanked by two men approached him and Casey, stopping within handshake distance but offering no such greeting. The woman spoke, then repeated herself, and this time he managed to sort out her accent. "Your aegis of travel?"

Another reason he was slow to understand was that he was staring more than was polite. Although short-pantsed and shortsleeved, these three were definitely uniformed: in light blue with white piping, they looked like fugitives from a marching band. Also uniform were their heads; except for brows and lashes, in the sunlight all three gleamed bald.

Which wasn't true of most people he saw here. Part of the regalia?

Pay attention, though: *Aegis of travel?* All right. "Frey sent us."

"You refer to *Lord* Frey?"

"That's right."

"Then refer correctly."

It griped Luke, but he said, "Lord Frey sent us."

"For what purpose?"

"You'll have to ask Lord Frey; he didn't tell us." The woman's face took on a look Tabor didn't like at all; quickly he put in, "He said we should find the Lady Aliira." Find? Well, not exactly Frey's words. But "be taken to" made him and Casey sound like pets or children, so let it stand.

"I will need your names."

"Lucian Tabor." And Casey said, "Karen Cecile Collins."

The officious woman pressed keys on a flat, pocket-sized device, compressed her lips and glared disapproval. "Neither name is valid in this jurisdiction. But that is not my concern; I shall advise Lady Aliira to extract suitable explanation."

Her phonestick looked like common everyday plastic, not wood-grained like Frey's. She said into it, "For the Lady Aliira: Subcontroller Svansek of Enclave Five-Seven-A-C. Two persons without valid registration, claiming aegis of Lord Frey, request they be remanded to your jurisdiction. With respect, message concludes."

Her gaze returned to Tabor—and how could eyes so mildly blue carry such steely intent? "If Lord Frey underwrote your transport here, no doubt his bounty extends to your next journey also." Luke wasn't sure what she meant—until, scowling, she said, "Back into the carrier and away with you! I have other duties."

So he and Casey began walking. But just as they reached the egg, Svansek shouted, "Clearance rescinded! I have received orders to hold you here!"

*Oh, no!* Tabor yelled, "Open the door!" and the slit gaped. He handed Casey up and in, pushing her by one arm while her other clutched the bundle of clothing she hadn't yet inspected. But before he could follow her, Subcontroller Svansek and her two stooges were upon him. One grabbed his arm and swung him around; the others brought out a pair of nasty-looking handcuffs.

"Oh bloody hell!" One small segment of Tabor's mind went cold and clear; with an observer's detachment he watched himself pull a book of matches from his shirt pocket, tear out three at once, light that bundle and jam it, flaring, into the ear of Svansek's stooge Curly. Then he lit the entire book and stuffed it down the open collar of her *other* stooge Curly. While both screamed and batted at themselves, getting in Svansek's way, Luke scrambled inside.

Casey occupied one front seat; Tabor took the other. "Close the door!" After momentary hesitation the egg obeyed.

Clear of her stooges, Svansek brandished a gleaming

object; from it a bright noisy blast splashed off the egg's hull. Luke yelled, "Get us upstairs!"

"Unclear. Please clarify," said the egg. Svansek moved to their front for a better, more direct shot.

"Lift off the ground; move from here. Get away from these people attacking us. So's you don't get *damaged*, you tin Socrates!"

The egg lifted. As it began to move, up more than forward until it cleared treetop level, the last Tabor saw of the Subcontroller was her resentful glare as she ducked sidewise to avoid getting beaned, and a last futile flash from her weapon.

Again the ground dropped away. The egg said, "Destination, please."

Lacking an answer, Luke said to Casey, "Any ideas?"

"Sheest, I dunno." She frowned. "How about this Lady Aliira?"

"She's a friend of Frey's; is that a good idea?"

"Maybe, maybe not."

Another thought came. "How about Derion?"

Her brows lifted. "You trust him more?"

Luke gave a snort. "Ask me something easy." But the egg, now up and away from Enclave Five-Seven-A-C, was basically hovering, going nowhere. "Well, okay." And to the egg, "Set destination. To Derion's location." Oops. "*Count* Derion."

"No authorized destination has been specified."

The response gave no clues at all! What ever happened to user-friendly? Curbing an impulse toward rude speech, Tabor said, "Specify any authorized destinations associated with Count Derion."

"None exist."

Well. Maybe Lady Aliira was the only game in town. "Specify . . ." Different name, same question.

The egg said, "Primary locus: coordinates Two Four Three W, Three Four Two J. Secondary loci: coordinates Two Five One K, Five Six Two R, alternate Four Two—"

"Enough!" The numbers didn't mean doodly. Luke

thought. "Are either of the first two loci mentioned, the destination originally specified by Lord Frey, before he changed it to Enclave Five-Seven-A-C?"

"Primary locus is superseded destination."

"Reinstate superseded destination."

Tabor knew that long pause; judging by Casey's expression, so did she. The egg said, "Awaiting confirmation by Lord Frey."

Through gritted teeth: "Lord Frey is not here. Lord Frey is not available at this time. Lord Frey may be most easily reached from previously assigned, superseded destination. Proceed to that place and initiate contact with Lord Frey."

"At what velocity shall I proceed?"

If it ain't broke, don't fix it. "One-point-six rambs. Same as before."

The egg swung course and accelerated. A bit north of west, was Luke's guess; backtracking slightly from their earlier, generally southward course. Aloud he wondered why Frey hadn't sent them straight to this Lady Aliira in the first place.

"Maybe he wasn't sure she was there," Casey said. "Where we landed could be some kind of locator center, among other things."

Luke didn't answer; he was brooding over Svansek's dogmatic assertion that his and Casey's *names* were not "valid."

"What does she mean, valid?" Suddenly he laughed. "Svansek? Or Zwanzig? In German, that's the number twenty!"

"Her accent wasn't German," Casey put in. "I couldn't place it; could you?"

"Not really. I've heard it before, though." But where? Then it struck him: "Derion and Frey." But theirs were so subtle, so nearly trained away as to be only subliminally noticeable. "Until we heard the undiluted form, it didn't hit me that they *had* any."

"Mmmm." Casey was sightseeing. Tabor also looked out and down, seeing clouds make darker patterns on sunlit terrain. They rode higher now, perhaps five thousand feet. Judging by his experience in both jet transports and lighter planes (he'd never ridden SSTs, either standard models or the more advanced suborbital scramjets), he guessed their speed at about one-fifty. Yet at this moderate altitude, where light planes bounced through thermals, the egg rode steady and unbuffeted.

Whenever they were, the technology was worth noting.

To the left, nestled against the end of a foothill range, Tabor spotted a patch of trees, perhaps a second oasis like the one they had briefly visited. And on the other side, near the horizon at an angle ahead, another. Presumably they were bound for something of the sort, but as yet no such place appeared along their present course.

Although Luke's stomach was still comfortable from the lunch Frey had shared with them, he was beginning to feel thirsty. He looked around the compartment, especially alongside and beneath the instrumented dashboard, but if anything like a storage cabinet or glove compartment existed, he couldn't detect it. Just like the door . . .

So *ask*. "Is there any water aboard? Anything fit to drink? If so, please disclose it." And why was he being polite to a machine? *Because it's in charge here.*

The same soft, barely inflected voice said, "There is water, protomilk, nalcwine, and several palatable juices. I know this because those compartments hold contents; I do not know, for instance, which juices have been stocked." At least it couldn't read the labels!

Luke said, "Would Lord Frey normally have nalcwine with guests at lunch?"

"He would."

So that was the stuff they'd had; file the term. "Then I'd like some. Display it, please." Booze, in this unfamiliar situation, wouldn't be a good idea. But this nalc stuff—short for nonalcoholic?—was safe enough. As with the door, below the dash a slit appeared and widened into an

opening, revealing a cabinet that held four flasks like the
one Frey had brought, and half a dozen stacked glasses.

Tabor helped himself. Without asking Casey he
poured for two; they touched glasses, then sipped. The
clink didn't sound like glass but had too much of a ring
for plastic as he knew it.

This wasn't the same beverage Frey had offered; it
held a deeper, pinkish tinge and more full-bodied flavor. It
felt the same, though: gentle, pleasant stimulation, with no
hint of the familiar effects of ethanol.

Slowly he enjoyed two glasses. But intake eventually
mandates exhaust. Luke had a time of it translating his need,
in a vehicle obviously lacking restrooms, to machine-
understandable terms. But finally the egg told him how to
pull from under the seat a device attached to a retractable
tube.

He looked at it; one design fits all. He and Casey had
gotten over being john-shy, so he didn't bother retiring to
a rear seat. When he was done he let the doohickey retreat
to its hidden position and felt much relieved.

Still no obvious destination showed ahead. Tabor
leaned back and closed his eyes.

Stimulant or not, Luke dozed off. Casey's elbow, and
her voice saying, "Hey! See that?" brought him awake.
Blinking, he focused on an uneven dark line crossing the
plain far ahead. At first it didn't look like much, but de-
creasing distance gave him more detail. He was looking,
from a very flat angle, at the near rim of a canyon and the
darker contrast of its farther lip.

As approach improved perspective, he saw he viewed
no mere ravine, but a big granddaddy chasm indeed. As a
child he'd seen the Grand Canyon; from what he could remember, this one had to be less wide but possibly deeper—
and here, close to the head end, its river tumbled in muddy
turmoil.

At first no sign of a destination appeared, but as the
near rim passed below he saw that where it made a wide
outward swing it left a great ledge far down, nearer the

river itself than the plain above. Over a mile in length, that ledge; at its widest point, well over half as much. And tree-covered. More knowledgeable now, Tabor looked for and spotted hints of structures showing, in late-slanted sunlight, past the foliage.

A thought came. Here, as at the place where they'd landed earlier, *now* the leaves mostly hid the buildings. In winter they would not. His camouflage theory self-destructed. Keeping his rueful grin totally inward, he responded to Casey's increasing excitement. Yes it *was* a sight to see; no he had never seen anything quite like it, and no he hadn't the faintest idea where on Earth it—not to mention *they*—could be.

Maybe when the egg landed, somebody might tell them.

Instead of finding a gap between trees the egg swooped down wide of the great ledge and came in level with it. Viewed at roughly ground level the place wasn't actually flat; overall it sloped gently inward and down-river, and that slope varied with minor rolling swells. Nothing for hill climbers, just enough to break the monotony.

Near the ledge's end, foresting thinned and stopped; there the egg swooped in, passing two similar grounded vehicles and a row of nondescript storage-type buildings to touch down a few yards short of a more distinctive structure at the row's end. That one sported a loading dock alongside what appeared to be an office entrance—before which stood perhaps a dozen persons gathered around a tall figure, facing away, with long blond hair reaching down its bare back, nearly to the low-slung beltline of loose-cut khaki shorts.

Several of the group, varying as much in overall appearance as those in Subcontroller Svansek's Enclave, began to look and gesture toward the egg. Within moments the tall one noticed and turned around.

At first glimpse Tabor was thoroughly confused.

* * *

Judging by the long, wavy hair, plus a subtle but distinct swell of hipline, Luke expected it to be a woman who turned to face him. But the handsome face told nothing of gender; somehow it hinted at immaturity. And the torso, bare to the waist, resembled that of a slim, relatively unmuscled boy, lacking any breast development whatsoever. In a clear, rather high-pitched voice, just audible through the egg's transparent segment, the person said, "As you may know, I am the Lady Aliira. Who visits here, unannounced?"

Tabor ordered the door open and clambered out, giving Casey a hand to follow him. Aliira approached. At closer range Luke made out small, pale nipples but no discernible areolae.

Stopping just short of arm's reach, she said, "Might you be those reported to me by Subcontroller Svansek? In any case, why come you here?"

"We're the ones, all right—uh, milady." *This time, let's not get off on the wrong foot.* "We were given the loan of the—the *carrier*"—he hoped he'd used the proper term—"by Lord Frey, who advised us to look you up. I'm Lucian Tabor, and may I present Karen Cecile Collins." He said the latter as statement, not question, and added, "Even if Svansek does say we're not valid."

"Svansek reported the fact that your names are not registered in this jurisdiction. What is your provenance?"

Stall, or tell the truth? Impulse took over. "We were brought to this jurisdiction"—hoping he had that part right—"by Count Derion. We come from the city of Pullman, in the state of Washington, one of fifty-two states comprising the United States of America, the predominant nation on the North American continent." *And that should hold you for a while.*

It didn't, though. "As of what date? Roughly speaking. Except for the continent itself I know not of the places you claim as origin; presumably their names antedate any era of which I have detailed knowledge."

Truly, this one didn't horse around. "Uh—" What

numbers might she know? Keep it general. "Give or take a little, the end of the second millenium after Christ."

Aliira's hands clasped tightly together against her boyish chest. "Then Derion succeeded; he has passed beyond the Waste Times. And reached a new, farthermost Island!"

Freeing her hands, she reached one out to Luke and the other to Casey. "Come. There is much you must tell me."

Escorted by a muscular, swarthy man whose black hair and whiskers bristled uniformly at approximately half-inch length, Luke and Casey followed the Lady Aliira. The man, who stood about Tabor's height, said no word and showed no expression.

All four walked around one side of the building; behind it sat a nacreous-gleaming object. To Luke it looked like a cross between a canoe and a bathtub, enclosing six upholstered seats paired to form three rows.

"Valmir?" said Aliira. The man touched the wain's rim; part of its near side opened down to offer a stepping-point for entrance, and he gave the woman a hand up. She took a rear seat; Valmir sat up front. Leaving the middle pair for Luke and Casey.

The side swung up to close again. Tabor couldn't see whether Valmir's hands did anything, but the boatlike object lifted gently, a foot or more off the ground, and moved ahead at somewhat better than walking pace.

"Derion brought you to Hykeran Outjut." Aliira's tone rang flat. "Yet you say you were sent *here* by Lord Frey. There is a contradiction; you may be liege to either faction, of course—but hardly to both. An explanation is due."

That point cut both ways. But first: "We know nothing about these factions of yours. The only ones we'd met, back home, were Derion and Frey. They—"

Her hand gripped his shoulder. "Lord Frey was there also?"

"Too right, he was. And very disruptive, I might add. Is that his specialty?"

She said only, "I'd known he could swim the river, of course—but not to *that* extent." The treble voice hardened. "You have not defined your liegeship, as I asked."

Tabor was out of his depth here, but being pushed around had never been one of his strong points. "Come to that, what's yours? Whose side are *you* on?"

"Neither. With some effort and more caution, I hold myself neutral. Until now, at least. I dislike the thought that Frey or Derion may have sent you here to destroy that balance."

Silence lengthened. Gliding along between trees, passing buildings Luke took to be residences of varied and imaginative design, the floatboat had covered nearly half the ledge's reach. Casey said, "We don't know anything about your disputes here—or for that matter, what Derion and Frey were trying to do in our own time. What we'd *like* to do," she said, "is get ourselves back there and forget the whole thing."

Her elbow nudged. "Isn't that right, Luke?"

"Right." Then suddenly he wasn't so sure. This was a new place, a new time; what might it hold? What *did* he want?

At the upstream end of the ledge, where it petered out in a sloping of talus from above, a building sat with half its bulk cantilevered out over the river below. What with Aliira's title, Tabor had expected a veritable palace, but the wain came to rest before a flat-roofed, split-level structure done in pastels and transparence. Not greatly larger, he guessed, than a four-bedroom home in his own era. Hardly ostentatious for a titled lady.

The wain's side opened down; the Lady Aliira debarked and her two quasi guests followed. Valmir did not; when the vehicle closed itself he turned it and departed down-ledge.

Aliira led toward a door-sized section, framed off by thin metal, of a wall which somehow looked like glass that

wasn't quite there. Pausing, she held one hand, fingers together and pointing ahead, a foot or so before her face,
which briefly held a look of concentration. What the section did, as near as Luke could tell, was change its seeming from ghost glass to thin air. All three walked inside,
into a largish area divided only by half-height partitions in
contrasting colors; the furniture and its arrangement made
no sense to Tabor.

The woman did nothing more about the doorway, that
Luke could detect, but sneaking a look behind he saw the
section revert to its original appearance.

He stepped back and reached to it, feeling coolness
and vibration, resilient resistance. He'd always thought
"force field" to be a non sequitur; now he reconsidered.
And noted that Changed *will* was good for more than
zooming beer cans and substituting for elevators.

But Frey hadn't used it to open or close the egg, the
carrier. Or had he?

"Come." Aliira sounded impatient; Tabor pivoted to
see a rectangle of floor swing aside to reveal a downward
stairway. Feeling more impressed than he wanted to be, he
followed her and Casey to a lower level.

The room lay damp and cool, moss-covered stone
walls streaked with trickling rivulets of rust-tinged water
which somehow drained without spreading onto the stone-
flagged floor or wetting the several resilient rugs scattered
across it. The slightly irregular ceiling looked like stone
also, but Tabor bet himself it was some kind of synthetic.
Amber light, bright for its softness, came from a sus-
pended, basketball-sized globe.

Also depending from the ceiling was a sort of couch,
like a porch swing upholstered in apricot plush—except
that its four supporting lines slanted outward, for stability.
Still, when their hostess gestured toward seats, Tabor
passed it by for one of several more orthodox, varicolored
chairs. At least these stood on the floor, their seats and
armless backs separated from platform bases by arcs of

flat metal. Seating himself, Luke expected elasticity and was not disappointed.

Casey made a similar choice. Going to the couch, Aliira picked up and donned a white bolero jacket. Then from a small cabinet she produced a bottle and glasses.

"Wine, Lucian Tabor? Or is Luke, as Karen Cecile Collins addressed you, more to your preference?"

"Luke or Lucian, either one. And among friends, Karen Cecile goes by Casey." Belatedly then, "Wine? Yes, please." And Casey nodded.

Deftly Aliira poured; after sniffing, Tabor sipped. Not nalc, this chartreuse-tinted liquid. But in the army he'd developed a fair head for booze, a prerequisite for any degree of success at payday poker. He'd gotten a little out of practice, was all. But pacing always helped. . . .

Aliira herself occupied the swing, which as Luke had guessed, didn't. She said, "It is difficult to believe: you two being here, from beyond the Waste Times. Before the Genocides. Derion has achieved what none thought possible."

Waste Times? Genocides? Tabor leaned forward. "How long has it been? From our time to now?"

Looking baffled, the Lady Aliira said, "We have no means of knowing that."

"But you said—" What were her words? "The farthest Island yet. So you must have some idea."

She shook her head. "No. We know of the calendar you cite, but during the Waste Times enumeration by it was irretrievably lost. I can only be certain that the Island encompassing your time must be far past indeed."

# SEVEN

**N**o wonder Derion hadn't named locations! Tabor thought he'd accepted the fact that time, not distance, separated the Islands, but the full gut realization came like a physical blow.

He took a deep breath. All right, ask questions. "Is this the earliest of the Islands you already knew of?"

"Hykeran Outjut? No, some few exist earlier: all minor, none over a year in span." At his and Casey's puzzled looks, the woman said, "You would not know, of course. The river of time is most likely a separate continuum, in which time and space partake of each other's attributes. The Islands are periods which serve as windows, during which a few of the Changed—a small minority—can enter or leave that river. If I, for instance, neglected to establish a preemptive presence at Hykeran's lower end and allowed myself to remain past it, I would be trapped in time's normal current for almost fifty years, until a small Islet—of only a few days' extent—breaks surface. Because one cannot sense the approaching end-boundary of an Island while living in normal time, only from outtime, within the river."

As Luke struggled to understand, Aliira paused. "I shall miss the Outjut; it has been one of my favorite times."

"But you can come back to it, can't you?" Casey said. "Any time you please?"

"In the same moment *twice?*" Aliira shook her head.

Tabor said, "I don't understand. I thought people like you could go anywhere in time at whim. Where there's an Island, I mean. What's to stop you?"

"It cannot happen. Once we have lived a period, we are barred from it by preemptive presence. Earlier in this

Island, only a little over two years at its beginning are still available to me. If I went there, then when I reached the point of my previous arrival I would be ejected into the river of time." Her nod was vigorous, putting an end to the subject.

"At any rate—" Now she laughed. "I am by no means ready to undertake a fixed existence. Any more than to—" She gestured toward her own body. "As you can see."

Casey's scowl denoted concentration. "I don't *understand* what I see. May I ask a personal question?" Aliira nodded. Casey cleared her throat. "Well, then. You look to have your height, and obviously you hold fully adult status. But on the face of it, you're not what *we* expect in a grown woman."

Aliira's puzzled frown cleared. "Of course. You know little of the Changed. And the Unchanged never develop as prepubertal adults; your sexuality finds you barely half-grown."

"Yours comes later, by nature?" Luke hoped his question was tactful.

"Partially. And, to a certain extent, by choice. Some opt to ripen early, others do not. I have lived a bit past three-six years and plan, if allowed"—momentarily she appeared anxious—"to wait perhaps another five."

"Any particular reason?" Luke's question came out before he realized how nosy it sounded.

She didn't seem to mind. "My work. I lead a research group designated by the Prime Peer. Our study is the focusing and modulation of *will* induced fusion, and all our effort is directed toward a specific goal."

Serious-faced, she leaned forward. "Pre-Genocidal humans walked upon our moon and at least two other planets. An uncrewed probe reached another *star.* Our aim is to regain those capabilities and exceed them; our first ship, now building, is goaled to full inner-system access. At any rate—when my part in this work is ended, I will find time for sexual maturation."

Solemn until now, Karen Cecile grinned. "I'd like to

see your face when you find out what you've been missing!"

Lady Aliira's own expression was perhaps too aristocratic for a true grin, but it came close. "You are mistaken. For as long as I can remember, I have been orgasmic. Clitoral function does not wait on puberty."

"I know that. I also know there's more to it; you still have things to learn."

"Not so much as you might surmise." This was getting franker than Luke was comfortable with; he began to feel embarrassed. But he kept listening as Aliira went on, "When a time came that I desired to compare the experience of true coitus with those of its several useful and pleasant alternatives, I consulted a practitioner and was advised how best to achieve the necessary dilation. The result has been quite satisfactory."

Well, goodie for her. And no contraceptive worries, either. Although maybe the Changed managed that by *will*, too. Tabor decided not to ask. . . .

Instead he changed the subject. "So you don't know how far out of our own time we are. But you do know time periods in your own history?" Aliira nodded. "Then how far back were the Waste Times? And how long did they last? When were the Genocides? How much time-dated history *do* you have?"

"These," she said, "are fruitful questions. Very well; we set the end of the Waste Times, rather arbitrarily, at two-three-two-five years ago. Our calendar begins then. It is impossible to state accurately the duration of that lost era; scholars' estimates vary between three-one-zero and one-four-four-zero years." Her smile came sad, rueful. "It was the Genocides which caused the Waste Times. And need not have lasted long to do so."

What there was of it, made sense. "Do you know what the Genocides were?"

Briefly she put both hands to her face, then clasped them in her lap. "That knowledge shames us all. Changed and Unchanged alike."

At this point, it seemed, she wouldn't say more. On

a new tack Tabor began, "It takes disagreements to produce factions. What's the beef between Frey and Derion? Uh—the difference."

Again Aliira made her slight frown. "How can I tell you? There is too much you would not understand."

"Give it a try." *Oops, don't forget who's boss here!*

Aliira took no offense; she said, "Certainly. But may I suggest we dine now? I can offer you—"

Rude or not, Luke interrupted. "Why don't you choose for us? We enjoy surprises." And appreciate saving time, as well . . .

The little cabinet was more versatile than it looked. Aliira touched parts of an ornamental molding—controls, obviously—then opened the front. No bottles inside now, but three covered trays. Distributing these, the woman showed how a smallish frame unfolded from under each chair seat and swung into position, how first the lid and then the tray itself nested into that frame.

While she was up, she refilled all three wineglasses.

The main course appeared to be roast chicken, but with more flavor than Luke was used to. Yet not unfamiliar, after a few bites he recognized the taste of the free-running chickens his parents had raised on their farm before moving into Lewis Gap. In later years he'd had only "factory chicken," bland and fatty.

As with the lunch Frey had provided, some of the side vegetables were new to him. Not bad, just different.

The utensils, at least, were more or less familiar, though subtly different in shape and proportion. And the fork with the cutting edge along one side required a certain amount of caution.

Once he had his gastronomic bearings, Tabor dug in and enjoyed the dinner. When all three were finishing he looked across to Aliira. "You serve a delicious meal; thank you."

As she nodded, looking pleased, he added, "Where can I wash up?" Spreading his fingers which were not only sticky but looked it.

"Ah. Allow me . . ." Not everything in the place operated by *will;* Aliira moved to the far wall and touched spots of apparent lichen on a seeming rock. Part of the wall pivoted sidewise; the basin that swung into view had spigots, but came out already filled with scented water.

Great, but that wasn't entirely what he'd had in mind. Perhaps his expression spoke for him; again she touched green-grey spots on brownish stone, and to the left of the basin another section rotated. The fixture that appeared resembled a wider, more enveloping version of a Western saddle; along its central axis ran a fair-sized, all-purpose oval orifice above a bowl with some water in it.

The Lady Aliira smiled as though she'd invented the thing. "Will this be satisfactory?"

Somehow it was easier to defy old taboos than ask her to put a screen around it. He sat bare-assed in the saddle; it accomodated to fit him snugly. He let his stream run and end. When he put a hand down to help push himself up, his crotch received a jet of warm spray followed by dry, even warmer air.

Clean and dried, Lucian Tabor rose and zipped his pants, washed his hands, walked to his chair, and sat down.

When in Rome, follow the yellow brick *iter.*

"Now," he said to Aliira, "you were going to tell us more?"

"Yes. Of course." Briefly she closed her eyes, then opened them to look from Luke to Casey and back again; until now, their green glint had escaped him.

"To the best of our deductive estimation, the Genocides' beginning came about in this fashion. . . ."

Genetic engineering: hailed and damned, federally funded on the one hand while at the same time legislated against at that and other levels, it proved to be a Pandora's box, and perhaps larger inside than out. From licit and bootleg labs alike came valuable discoveries—but also abominations.

Several diseases and genetic impairments, their very

names now lost, had been eradicated—sometimes with unforeseen repercussions. An effort to program genius produced a cadre of conscienceless egotists who came near to destroying a society before their victims rebelled—and by sheer numbers, conquered. The genetic strain was completely exterminated.

Behind closed borders a paranoid government bred the equivalent of soldier ants: single-goaled warriors with thrice the strength and endurance of normal men, able to wage war with lesser and poorer equipment yet still prevail. After two of their invasions succeeded, the next and all future attempts were ended by hellblasts in quantity—the single case, to Aliira's knowledge, in which legend told of massive fusion bombing. "Only in fairly modern times have the bombed areas once again become safe to inhabit."

As folklore had it, nearly any genetic experiment that could be tried had been. One such was the proposal to double or triple, in one generation, the world's capacity to feed humans, by altering genes to produce offspring of half-normal mass or less. Tabor saw problems: pelvic girdles too small for passage of the infant braincase; also the simple fact that since the population couldn't possibly be changed all at once, the new Little People could very well get pushed around a lot. *Jock City,* he thought, then decided perhaps he was being unfair. And found that while musing he'd missed the part of the legend that told what actually happened to that experiment.

He did follow, in outline, the long haul of lost history. Inevitably there developed genetically advantaged subpopulations, and estrangement between those haves and the "normal" have-nots. Leading eventually to open, catastrophic conflict.

"It couldn't have been quite that simple," said Casey. "All the tinkered-genes rich and powerful, and the rest downtrodden."

"There were, we believe, aggravating factors," Aliira said. "Aside from government programs, designed to eradicate defects and disease so far as might be done, most genetic alterations were privately financed. Providing automatic priority to the wealthy." And as Casey nodded, "One such achievement was increased longevity, giving the individual a much longer productive career, more time to *build* wealth."

"I read a story like that once," Luke put in. "In general the short-termers were outclassed, couldn't truly compete."

"However it may have been," Aliira resumed, "it is told that the masses turned against the new elite, mounting veritable pogroms. And the intended victims, hardly powerless, struck back in kind." Her voice dropped near inaudibility, as she said, "Bacterial and viral agents were loosed, specifically tailored to attack normals and spare the elite. The effort came very near to total success." She shook her head. "That shame we still bear."

Slowly, Tabor asked, "How far did it go? Where your current history begins, how did things stand?"

"World population, we estimate, numbered to not much over seven zeroes. This after the uncounted devastating Waste Times years. Those people believed all trace of the oppressor class was gone, wiped out. But one strain survived."

"The Changed." Luke stated the obvious. And then, "How?"

"The gene quirk which produces *will* must have been a serendipitous variation; none of us can conceive how it could be deliberately wrought. It has several side-properties, such as the ability to increase longevity or—or achieve other physical changes. Another is that it is recessive."

It took a moment; then Tabor said, "So throughout the Waste Times, some of the supposedly Unchanged were carrying your heritage around in their own gametes. But when two of those matched up, what happened? To the offspring, I mean."

"The ability to sense or influence emotion is not obvious to detection. More apparent attributes could be exercised only with great discretion. And longevity, as an anomaly, poses no danger to one who moves occasionally from one isolated community to another. In those grim times, doubtless some Changed did reveal themselves—and died for it. But as our numbers grew over the years, my ancestors devised codes of living to guide them, to make a place for us." Shame was gone; now Aliira showed pride.

"And it's worked?" Luke asked. "No big problems?"

Her expression saddened. "Not until quite recently. Not until now."

Luke and Casey waited until she continued. "The skills of those who changed us were lost during the Waste Times or before. But knowing of what can be and has been done, both we and the Unchanged have studied and experimented. Over the past few generations progress was made—gains in elimination of defects and diseases affecting our own time. But the result is that many, perhaps most, of this period's so-called Unchanged may and do differ considerably from our common root stock."

Grimacing, Casey said to Tabor, "Nothing like knowing our place. Hello, brother Root Stock. Are we here for a little grafting, do you suppose?"

The Lady Aliira seemed puzzled. Luke said, "I think Casey's asking, why *are* we here? At Hykeran Outjut, I mean. Do you have any idea?"

Side to side her head moved. "The true thought of Derion, I have never known."

"And Frey?"

"Lord Frey's apparent objectives change like the wind at break of spring. He seeks to hold sway over all that touches him. So that he is often at odds with Count Derion."

Aliira stood. "I have had a very long waketime. May I show you to your quarterings now—and, until morning, leave you?"

There wasn't much to say to that, except yes.

\* \* \*

Upstairs the ground floor had changed; instead of the large semi-open area they emerged into a foyer that led to the front entrance. Only that end was transparent; the side walls, and the two doors on either side, looked like wood paneling.

Skeptical, Tabor brushed a knuckle against the wall to his right. Not to his surprise, he met the same cool, almost subliminal vibration he'd felt when the front door reappeared.

So the walls were subject to change without notice.

Aliira led them to and through the second door on the right. Inside she walked to the far wall, the one containing a large window which overlooked dimly lit trees. She pointed to a small knob at the window's corner. "This governs opacity. If you like, you may close off outside view." She demonstrated.

Now she touched colored spots on an oval panel, first evoking from the wall some facilities like those Luke had seen below: the basin and formfitting potty-seat, a cabinet like that from which Aliira had taken food and drink. Next, a section opened to reveal a sunken bath. And last, from the floor rose a low, spacious bed.

All very interesting. Not least, that everything came out of the far wall and the floor. Ergo, those two surfaces were real, not field-generated pseudomatter.

As before, Aliira touched fingers to the molding that girt the cabinet's top. "I have taken the liberty to program a few items of food and drink. Should you thirst or hunger ..."

"Thank you." More or less together the two guests said it, as Aliira moved to the door.

"Then sleep well. I shall visit you next at morning."

She went out; Tabor noticed that the closing door made no sound. He looked at his watch: ten-eighteen. Not too early for sleep, except that he wasn't sleepy.

He was, however, rife with sweat and grime. "Casey! Want to share a bath?"

"Why not?" So they climbed down into the tub, fiddled the confusing and unfamiliar controls until water came at proper heat, and played a little splash. Lucian had more in mind but Casey said she, personally, *was* tired. Umm, yes—he figured back; by her timing, she'd been up all day and all night, and this was ten-thirty the next morning. Or close enough.

So he helped her up. When they stood, the blow-dry came on, taking only a short time to do its chore while the tub drained. Casey stretched to kiss him good-night, went directly to the bed and lay down, pulling up one thin coverlet. The lighting dimmed partially, so that none shone directly on her. This place had more tricks than a stage magician.

Restless, Luke checked the cabinet. He rolled a thin slice of meat and a stick of soft amber cheese up in a palm-sized sheet of something like seasoned pita, and munched happily. With his second one, adding a slim, tangy pickle, he sampled a small flask of something that looked like beer but had a somewhat different, equally pleasant taste. He couldn't quite place it.

Then, after a brief stint back in the saddle, he washed his hands and went to bed. Soon after he lay down, the overall lighting dimmed near to darkness.

A little surprised, he woke to the sound of Casey showering. The window was clear again; sunlight filtered through foliage lit the room. When the water stopped and the blow-dry had done whooshing, he said, "I'd've thought you were still clean from last night."

"I ran it cool, to wake up on." Her hair hadn't dried thoroughly; it hung damp but not dripping.

From the bundle of clothes she extracted and put on a shortsleeved V-necked blouse, sheer except over the breasts where transparency changed gradually to central patches of solid color; the whole was a pale blue. With it she donned slim knee-length breeches in an equally pale yellow.

She looked at a dressy pair of shoes and one of comfortable-looking slippers, shook her head, and pulled on the sandals she'd worn yesterday. Standing, she said,

"I'm going out and walk around. Get the cobwebs out of my head." She made a mild grimace. "Jet lag, it feels like." And as Luke had noted to himself last night, well it might.

"How about breakfast?"

"When I get back." She went out; again the door closed without sound. Lying flat, Tabor stretched. He hadn't thought to caution Karen Cecile, but this *was* Here There Be Tygers country. Oh well; Casey wouldn't know how to work the disappearing door, and certainly Aliira wouldn't let her go anywhere dangerous. He kept telling himself . . .

Casey's wakeup plan sounded good. Going to the tub, he wished he'd asked her how she finagled a shower out of it. But by persistent tinkering he found the way—and was struck by a fire hose blast of icy water.

When he was done yelling and had the thing adjusted to his liking (a coarse, vigorous spray, slightly warmer than tepid), he stood, eyes closed, turning slowly for uniform effect.

He wasn't expecting another wet, naked body to embrace him from behind.

"Casey?" But the chin rested on his shoulder; Casey's couldn't. And he knew exactly how high on his back her breasts would press against him. They weren't doing that.

So he looked around. Two inches away from his left eye, the Lady Aliira was smiling.

Moving to cut the water flow, he got it on the second try and turned within Aliira's grasp, gently pushing them apart. He didn't wait for drying but stepped up and out as the blower whipped waterdrops off Aliira's child-smooth skin. She hadn't gone into the spray far enough nor stayed long enough to more than dampen the lower reaches of her hair, swinging free. She shook it back; still moisture-specked, she left the tub.

Except when his cousin Lily's daughter ran out of her diaper, Tabor had never seen a young, undeveloped girl naked. Now as he backpedaled he couldn't avoid seeing a quite undeveloped full-scale woman.

He'd already noted the lack of breasts, of nipple-area definition. Added now was the sight of a child's crotch grown larger but otherwise unchanged: plump smoothness, marked only by the vertical fold that hid her potential for genital function.

As with Lily's toddler it brought no sexual response at all; he saw her disappointment. "I do not incite your desire?"

"It would be—" He tried not to say it but couldn't stop. "—like raping a child."

"I assure you it would not; lubricant has been applied." She must have seen she wasn't helping matters; she said, "Or consider: my alternative orifice is fully adult. And—" She licked her lips. "I am also skilled . . ."

"No—" His hands pushed air; he backed away. He saw her expression firm to purpose; her eyes widened, then slowly narrowed. He felt a twitch, a moving tingle. Then, like it or not, he began rising to the unwelcome occasion.

Like a ten-year-old in the schoolyard he heard himself complain, "No fair! That's cheating."

His yelp jarred her; the stimulation faltered, then died. Tension left her face, leaving only serious concern. "In your culture, sex with the immature was a firm tooboo?"

"Tooboo?" Portmanteau of taboo and booboo? Fighting a sudden impulse to laugh, he said, "Taboo, we'd say. Yes, it was. Those who violated it were despised, viewed with loathing."

She nodded. "I see. Very well. I had thought you only needed an urge of *will*, but I shall not do that again." And ruefully, "Had I come to you in darkness, you would find no cause to withdraw."

Seeing where he looked then, she touched her pubes. "Surely some of your women depilate? For one reason or another?"

"Uh—I suppose so." How far did a bikini wax go,

anyway? Never mind. And don't quibble about breasts, either; more than a few adult women showed practically flat except when the function was appropriate. Choosing words carefully, he said, "The concept of undeveloped adults—their being *eligible*—is too new; it hasn't sunk in emotionally." Then, quickly, "But aside from that, Lady Aliira, Casey and I are paired up. We don't play around." Actually, he realized, if that agreement existed between them it was tacit; they'd never discussed the matter.

"Monogamy, yes," Aliira responded. "It is practiced by some few of us, also. Not a high proportion, due to the need for outbreeding: with the Unchanged to produce Chi-carriers, and then with those to augment the Changed population. Of course our men fill the greater portion of that requirement, though by no means all. At any rate, I respect your right to make your own choice."

Her smile came close to being impish. "You might have told me."

"You didn't ask."

Evaporation had dried them both; Luke was walking over to where his clothes lay when Aliira said, "Do you desire the growth of hair to obscure your facial features?"

"Huh?" He felt his chin; the two days' growth—or was it three by now?—didn't feel like much. Still, "Not especially. But I don't have anything to shave with."

From a recess beside the washbasin she brought out a small grey ovoid object, twice as long as wide, with at one end a flat, slanting surface; the sides had finger-grip indentations. She held it out to him, turning it to show him all sides, and said, "This device depilates by shaking dead protein to dust using ultrasonic vibration. You must move the flat face gently along the desired skin surface. Do not allow it to linger too long at any one place, because surface skin cells are also dead; too much exposure acts to uncover a more tender layer."

She was obviously waiting for him to try it out, so he did. Lacking a mirror (there had to be one, hidden in the works somewhere, but he didn't feel like asking) he used the fingers of his other hand to monitor progress.

The thing gave him a slight tingle, not at all painful. When he decided he was done he turned to Aliira, only to see her tilt her head to one side as though she were listening. He heard nothing; she said, "Casey has returned," and for a moment her face took on the *will* expression. Blanking the front door? Probably. His original intention sidetracked, he was still standing there when Casey walked in.

"Hi! It's great outside. The air alone takes ten tired years off your karma, and—" She looked at Luke and at Aliira.

"Setting up for breakfast *au naturel,* are we? Do I peel too? Or should I go out again and come back later?"

She didn't seem angry: just talking aggressively to cover surprise. Before Tabor could think of some way to defuse matters, Aliira said, "I discovered Lucian bathing. He did not know I had entered until I embraced him from behind. I then made an amiable suggestion which he did not find acceptable. His refusal took place perhaps six-zero-zero seconds ago."

Very few times had Luke seen Casey Collins at a loss; here was one for the book. Her mouth opened and closed once before she said, singsong, "Thank you for sharing that." Nobody kept Casey down for long. . . .

Plaintive-toned, she added, "I wasn't kidding about breakfast; either way is fine."

Aliira had no clothing with her and obviously didn't care. As she juggled the cabinet's controls to produce food and drink, and the wall's to elicit a table and chairs, Tabor took the opportunity to get dressed. Two clothed and one not, they sat and ate.

Eggs hadn't changed. The meat was vaguely hamlike but less salty; taste and texture of some rounded objects resembled whole grain toast. Luke couldn't identify the source of the fruit juice, but he had two refills.

Along with some of the best coffee he could remember. He was sipping the last of his second cup when Aliira broke silence.

"There has been a message, purportedly from Derion. It came during my sleep, which is well because I did not have to answer without time for thought."

That couldn't be the full story, but Aliira stopped. After a pause, Tabor said, "Did the message concern us? Casey and me?"

"Derion's representative asked if I had knowledge of your whereabouts." She looked from one to the other. "What should I answer?"

"Is there any reason," Casey said, "why you shouldn't just tell him we're here?"

Aliira frowned. "Not with regard to Derion. But such disclosure might run counter to the wishes of Lord Frey."

"And Frey scares you."

Luke wished Casey wouldn't push it, but the thing was said. He cleared his throat. "Derion warned me Frey was dangerous. To me, at least. Is he a threat to you, too?"

The clear childlike voice couldn't drop much in pitch, but its level ebbed to faintness. "When Frey is moved to avenge a slight he has been known to destroy without restraint."

Casey nodded. "So you'll have to stonewall Derion?" Aliira frowned; Casey said, "Not tell him where we are."

"Derion has not Frey's violence," Aliira said slowly. "Yet the weight of his displeasure—"

Tabor stood. "Where is Derion, anyway? Did he say?"

"He gave no location. That he needs to ask of your presence, places him beyond useful farsight distance. At his primary locus of operations, perhaps." She frowned. "It matters not. If I tell Derion, I anger Frey. If not—"

"So they've got you coming and going. Well, I have an idea." At that point he had only about half of it, but Aliira needed a jump start. So he said, "Can you program that carrier to ignore the past? Forget Lord Frey and take orders from *me?*"

Hesitantly, Aliira said, "I would assume so. But where would you go?"

"Well, we'd need a map. And plenty of food and water stocked in the egg. Any problem with that?"

"No. But *where—?*"

"That's the whole point, Aliira. If you don't know, you can't tell Derion, can you?" *Or* Frey . . .

As Luke and Casey got into the grey-bronze carrier, loaded with their own meager gear plus items supplied by Aliira, the Lady kept up a nonstop stream of advice. Leaning inside, she said, "—and if you venture near the great river's mouth, you must avoid the swamps surrounding it. For these—"

"I know; you've told us," Tabor put in. He looked at the map, marked with the few destinations she'd recommended as possible safe havens. One was Derion's primary locus; he'd made sure of that one, then requested others as a measure of misdirection. But from Aliira's expressions and tones of voice he guessed she doubted the dependability of some.

No matter; he said, "We'd better go now. You do want us out of here, in case Derion or Frey come looking." She didn't protest, so he said, "You want to move back out of the way now?" When she did so he told the egg, "Close the door."

She was still trying to get in a last word, faint through the transparent panel, when Luke said, "Lift off, rise to cruise altitude, and head south at two rambs per second." Whatever *they* were. Well, one-point-six had seemed a fair clip, earlier.

Then to Casey, "Now we should have time to sort things out."

# EIGHT

"**W**ell," said Karen Cecile, "now what?"

She shook her hair back; puzzled, Tabor waited. Then Casey said, "Here we go, just as if we had good sense. And you didn't ask Breastless Mahoney several of the important questions."

It took him a moment to get the reference. *Dick Tracy* was one of Casey's favorite cult discs; she always exclaimed over how *young* Madonna looked. As though the woman hadn't been on the sunny side of thirty, then. Nettled, he said, "Such as what?"

"Like what are some other iffy spots to stay away from, how to dodge Frey, or get hold of Derion if he's not at his home fief. You—"

The egg, the carrier, lifted past the canyon's rim. Trying to keep his tone reasonable, Luke said, "Neither did you."

"But—" She sputtered. "You were here *first.*"

So it was his place to lead? Oh, sure! Suddenly they were both laughing. And hugging. A kiss threatened to get out of hand; Luke wasn't sure which of them first pulled free. He said, "If Aliira knew what she was doing, Lord Frey's restrictions on this machine should be looser now. We might have better luck with its Answer Man."

Casey nodded. "Can't hurt to give it a test run."

Nothing ever lives up to first hopes; Tabor knew that. But his inquiries began well. While the map was scaled in rambs, and their length was something else he hadn't thought to ask, its orientation was clear enough. The spot Aliira had marked to approximate the site of Derion's "primary locus" lay well past the mountains to the south, at about fifteen degrees east of that direction and perhaps twice Enclave Five-Seven-A-C's distance from Aliira's canyon.

Actually the mark itself was a bit vague, slopping across a coastal shoreline so that their destination could be equally predicated to lie on land or offshore. Squinting at the coordinates along the map's sides, Luke estimated a pair of readings, recited them to the egg, and asked, "At our current rate of speed, how long will it take us to reach that point?"

Instead of answering, the machine said, "What is the significance of this locus?"

"It's—" Whoops! No acceptable destinations were indexed to Derion, the egg had said. Frey's doing, no doubt—and maybe Aliira hadn't defused all the big Viking's shibboleths. "It is a destination suggested by the Lady Aliira."

"Very well. The time interval is approximately seven plus exponent-four seconds."

Seven—uh, seventy thousand? More than nineteen hours? How long had it been from Enclave to canyon—five, maybe? And they were going a quarter faster. . . . Eight should be more like it, nine at most.

He'd mumbled loud enough for the egg to hear. "What is nine?" it said. "And define—" It began a list.

"Stop!" How to begin. "Nine is three times three, and—"

"I am recording this new term for the integer one-one."

One-one? What was wrong here? A thought struck. "Start counting, by integers."

One-zero came after seven. The egg spoke not decimal, but octal. He said so.

Casey frowned. "Octal?"

"Base eight. It counts by eights, not tens."

So how long to destination? Round-numbers approximation told him that eight hours, maybe a bit under, was fairly close after all.

* * *

A sudden thought struck. "Jeez!" At Casey's surprised look he said, "All those numbers Aliira gave us— the time periods. I took 'em all for decimal. Hell—the two-three-two-five years since the Waste Times wasn't any twenty-three hundred. More like twelve hundred and something."

The same grade of thinking told him that two rambs was *not* a quarter faster than the egg's definition of one-point-six, but only a seventh. Hell with it; why get picky? Instead, "Is this speed—two rambs per second—your best normal cruising speed?"

"Best in what fashion?"

His exasperation must have shown; he could see Casey suppressing a bad case of the giggles. "The highest speed in your normal working range."

"No." Just plain no! Damn machine . . .

"What is that speed, then?"

"One-zero-point-four rambs per second."

Eight and a half. Maybe two hours for the run. All *right*. "Proceed to destination at that rate."

"At optimum altitude?"

"Roger. I mean, yes."

"Confirmed and executing." Acceleration both forward and upward made itself felt, not burdensome but implying plenty of horses. After a time it eased off and vanished.

Upstairs here, the sky looked a little funny.

One hour brought them to the mountain range: its foothills, at least. Snow capped the peaks and reached well down their northern slopes. The map, with only a fringe of coastline along its west side, gave Tabor no clue to location; no names of places or geographical features bore more than hints of familiarity, nor did their arrangement. Of course, he reflected, there were large parts of the world he didn't know worth doodly.

It was far too early for lunch, but to relieve boredom Luke brought out a pair of rolled-up snacks and some nalcwine. Neither he nor Casey recognized the tasty stuffing inside the pasta wraps; they merely nibbled away appreciatively. Finished, Casey poured second glasses and lifted hers. "Here's to—"

As the carrier took a violent dip, swerved, and plunged downward, nalcwine flew all over the place.

He couldn't yell What the hell happened?—the egg would ask him to define hell. "Pull up! Level off!"

The egg didn't. "Order cannot be executed."

A few times, in emergencies, Tabor had experienced timestretch. Not now. Events outside himself moved fast; only his own thoughts and action seemed slow. Casey was gesturing violently but at least not giving him cross talk as he said, "Why can't it?"

"Outside impulses control me."

"Override!"

"Control signals emanating from a human source have priority over my status as automated vehicle."

Damn all! "I'm a human source too, and I'm closer. Level off!"

"Impulse receptor holds precedence over sound receptor; I—"

*"How can I gain precedence?"*

"Manual controls are—"

*"What* manual controls? Where are they?" The egg was still zooming down; Luke gazed out at an increasingly serious lack of altitude.

"Concealed inside instrument array. Not extruded to operating position."

"Well get the fuckers *out* here." Cutting the egg off in the middle of "Define—" he rephrased it: "Extrude the controls!"

Out from the dashboard popped a slanting shelf that bore two lever handles.

As he took tentative hold of them the hum of power died; now the egg fell free.

"Tell me how to *work* these things!"

Calm and unhurried, the egg said, "Your right-hand

lever controls vehicle attitude." Luke wobbled it around; the egg spoke true, so gingerly he brought the nose up. "The left applies power, positive or negative, to direction of motion." On a guess he pushed it forward, and felt acceleration.

Gradually the egg came out of its dive and began to climb. Sounding unbearably superior the egg said, "It was not wise to preempt controls unfamiliar to you. Accordingly—"

"Yeah, yeah. Tell me the rest of it. And *fast.*" Something was pushing and pulling at the vehicle, trying to throw it off course or change its aim. "And what's interfering with us?"

"A Class C carrier follows, of greater power than mine and possessing manipulative devices which I lack; its occupant employs force beams to interfere with your guidance. But hear now: am I correct in deducing that my own occupants are of the Unchanged?"

Now Tabor had the egg level and heading south; for the moment, maybe, he'd lost their pursuer. "So what if we are?"

"Then I must restrict the parameters of the manual controls to those stresses unharmful to the Unchanged physique."

"You mean g-forces? Acceleration?"

"Correct."

Something nudged the egg down and to the left; Luke pulled back on line. "Is the Class C carrier restricted the same way?"

"It is not; thus, its occupant or occupants would be of the Changed."

"Frey?" Casey said.

*Oh no! Don't remind this tin can!* But the carrier said, "My identification register circuit is inoperative—a malfunction not evident until now. So—" Maybe Aliira had gimmicked it. . . .

Luke cut in. "This Class C is behind us, you say. Can you show it to me?" The egg started to yaw; he yelled, "No! Don't turn. I mean, can't you give me a rear view on a screen or something?" They were lower than he liked; the highest peaks of this range's central ridge towered above his course. Again he pulled up, and again a push of force flattened his angle and sent the carrier veering until he compensated.

His forward vista vanished, replaced by an expanse of sky with a bright dot—another egg—skittering along a tight curve toward him. "Not *all* of it!" he yelled. "I need to see ahead, too. Reduce the rear view to—"

Fast thinking: how to define an area, when the transparent part of the egg's shell included sections of top and sides? He reached forward. "Put it in *this* space," and outlined a fair-sized patch above his direct forward line of sight.

Obediently the rear view shrank, letting him see ahead again; no immediate danger there. Inside the roughly oval border he had drawn he saw the other carrier, still pursuing a curved approach. A black dot, which did *not* move onscreen when he tilted the craft, showed him a point directly astern. Useful—and he hadn't even asked for it!

Sudden impact slued the egg, almost throwing him out of his seat; at the same time the rear view blurred and shimmered. The force beam? Probably. With scant hope he asked, "Is there any way to dodge that beam? Fool it? Throw it off track?" Because the carrier had said it couldn't outrun its big brother . . .

"Only by providing a solid material background, so near the same distance that no Class C could isolate and focus on this vehicle. Such background does not, of course, exist at this altitude. The mountains—"

It took him a moment; then "Gotcha!"

Downstairs, sure; that could be the answer. He took the egg down fast, veering to match the slant of a major snowfield, then skimming along it. As he slowed, furrowing and then plowing a tunnel, snow blocked both fore and aft views.

As the egg shuddered to a halt, Luke waited. When

nothing happened he turned to Casey and grinned. "Our boy's gone off and left us, looks as if."

"Well, bully for you," said Casey. "What do you plan for an encore?"

As she tipped the nalcwine flask up and drank from it, he looked at her. When and how she'd retrieved it, he had no idea. "Are you bombed on that stuff?"

"I'm working on it."

Seeing the fear behind her flip facade, he realized he'd had the easy part: reacting to urgency while she could only sit and watch. He grinned. "Let me help." He took a swig himself. His body's reaction surprised him; until then, he hadn't noticed how far adrenaline had drained him. Handing the flask back, he asked the egg, "Has the Class C gone away? If it's still hanging around—uh, nearby, I mean—could you detect it?"

"My receptors are blocked by the snow above me."

"How about *its?* Can it find us under here?" What difference? Certainly the human pilot had seen where they went to cover, and the snow surface would betray their tunneling with at least a ripple. But keep asking. . . .

It said, "The carrier cannot; its pilot, being a thinking human not subject to the inherent limitations of its devices, is another matter."

Just as he'd thought. All right; what was the next question? Casey asked it. "If the pilot's one of the Changed, how come he didn't use *will* on us?"

The egg hesitated, then apparently translated the slang term. "Emanations of my propulsion system interfere with the use of *will* from outside me with respect to my occupants. And, of course, vice versa."

Whoops! Hastily Luke asked, "How about right now? When you're shut down?"

"I am not deactivated, merely at rest."

*Good.* What next, though? "Can you move us up close to the surface, and see out, without exposing yourself to detection?"

"Not entirely. But I can extrude sensors which will

exhibit a minimum of detectable cross section. Shall I do so?"

"Please do." Courtesy again; well, in its own peculiar way, sometimes the thing sounded so *reasonable*. . . . Luke waited, then said, "Well? Is the Class C still up there?"

"I do not know whether or not it is airborne; I do not detect it in my fields of view."

Tabor looked at Casey, who was looking right back. "What do you think?"

She shrugged. "Sitting here won't accomplish much."

Luke nodded. "Let's lift again. Speed and destination as before."

Taking its snow cover with it, the egg rose. As it circled for altitude, airspeed blew the snow away, leaving streaks of water which lasted only for seconds. Soon the carrier straightened course and climbed toward a notch in the horizon. Luke was happy to see no sign of their Class C nemesis; whoever the guy was and whatever he wanted, he seemed to have given up.

"Not Frey himself, probably," he said.

"Huh?"

"Oh. I was just wondering who was on our tail, there—and decided Frey would have stuck around to nail us."

"Maybe so." Indifferently.

"Lord Frey," said the carrier, "does not have free passage in this sector. Nor, of course, do we. We were pursued, I would guess, by a sector patroller, and perhaps went to ground just outside its border."

So that was why the pursuit ceased? Could be. As Tabor put the matter out of his mind Casey pointed forward, down the range's southern side toward a rolling downslope of foothills, brown at first but greener as they descended. "Do you see anything that looks promising?"

Not near at hand, he didn't. But *way* ahead—a quick guess said the predicted timing might fit—a big valley, its river cutting right-to-left across their eventual path, flowing east. Its mouth lay hidden behind an outlying rise of almost-mountains, but to their either side showed glints of light reflecting off water. "Over that way." Luke pointed. "Coordinates look right." Though precise distances were still sheer guess. "Behind those rises somewhere. We'll have to wait and see."

They saw, all right. Feeling a need for caution, Tabor had the egg slant its approach, slowing and dropping as it neared the west end of the range of wooded hills. Beyond lay the river, widening in spread until, before it reached a curving shoreline, it became less a stream than a vast stretch of swampland.

"Luke?" Casey caught at his arm. "That could be the place Aliira told us to stay away from."

"True. So we won't land there."

Downriver, where the shoreline crossed, Luke anticipated a delta formation. Instead the apparent swamp made only a slight bulging interruption to the curved sweep of beach; not far offshore the water shone clear, its deep blue indicating depth.

What brought him up straight, though, as their ground-hugging flight path passed the hills and gave a clear view east to the sea, was something quite unexpected.

Out of that sea, perhaps a mile offshore, rose a tower.

Armored and ornamented, shining with varihued aurae that flickered under moving patterns of sun and cloud, the thing thrust its tapered shape high.

How high? From his perspective, altitude less than a hundred feet and nearing, Tabor knew his guess couldn't be very good—but a quarter of a mile, he decided, was conservative.

"What *is* that thing?" His voice came out plaintive.

"Our destination, of course." She didn't have to sound so smug about it!

"Well, let's not be in too big a hurry. I—"

But with a rakish swoop, ignoring Luke's movement of the manual controls, the carrier soared out over the water. Halfway between shoreline and tower, abruptly it slowed and dropped. Until, far short of the structure that rose ahead, the egg's steep slant made jarring contact with the water's surface.

For a time the steep plunge continued; then Tabor felt deceleration as their path leveled off. At quite some depth, it appeared; outside light had dimmed considerably.

Now the dimming ceased; they were riding level.

In a calm, reasonable tone, Karen Cecile asked, *"Now what the hell?"*

The egg made no response. Not even to request clarification.

For minutes nothing more happened; then a spot of light appeared and grew. Tabor squinted. Ahead he saw a rise in the ocean floor; from an opening therein came the light. At first the hole seemed small, but closer approach revised his estimate: at least forty feet wide and nearly as high.

The egg passed inside, into a tunnel that rose steeply. Within a hundred yards they broke surface and were airborne again, but now inside a huge, dimly lit cavern. Slowly, hovering only a few feet above the water, the egg moved to a brightened area at one side of the underground enclosure, passed over a short dock and grounded alongside a long, squat building that stood before a large pair of closed gates. Hot muggy air rushed in, popping Luke's eardrums as the vehicle's door opened.

"Destination reached. You will now disembark."

"Who says so? Since when are *you* getting bossy?" Casey was sore, no doubt of it.

Luke put a hand to her arm. "Easy." And to the carrier, "Have you received instructions we don't know about?"

"That is correct. Outside impulses. Impulse receptor—"

"Holds fucking *precedence;* I know that." Regretting his vocabulary lapse he reached for the two control levers and jockeyed them; as before, when the carrier had made its dive, he got no results. "All right; what's going on?"

"Impulse receptor also directed me to disengage manual control."

"Somebody's a real smartass, right?" He ignored the egg's request for translation. To Casey: "Let's gather up our stuff; may not do us much good, but it can't hurt."

All right: their clothes, including some supplied by Frey to Casey but not yet inspected, let alone tried on. Some well-wrapped foods, a flask of juice and one of nalcwine. And the miscellaneous items Aliira had given them. "Why all this?" Casey wanted to know.

"Do you see anybody out there? We could be on our own for a while."

She nodded. "Sure; I can stash a couple of flasks, too."

They climbed out of the carrier. No sooner did Luke clear the door than it made rapid closure. "Just can't wait," Tabor grumbled, then saw the truth of his words as the egg rose, turned to move off the dock, and submerged. Headed, he noticed, back the way they'd come in.

Words to express his feelings came easily to mind; he looked over to Casey and didn't say them.

The drab, pinkish-grey building had in all its length and breadth no windows and only one bare door: bare in the sense of lacking any features whatsoever. No knob, no latch, no keyhole. It wouldn't push open, either. Nor did knocking bring response.

The gates—heavy grillwork at the entrance to a sparsely lit tunnel which curved out of sight within a hundred feet—stood about twelve feet high and spanned a similar width. Each of the pair bore an oversized handgrip at convenient height, but pulling on them accomplished exactly nothing; the portals were so massive they didn't even rattle.

Or else—frowning, Luke felt the handles again, paying more heed to the sensation. And bingo! Not matter, but force fields. These things wouldn't necessarily swing open; like Aliira's door and some of her walls, they might simply vanish and reconstitute.

Trouble was, Tabor had no idea where the controls were. He saw nothing that might operate a doorbell, either. Well, then; stepping back, he walked out onto the dock and turned to look.

What he saw was a level paved surface, less than an acre in extent, forming an arc out from the irregular cave wall. On it sat the building; extending from it was the dock; its only exit was barred by the gates. One corner of the building was perhaps ten feet out from those gates and a little over a yard to one side. The building itself stood only a foot or so higher than they did.

That's all there was. From where he stood, Tabor saw nothing that might be of use.

But—walking around the building he'd looked only for a way in; maybe he'd overlooked some other possibilities. As he started off toward the structure's right side he saw Casey looking after him with apparent puzzlement and obvious impatience. No matter; another circumnavigation was in order.

At the back side, piled against the building itself, lay a stack of thin-walled metal tubing, twenty-foot lengths, each about two inches in diameter. What use . . . ?

Let's find out: he pulled one aside, finding it very light to handle, and laid one end across the pile. Then with one foot he applied weight to the center. It flexed until it touched ground, but recovered when he lifted his foot.

The pile wasn't high enough to give him much of a bend. He set one end against the building, slanting the tube at about thirty degrees from the horizontal, and put all his weight on it. Before the lower end skidded, letting the other grate down the building wall, he'd made a bend that didn't straighten fully.

So one tube wouldn't support him. But a bundle could.

"What are you trying to *do?*" He'd brought six tubes around the building to the gates, stood them on end and asked Casey to hold them for him while he climbed the grillwork. If someone vanished the force field while he was up there, he was in for a nasty fall; he hoped nobody would.

"Get on top of the building," he answered her. "Sometimes roofs have trapdoors." The grill was widemeshed and its members rounded; climbing was easy. When he reached the top he gestured to Casey; one at a time she handed up the tubes and he placed them: one end through an upper level grill square, dividing them between the three such openings nearest the "hinge" side, and the other across the edge of the building's roof, starting a couple of feet from the corner and spread a bit.

The angle wasn't too bad; now for it. Tabor hadn't enough confidence in his gymnastic ability to make the tubes a tight bundle and try hand-over-hand, nor to hands-and-legs it hanging underneath and then swing up at the far end; that's why he'd spread them horizontally. Gingerly he pushed up, easing his weight gradually onto the row of tubes, trying to keep it distributed across the lot. One and then another bent alarmingly but he managed to shift, to spread the load as evenly as he could, and for the first few feet his plan seemed to be working.

But as he neared midpoint the whole array sagged, leaving Tabor with a considerably steeper climb. Breathing hard he gripped the two outermost tubes and pulled—but only briefly, because the damn things came sliding. Only friction to hold them: if he kept that up, the far ends would come off the roof!

All right; either he knew the laws of physics or he didn't. Friction can be your enemy or your friend. You can move a raft by walking on it, building speed gently and leaping for impact, then returning slowly to your starting point and repeating.

All he had to do was apply the principles. The combination he came up with, exerting as much friction as possible with hands and arms while he brought his legs forward, and the other way around while he extended himself again, lacked both elegance and ease. Not to mention efficiency; the last five feet to the roof must have taken nearly twenty minutes.

Moving carefully off the tubes, though every impulse urged him to scramble, Luke rolled over on his back and breathed deeply, waiting for his pulse to drop back into two figures.

What roused him was Casey yelling; screeching was more like it. Luke levered up on his elbows; on hands and knees he moved to the roof's edge. "—you all right? What are you *doing?*" Then she saw him. Standing, red-faced, hands on hips, she shouted, "Well it's about time! Did you find anything?"

"Not yet. Hang on; give me a minute to look around." He turned away and scanned the roof. Several vents, none large enough to be useful. A skylight shaped like a flattish pup tent; inspecting it he saw no way to open any part, and rather doubted the transparent panels were as breakable as they looked. Also, directly below he saw unfamiliar machinery, studded with levers and handles and other projections he wouldn't care to land on.

Beyond the skylight, though, lay the structural feature he'd hoped to find: a rectangular hatch cover, about three feet by four, sitting atop the roof's surface.

It looked so much like what he expected that he wasn't surprised when it came clear easily, revealing a rimmed opening.

He looked down, directly into the building. Directly into a vat of colorful boiling liquid; with the lid off, the opening attracted a billow of fumes that damn near strangled him before he wrestled the cover back into place.

Coughing, he turned just in time to see the ends of his six metal tubes tip up and slide away, off the edge of the roof.

"*What—?*" Then he saw: in the opening the gates were gone. He went to the edge; Casey, apparently unharmed by falling tubes, stood looking into the tunnel.

She said something he couldn't make out to someone he couldn't see; his angle of view was too steep for him to see more than the first few feet of tunnel.

Then the woman emerged. Even from where he stood it was obvious that Casey dwarfed her, yet her body and movements were those of an adult female. She said something to Casey, who in apparent reflex looked up toward Luke, then froze in place.

The woman lifted her gaze also, and then one hand. She seemed to tense, and something jerked at Tabor. He struggled for balance but fell forward, hands missing the edge but knees smashing against it, and toppled off the roof.

In Phys Ed, the semester he'd taken elementary martial arts, he'd learned a little of the art of falling. Now it did him no good; he was spinning and lacked any reference point. Trying to relax, at least, he waited for impact.

It was unnaturally long in coming; he touched ground in an awkward position that could have caused serious injury—except that he landed *lightly*.

Like Frey going out the window.

Luke rolled over and sat up. Whoever this woman might be, she was of the Changed.

# NINE

**A**s he clambered to his feet, not hurrying, Tabor gave this new factor a quick look-over. She was short, all right, not much more than five feet. Scaled up to Casey's height the woman would have seemed stocky; as she was, though, her look did well to escape fragility. Her electric blue costume, of a silklike fabric decorated with rows of studs and buttons in varied, contrasting colors, clung closely almost to the knees; from there down, the legs flared a bit.

Her face, darkskinned with a hint of ruddiness, showed at this moment the calm perfection of a cameo. Dark hair, center-parted, bulked out in waves, not quite reaching her shoulders. Except that a diamond-shaped area of iridescent green began at a point between her eyebrows and rose to its widest span at the hairline, which it interrupted; the bare patch tapered to a point again a few inches back, and there the center-part began. He'd first thought this to be some sort of badge covering forehead and hair; now he saw it was all smooth, tinted skin. Remembering Svansek and her two stooges, he wondered what this marking conveyed of the woman's place in the hierarchy.

She gestured toward Casey, who unfroze and almost stumbled; then she said, "You will account for yourselves, your presence here, and what *you*"—a nod toward Luke—"were doing on the roof. I am addressed as Yrr."

"Ear?"

"Yrr."

"Yur."

"In the Inklizh alphabet, wye-arr-arr. And you are . . . ?"

He recited his name and Casey's, saw her reaction

and said, "Yeah, I know; we're unregistered. We're from a year you don't have data to relate to, before the Waste Times. Brought to this time by Count Derion." She was listening, so push it. "He sort of mislaid us; we came here hoping to find him."

"On the roof?"

"The gates wouldn't open!" Casey sounded peeved. "Luke was looking in the only place there might be something to help us."

Yrr smiled; in her expression Tabor read amused tolerance. "Had you gained entrance you would have been disappointed. Perhaps fatally."

The fumes, yes; Luke didn't argue. "Can you take us to Derion?"

"I can conduct you according to my instructions." On her left wrist, Tabor saw, she wore a wide bracelet which sported a miniature keyboard layout and tiny screen.

Yrr punched buttons like an expert, then watched her screen. Her expression did not encourage comment, let alone questions.

After a time the woman nodded. "Come here. You will both embrace me closely."

*That's what Derion had us do.* "Where are we going? Or should I ask, when?"

Luke was braced for the usual line: "The name would mean nothing to you." But Yrr said, "To an interim staging area. And we do not swim the river of time; that is beyond my powers."

He looked at Casey; trading shrugs, they reached to the small woman. She said, "Close your eyes, relax your thought, and breathe deeply."

*Okay, lady.* He was on his third breath when he felt them all lift and move and drop—into the water! But his involuntary gasp brought air, not strangling liquid. His eyes flipped open, to see water a foot or so away. Dimming light showed their heads to be surrounded by a bubble of air; its lower boundary wavered, alternately covering and revealing their shoulders.

As light dimmed further, the bubble shrank. Sure; more depth, more compression. He hoped to hell the woman had brought along enough air to last them!

The light died almost entirely, then reappeared, still not bright but more so than the cavern's best, and increasing. So they were outside now and rising toward the surface. When they broke it the bubble vanished; Luke hadn't noticed the air getting stale but his first breath outside told him about it.

Now what? "Hold to me," Yrr said, "and be easy." Lying on the surface, riding a little higher than normal flotation would allow, the joined trio moved shoreward. Not fast, but steadily. Well, if action by *will* were fueled by energy from the body, there would be limits. And also optimum trade-offs: they were, Luke guessed, out of the water just enough to minimize the combined energy drains of lift and drag. However it worked, they did keep moving.

Toward the swamp Aliira had warned against. Tabor felt less than reassured. And in the water he saw shapes moving; one, emerging briefly, looked distinctly predatory. Big, too.

As they reached the outskirts of swampland he must have fidgeted noticeably; Yrr said, "The water denizens will not approach me; we are quite safe." A soft laugh. "Without me, of course—"

Luke didn't need a translation.

Yrr's face ran sweat; her breathing had become a series of gasps. Tabor tried to estimate the effort she was putting forth: lifting at least a portion of their combined weights, while hauling their total bulk against residual water drag. For a small woman, he decided, she was in damned good shape.

Through narrow, winding channels between reed-grown hummocks she took them. Until they reached a slope, muddy but solid, leading to an apparently sizable patch of ground; trees and underbrush blocked view of any distance.

Standing now, they waded ashore and walked up the

bank, as Yrr quickly brought her breathing under control. She said, "I am glad that passage is done with; it was altogether long enough!"

Luke nodded. "Quite."

Strangely, she stared at him. "Was that a request? For now? This present moment?"

"What—?"

Cocking her head to one side, Yrr said, "Since I find you accompanied, the thought had not come to me. Yet given time for it, and privacy, I might well like to quite with you. But—"

"I don't understand." From Casey's look, neither did she.

Yrr's eyes narrowed. "It is simple enough. Naturally I enjoy quiting. And sometimes I find it pleasant to consort with the Unchanged, since there is not the need to avoid inadvertent conflict of one *will* with the other. Now, though, time does not permit us to quite together."

Shaking his head, Luke said, "Wait a minute; define 'quite' for me. Or—" Another idea. "Spell it."

Exasperation showed. "Cee-oh-eye-tee-ee. Coite: to engage in sexual embrace. What else might it mean?"

"Cue-you-eye-tee-ee, quite. Meaning: yes, indeed. Or, as an adjective—"

Suddenly Yrr laughed. "Oh, I see. I would have realized, but you—your accent is atrocious."

Tabor felt himself redden. "I'm sorry. I—"

With an exaggerated expression of wide-eyed innocence, Yrr said, "Then you withdraw your request?" She laughed; then, suddenly businesslike, pointed inland and slightly to the left. "Follow that direction; you will find other persons. Perhaps they can inform you further." A line that could be taken more than one way . . .

"What about Derion?" Casey asked. "Will he know we're here? How to find us?"

Shaking her wet hair back, Yrr gave no smile. "What Count Derion knows is not my concern. I am constrained to act for Lord Frey."

With no other word she turned, walked down the muddy slope, and plunged into the water.

"Oh, superb!" Casey's voice rang with sarcasm. "All that work to find Derion, and one of Frey's people picks us off. Why didn't you—"

"Ask? Sure; why didn't I? Just when would have been the proper moment? And what good would it have done, anyway? *Dammit*all, Casey—"

She reached to clasp his shoulder. "I know. I didn't think, either. And you're right: the way she rushed us, there *was* no good time or way to dig in our heels. If it would have done any good anyway, against that *will* they have." Now she leaned against him, head on his chest. "Luke? What do we do next?"

He considered. His pockets held a few items, but everything they'd been hand-carrying was left behind. "In your jacket do you still have either of those flasks?"

"Both, in fact."

"There's a dry spot over there. Dryer, anyway. Let's sit for a few minutes. I'm thirsty; aren't you?"

"Quite."

He couldn't help laughing with her.

One flask was juice, the other nalcwine. They decided in favor of the latter, and drank sparingly.

Afternoon had latened; the sun, almost directly upriver, rode low. Relaxed after a few minutes' sitting with his back to a tree, Tabor said, "Yrr said there's people here. Do we want some? They could be either help or danger; how can we know?"

Casey shrugged. "It's like when we were stuck in the snowfield; sitting here won't get us anyplace."

Sigh. "I suppose not. Okay; stopper the jug and let's go."

Pushing through reeds and brush, slogging in the direction Yrr had indicated, after a short while they came to a path. Or the semblance of one; someone or something had passed this way more than once or twice. Whatever it might be, Luke noted, it wasn't a very *large* something.

The ground bore an upward slope, barely noticeable; after a few minutes' walking it mostly leveled off. On this plateau trees and brush grew more thickly; visibility, for more than a few feet, was largely obscured.

Ahead Tabor began to hear sounds—faint at first but growing as they continued—of human activity. In particular, voices, which still seemed to be some distance away when, without warning, a man stepped out of the brush to face them.

"You were not announced. Which quota do you represent?"

His version of Yrr's garb was grey-green, and the trouser legs did not flare; his forehead patch shone dull bronze, and the upper triangle that ran up his scalp displaced stubble-cut sandy hair. Though he stood taller than Luke, his rangy build carried little more weight. He did, however, hold a device which, by the way he pointed it, was probably some kind of weapon.

Quota? Luke shook his head; stick to facts. "Do you know Yrr? She brought us ashore. Back there." Pointing. "And said to come here and join you." *Chew on that, buster!*

"Then you are of Lord Frey's bringing, not Count Derion's. That is well." He turned away. "Follow me."

"And I'm Luke Tabor; pleased to meet you." Sourly, Luke muttered this to Casey as they resumed the walk.

"More important," she said, equally low-voiced, "this one's probably a Changed, too. So let's watch our step."

The man ahead led them into a clearing, two or three acres, containing about a dozen scattered, identical flat-roofed huts. At a quick glance the design seemed to include only one door, with two windows per wall. The beige-colored structures had the look of hardboard or plastic.

Here was the voices' origin. In the area stood or sat or walked at least three dozen people. Most but not all appeared young, college age; several were dressed as for a dance: suits, even tuxes, and long dresses. From the looks of that clothing, it had been worn for some days.

Before he had time to see if there was anyone he knew, from one side he heard, "Hey, Tabor!"

As their conductor walked away, Luke turned to see Jay Rozak and Carla approaching. Their clothes weren't exactly fresh, either, but looked better than what the prom refugees wore. "Well, compadres," Jay announced, grinning through more than a few days' growth of beard, "I see Varj corraled you safe and sound. And just in time for chow. Welcome to the farm."

To some extent the place was organized. Under a tarp stretched between two huts sat a sort of field kitchen, with tables and benches alongside. Jay shepherded Luke and Casey through the routine, picking up camp-style tableware and dishing stew from a huge kettle. With bread and fresh fruit and coffee, it made an appetizing meal for hungry folk. "Frey's people bring supplies by carrier," Carla reported. "Every other morning."

"Frey," said Luke. "This is his, then. How about Derion?"

Jay's grin came lopsided. "It's a longish story. . . ."

Nearly two weeks ago he and Carla had been dropped into the coastal fringe of a rain forest. Where? They had no idea. They had subsisted on tropical fruit—and gotten violently sick from some part of their diet. "Worst of it was, we didn't know *what*."

"A few things," said Carla, "we were sure of. For being safe, I mean. And when we got down to the shore there were clams and such."

The fourth day Lord Frey had arrived in an egg and brought them here. "And then some of our others, the past week or so."

"Which is not," Jay put in, "all to the good. For instance, we have—" He broke off, nodding to one side where in peripheral vision Tabor saw someone approach.

"Well, now! Twarn't good enough, havin' jest ol' Jay

Rozak to bird-dog. Now I got me Rozak's asshole buddy, too."

Junior Yancey! Bristle-jawed, gut bulging over his belt, moving with a swagger, hand to the butt of some holstered gizmo. Maybe the same kind Varg, their discoverer here, had wielded.

By reflex Luke made to stand; Jay pulled him down. Whispering "Eat crow if you have to. That ultrasound thing he carries, fries your mind through the ears. And he loves it."

Clapping a hand to Tabor's shoulder, Yancey said, "Jest keep in mind, ol' buddy—this here, it's like we're in the slammer. But you're the cons, see, and I'm the trusty." Giving them the benefit of an unpleasant laugh, he strutted away.

"Who," asked Casey, "gave *him* any authority?"

"Varj seems to have taken a liking to him." Jay's grimace emphasized his opinion of that bias.

"Liking's not quite the word," Carla said. "Fascination's more to the point. What was it he said to Frey?"

Jay cocked an eyebrow. "Umm . . . 'a specimen unlike any I have ever seen. As an experiment, I've made him my deputy.' "

"Experiment?" Luke snorted. "That's all we need, isn't it? A test-tube gorilla."

Casey clutched his forearm. "Wind down, won't you? Jay—is anyone else here that we know? From the tank at Pullman, for instance?"

Draining his coffee cup, Jay said, "The best I remember, it was seven of us Derion tried to bring along. Sprainbrain over there"—he gestured to where Yancey stood—"he was an accident, either playing tackle drill or just plain pigpile." Jay scowled in concentration. "There's the four of us. And the young couple that got roped in; they're around too. Matter of fact they bunk in the same hut we do."

Bruce Garner and Alycia Frazier, sure. "It's good they're with you," Luke said. "Those kids may need some looking after."

Rudely, Casey's elbow jarred his ribs. "Real up, will you? So far, we're hardly star class at looking after *us.*"

For being dumped into a strange time in total ignorance, Tabor felt they hadn't done all that badly. But he let it go. "So of the lot, we're all present but Derion and Vivi." Jay nodded; Luke said, "The rest here: who brought them?"

"Frey, sort of," Carla answered. "But that's *another* story." Lord Frey, it seemed, ran his own operation more like a log drive than a conducted tour. Over a period of time, back in Pullman and possibly elsewhere, he'd been inserting people—usually by ones or twos—into the river of time, pulling them upstream a bit and leaving them to drift. When he decided to leave, presumably on learning of Derion's departure, he rounded them up and herded them downtime by *will* as well as physical contact. Then, reaching destination at Hykeran Outjut, he had "beached" them.

From an exchange Carla had overheard between Frey and Varj on one of the two occasions Frey had visited here, at least a few persons had been lost from the Viking's roundup, most probably tossed "ashore" in some minor eddy along the way. "He didn't seem disturbed about it," Carla said. "Said there were enough without them."

"The man's all heart," said Karen Cecile.

Unchallenged by any outdoor lighting, twilight came. Jay first showed the new arrivals where to wash utensils at a tank-fed washrack, then pointed out the two outhouses at the clearing's downhill side. Primitive and lacking privacy within, the facilities killed odor with probably much the same chemicals used centuries earlier.

Coming away, Jay said, "There's only the four of us in our hut, if you'd like to join us."

"And eight sleeping mats," Carla added.

"Sounds fine to me; thanks," said Luke. It didn't, really, but it was the best offer he was likely to get.

The hut was about sixteen feet square. Going in, Tabor saw that the bunks were arranged in four pairs, one at each corner, and set crosswise, leaving a central aisle front-to-back and another crossing it. At the intersection sat a small cylindrical object, metallic-seeming and perhaps a yard tall, above which hung a dimly luminescent globe. The cylinder, when he passed near it, radiated mild warmth.

And that was it. No running water, no partitions, no closet space, not even hooks to hang clothes on.

"Does Varj live in one of these?" Luke asked.

"Not hardly," Rozak said. "Doesn't use our same biffy, either. That slicksuit has his own digs somewhere out in the brush, nobody knows exactly. We think it's at the upriver end of this mudbar—because if you try to walk up that way, you get to feeling so jumpy you decide not to go any farther." He shrugged. "Just another of their gadgets, I expect."

Luke nodded. "It sounds reasonable."

"The mats, now," said Jay. "Those are ours," pointing far left. "Garner and Frazier have these." Near right. "Two corners free; take your pick."

Somehow the right rear corner seemed more sheltered; Luke nodded toward it. "There, Casey?"

"Why not?" She scowled. "Does the light turn out?"

"Sure," said Carla. "Just touch it. On, off, either way."

The Changed, of course, probably did it by *will*. Oh, well; Tabor walked back and inspected the farther mat: a combination of mattress, pillow, and cover, all in one blue-grey piece.

Without warning the long day hit him. Hard to believe it had begun in one of the Lady Aliira's force field–walled bedrooms. If anything were certain, it was that this hut was solidly material. Stretching, Luke yawned, and said to Jay and Carla across the room, "I don't think I'll wait up for our cohosts."

No privacy at all; the hell with it. As though he were in the Rho Delt house or army barracks he undressed, laying his clothes more or less neatly alongside the mat. As a sop to propriety he retained his undershorts until after he

crawled into what was almost but not quite a sleeping bag;
then he put them out on top of the rest. Across the way,
past the foot of his low bed, he saw Jay and Carla doing
roughly the same things.

Standing, waiting until the other three had crawled in,
Casey touched the globe, bringing darkness. He heard rustlings, then sensed her coming nearer. Kneeling, most
likely, she put a hand to his shoulder, then bent and kissed
him. " 'Night, Luke."

"Yeah, g'night."

Right; under the circumstances, that was that.

Fatigue had Tabor near sleep, but he couldn't ignore
sounds from across the way. Then he heard the door closing, a muted giggle, rustlings, and what had to be Garner
and Frazier getting into bed. It didn't stop there; he heard
movements and gaspings, and after a moment realized he
was hearing them all in stereo. From the other occupied
corner as well.

Fully awake, he sat up and leaned far over, to touch
Casey. When he found her ear he whispered, "You know
what? They're *all* screwing."

"Yes. Do you—?"

"I—not now, Casey."

"Me too. We'll probably have to get used to the idea,
but not yet."

"Well, they've been here longer."

He didn't get to sleep until things quieted.

Tabor woke to half-light, grey at the fixed single-pane
windows. He felt surprisingly good: a little hungry but not
uncomfortably so, the same with thirst, a moderate urge to
visit the outhouse.

Sitting up he saw no signs of wakefulness in any of
the other five. He rose, dressed, ferreted out Casey's juice
flask for a few sips, and quietly went outside.

Breathing deeply of morning-cool sea-tinged air, he
worked his arms to loosen neck and shoulder muscles.
This was great! Not the overall situation, of course. But

the feel of this one moment, the tang of cool air, exhilarated him.

Heading across the area he came to the field kitchen. Even this early, someone was trying to kindle a fire. In no great hurry, Luke paused. "Hi. Getting an early start, aren't you?"

The person who straightened to face him was a woman pushing fifty but not too hard. She scowled. "If this is the future, give me the Middle Ages. Superchauv—that Varj person—I'm a woman so I'm assigned kitchen duty." She spread her hands. "Me, an associate professor. Garland Feltzer, if you're interested. I teach modern dance, for heaven's sake. And can't cook for sour owl shit." Shrugging, she began to turn away.

Quickly Luke said, "I know what you mean; in the army I made a lousy KP. Hey—I need to run down to the little house for a minute. But coming back I can give you a hand with that fire. I'm Luke Tabor. Grad student, physics."

Moving on, he heard her say, "Good; I can use the help."

His outhouse visit was brief; returning to the cooking area he stopped at the washrack to cleanse his hands, and was moving toward the field kitchen again when all the yelling began.

It came from near the hut he'd slept in; Tabor forgot the kitchen and broke into a sprint.

A number of people, some more dressed than others, were milling a little but basically doing it in place. Luke shouted things like "Party through!" and even "Lady with a baby!" to startle half-awake gawkers out of his path. When he came near the hut, he wasn't so sure his haste had been a good idea.

What he saw came through to him in installments. Alycia Frazier with her hair like tumbleweed, face bashed on one side, dress more ripped off than not. Casey and Carla with arms around her as she crouched, crying, over

Bruce Garner, that one lying with purpled face contorted, screaming like halfpast death, body convulsing . . .

Standing over them, movement! Junior Yancey leveling his ultrasonic weapon that looked like a plastic toy handgun, Jay Rozak on hands and knees, blood running from one ear, coming up to make his try . . .

Forty feet away, Luke was. He found himself scrabbling at the ground and came up with a stone not quite fist size. Rearing back, he went for the peg to home plate.

He almost made it, but instead of imploding Junior Yancey's skull, the rock caromed off the man's shoulder; Yancey dropped the weapon. Not for long, though; left-handed he scooped it up and swung to take Jay Rozak in midcharge.

You could see Yancey hadn't trained lately; his reflexes didn't measure up. Coming fast, with his left hand, Jay knocked the mindfryer to one side; the extended knuckles of his right—*not* a fist—smashed into the larynx. The hulking redneck fell like a tree.

All at once, Tabor believed the secret agent stories.

As Garner's paroxysms eased and his color improved, others helped get him and Alycia into the hut. To Luke the mess needed some sorting out; after a few questions he thought he had it partly straight.

Seduction was for sissies; Junior Yancey liked his rape. With one big hand over Alycia's mouth he'd hauled her out of the hut without waking anyone else. He took her no farther than around to the side before he escalated his assault: tearing clothes, slapping her to silence which didn't last, wrestling her to the ground, and trying to climb aboard.

Her shrieks woke the others. Nearest the door, Bruce Garner got outside first; Yancey hit him full-face with the ultrasonic and held the beam on him until he collapsed, and after.

That's when Rozak made his first try; after one look he came fast and yelling, saw the hand weapon swing up, made a fall and tried to roll under and past it. The beam caught him at close range but not for long; it rang his bell badly but didn't put him away. He was coming up for seconds when Luke reached the scene.

"And your throw got me to him. Thanks." One finger wiping blood from his left ear; Jay said, "Hearing's beginning to come back; sumbidge didn't totally wreck my eardrum, after all."

He and Tabor went back outside the hut; along with a number of others, most standing farther back, they looked at Junior Yancey. Not a pretty sight: hands to his battered throat, tongue protruding from a purpled face. His ragged breathing made a series of moaning grunts.

A tall young man, wearing a tux that had totaled its damage deposit, cleared his throat. "What are you going to *do* about him?"

Luke resented the challenging, demanding tone, but Rozak spoke first. "Glad you asked that. You, and"—he pointed to two other spectators—"you, and you. Take him to whatever hut puts up with him, and if there's any kind of medical help in this place, round it up."

"Just who do you think *you* are?"

Then the tall one fell quiet. Jay had picked up the weapon. "I'm the guy with the gun."

As the three carried Junior Yancey away, about half the crowd followed. But as they neared a hut at the clearing's edge, Varj pushed brush aside to stand in their path.

"Who has done this?" Pointing to rasp-breathing Yancey. "What act of rebellion do you now?" His finger moved to scythe across the group. "Punishment! All of you, without mercy."

Luke sensed what was coming; even as Jay tentatively raised the small weapon he held, Tabor's mind cried *Don't try to talk—shoot!* Too late: Varj went tense-faced. Emphasizing his effort of *will* he said, "Put the sonic down now."

In Rozak's expression, struggle showed plain; his gun sagged. *No, dammit!* With a rebel yell Tabor began doing jumping jacks; he shouted, "Make noise, everybody! Jump around. Get mad! Shake this bastard up; you can do it!"

Beside him Casey said, "You can't. Remember how Derion—?"

"Not the same," between yells. "This stooge isn't Derion." Then, "Yay! Yippee! A little pepper out there!"

And by damn, it worked! First a few and then more of the bedraggled dress-ups began to shout, jump, chant, what have you. Varj's look of purpose slackened; his stare shifted from side to side. Belatedly he reached for his own sonic—but Tabor, surprising himself, jumped for it. A cutting shriek, at the upper limit of his hearing, shot pain through his head and blurred his consciousness—but momentum carried him close enough to grab the thing away. Ears ringing, he scuttled back.

The uproar ebbed. This would not do! "Hey, keep it up!" Luke shouted. "Stay hot! Don't let Varj catch his balance."

Nobody seemed to listen; the group quieted. Obviously regaining confidence, Varj compressed his lips; in his features, again tension grew. *Oh bloody hell—!*

As Luke hesitated, Jay Rozak aimed the weapon he held. Not at Varj's head but at his midsection. Abruptly Varj bent, retching all over his shiny pant legs.

"All right; who's got some rope? String? A belt, maybe?" Jay barked out his questions. "Anything. A blindfold, earplugs. We have to disorient this fucker, keep him offbase so he can't use *will* on us." Someone had a canteen; Jay took it. "Here; let's wet him down some." Starting with a choking splash into the now-upturned face.

Hog-tied, gagged and blindfolded, Varj was half carried, half dragged over to the field kitchen. Jay had him set down alongside a full dishpan. "If you feel him starting to influence you," he told the two women he assigned as guardians, "dunk his head for about half a minute." Starting to walk away, he looked back and said, "Don't drown him, now. He's not all *that* bad, and we may need him for trading points."

He turned to where Luke stood watching. "All right, we got us this far. *Now* what do we do?"

If the question had an easy answer, Tabor couldn't think of it. One of the prom leftovers, this one missing his tux jacket but still sporting a wilted black tie, said, "It's getting close to time for food delivery. How are we going to handle *that?*"

"I don't understand," said Luke.

The fellow, a gawky kid with a world class Adam's apple and very patchy growth of beard stubble, turned to him. "That's right; you're new." He stuck his hand out. "James Wilson, Phi Delt. Uh—pledge, that is."

"Luke Tabor, Rho Dammit Rho. Ex-pledge."

Wilson blinked, apparently decided not to ask anything, and said, "Before we unload, Varj always signs a receipt for the carrier pilot. Once or twice he had Yancey do it instead. So—"

"Just a minute," Rozak said. "Does Yancey have a badge or anything—symbol of authority from Varj?"

Wilson looked blank. "When he did the accepting he might have held out something in his hand, to show. I'm not sure."

"Maybe it's on him now," Tabor said. "Let's go look."

In the hut where Yancey lay, the fragile blonde with the ruined dress and black eye protested their intrusion. No matter: Jay searched Yancey thoroughly; Luke pawed through the pockets of the ex-tackle's coat. Neither found anything that looked useful.

"If you'd just tell me what—" Jay did. With an upstage smile she reached under Yancey's sleeping mat and handed Rozak a small, ornate medallion. "All you had to do was *ask.*"

Giving her a brief stare, Jay said, "Thank you very much; I'll remember you in my prayers." And to Luke and Wilson, "Come on! I think I hear the carrier."

For a moment Luke doubted the statement; in his experience, carriers arrived almost in silence.

This one, though, was different. Decelerating from what must have been considerable speed, the thing screamed in to land.

Nothing like the now-familiar egg, this vehicle. Nearly twenty feet long and eight wide, it had a small cablike protrusion at the front, resembling an egg's forward section. The remainder, Luke deduced, would be cargo space.

"That's not the usual delivery car," said Wilson. "Maybe they're bringing in some more people."

As the carrier grounded, its cab's left side opened to extrude a boarding ramp, and the pilot clambered out.

"Oh, shit!" said Jay Rozak. "We can forget the scam."

Debarking, looking curiously at the group assembled to greet him, came Lord Frey.

# TEN

Standing in the forefront, largely because everyone else had edged away and shuffled back, neither Jay nor Luke tried to flaunt their sonic weapons. The butt of Tabor's showed at his belt in front. Jay's didn't; Luke's quick look spotted it at the back of the waistband. Chalk one up for special training.

Whether Lord Frey read minds or merely body language, he came right to the point. "What are you two doing with the behavior control weapons issued to my overseer and his assistant?"

Luke turned to find Jay looking at him with the same unspoken plea that filled his own mind: *You* field this one. Frey's calm air might be real or might not; Tabor remembered what Aliira had said about the dangers of crossing the man. Clearing his throat, he hesitated and then said, "The assistant was a bad choice. Very bad. Anyone who knew him . . ."

One of Frey's eyebrows began to rise. *Make it march!* "This morning Yancey brutalized a young woman, tried to rape her. There was a fight." Luke spread his hands. "Varj wasn't there, didn't see it, but he took Yancey's side anyway—"

"Said he'd punish *all* of us." Someone behind Luke.

"—without mercy!" Sounded like Wilson.

"So what happened," Tabor began again, "we—"

"Enough!" Frey's brows lowered. "Where is Varj?"

Tabor gestured toward the field kitchen. "Over there. Uh, you see, he tried to—we had to—"

But ignoring words, weapons, and bystanders, Frey strode off in the indicated direction. Following, Luke looked helplessly at Rozak. "Jeez—what'll he *do?*"

137

* * *

Asking no more questions, Frey made short work of the situation. In minutes Varj was freed of bonds and the rest of it. Frey said, "You are demoted to Subcontroller. Go into the carrier and make the necessary changes." Then to the others, "Gather all your gear and form up at the carrier. Tell the rest to do likewise. You have oct-two minutes." *Ten, that would be.*

As Luke turned to obey, the Viking added, "You two—Tabor and Rozak—stay a moment." As they faced him, he looked for a moment before saying, "Is this Yancey dead?"

Tabor shook his head.

"Then see to it."

Just like that. Not looking back, he stalked past them. One or maybe both hollered, "Hey!" Then, "We can't do that," Jay said. "Not in cold blood."

Frey turned; his eyes narrowed. "Then bring the fool along; he will be your responsibility. And you will give me those weapons now. Also, I believe, Varj's sigil which delegates authority."

Varj was one thing, Frey quite another. Watching the man walk away, both guns gripped in one big hand, Rozak said, "Me and my big mouth! My mother never raised me to be a Boy Scout."

Not only that: Junior Yancey was no light load to move.

Five hours in the overcrowded carrier was not fun; it seated fewer than it now carried, leaving a dozen or so to find deck space where they could. Semicomatose, Yancey lay sprawled in an aisle. Now and then a small, silent woman in grey hood and robe came and looked at him. Looked, and went forward again.

Water was available, and in a rear corner, one of the saddle-type johns. An hour or so into the flight, ration packets were distributed by Varj, who now sported a blue-and-white jumper suit similar to those worn by Svansek and her stooges. A further similarity was that Varj's forehead diamond had lost its color, the skin showing only a faint pink; also, the rest of his hair was gone. Along with his officious airs; quite subdued, the man was now. On the outside, anyway; inside could be considerably different. Accepting a packet, Luke took care to thank Varj with full sincerity. Politeness couldn't hurt. . . .

Along its sides the passenger section had no windows; only up front, to either side of the protruding "cab," was there any outside view. Early on, before Luke realized the shortage of seats, he stood for a half hour looking forward. The carrier lifted heading west, upstream, then turned north and climbed rapidly. Immediately Tabor saw that this machine managed considerably more speed than the egg; even at higher altitude the ground below moved noticeably.

Long before snack time they passed the nearer mountains. When Tabor went forward for a later look the carrier was leaving the great plain, moving toward the more northern range. The one he had seen, upriver, when he first appeared in this time.

Mostly, though, he sat. He'd lost his seat on his first look-see, ate sitting on the deck, but lucked into a space after his second time of forward viewing. Actually, seating was no major problem. There seemed to be an unspoken agreement that no one could hold a place for anyone else. If you want a seat, wait for someone to go to the john.

What Tabor wanted was to sit beside Casey—as, over toward a rear corner, Bruce Garner and Alycia sat together, and a little nearer, Jay Rozak with Carla. Luke watched, but Karen Cecile's immediate neighbors never budged. Finally one of his did; Casey noticed his wave and made the move.

Once he'd told her his and Jay's experience with Frey, they didn't find much to talk about. The seats did not recline, but the backs were high enough to rest a head against. As most of the passengers were doing by now, Luke and Casey tried to catch a doze. He, at least, succeeded.

* * *

Sounds woke him to see nearly half the passengers crowded up to the forward view, oohing and aahing. He looked to Casey; she shrugged. "It's too jammed up there; we couldn't get close enough to see much."

The carrier was dropping steeply, and soon came the sensation of an elevator stopping fast—except that it continued for some time. Killing a *lot* of speed in a hurry . . .

Then, smoothly for a large craft, the carrier landed. A few persons stood up, but when the forward door remained closed, one by one they sat again. Minutes passed; then the grey-robed woman came in with two men and a stretcher. Quickly, Junior Yancey was strapped to the litter and carried out. Luke felt relief; Frey wasn't loading him and Jay with Yancey's care after all.

Now in the doorway appeared a tall man, wearing the same style of uniform and forehead/scalp patch Yrr and Varj had displayed. The clothing was brown, the patch ocher. "I am Terrell. Take up your personal effects and follow me to debark."

Outside in warm sun and cool air, Tabor looked across a downward-sloping area to the near side of a great blue lake; nearly to the horizon it stretched, with purple-hazed hills beyond. Upslope lay a varied lot of wooden and concrete buildings, mostly two-story but a few higher, set among spindly conifers of which few topped more than ten or twelve feet.

From his Alaskan tour of duty Luke knew they had picked up some serious latitude, something like the area near Fairbanks. This place was fine for now, but summer would be brief indeed.

Once the last passengers straggled out, the overseer Terrell allowed no more time for gawking. "You will form up now! Men to my left, and," pointing to a bulky woman, similarly clad, "women here with Nalra, my counterpart." As the assemblage sorted itself, moving hesitantly, he made vague sounds and gestures of hurry; when it had become two distinct groups he said, "We will lead you to your respective quarterings."

Out of a rising babble of protest, Casey's voice rang. "Just a minute there, buster! If this school isn't coed, count me out. You can't—"

Impassive, expressionless, Nalra drew her sonic weapon. Luke yelled, "Hey, no!" and started to run toward her. His path took him too near Terrell; the big man tripped him. Rolling to hands and knees he looked at the business end of Terrell's own weapon, then to Casey who stood staring at Nalra's. Rising slowly, Tabor said, "Look; can't we talk this over? At the—the staging area, we weren't segregated. So—"

A sharp whistle shut him up. Him and everybody else. Down the ramp walked Lord Frey. "Tabor. Rozak. I may have erred, this morning, in dismissing your disruptive behavior so lightly. If so, I shall not repeat the mistake. At this point you—all of you—will obey my overseers. And tomorrow morning you two will be escorted to report to me personally. Do you understand?"

Luke forced a nod and a mumble, Jay much the same. With a sudden smile, as if greatly pleased with himself, Frey walked past them all, setting a good pace toward the tallest building in view and not looking back.

"Come," said Terrell, and led off in the direction of a group of barrackslike structures. Still angry, but feeling curiously passive, Tabor fell into line. The pacifying influence, he assumed, had to be the tall man's *will;* Terrell probably wasn't in a class with Frey or Derion, but he had a lot more of the ball than Varj did.

Coming up alongside Rozak, Luke said as much. Jay nodded. "No shaking this guy up with yells and jumping around," he said. "And what's the point? Before we can have any idea how to improve things, we have to figure the setup."

"I guess." Now they reached a building and filed inside, through a pair of doors centered in its length, to enter a compact central lobby extending nearly all the way across it. At either side of this space, next to stairways leading to the upper floor, a central longitudinal corridor opened. Toward the lobby's rear, straight ahead, Terrell gestured. "Bathing, laundry, and so forth. Basic facilities, though, are provided in each room." He scanned a list he held, then shook his head. "I will not trouble to assign you. The rooms hold two each; choose your own. Initial supplies are in place; later you will be shown how and where to obtain replenishments. Have you any questions?"

"Yes, sir," said James Wilson. "When do we eat?"

"Feeding arrangements are still in progress. For the time being, provisions carts will visit each residence hall in turn." The man had no poker face at all; when an idea struck him, Luke could practically see the bulb light up. "Later today I will need volunteers to help provide this service."

Moving to nudge Jay in the ribs, Tabor's elbow met Rozak's coming the other way. Together, "Aye, sir!"

As soon as Terrell left they moved fast and laid claim to one of the rooms nearest the lobby and washroom. Its single window faced front, giving advance notice of any official visit.

The room also offered two beds considerably better than the mats at the staging area, two spartan pedestal chairs and a small matching table, a closet for which they had no immediate use, a washbasin with fully furnished towel rack, a shelf and drawer with miscellaneous utensils, and the usual saddle-type john.

It seemed a shame to let the showers go to waste. The new roommates were reveling in a hot soak when James Wilson came in with Bruce Garner. Those two, it turned out, had a room across the corridor and two doors away. Right; nice to keep track. But for the moment, Tabor couldn't focus much interest on these people he knew only slightly.

Returning to their own cubicle, Luke and Jay lay on their cots, awaiting summons to the food cart detail.

That chore, the two figured, would make fine cover for a little recon. Dutifully they followed a short

Subcontroller past two other barracks, picking up two more volunteers at each, and finally to a sprawling, barnlike structure alongside the taller one Frey had entered.

Inside, Tabor saw it was working on being a mess hall. At one end the kitchen was going well. The improvised chow wagons each held three large kettles, plus niches for side dishes, beverages, and condiments. All in all, not a bad job of design.

Not high tech, exactly, but with six men to move their cart, it rolled easily enough. Their route led back the way they had come, visiting each barracks in reverse order. Volunteers ate at their own buildings; by the time Luke and Jay reached theirs, Tabor had an appetite of predatory dimensions.

Filled up, he could have used a rest to let the meal settle, but no such luck. Four stops pretty well exhausted the cart's resources; it was back to base for refills.

The second run visited two more men's barracks; then, as Luke had hoped, the next two stops were women's. Neither was the one housing Casey and Carla. But maybe if they drew a third routing . . .

And bingo. Second stop on that run, crowding the chow line were Casey and Carla—and Alycia Frazier as well.

Dishing up from the stew kettle, Tabor couldn't spare attention to say much, and the line moved Casey past before she or he could pass more than a few words. He did manage to point to his barracks and say, "Sneak out later?"

"If we can," she said, and had to move along.

Trundling toward their third station, Luke did his pushing alongside Jay. "You and Carla going to try to meet?"

"Try, sure. I have a nasty hunch it may not be that easy."

\* \* \*

By the end of the cart's fourth and final run, sunset was past; the air began to chill. What with all the exercise, Luke was pleased to find that before the mess crew did final cleanup, the working complements of all three carts had first dibs on whatever food remained.

Walking back, no one said much. The first two men dropped away at their own barracks; then Luke and Jay reached theirs and the other pair went on. Partings amounted to "See you . . ."

Standing at the door, Luke nudged Jay. "Should we take out for you-know-where?"

"Umm. One of those guys keeps looking back; maybe we'd better step inside for a couple minutes first."

So they did. To face newly demoted Subcontroller Varj. He fiddled with a small, flat, hand-held screen-keyboard combo and said, "Since you two are the last to observe curfew, I may now seal this residence until morning."

Luke didn't see how Varj worked the lock, but it made a very convincing *thunk*.

*"Now* what the hell . . . ?" In their room, Tabor and Rozak sat facing across the little table and fairly simmered. Why hadn't they guessed—but how could they have known?

The place had only the one door. And no fire escapes; on both floors the central corridors dead-ended. "What if there's a fire?" Jay asked.

"Give them a little credit. The place has to be fire-proof."

Rozak glared with lowered brows. "If you say so."

Windows were fixed in place—and probably not breakable, even given the willingness to use such flagrant means. After all, they weren't planning escape, just a brief time out.

Rummaging from his jacket pocket, Jay got out a flask. Something more than a pint, it looked like. "I finagled one of the cooks out of this. Dunno what it is; tastes something like cheap bourbon. We could do worse."

After sipping a little of the stuff, Tabor tended to agree; it had his mind buzzing like a bee in clover. "Jay. There has to be more than one way out of this overgrown rooming house."

"Right. We're not in Hut City now. May look like it, but this is tech country. F'rinstance"—he waved a hand—"no open windows, but good air. Ventilation, Luke. The question is, where's it come from? And go to?"

Inspection gave no clues, but a hand held high near any wall felt slight air movement. Luke frowned. "Well, the *building* should have some kind of major ducts leading in and out."

"Like where?"

"Like let's go looking."

Existing knowledge limited the options. Their own room offered no egress; even if others might, they could hardly go barging into all of them to find out. On the face of things, the building's walls were a dead end.

Except, Rozak pointed out, maybe somewhere in the washroom area. All right: scouting time. Warily they peeked out into the corridor and approached the lobby; Varj the keeper could be on station anywhere.

He wasn't, though. And his absence was welcome.

The washroom—showers and laundry, among other amenities—was fairly large. Separating, Luke and Jay prowled its perimeter and met at the rear, where unmistakable, familiar-looking tanks presumably stored hot water. "Anything?" Rozak said; Tabor shook his head. "Then we're stonkered."

At the back of Luke's thinking, something tickled. "Maybe not." What was it? Oh, yes. "There's still the roof."

The second-floor corridor ceiling was at least ten feet high, the passage itself over six feet wide. With no way to brace against a wall while one man boosted the other, the centrally located ceiling hatch was nowhere near as accessible as first appeared. Neither the room-issue chair nor table had enough height to make it a one-man operation, and pedestal construction made stacking too wobbly.

Well, dammit! Luke was no gymnast, but Rozak, standing in a spraddled half-crouch as though bracing to play Atlas, coached Tabor up until he stood on the other man's shoulders and could reach the hatch cover. Cautiously he raised and eased it to one side, enough to look out over the flat roof.

"You see anything?"

"Just the roof. And some vent pipes, little ones. Hold still while I get this put back." Legs beginning to tremble, Luke reseated the cover. "All right; here I come."

It wasn't a great descent, but their awkward collapse didn't make enough noise to bring investigation.

Back in the room Jay poured more of the cook's bounty; Luke took a healthy first snort and said, "I earned that."

"Tell me. I'm the one with the bruised shoulders."

"And I know how we can get out of here," Luke retorted. He gestured. "I get up topside. First we swipe some rope, or cut bedding into strips and tie it together." There had to be knives in the mess hall. "Throw a hitch around one of the pipes I saw at the back, above the washroom, and slide down." He paused. "You can probably climb back the same way. Put enough knots in it, maybe I could too."

Rozak nodded. "Good, so far. One problem though. Do you see Carla and Casey getting out the same way? I don't."

Oh *shit;* Luke pushed his tumbler forward. "Shut up and pour." But at the half-inch level he signaled enough.

"You two," said Lord Frey, "pose a vexing problem." In the luxurious room, the entire top floor of the taller building beside the developing mess hall, the man sat behind a large desk. Tabor and Rozak stood before him. "You are both good stock, with above-average potential. A shame to see your possibilities wasted through senseless recalcitrance."

Shortly after sunrise Varj had roused the barracks, giving everyone time to get ready and form up outside.

Luke started to use the ultrasonic "razor" Aliira had given him but found no need; apparently the gadget dissolved whiskers slightly below skin surface; they might take a day or so longer to reappear. Jay, however, was interested, running the appliance over his cheeks and under his chin; the resulting sideburns, mustache, and goatee gave him a Mephistophelean look. Or maybe, Luke thought as the two faced Frey, Loki was a better analogy.

They had expected to resume cart detail duty but Varj said otherwise. For that job he chose Garner and Wilson; Tabor and Rozak he escorted personally to Lord Frey. Without breakfast.

Now Frey said, "What had you in mind, for instance, when disturbing the ceiling hatch in your building?"

Huh? Luke and Jay looked at each other as Frey continued, "At the time indicators showed it uncovered, your living space was the only one unoccupied." So the place was bugged; in spades! Frey leaned forward. "What causes your dissatisfaction, impels you to attempt infractions?"

Trying to frame a reasonable-sounding protest, Luke waited too long; Rozak said, "It's like this. Tabor and I get along fine. But for the long term we're not each other's prime choice of roomies."

Brows hoisted, Frey said, "But there are no restrictions; in your building you may pair off as you choose. Whom would you prefer?"

"Carla!"

"Casey!"

A nod. "So that is it. Then I have a proposal for you. Should I relocate you and the two women into quarterings more to your liking, will you repay me with conscientious service?"

Any used car buyer knows better than to bite on the

first offer; Luke said, "Can you extend that option to the whole group?" Jay frowned. . . .

Frey shook his head. "By no means. Your improved situation would relate entirely to your appointed positions as overseers' assistants. Extending such amenities to all is not feasible."

Surprising Luke, Rozak said, "How about just one more couple? Friends of ours, from Pullman; they don't know anyone else here—and they could assist *us.*"

"I've worked with them before," Luke put in. Well, in a way, though Physics Seven seemed a long time ago. And come to think of it, *was* . . .

Better, perhaps, to let that request simmer a while. He said, "Just what would our duties be?"

"To supervise and monitor the scheduled progress of my genetic enhancement program, and the accuracy of its day-to-day records."

"Huh?" Luke's hand pushed air. "We're not any kind of genetic engineers." A thought. "Garner's studying in that field, though, so maybe—"

"Seat yourselves. I shall need to explain at some length."

It was a lot to digest in one lump. This camp held persons Frey had extracted over perhaps a decade of Tabor's home time. The Viking hadn't experienced the entire period; typically he scouted for a few days, made his choices, inserted them into the timestream, then skipped ahead a bit and set up in a new location. The Apple Cup weekend had been his final stopover.

But why? What was it all for?

Frey answered. Aliira, Luke realized, had hinted at the problem. Since the Rebirth, genetic tinkering had eliminated much heredity disease and other defects. But the processes had somehow altered the so-called Unchanged; crossbreeding produced a lessening proportion of offspring carrying Changed genes.

And the Changed themselves constituted only a marginally viable gene pool; left to its own capabilities, the strain would have died of excessive inbreeding. That hazard still threatened.

New genetic material could not be had from the few known earlier Islands. Post-Rebirth population had always been relatively small; extracting persons from their original time frames could cause catastrophic changes, down time's river to farthest future. Rarely, that peril *had* been risked. . . .

All right; Luke had read stories, fiction concerning time travel and its theoretical paradoxes. "But back in our time you don't care what happens; is that it?"

"In your era, your sheer numbers endangered the biosphere itself. Removal of a mere few hundred, from loci well separated in space and somewhat in time, could hardly cause changes that would survive the grim ordeals of the Genocides and Waste Times."

Frey smiled. "In all timeshift activities, minor change affects the stream. But the fabric of events, it appears, is to a degree self-healing. Proceeding futureward from a given alteration, its *effects* seem to smooth away like a ripple spreading in water. Believe me, we have studied these matters."

"And that gives you the right," said Jay, "to destroy people's lives, bring them up here and stick them in boot camp?"

Color touched Frey's cheekbones; Tabor gave Jay a cautionary nudge as the Viking, his voice unnaturally flat and even, said, "Not their lives, only their circumstances. It is *our* lives, our future existence, standing in peril." His tensed features eased a bit. "In your own time, did no persons or groups receive somewhat cavalier treatment in the name of the greater good?"

Frey couldn't know about the internment, Japanese-Americans sent to camps in 1942 by Executive Order without due process. But Luke did. He gestured. "Okay; we're not perfect either. It's beside the point now, anyway. We're here. And somehow I don't think you're going to swim us back. So I'll work, yes."

Jay moved a hand. "All right; that goes for me too.

But we still haven't heard what this setup does, you want us to honcho for you. You and Derion together?—seeing as he's the one who brought our group. But I thought you were on different sides . . ."

"Indeed we are. This is my program; against all reason, against the very instinct for our survival, my cuz-cousin opposes it. Knowing that, I assumed he conveyed you here in some move to block my plans. Therefore, I located and sequestered you myself."

Curious, Luke asked, "How'd you know who-all to look for?"

"Your disappearance caused quite a turmoil. A Sergeant Manning was kind enough to list me the missing parties. As yet," Frey added, "a Vivi LaFleur still eludes me. As does Derion."

He paused. "More immediately, I shall instruct Varj to see that you and the two women are issued proper garb and suitably quartered before midday. After that hour's meal he will show you to your place of duty. He will also provide your initial schedules and instruction sheets."

"We work under Varj, then?" Jay sounded unwilling.

"He acts for me; he gives no orders on his own account."

Good. There was more, though. Luke knew he should let it drop for now, but still . . . "How about the other couple: Bruce Garner and Alycia Frazier? Can we have them on the team?"

Pausing, Frey nodded. "I see no harm in it. But that will be all; do you understand?" Voice edging with impatience, he said, "Sperm extractions will be scheduled on a three-day cycle, to maintain a steady workload. And technicians will provide you a chronological chart of each woman's fertility, so that impregnations may be arranged as expeditiously as possible."

He stood. "We are finished here; Varj will now escort you."

A few minutes later, outside and following the wooden-faced Subcontroller, Jay said, "Y'know? That guy really knows how to save up a punch line and throw it all at once."

First back to barracks, where everyone else now wore lightweight beige jumpsuits. Next, put their gear together and hike over to pick up their own new clothes—much like the others except for olive green stripes down the sleeves and the sides of pant legs. Third, on to the barracks where Casey and Carla, also jumpsuited, brought their own possessions out and joined the trek. Under the eyes of Varj and the remaining residents, the four exchanged only verbal greetings. Then, still dutifully following Varj, to two facing rows of four semidetached units each, behind and to the right of Frey's HQ building.

Here Varj stopped. "Units Two, Three, and Five are not occupied; you may choose for yourselves."

As he turned to leave, Tabor remembered something. "Hey! Frey—uh, Lord Frey—said we would have two more people here with us. That's Bruce Garner from our barracks and"—pointing to Casey and Carla—"Alycia Frazier from theirs." He looked into Varj's stony gaze. "See to it, would you please?"

"Understood." Varj walked away.

Luke pivoted toward the nearer row of housing. "Dibs on Number Two. Come on, Casey."

Inside wasn't lavish: a bare-bones version of the bedroom they'd shared at the Lady Aliira's residence. Except that no part of this was likely to be immaterial force fields. The bath was small but held most of the trimmings. With their gear set down, Casey faced Luke. "Wanna share a splash?"

"I haven't had any damn *breakfast*." Then his mind pictured Jay and Carla, last seen entering Number Three. Would Jay cavil at a romp, merely to avoid starvation?

"Last one in's a rotten egg!"

# ELEUEN

It worked out fine. They needed a second rinse-off after; then Varj showed up to escort them to their workplace.

Hoping to work directly with Casey, Tabor specified her as his own assistant; Jay followed suit regarding Carla. Varj, it seemed, had no instructions to the contrary.

As they set off, Tabor spoke. "We're to have our midday meal first." Griping about the missed breakfast wouldn't change anything, so he didn't.

The mess hall was coming along well, with nearly half the bench-type tables in place, but meals carts were also being loaded. Even when the setup was complete, Luke judged, more than one seating would be needed to feed the whole area.

Joining the line, they were served in typical mess hall style and sat to enjoy a rather good stir fry. Luke and Jay went for seconds; maybe you can't catch up, but trying never hurts.

On, then, to the original destination. Duty station, it turned out, was ground floor, right-hand half of the HQ building. Varj handed papers to a stout, thirtyish-looking woman wearing a small green cap, then left. Also on hand were nearly a dozen medical flunkies; the costumes hadn't changed much.

Jay came over and nudged Luke. "Our colleagues here aren't all locals. Frey dragged some back from *this* time's future, which seems to be his own major stamping ground."

"How did you—"

"One guy was griping, wishing he was still up at the Node of Terlihan, instead of back here where whizzgizz isn't available. And just because Lord Frey likes to rough it—"

"Whizzgizz?"

Rozak shrugged. "That's what it sounded like."

So. Timeswimming or no timeswimming, the various eras of this future time had not become homogenized.

Time to get the works in gear. Stepping over to the green-capped woman, Luke said, "I'm Luke Tabor. Those papers Varj gave you: I expect one of them concerns us?" With a gesture toward his companions.

Somewhat bulky but generally well proportioned, with a squarish face and short brown hair, she stood near enough his height to favor him now with a level gaze. "You may call me Dennet. I am told that all subjects at this facility are of the far past. Lord Frey sees fit to assign you responsibilities in my clinic; be certain you discharge them properly."

Was this one a Changed? Best to assume so. "Of course. But being new here we'll need some instruction, at first."

"True. Your combined work station is there, to the rear." A U-shaped item of office furniture, like several desks in one piece. "Here are your printed schedules, also a map showing the designated residences. Deliver the groups here promptly, collect the tasksheets from my technicians and transcribe the entries onto those schedules, indicating that all specified procedures have been accomplished as directed."

She consulted a paper. "Blood and tissue samples are first required, for genetic typing. After you four have provided your own, you may go and bring us the first scheduled contingents."

The implications of giving DNA samples had Karen Cecile pretty well worked up. It didn't help that without prior warning they'd also been given several shots apiece; one of Luke's, at least, still stung like crazy. As he and Casey walked to pick up their first contingent for testing, she continued to protest. "All I can say is, you'd better get us off the hook."

-      She strode like a trooper. "It's all well and good, Luke, you depositing to their sperm bank. But on my side, remember, they use the word impregnation, and I don't like it a damn bit!"

He was going to say, jesting, that he and she could always preempt Frey's program to that goal. But a sidewise look at her expression changed his mind in a hurry.

A Subcontroller had half the barracks complement out and ready. Luke read the names and Casey checked off responses; then they all walked to the clinic, where Dennet's crew of techs did their extractions and insertions with speed and efficiency. By then, Jay and Carla had a similar group on deck.

To Luke it seemed inefficient to escort groups from barracks to clinic and then tag along while their Subcontrollers walked them back. But it's never the new boy's place to nitpick established routine, so he said nothing.

Their fifth trip went to his old digs; Bruce Garner was one of the group. As they walked, Luke said to him, "Jay and I got you a new job; why hasn't Varj pulled you out of there?"

Varj had begun to tell him something, Bruce said, but then was called away. "So I didn't learn what it was about."

"Don't worry; we'll fix it at the clinic."

But Dennet did not agree; neither Garner nor Alycia Frazier appeared on Frey's appointment list, and that list was scripture. Tabor knew he was close to hot water; for the moment he shut up. Looking at the status of the processing lines, he edged out the clinic door and made his way to the top floor.

He was just entering Frey's domain when it occurred to him that he might be badly overstepping the limits of his position.

Frey, though, seemed not displeased to see him.

Quickly Luke stated his problem; the big man nodded. "An oversight," and scrawled briefly. "This will authorize."

"Thank you; thank you very much." For that moment, Luke almost liked the big, gaunt corsair.

Dennet, downstairs, showed peeve: leaving was unauthorized, invading Lord Frey's privacy was unthinkable, and—Luke's worst offense, it seemed—getting away with it was unpardonable.

Grudgingly she gave orders for the transfers and proper reclothing of Garner and Frazier. Then she glared at Luke Tabor.

Say something *first!* "Look, I'm sorry. Lord Frey *had* assigned those two to work with us; I just wanted to clear things up." Did her glower ease, even a fraction? "I didn't know what else to do. But I'll try not to make the same mistake twice."

Amazing him, Dennet smiled: a true, wide-open grin. "Very well. Honest error, honestly admitted. Your board is clean."

As they trailed that batch, minus Garner, back to barracks, Luke said to Casey, "You know? That woman's not half bad."

He was glad he hadn't, earlier, protested the needless walking; anyone's tolerance has its limits.


When they delivered the other half of the same barracks, Dennet beckoned to Luke. "This is your last section for today. You need not accompany its return."

She gestured toward a portable screen shielding one of the room's rear corners. "Coffee, and small foods, if you and your assistant choose. Had I thought to tell you earlier, you could have indulged during any of your waits here. I regret."

She turned away. Well now; the boss lady could even admit a mistake of her own. Tabor motioned to Casey; she and Carla and Jay came to join him at the screened-off corner.

Sure enough, the coffee break had survived the Waste

Times—or been reinvented. There sat a filled transparent urn, several cups, and two trays of unfamiliar snack items. Plus, unscreened from the rest of the area, the ubiquitous saddle-shaped toity.

Luke didn't need it just now; twice this afternoon he'd used washroom facilities at barracks. Carla, though, stared at it. "Damn! I suppose I'll get used to this, but—"

Jay snorted. "Pretend it's a picnic and we'll all turn our backs."

Released from duty the four strolled to their new quarters. "Anybody for a drink?" Jay asked. "I've got most of a flask left; Luke and I didn't dent it much last night."

"You called the right number," said Casey. "Lead me to it." Inside Unit Three, next door to Luke's and Casey's, Rozak poured. Talking quietly and sipping, the four sat at ease for a change.

At the door came a knock; Jay stood and admitted Bruce Garner and Alycia, both suitably green-striped. He apologized for having only one more glass; the newcomers agreed to share it.

One side of Alycia's face still looked like ten rounds with the light gloves, but she seemed cheerful. "Look; you guys *saved* me from that animal, and I haven't even thanked you. I—"

Jay raised his glass. "Shut up and drink." She nodded, and said no more about her ordeal with Junior Yancey.

Garner spoke. "Alycia and I really appreciate your going to bat for us. But I wonder—do you suppose you could get James Wilson out of barracks too?"

Rozak's hand knifed air. "Forget it. Wilson's a good guy, sure, but we've stretched our luck already."

Bruce looked abashed; Casey said, "What I can't figure is—Jay, back at the hut camp, you and Luke were the focus of the trouble. How did *you* two get picked for the gold stars?"

Rozak laughed. "I could say we just got lucky, and

we did. But it's an old principle; teachers used it in grade school. To keep order, take the most rambunctious kid in the class and give him a title. Put him on his honor. Works every time. Unless he's a bully—as Varj found out the hard way, with Yancey."

Alycia shivered. "I thought we weren't to talk about him."

So Luke suppressed his urge to ask if anyone knew what had happened to the big troglodyte....

Garner broke the silence. "Dennet told us where to find you, and that we're to be in Five, two doors down." He looked around. "Say—this isn't bad at all, is it?"

Feeling good, not high but relaxed, Tabor chuckled. "Beats hell out of those huts." Not to mention the barracks.

Back at the clinic he hadn't sampled the snack trays much. "Anybody else hungry? We could hit the mess hall."

"Or vice versa." Rozak gave an *I*-know-something grin, then relented. "Algar, one of the Subcontrollers we tagged around with today, is a helpful dude. Told me we rate room service."

From a small wall cabinet he brought out a phonestick and touched a button. "Dining hall?" And then requested six dinners for Unit Three. He turned the stick over. "Here's how you punch On and Off." Before putting the device away, he demonstrated.

Casey shook her head. "Rozak, you're a wonder."

"No need to butter me up. I was gonna pour you another, anyway."

After dinner was delivered and consumed, the flask still managed one more short one all around, to go with the coffee.

In bed, steamy from bathing, tired yet not ready for sleep, Tabor said, "You didn't bring up the major problem."

"Neither did Carla. But we talked, she and I. And

when it comes to impregnation, we have here a case of serious won't."

"Then how come neither of you spoke up?"

Against his side he felt her shrug. "Maybe it's better we hold off, let you guys try to come up with an out. Because with Frey, you two seem to have the *in.*"

*Don't hold your breaths, is all.* Leaning over, Tabor kissed her forehead. "Case, I hope to hell we can."

Waking early next day, Luke felt a bit feverish. Not bad otherwise, though; he and Casey exercised abed before showering, then hit the mess hall. And still reached the clinic on time, to find their four associates there already, and a few of the staff.

Some minutes passed before Dennet herself arrived, obviously on edge, as were several of her technicians. Tabor had no idea why; from the puzzled expression of the other staffers, neither did they. Asking wouldn't be a good idea. . . .

Reporting to a women's barracks for fetch-and-return, Luke and Casey found its Subcontroller, also female, every bit as antsy as Dennet. Curious, Tabor angled over to walk beside her; maybe she'd be easier to pump. Less risky, anyway.

*The trick is to act as if you already know.* "What do you really think will happen?" Concerned tone, serious face.

Startled, she looked up. "If he has been able to bring enough men and weapons, there is no doubt that Ahearn will attack. You know his record!"

"Uh, well, only sketchily. Maybe not even the highlights."

She nodded. "Ah. You have heard of the Three Sectors uprising? Against Baron Dol Hakor?"

"Only in large. Do you have details?"

"It was midwinter, a year and more ago. Ahearn himself spearheaded the drive to the heart of the Sector group. Dol Hakor, though not a full potant, was able to save his own family and a number of his household retainers, but—"

It was a tale of unbridled violence and little mercy. The man Ahearn was an exile from the Node of Terlihan, brought back by order of the court itself. Time displacement, it seemed, was used to remove key dissidents from their spheres of influence; several hundred years into his own past, Ahearn had no power base, no prestige.

He still had his wits, though. Within a month he vanished from official purview; now, some years later, he directed a widespread network of rebellious Unchanged with a surprising record of slayings, abductions, and miscellaneous destruction.

"With his knowledge from our future he has synthesized the berserker drug, which—among other effects—makes the Unchanged highly resistant to *will*. To some extent it even shields them from farsight. Thus prepared, his men—"

As they neared the building entrance the woman fell silent. "His men *what*—?" Tabor prompted, but she shook her head, mumbling that talk of Ahearn was not encouraged by the higher echelons. Which, Luke guessed, probably included Dennet.

Indoors he found he was feeling worse, so he caught Dennet's attention and told her so. The woman frowned. "It's the injections yesterday; you're not the first to complain. Really, the L-series shouldn't be given all at once; some persons do react poorly. But Lord Frey wanted the process over and done with, and you're lucky to get them at all. Few Unchanged do, these days; Lord Frey must value you six a great deal."

She shrugged. "Well, the discomfort is soon gone; in octades to come, you'll be grateful. Meanwhile swallow a couple of these." The big capsules took some gulping, but soon he felt better. But wondered, what in the world *was* the L-series?

When their contingent, duly sampled, was ready for return, Tabor had the chance to tell Casey as much as he could remember about the man Ahearn. She said, "So for us personally, would this guy be good news or bad?"

"Bad, I think. Sounds too trigger-happy for my taste."

"Then let's hope he doesn't show up."

Their second quota was the other half of the same barracks; the third was, again, women. One, a slim young brunette with high cheekbones and a wide mouth, looked somehow familiar. From when, though? Not more than a couple of years back, or she'd have been just a kid. But for that time he drew a blank.

He had to ask. Moving over to her, he said, "May I check your name, please?"

As she looked up, slantwise, her expression triggered memory. "Seena Haymes!" He said it almost in unison with her. Then, "But you disappeared nearly ten years ago." A popular starlet with a major role in a hit holovid show didn't vanish without news coverage and speculation; consensus eventually postulated a serial killer.

Unfazed, with the premature air of maturity some young entertainers achieve, she said, "It's more like fifteen hundred, they say. But for me it's been—umm—three days." So Frey's far-past operations had indeed covered several years.

Impressed, Luke said, "You're taking it well."

Seena shrugged. "Nobody ever wrote up my real background. Compared to my childhood, this is gravy."

She couldn't know yet what she was up against. "Keep thinking that," and Tabor moved ahead to walk with Casey.

At the clinic they took a coffee break. Behind the screen Jay and Carla sat with Bruce—whose duties, it turned out, included upkeep of the refreshments corner. "And where's Alycia?" Tagging around with Dennet's messenger, to learn the layout and take over that job. She could do worse. . . .

Luke cut through the trivia. "Listen—I think you'd like to know what I've heard about the bogey man. The one who has Dennet chewing her toenails."

* * *

As he told it, Carla nodded. At the end she said, "I have some dope, too. One of the Subcontrollers, brought back here from the Node, is part Afran. Sort of beige, which is about as much as you'll find in these homogenized times; when she saw me she got positively chatty. Not so much about what Ahearn does—she was cagey on that part—but what he is and how he got that way." She made a pause. "For one thing, he's a Chi-carrier."

"A what?"

"Father a Changed, mother not. Remember Mendel, brown eyes dominant over blue? Unchanged is dominant; in second generation crossbreeding, on the average you get one Changed and three Unchanged, but two of those carry the Chi gene arrangement.

"Except that with modern-day Unchanged, more and more the law of averages is skewing. Fewer Changed than the rules say—and even less of what they call full potants, the really high-powered Changed like Frey and Derion. And of course that's why Frey's mounting this project."

As Frey himself had said, yes. Luke made an interceding gesture. "Then if Ahearn mated with another carrier, the children would be Changed. Or Chis, or whatever."

Carla nodded. "Except that Ahearn's bitter about Chis. Seems his dad treated his momma like dirt. Ahearn tried to kill the old man, didn't quite manage it, and ran off. He's well educated on the scientific side and a natural organizer. What he's out to do is exterminate the Changed. One way is to discourage crossbreeding." She frowned. "I gather he can get pretty drastic about it."

"And no wonder," said Rozak, "that he'd pick this place for a target."

Luke wanted to ask if anyone really knew how serious the current threat might be, but a tech stuck her head in. "Tabor and Collins, your group is ready for return."

So that, for now, was that.

That day finished the taking of specimens. Dennet announced that the next stage, sperm deposits and impregnation, would begin. Aside to Tabor she said, "For myself, I do not care to conceive by syringe. Six days hence, I ovulate. I shall receive your sperm directly, and in private."

While he absorbed that bit of news she said to the group at large, "Impregnation, of course, must wait upon each female's charted fertile period."

Casey was scowling up a storm; Luke squeezed her arm in warning. Carla didn't look too happy either, but her poker face worked better; Alycia's betrayed only confused apprehension.

Tabor certainly couldn't blame any of them. Also, he couldn't think of a damn thing he could do to help. Jarring his introspection, Dennet spoke. "Lord Frey will join us shortly. Tlegg, his deputy, is unavoidably absent, on reconnaissance patrol. To expedite matters, Lord Frey himself will conduct this morning's sperm withdrawals. You three will be the first."

Luke wasn't sure what he'd expected: duck behind the screen, maybe (or maybe not), and jerk off into a bottle? Instead, Frey simply ordered the three men to take it out and hold the bottle ready; then, with no volition on his part, Tabor's body readied, aimed, and fired. All done in a matter of seconds, with one stab of sensation too intense for pleasure yet not quite pain.

The pain came later, a urethral burning, much like the time he and Casey had tried for one too many and went nearly an hour before giving up. Walking, now, to bring in a group of men for similar treatment, was no fun at all. And Casey, tired of hearing him complain, marched a good three paces ahead.

Their first batch included Junior Yancey, who seemed to have recovered well enough. He cast a sullen gaze at Luke and Jay but said nothing; Tabor for one was glad to return the favor in kind.

As they reached the clinic, down swooped a wain similar to those they'd seen at Aliira's, but larger and sporting a transparent canopy: Tlegg, Frey's deputy, now returned from patrol. The thin, dark man first assisted Frey in collecting sperm, then after the midday meal had that chore all to himself.

Late that afternoon Luke and Casey were sent to fetch three women: the starlet Seena Haymes, and two who looked vaguely familiar though Tabor couldn't put names to them. He moved, Casey following, to talk with Seena.

"You know why they called you?" Hoping to ease the jolt.

At the corners of her mouth, her lips quirked. "Oh, sure. To bear a member of the Master Race, just like when I played a Hitler Youth fräulein in *Nazi Love Camp.* Except that I don't have to learn any German."

Think again, Tabor! Casey said, "And you don't *mind?*"

"No. Because I don't have to do it."

Puzzled, Luke asked, "How do you figure that? These people can bend your mind; didn't you know?"

"Hints, yes. And they say I'm ovulating. But screwing my brains out still won't get an ovum down my tubes; they're tied."

"Oh." So much for comfort from older and wiser heads. "You don't think they can short-circuit that too, someway?"

Seena shrugged. "How should I know? All I can do is play the hand one card at a time and see how they fall."

She was done talking. Leaving Casey with her, he moved over to walk beside the newcomers.

The nearest was slim, fairskinned, with dark brown curly hair now tied back. Luke said, "Hi. I'm Luke Tabor; I think we've seen each other around campus."

"Yes." Shelley Lenoir, she identified herself. Then, "I've seen you walk by our house—the Thetas; y'know?"

"Oh, sure." Kappa Alpha Theta was on his way to Casey's apartment. "Good to meet you." Though this wasn't what he'd have picked in the way of circumstances.

He turned to the other, a chubby, pink-faced woman. "Are you a Theta too?"

She shook back longish, straight blond hair. "I was in

the dorms. But Shelley and I studied European history to-gether. We were on our way to the library when that big man grabbed us. Why, we thought—" She paused. "My name's Carol; Carol Harper."

"Pleasure." Then to both, "How are you getting along here?"

Lenoir shrugged. "Hysterics didn't do me any good, so I'm taking it all one bite at a time. I don't suppose you know a way to get back home?"

" 'fraid not." Not without help from Frey or Derion. "And you, Carol?"

The plump face set into surprising firmness. "They think they're going to breed us like animals; I've heard the talk. Well, they can think again."

She made a face. "I'm already pregnant. Just that day, I'd found out. And I thought *that* was the end of the world."

It was a hard line to top; Luke didn't try.


At dinner he felt uncommunicative; afterward he de-clined the offer to share in a new flask Jay had wangled, and went straight to Unit Two. A few minutes later, Casey joined him there.

She looked more than friendly, but sore plumbing was no help to the libido. Also, Tabor hadn't yet told her of Dennet's intentions. He *wanted* to feel like lovemaking, but mind and body wouldn't cooperate. "I know," said Casey when he begged off. "Actually, this whole damn sit-uation tends to shut me down, too."

"Tomorrow, for sure." And sometime that day he'd get the Dennet thing off his chest. So they kissed good-night, and after a time he slept. What woke him was a dream in which Lord Frey was blasting a mountain down on his head.

The noise terrified him; he found himself sprawled on the floor and coughing dust.

Some dream! Where most of their front wall had been, now gaped a large, ragged hole.

# TWELVE

✳

"**C**asey!" He looked; wasting no time on comment she was scrambling into her clothes. Quickly he did the same.

The wall between units One and Two was also breached, and next door lay carnage. Luke hadn't known that couple; now he never would.

Banging on the door. "You guys okay?" Rozak.

Casey beside him, Tabor swung the door open. "Yeah, sure. Not them, though." Pointing. Then asking "What—?"

"Who the hell knows? Come on; Tlegg's yelling for everybody to group up with him." Rozak turned and left.

It made as much sense as anything else. Luke followed.

Hunkered down at one side of the HQ building, away from the crashing barrage that still persisted, the survivors from the apartment complex looked to Tlegg. With the man were a number of other people including several Subcontrollers; Varj, crouched beside a pile of weapons, was one. Tlegg shouted, "Who among you has skill of small arms? Come forward!"

"That's us." Rozak nudged Luke. As they moved, Casey and Carla followed.

Less than half the group was taking Tlegg's offer but he seemed satisfied. "Varj, disburse weaponry: our few alloted bolters to the most expert, then sonics as far as they go." Eyeing the volunteers he said to Rozak, "How rate you your own prowess?"

"Tops. You want to try me?"

Tlegg laughed, motioning to Varj who handed Jay an

angular pistol-shaped object with a flanged muzzle. "That is a bolter. No mere stunning tool; its energies are quite destructive."

Up next, Luke temporized. But Jay said, "He's good too; arm him heavy." And to Tabor, "Jeez, man, take all the firepower you can get."

The next in line settled for a sonic gun; so did Bruce Garner. Alycia, clinging to him, refused any weapon.

Not Casey, though, nor Carla; from where he stood, Luke couldn't see what they were issued, but neither came away empty-handed.

Meanwhile Tlegg and two other Subcontrollers were pressing other weapons on everyone, volunteer or not, who lacked a gun. Knives, swords, clubs, staves: "You're sending people up against bolters with *that* stuff?" Jay protested.

"As does Ahearn," Varj said. "Active weaponry is always the minority; when one side's shooting prevails against the other's it is club and sword which must convert advantage to victory."

Maybe so—but if *anybody* was going to be shooting, Tabor felt, he'd just as soon be one of them.

Quickly now, Tlegg gave Varj low-voiced orders, then said, "I must organize other teams; Varj will lead you." At a fast trot he moved to the rear of the building and out of sight.

Varj said, "We go up the slope until we reach cover, then to our left. You without guns, spread out and follow; when engagement begins, take care not to obstruct our field of fire."

Up the hill, making enough noise for a herd of goats, the group straggled.

But against the blasts and crashings from farther along the lakeshore, a migration of buffalo could have passed unheard.

Edging through underbrush and skinny trees, Varj's meager platoon reached a vantage point. Below, in wavering light from incendiary blazes and sporadic flashes of energy weapons, Tabor saw armed personnel firing, charging, falling back ... One group was overwhelmed and silenced; he had no idea which side was which.

Varj's droning voice, speaking to Jay Rozak, caught Luke's attention. "... cannot pacify men dosed with the berserker drug, any more than Baron Dol Hakor was able. But Lord Frey has a new and different stratagem. When the time comes ..."

Maybe so, maybe not; Luke's thoughts drifted. Until he heard Rozak's voice sharpen. "Varj? How come you're not gunning for our asses, Tabor's and mine? After all, we did you one hell of a bad turn."

The Subcontroller's answer came slow. "With the man Yancey I made grievous error. Had I not, I would still hold my former position. Your acts, while painful to me, were necessary."

Shouts rose from below—and now, from a device Varj carried, blared sharp-voiced commands: "Tlegg speaks! To me, all units!"

Without thought Luke found himself moving in a disorganized mob. Some brandished guns, others miscellaneous instruments designed to bash or cut. Now the lot of them broke into a run, toward the hellish melee of screams and explosions erupting down near the lake.

Once out of cover they converged with other groups moving downhill. The moon had risen, not yet full but more than half. As clouds passed across it, light came and went. Tlegg's voice rose: "For Lord Frey, *forward!*"

Tabor saw Tlegg himself stand fast, watching his troops gradually form into movement down the slope. Feeling somehow disconnected from reality, Luke moved up beside the Changed man who had become leader. "What's going on?"

Hooded eyes noted his presence, then looked away. "It is Ahearn, with his drug-created berserkers. They overrun us."

"And Frey can't pacify them."

"No one could. Lord Frey will not attempt it.

Instead—" Below, a flare went up; by its light Tabor saw the combatants momentarily freeze in place as high above appeared a wain, hovering. At one side of it a man leaned to fire a bolter into peripheral attacking ground forces. As they scattered it struck Tabor that aerial combat here and now hadn't developed very far. This was like mid–WorldWarOne, when observation plane pilots shot at each other with pistols. And maybe just as well . . .

From the ground sprang return fire, flaring off an opalescent bubble which suddenly enveloped the wain. Automatic shield? Luke didn't know. The man inside—and now Tabor recognized Lord Frey—shouted at full volume:

"Attack!"

A burning surged through Luke's nerves; all that he saw came preternaturally sharp. The pulsing of his own blood roared in his ears, and that pulse raced. Fury struck; in great leaps he plunged downhill toward the fighting. If the central, defending contingent were Frey's men, the encircling group had to be Ahearn's. Tabor aimed and triggered his weapon; where it pointed, a burst of blue and orange spattered and a man fell.

Part of Tabor's mind questioned: was this Frey's doing, forcing the berserker state by *will?* But if Frey's effort had this effect on *him,* how much more terrible would it make the enemy, already impelled by Ahearn's drug?

Now gunfire came at him; from behind, Tlegg yelled "Down!" Varj made another grievous error; he didn't drop fast enough. At least his head didn't. The rest of him landed safely. . . .

Briefly retching, Luke scrambled up and charged again.

At no time did he lose consciousness; all through the fight his mind seemed clear, his senses keen. He saw the wain, its shield apparently breached, emit an arcing flare and then limp wobbling back toward Headquarters. But at the end, when most survivors of Frey's forces milled among scattered dead while some pursued the fleeing remnant of Ahearn's raiders, he remembered very little. He had killed, certainly, and hand to hand as well as by energy bolt. He'd taken punishment also; the left side of his face was one oozing, aching bruise, and other pains forced themselves on him. But when and how these things had happened, he had no idea.

What he did know, as he gazed at what Frey's *will* had wrought, was that no man should have such power over another.

The heightened state, the unnatural stimulation, those were gone; in flickering light Luke forced himself to move from one group of fallen bodies to another, looking in fear of what he might see. But the only dead face he recognized was Junior Yancey's, and he couldn't bring himself to care much. When a hand grasped his shoulder, bringing pain he hadn't known was there, and Jay's voice cried, "Here he is, Casey," Tabor almost collapsed from sheer relief.

Behind them came Carla, insistently querulous: "—no marks at all! Just limbs rigid and faces contorted, some gorged black with blood. What—?"

Enemy dead, she meant, and by a Subcontroller's handlight Luke saw what she was talking about: bodies with the look of insupportable strain but no wounds evident.

Another voice overrode Carla's; Frey approached, speaking to Tlegg and a few others following him. "—limit of tolerance. The berserker state, whether produced by drug or *will*, stresses the body into overload. Ahearn's drugged troops received roughly twice the stimulation. As I theorized and gambled upon, the doubled effect killed many."

Luke didn't hear Tlegg's question; Frey laughed. "Oh, heart rate, blood pressure, level of neuron excitation: any parameter susceptible to critical breakdown. Resulting in cerebral hemorrhage, aneurism, fatal convulsions, and the like. Think of it as bursting a balloon." And after another query unheard by Tabor, "Ahearn? Cede control of his mind to a chemical? Not likely. If he lies among these dead, my nephew fell to weaponry. But I think not. . . ." No longer chuckling, Frey led his entourage past the scene of death and up the slope toward Headquarters.

"So that's why he *willed* everybody berserker!" Rozak added an admiring curse; then, "No getting around it, colleagues; when it comes to strategy, that man's a major force."

"But not," said Casey, "a very likeable one."

Jay shrugged. "Who said anything about liking?"

Under the direction of two Subcontrollers, a dozen or so people began inspecting and searching corpses, putting tags on them for reasons unclear to Luke. Now as those not assigned to the body count began straggling back along the lakeshore and up toward the complex of buildings, he moved with them.

Another nagging pain caught his attention; in his frantic haste he'd fastened his left shoe much too tightly, but only now did he feel it.

"Go on, Casey; I'll catch up." He stepped aside into underbrush, out of the path of those behind. A sudden twinge told him he'd been out here overlong, so first he relieved his bladder. Then he knelt to attack the problem.

In the dark he pulled at a lacing end, but the knot only tightened. "Damn!" He sat, turning so the shoe could catch what little firelight reached this far, and picked at a loop until he had some slack. When the snarl loosened he spread the shoe's flaps a moment, savoring the release of pressure. As the last of the stragglers walked past him and out of sight, he brought the shoe to proper snugness and secured the knot.

He was bringing his feet under him, preparing to stand, when a hand snaked forward over his right shoulder and gripped his throat. At the same time something pricked the left side of his neck at the jaw hinge.

"Remain silent and listen." A harsh voice, muted. "I need your help."

Thumb to one side and fingers at the other, the hand

constricted his carotids; feeling dizziness mount, Luke gasped a whisper. "Ease up, will you? I'll hold still."

A squeeze, then the pressure lessened. "Be certain you do so." And after a moment, "Name yourself and your time. Are you of the Outjut, or elsewhen?"

What the hell? Who was this, and what did he want? More importantly, what would make him happy enough to get that knife point off Luke's neck? Tabor made a mental shrug; the truth was all he had, and it might even work.

"Lucian Tabor. I'm not from here, but from the far past; I don't know what this fight's about, or who's on whose side. I—"

"Enough!" The sharp thing went away, but Luke heard no sound that might be its sheathing. "You will help me to stand and to walk; I will tell you which way to go." After a hesitant sound, the man said, "None must see us."

Quite an order, that. But Luke answered, "I understand." And to an extent he did; this was Ahearn's man, not Frey's.

The hand moved from his throat to his upper arm; taking the change as permission Luke stood, turning to face someone crouched half-hidden in the brush. Putting some weight on the grip the man pulled Luke farther into cover and brought himself upright—to stand considerably the taller and to show, dimly lit, a familiar face.

It couldn't be. Frey had gone ahead, up the hillside. But on second look this face was younger, the body slimmer. And Lord Frey had no scar from the left corner of his lower lip to the point of his chin.

What had Frey's words been? Without thinking, not knowing why he said it, Luke blurted out, "Your uncle Frey guessed you'd survive the fighting." The wild hunch bloomed and he went along with it. "He is your uncle, isn't he, Ahearn?"

The knife flashed altogether too close before the man's teeth-bared snarl subsided. "He's told everyone? I thought he'd be too proud."

So this *was* Ahearn! Careful now . . . Luke said, "Not everyone. I—uh, overheard something and made a guess."

Ahearn's grip tightened. "Yes. No matter. Come; we will go eastward, where cover extends downward to the shore."

Slowly they moved through brush until they intersected an overgrown path and followed it. Now Ahearn's right arm lay around Luke's shoulders for support; side vision showed light glinting from the blade the left hand held. The man's steps were slow, even a bit shaky.

"Are you hurt?"

Tabor sensed rather than saw the headshake. "No. To negate Frey's *willing* of battle rage, holding my mind clear for tactical work, I ingested sedation. The conflict drained me, and the excess now, of sedative—not easy to struggle against. Otherwise I would not need your aid."

Maybe so—but with one massive hand on his shoulder and the other wielding a knife, Luke couldn't bet Ahearn's reflexes were slowed enough to give good odds on breaking free and running. *Color me chicken,* he thought, *but not with my own blood. . . .*

The path led where Ahearn had predicted, to a stretch of shore covered with brush and the skimpy trees. At the water's edge the man looked both ways, nodded, and impelled Tabor toward the right. "A bit farther."

Not many minutes later they reached a small, high-banked cove; from where Luke stood, he couldn't see the shoreline. Ahearn emitted a low whistle. Almost immediately someone popped up, head and shoulders looking over the top of the bank. "Ready to move, Ahearn." A light, clear voice, softened by the need for quiet.

The black-hooded head, barely silhouetted against vagrant reflections off the water, turned to face Luke, and the voice went stern. "I agreed to risk my boat on the chance of your besting and taking Lord Frey, though how you thought to do so still lies beyond my knowing. And the rescue of yourself is valid use, also. But I did not contract the transport of miscellaneous captures. What is the importance of this person?"

"Absolutely none" would have been Luke's preference; he had no desire to go anywhere with these people. But impelling him toward the cove's head, where a minor ravine cut the bank, Ahearn said, "From the far past, he claims to come. We have heard rumors of such. If his claim is true he can tell us much."

"Humph!" The one below made a sniff like an outraged dachshund puppy. "*If.* Oh, well enough; bring him down."

The partial burden of Ahearn made the little canyon's uncertain footing even harder to manage; several times Luke slipped, but escaped any actual fall. At the bottom he stood panting. Now what?

"This way!" To the right, at the edge of a shelf of bank, stood a small figure, black clad in something resembling a wet suit. It came to take Ahearn's other arm. Together the three moved along to where a long, flattish oval object floated, almost touching shore, its top open or missing to reveal four couches. Or cots, or mats—something like that.

"Get on." Turned toward Luke, the small person's suit exposed the face only from chin to eyebrows; Tabor saw a sharp, strong nose, large eyes, and taut-stretched lips above a small, pointed chin. *A woman,* he thought, but couldn't be certain.

"Sure." Gingerly he stepped onto the vessel; surprisingly, it tilted not at all. At one end he saw dials and levers; he wouldn't be wanted near the controls, so he chose one of the other positions and lay on his stomach, facing forward. And got another surprise when Ahearn took the place beside him. But on second thought, that move was simple precaution: prisoners don't ride in the backseat unrestrained and unattended.

Taking the left front position, the small person tapped at the control area; on either side transparent panels emerged and came together to form a canopy. As with the egg, Tabor couldn't spot where they came from, or how.

No matter; Ahearn said, "Udeen. Subsurface, please. Viewpipe and breather to extend as need be."

Again the dachshund puppy snort. "I came here, Ahearn, in full daylight. And without detection."

For the first time Luke heard Ahearn laugh. Well, barely—a brief bark, but good-humored. "Of course, Udeen. My anxiety regarding details, you must understand, has become reflexive."

This time the puppy's sniff sounded conciliatory. Ahearn turned on his side, facing Luke. "The far past, you said, yet prior to Hykeran Outjut only few and minor Islands are known. Is there yet another, near the Rebirth after the Waste Years?"

The boat submerged and began moving. How much, thought Tabor, should he tell this man? Or did it make a difference? So far, Ahearn hadn't done much threatening—only enough to enforce his demand for help. On balance, Luke decided to be open and direct. Two reasons: he didn't see what harm it could do, and it was a hell of a lot simpler than lying.

"Before the Waste Years? Even the Genocides? What was it like? Did the Changed rule then, as now, with little thought to the well-being of the Unchanged? Tell me—"

"In my time there were no Changed; they hadn't been produced yet." Now what? "Actually, the beginnings of genetic engineering emerged late in my century of birth; the first Changed may have appeared not much later. But what *we* had were something like eight billion of us Unchanged, about to drown in our own excesses because nobody had the will or authority to stop us." *Some soapbox!* Luke took a deep breath.

Ahearn whistled. "Eight *billion?* How could they all be fed?"

"We never did get that part figured out too well."

"But if you were all Unchanged together, then none held power over the rest. You had no oppression! Wonderful!"

Right. The Imperial Caesars, Napoleon, Hitler,

Mussolini, Stalin, Mao, Perón, Castro, Pol Pot, Idi Amin, Khomeini, Ceausescu, Saddam, Fercznath, Klewstouyn . . .

Mildly, Luke said, "Well, not exactly."

In near silence the boat continued; above, the water paled and darkened as more or less moonlight impinged. After perhaps twenty minutes Tabor felt the air growing stale; before he could decide to mention it Ahearn said, "Breather up, I think," and Udeen nodded. In seconds, fresh air entered.

Ahearn held out something like a floppy pot holder. "Your face, Lucian Tabor. Apply this healpad; it will bring a measure of ease." Surprised as much by Ahearn's remembering his name as by the man's consideration, Tabor blurted thanks and followed instructions. The thing carried a sweetly spicy odor and put a coolness to his rasped bruises; in moments he felt aches and tensions shuddering loose, relief felt not only in face and neck but gradually spreading outward from those areas.

However this gadget worked, Luke was all in favor!

He expected more questions, but none came; now Ahearn lay quietly, and finally Tabor realized the tall man had gone to sleep. So much for guarding the dangerous prisoner.

Not that he felt like much of a threat: here he was, underwater in a boat he didn't know how to handle, going from one place he couldn't locate on a map to another which might be anywhere on this lake's shore. Wherever that was . . .

*So I take Ahearn in his sleep and overpower Udeen. Maybe. Then what?*

It hardly seemed worth trying. Instead he crawled forward, almost alongside the boat's driver. "Hi. Ahearn's sleeping. How much farther do we go? I mean, how much more time until—"

In dim light from the control instruments, Udeen's face showed disapproval. "You should remain back there."

A woman, all right; unmuffled, the voice made its gender clear. And young-sounding, possibly not too sure of herself. Moving ahead to put more light on his own face, Tabor grinned. "I got lonesome. Sleepers aren't very good company."

For a moment the visible side of her mouth twitched upward, but then she said, "Neither are boatners, while on duty. And captives do not move freely without specific let. Return to your place, or I shall have to use my stunner."

"In *here?*" With that sonic gadget? "You'd shake the lid loose." But he wriggled back alongside Ahearn and rolled over on his back.

It had been a long day's night. Luke had no idea how much he'd slept when Ahearn's hand on his shoulder brought him awake.

Canopy opened, the boat lay at rest, bumping gently against a low dock where Udeen already stood. Ahearn lumbered to his feet; unaided now, he stepped ashore. "Udeen. I must see to communications with the field teams, coordinate efforts in rescue of our surviving raiders." He gestured. "For now, place this man in one of the holding areas."

Udeen nodded. "I suppose the chore lies within scope of contract. Very well; if he makes trouble I will use my stunner."

This woman definitely had an attitude problem. Luke said, "I won't. Except to ask if I might be given something to eat."

Her lips tightened, but Ahearn turned back and said, "See to it. I seek allies, not antagonists." Still slow-paced he walked away, up from the water and angling to the left.

Pointing the other way along the shoreline, Udeen said, "Lead; I will tell you where to go. Stay before me at all times, or—"

"Or you'll shoot that thing." Obediently, he walked. "What makes you think I'm an enemy?"

"You—" She broke off. "That light ahead, up the slope. We go there." Luke turned in that direction and kept walking. Udeen said, "You are from Lord Frey, one of his people."

"Hah! The guy captured us, same as Ahearn did me." Come to think of it, capture was the story of his life lately, starting with Sergeant Manning nabbing him in his own apartment.

"And brought you from the far past. If he did not favor you, why choose you?"

The light, nearer now, came from a long, low building which even in this dimness looked more than not like a prefab. Flanking it as lean-tos were several tents, only one of which showed any light within. It took Luke a little time to make out even that much detail, because some effort had been made to use tree cuttings for camouflage. Maybe from the air it worked. . . .

"He didn't." They reached an entrance, its door inset to allow a guard to stand in shelter. The middle-aged woman held her weapon at the ready, then lowered it and opened the door. Inside, a door-lined corridor led straight back. "It was Derion who brought our group forward in time; Frey found us later. You know Derion?"

"Not well enough to omit his title. Nor Lord Frey's, for that matter. Enemies though they both be, to us."

About halfway along the corridor stood a pair of double doors. Udeen touched Luke's arm. "In there." Inside was a mess hall, smaller than the one at Frey's encampment but otherwise pretty much standard issue. A bored cook dispensed stew and coffee to both newcomers. Across from Udeen at a small table, Tabor acceded to her demand and began his story from the start.

As he talked, she peeled back the wet suit's hood to reveal a scant quarter-inch growth of light brown hair. At his querying look she interrupted his narration to say, "Not many days ago I had occasion to impersonate a Subcontroller. Most such, of course, are of the Changed, their less able. But not all; the ruse was plausible." She grimaced, the fading oval of crease from the hood's rim adding grotesquerie. "I did not wholly succeed—but did withdraw unsuspected and may try again."

The combination of large eyes, strong nose, prominent ears, and fuzz of hair gave Udeen a fey elfish look, almost childlike. But, "Be on with it," she said, not child-like in the least.

For the most part he told it straight. He omitted, though, the Lady Aliira's comments on both Frey and Derion, and when the odyssey reached Frey's lakeshore base he began serious editing. What had he been doing there? Helping escort the camp inmates for physical exams and immunization shots. Who were these inmates? The truth couldn't hurt there, so he told it. But avoided any reference that might lead to mention of Frey's breeding program; that aspect, he felt, was best left untold. By him, at any rate.

Time for a breather. He went for coffee refills. When he sat again, he could see he was in for it.

"What, then, is Lord Frey's purpose?" Scowling, Udeen leaned forward. "What wants he with so many captives, and why from such distance in time past?"

"How would I know? Do you think he tells *me* his problems?" And another thing, "Why do you care? The last I heard, your only connection with Ahearn was contracting the use of your boat."

Her hard, fast slap caught him wholly unprepared. At least it was on the unmauled side of his face. "You will not question me." She stood. "Up! You have eaten enough; it is time you go to a holding room."

Obviously still angry, once out of the mess hall she herded him ahead of her, first for a brief washroom stop and then to a door opening onto a side corridor. Its other end abutted a largish tent, unlit except for a small pane in the sturdy door, with perhaps two dozen sleeping mats lying in rows.

Udeen gave him time to locate an unoccupied mat before the door closed, its lock clunking with finality. He also had time to notice that the tent was not simple canvas or plastic; woven into its fabric, floor and all, was a mesh shaped like that of chain link fencing. High-tech confinement, done on the cheap.

Tabor sat, listening to the breathing of men asleep and possibly some who weren't.

There was one good thing about it. She hadn't stopped him from bringing along his coffee refill.

"Up and out, now!" The commanding voice was peremptory but not bullying. As Tabor rolled to hands and knees, then stood, daylight through the translucent tenting showed him nearly twenty other persons also getting up. Not two dozen; the place had not been filled. He was surprised to see that this was another coed tank; several of his fellow inmates were female.

"I am Milot. You will heed my instructions." The stocky guard, a youngish man, armed but holding his shoulder weapon at a relaxed version of Port Arms, stood just outside the door and motioned the emerging persons to move faster. "Washroom first; two-tri-zero seconds, then form up for feeding."

Shuffling in line along the corridor, Luke calculated: two-zero-zero-zero, octal. After a moment he had it: seventeen minutes, a bit over. Not exactly lavish, but what could you expect? Being toward the head of the line, Tabor was able to get in the saddle on the first wave with no wait, and could take his time washing up afterward.

The mess hall was about two-thirds full, but to one side several tables were empty or partially so. Going through the line and finding a seat, Luke began to notice things. Such as that most of the contingent seemed to know each other and talked together, ignoring several others including himself.

The woman sitting beside him, tall and thin-faced, with black hair cut square-around an inch or so below the ears, was also getting the outcast treatment. For openers he asked her to pass the salt, then said, "Thanks. Say, what club is it that most of these folks belong to and we don't?"

Over grey eyes her brows made a frown. "That group is all of this local area and this time, an extended community. Ahearn has collected them here, partly for their own safety and partly to make use of their labors. An ingrown, insular people."

She looked a question; hoping he guessed it right,

Tabor said, "This is not my time and I have no idea where this place is. Yesterday I was Frey's prisoner, now I'm Ahearn's. I'm not really on anybody's side. But these people don't seem to give you much of a choice."

He told his name; she said, "I am Deba Sayan. I left Lord Frey's holding to join Ahearn. But his other face, the woman Udeen, insists I may be a spy and gives me no opportunity to speak with Ahearn personally. So I have gained nothing."

"Too bad. That Udeen—hey, wait a minute. From what she and Ahearn said to each other, she's nothing but a—a *boatner*, I think it was, contracting her boat out to Ahearn's use."

She made a gentle snort. "That is mere banter, a game between them. As I understand matters she is his protégé; in some ways they are closer than sibs. Were she not a Chi-carrier also, they would be fully quiting lovers, not restricted to other sexual expedients. But rather than sire one of the Changed, Ahearn would neuter himself."

Wow. No mention of contraceptives; maybe with such a small population there'd been no incentive to devise them. But more to the point, assuming this woman really did have the inside dirt: "He must hate his father very much."

"The Duke Mardeux? Who does not? Even the Prime Peer, whose name is not to be spoken and to whom Mardeux stands next in position. Which," she said with a knowing look, "is why, all his powers notwithstanding, the duke will never rise to that station."

Well, now . . . "But how do you know these things? I thought Ahearn was exiled back here from the Node of Terlihan."

"Through others brought from futureward, word reaches us."

"Yes. I see." A different thought came: "A community, you said. There must be children. But I haven't seen any. Where are they?"

"Another place. Farther away, thus presumed safer. Women with children, old persons, the physically impaired—as best he might, Ahearn has placed them out of danger."

And Frey? What concern, if any, had he shown for noncombatants? Yet aside from those kidnapped out of time, the big Viking's personnel formed something on the order of a military group; normal civilian standards might not apply.

Luke hadn't noticed Milot leaving the place but now he saw the man, flanked by two others in uniform, come in again. Rather than quiet the talk by voice order the guard blew a whistle, then said, "Word from Ahearn: marching orders. We are to dismantle and transport such facilities as we can reasonably manage; others will come here later to complete the task."

He beckoned to his own charges, who moved to gather near him. Luke got in line and followed, noting that the rest of the recent breakfasters divided, joining the other two guards to leave the place. Outside it, one cadre split off at the first junction and the other at the next.

Milot led his own group back to the tent and appointed the three nearest persons to disassemble and pack it. Deba Sayan was one of these; Tabor, standing next to her, another. The third, an older man whose name sounded something like Clofe, was the only one who knew how to take the damned tent apart, or fold the separated sections for transport.

Unfortunately he was nowhere near as useful when it came to helping carry it.

# THIRTEEN

✳

By late afternoon of the march, Tabor was ready to shuck his fifty pounds of pack and vamoose. Except that there was no place to go: just more miles and miles of spindly conifers, spread over rolling hills and shallow valleys. Plus, these latitudes were no place to try to live off the land—and no part of his burden was either food or water.

Some of the folks, he noted, had it easier: lighter bundles, and among the cohesive local contingent an apparent arrangement for swapping various-sized loads back and forth. Even Clofe found a partner to carry his heavy pack part of the time, while the older man took a smaller one. But Tabor encountered no one who seemed approachable—and neither, he saw, did Deba Sayan.

Maybe when they stopped for the night, or for an evening meal if that occasion didn't end today's leg of the trek, he could try harder and make some useful contact.

Meanwhile Luke slogged along, about halfway back in the column, tired and a little uncomfortable but in no real distress. He could keep this up a long time, but he didn't have to like it.

Starting from a point on the lake's northern shore they had first headed northeast, then gradually circled to the right until now their course lay roughly south by southeast. Not only to get around the lake, Tabor guessed, but to stay well clear of Frey's installation while doing so. What their destination might be, he had no idea and was caring less by the minute.

A shadow crossed his path; looking up he saw an egg home in on the front end of the trudging column, something more than a hundred feet ahead. At a rough guess it was about the size of the flyer Frey had summoned when he surprised Luke and Casey. Frey wasn't in this one, though. Or at least nobody thought so; when the vehicle landed, the column leaders gathered around it.

Everyone else stopped, too; Luke shucked his pack and sat on it. In the army he'd learned a basic rule: any time you get the chance you sit down, or lie down, or—best of all—sleep. For now he figured sitting was the most he could manage. Also it let him watch up front, try to figure out what was going on.

Which was, at the moment, two persons marching purposefully back along the column, heading more or less in his direction.

Even before they came past the group just ahead, Tabor recognized Milot escorting the woman Udeen.

"Those two," she said, pointing to Luke and to Deba Sayan, who had reslung her pack. "Milot, you will attend until I have them secured; then you are free to resume your usual duties."

As she gestured with her stunner, Luke decided she'd feel naked without the thing. She was hooded again, the oval from chin to eyebrows framed in pale, finely meshed fabric. Not moving, he said, "I don't imagine you want us to bring two-thirds of a tent, so I guess somebody else is stuck with it."

Frowning, Udeen looked irritated. "Milot, you'll have to redistribute some of the smaller items so as to make two fewer packs. I hope the process will not delay you greatly."

When the young man nodded, Sayan set her pack down. She and Luke began walking, Udeen's presence close behind as they picked their way through and around the waiting groups.

The egg's door sat open. Udeen climbed in first and stood just behind the front seats, facing the rear ones. Under her and Milot's guns Deba climbed in and took right-hand rear; then Tabor sat beside her. Following Udeen's instructions, Milot left his weapon outside to come in and—keeping out of her line of fire—strap both passengers in place.

Just because Luke hadn't found seat belts in Frey's egg didn't necessarily mean there weren't any. What he couldn't find now was any way to unfasten one.

"Udeen?" As the egg lifted. No response. Not expecting an answer, Tabor asked anyway, "Where are we going? No, scratch that; place-names wouldn't tell me anything. But how about *why?* Not that I'm complaining; this beats toting that pack."

Deba gave him the pitying look one gives to a child who has spilled its dessert in its lap; Luke guessed she was as surprised as he when Udeen looked back over her shoulder and said, "Farsight. It struck me as likely that Lord Frey has registered you both, in his mind, to render you findable. But—"

"Yes, I know." Luke nodded. The other egg had told him its drive fields shielded against *will;* presumably the effect applied to farsight also. "In here he can't see us." Another thought came. "What about Ahearn? I'd expect Frey's registered *him,* right enough."

"Which is why he does not march with his people. Some few Chi-carriers, Ahearn among them, can by considerable effort make themselves unsusceptible to farsight, though not indefinitely. But wherever he makes his temporary bases, Ahearn takes with him an interfering device, adapted and simplified to minimum weight and bulk, yet still a considerable load for one person to carry."

"Then you pulled us out so Frey couldn't use us to spot the column. That's good thinking."

"Which denies you the chance of rescue."

With a few hundred feet of air under it the egg gathered speed, heading roughly southeast. Peeved, Tabor said, "Once and for all, I don't view that big pirate as any kind of rescuer. I'm not on his side and never have been. I—"

"You fought and killed for him!"

And he had, too; no denying it. But—"Ahearn attacked our camp. Hell, the first I knew of it was when he blew the front wall out of Casey's and my apartment and killed the couple in the unit next to us. Of course I fought. And with Frey's *will* putting us all in berserker mode . . ."

He snorted. "You talk like you think I had a choice."

More silence, until Udeen said, low-voiced, "This is what the Changed do to us. We who have no valid grievance against each other are manipulated and used, giving our energies—our very lives—to their purposes." For a moment Tabor felt he and she might actually be on the same wavelength about something. But then, once more strident, "If only they did not exist!"

There it was again. Thinking back to Ahearn's fantasy of a pre-Genocides utopia populated only by Unchanged, Luke said, "You don't know what you're talking about. In my own century, before the Changed ever developed, we had cruelty and violence and mass slaughter on a scale you couldn't imagine. My grandfather fought in a war that killed more than five million from just one country. The manipulation was as bad as anything the Changed could possibly do, and all by Unchanged humans. The Changed just have an easier time doing it, is all. And from what I gather, they're not a patch on some of the evils *my* times saw."

Udeen didn't answer. Luke's seatmate's normally lazy-lidded eyes stood wide, unblinking; she said, "Before the Genocides, then, you were *all* predators? No wonder such things came."

"*Not* all; just a few, with the twisted genius to gather support and manipulate it." I was only following orders— the classic excuse of the twentieth century from Nuremberg to Contragate and beyond. Thought strayed to his observation during last night's combat, that in this time air war was only into its relatively benign infancy. But another idea preempted: "Come to that, what was Ahearn trying to accomplish with his attack?"

"Why, to disrupt Lord Frey's plans."

"Sure thing. He couldn't touch the boss man himself, so he cut loose with the artillery and killed off a bunch of

Frey's *captives*. And you bitch about the Changed manipulating people."

"But that is different! Ahearn must do what he *can.*"

And the end justifies the means, and the cheese stands alone, and this is the house that Jack built.

Fuck it. No . . . in these times: "Quite."

But with his lousy accent she probably wouldn't get it.

Across the land below, shadow crept. Higher now, for minutes longer the egg rode in sunlight. But inevitably came the moment when the sun, one thin red segment still showing above the horizon, made the anomalous blink which atmospheric refraction can produce, and vanished.

Even an hour later the western sky glowed paradoxically bright. During his army hitch, on a summer night in roughly these latitudes, Luke had lost a sucker bet that he could read newsprint outdoors in just such light; it could fool you.

Beside Tabor, Deba Sayan made a throat-clearing sound. Okay, so she wanted to talk; he waited, until she said, "You think Ahearn no worthier than Lord Frey?"

"How should I know?" Suddenly he was too wound up to speak reason; sarcasm would have to do. "Hey; maybe Ahearn lights a candle every night for the tooth fairy. Maybe he gave at the office. Maybe he's kind to wallabies and little buckaroos. But he also blew all to hell the man and woman who were bedded down in the next room to Casey and me, people I doubt he'd ever even heard of." So stick that in your pipes and play it, lady. . . .

Her tone remained calm. "These buckaroos and such: you speak in terms from your own time? I know nothing of them."

She sighed. "But we both deplore senseless killing."

He reached and squeezed her hand. "That we do."

Anything else he might have thought to say, left his mind as the egg tilted in rapid descent. Below and to the side Tabor glimpsed, briefly through the deepening twilight, a scattering of yellow-orange glows. Nothing big or especially bright; lighted windows, most likely, and maybe a few outdoor lamps.

Circling, Udeen brought them down, arriving in a clear space among smallish buildings and grounding in front of a larger one sporting a small floodlight over its entrance. She muttered something to the control panel; then, opening the door, she said in Luke's direction, "I'll bring someone to help release you."

To undo the belts while Udeen held the stunner. "Damn it all, you don't need a gun with us! Look—I give you my word, my solemn parole, that I will not try to attack you or to escape. What kind of idiot fanatic do you think I am, anyway?"

Standing with her mouth open, in the hood she looked a little like a frog. "Why, I—"

"And I didn't even come to Ahearn of my own accord. But Deba here, she did just that, and still you treat her like an enemy prisoner. Ahearn said he wants *allies*— you heard him, same as I did. How about trying to help him out on that?"

"Well—" Momentarily Udeen grinned, but it didn't take. Stern-faced again, she said, "Once you are secured and inside, there will be time to talk of alliance." She climbed out and walked toward the building.

The muffled sound Luke couldn't immediately identify turned out to be Deba Sayan giggling. "What's so damn funny?" After all, she was strapped into a seat too, the same as he was.

"That little tree toad, and we can't manage her! Here we sit, and she's not even here, but still—"

He clutched her arm. "Hold it. I want to try something." Thinking back, he said, "Carrier, close the door."

It closed.

*Well,* now . . . ! Quickly, before common sense could overrule impulse, Luke said, "Lift off."

It did.

Silent, Deba let her expression speak for her; what it said was, *now* what do you think you're going to do?

Since Tabor had very little idea, he hoped his own face wasn't answering. To the egg he said, "Are you under any specific orders at this time? If so, what are they?" And saw the woman nod in approval.

"On completion of my most recent assignment, which was to bring Group Leader Udeen and yourselves to Commander Ahearn at Resolve Village, she told me only to await further instructions."

But hadn't specified who should give them? Better and better. "Then your next instruction is to release these restraints." If it could . . .

With the faintest of clicks, the belts slipped free. Tabor climbed over the front seat and sat himself at the controls. Looking out, in this night's brief period of true darkness, he saw that the egg was making a leisurely circle over Resolve Village, altitude perhaps three hundred feet.

Now then. "Has any restriction been placed on selection of destinations?"

"The only major limitation is upon you, not on myself. I am currently stocked with food and water sufficient for two persons for perhaps two days." This machine, Luke noted, spoke in a deeper and more resonant voice than Frey's egg. More masculine? Not necessarily. It continued, "Further, I am not to enter a patrolled area without giving warning of the danger involved."

*But of course.* Luke turned around to Deba Sayan. "Do you have any good ideas where to go?"

"Of advantage to us?" She shook her head. "Childering and maturing in a lord's domain gives no knowledge of otherwhere."

Unexpectedly, she laughed. "And would you hear me now, thinking back on the whole of it, talking partly in Liegespeak?"

Interesting, but not productive. Luke said, "This is your own time; right? But mostly you were stuck in one place and don't know your way around?" Taking silence for agreement, he asked, "Where have you *heard* of, that might sound promising?"

"I cannot be of aid," the egg said, "unless given some criteria defining your wishes."

Tabor grimaced. "Now why didn't *I* think of that?"

All right. "Are you allowed to enter the holdings of Count Derion?"

"Patrols may be encountered, in which case I must—"

"Yeah, yeah. What would these patrols do? Shoot us down?"

"If we did not obey their orders to land and submit to capture. Count Derion is, by definition, Ahearn's enemy."

"But not mine." I *think* . . .

"By interrogating my log, his people could locate Resolve Village, thus betraying Ahearn. I cannot—"

"Okay; hold it. I have no intention of that. Can't you seal your log, or something? So they can't read it?"

"I cannot. But you could."

"How?" Order it sealed, the egg informed him, with a password provided as key. "Okay; I so order. The password is—" Something no one here at Hykeran Outjut could possibly think of. All right . . . "Cougars 33, Huskies 28," the final Apple Cup score.

Even before he looked around to Deba he knew she was giving him her patented you're-crazy look. He stared right back at her. "Whyn't you come up front now?"

Scrambling a bit, she did. "What did *that* mean?"

He shook his head. "If I told you, you might remember." Then, to the egg, "Is Count Derion's major headquarters available to us in terms of supplies here on board, and accessible with regard to the patrols you've mentioned?"

"By the most direct route, at peak recommended speed I could reach that locus in approximately six-one-trizero seconds."

Bloody octal! Just over seven hours, Tabor finally guessed. "Let's do it."

"Be advised that I cannot vouch for the behavior of patrollers unknown to me."

"Or vice versa, I'd expect. Put a move on. Go."

The egg swung about seventy degrees starboard; acceleration pressed Luke and Deba firmly against their seatbacks. Fumbling under the seat for the toity-tube, Tabor wished he'd waited to invite Deba up front until after he'd relieved himself.

But the device *was* a product of her own time. . . .

Course was set. Now it struck Luke that they'd all skipped dinner. On order, obligingly the egg opened its food and drink lockers. "Oh, hell." The pampered tastes of Lord Frey and the Lady Aliira, as sampled aboard Frey's egg, now led to profound disillusion; this carrier stocked foods on the order of granola and trail mix, and the flask he opened tasted like flat soda pop.

Sharing with Deba Sayan he said, "At least the price is right." And found he couldn't get the line across to her; she simply lacked the context.

Toward the end of their second hour of flight the sky began to lighten again, though only featureless blank lay below. Despite an annoying whine that had developed somewhere in the carrier's innards, Luke dozed off; what woke him was first the egg dipping into steep descent, and then its voice: "We are entering a patrolled area. Our direct route crosses a holding of Lord Frey's. I do not sense patrol vehicles nearby. However, to avoid detection by the mesh of high-altitude beams favored by Lord Frey, I now drop near to ground level and in the interests of safety will proceed at considerably lower pace."

At this height the whine, now with a vibratory component, echoed from the ground and set Tabor's nerves on edge. True to its word the egg hedgehopped at something on the order of highway speeds. So when Tabor spotted, ahead, a small, flashing light, he had plenty of time to observe it. At first he was only mildly curious. Then, abruptly, he sat up straight.

Somebody out there knew Morse code. At least a little. Because three shorts, three longs, and three more shorts spelled S-O-S.

\* \* \*

His first impulse was to go see what the problem was. But first impulses, he'd learned the hard way, weren't always the best. Instead he said, "Carrier? Deba? Do you see that light signaling?"

"I see an intermittent light," the egg said; Sayan asked how he knew it was a signal.

"So neither of you knows what it means." Right, and right. "Well, I do. Somebody's hollering for help. And it's somebody from my time; has to be."

The flashing was quite near now, a bit to the left of their course. He said, "We'll land a little this side of it."

"What distance is specified?"

You mean, how much is that in rambs? Think fast. "Set us down, twenty *paces* from that light. And"— afterthought—"with your door facing away from it." At Deba's puzzled look, he said, "For cover. Just in case they're not friendlies."

The egg landed. Here at ground level Luke could make out that they were clear of forested country and into prairie: low swells of ground covered by long grass and scattered bushes, with a very few deciduous trees looming ghostlike in the low mist.

The door opened to his command; first he and then Deba climbed out into cool damp air. The light had stopped and he couldn't be sure where he'd last seen it: off to the egg's right, sure, but at what angle and how far away? Edging forward to peer past the carrier's front, he felt acutely his lack of any weapon.

But he his very own self had decided to land here. *So get on with it.* One deep breath. Then, "You out there flashing the SOS! If you want help, give us a light to home in on."

The light shone, wavered, and then aimed straight at him. "Lucian Tabor! Am I ever glad to see *you!*"

The woman's voice sounded familiar but he couldn't quite place it. With Deba following, he headed toward it anyway.

\* \* \*

"Luke!" The light beam went skyward as someone grabbed and hugged him, gave him a warm, fervent kiss. "You're a lifesaver!"

He'd already known it wasn't Casey's voice. Casey didn't kiss like this, either. Not better, not worse, just different. He cooperated until she was done with it, then eased back from the embrace. Reaching for the light he said, "That's nice. Just whose life am I saving?"

As the beam caught the flushed, grinning face of Vivi LaFleur.

The woman had changed. Her carefully tended cover girl complexion showed sunburn and freckles, her cheeks were leaner. Hair fell forward of her left shoulder several inches longer than he remembered. And her stance was active and aggressive, not the graceful posings of an entertainer.

He knew she hadn't left the river of time before he did. So he asked, "When the hell have you been?"

She shook her head. "That can wait. I have a sick person here; we have to get her to—I'll give you the coordinates later. Help me get her into your carrier."

Suppressing irritation—Vivi was taking over a bit too fast!—Tabor moved to help her. Deba said, "You trust this woman? You take her at her word, without bona fides?"

Now he was getting flak from both sides. "We grew up together," he said, and left it at that.

Wrapped in a bulky robe or blanket, the invalid was a big woman. Tall, anyway. As Tabor took the head end and Deba the feet, Vivi aimed the light to show them their footing. Slowly they moved to the egg and propped their load against it while Luke climbed in; then he and Deba hoisted until the woman was sitting in the doorway and Deba could scramble past her.

Awkwardly they got her into the right-hand rear seat. Tabor said, "Carrier. Extrude the restraining belt for this seat," and without actually seeing the latching parts, shoved the two ends together and heard them click.

When he let go, the belt tightened. He turned to see

Vivi climbing inside. She said, "I can take it from here," and started for the control seat.

Tabor's hand on her arm stopped her. "Not so fast; I need to know a few things." He gestured. "Like who is this? And whose side is she on? And you still haven't told me where and when you've been for—well, obviously quite a while—and what the hell has happened to Derion." When she stayed silent his voice rose. "Now look, Vivi. I gather I haven't been up here as long as you have, but it's long enough to know we're playing in a hardball league. And I'm fed up with being shuffled around, not knowing my ass from third base. So before we move an inch, you start talking."

Vivi's sigh was half snort. "I wanted to save this for later, when there wasn't any hurry. But all right. Derion and I spent several months on a small Island between here and the Node of Terlihan, where he underwent chromosome regenesis. The idea was to circumvent identity exclusion, to be able to revisit a time he'd already experienced. We don't know, yet, whether it's going to work. But she tried too soon, swimming the river of time. We came close to losing headway and being swept on to the Hiatus. And the strain on Derion!—I'm afraid she'll die."

Pulling the cloth aside and brushing longish tangled hair back and away, she shone light on the sick woman's face. It was pale, dirty, and gaunt, but for all the world it looked like Derion's twin sister. If he had one.

"That's Derion? A sex change, for Chris'sake?"

"Not the kind we had in our time. It's—I have no idea how it worked, Tabor: partly *will* and partly drugs, and there was something about a gene-altering virus. I do know it was a bitch on wheels for him; one way or another, every cell in his body had its XY chromosomes converted to XX."

Vivi shuddered. "In between, during part of the sexless stage, he wasn't exactly human. His body needed nearly five times the normal fuel intake. The bones have to soften and reshape: massive replacement, bone loss filled in by cartilage and then the reverse. And going through puberty all over again, only in a matter of days. But by then she was back to making sense, at least. Except that she was so eager to get back here and *do* something, she overestimated her state of recovery."

"Who saw Derion through all that, looked after him? You?"

Headshake. "Oh, no. He assembled people around him who knew what they were doing; I was just a nice helpful flunky who could hold his hand and do various chores. At first, anyway. But you hold somebody's hand long enough, while they're going through really deep crap—there's a bond that forms."

She looked him eye to eye. "I'm her best friend, Luke. And right now I need your help to save her life."

"If you know where to go and how to get there, take over. You can tell me the rest on the way."


Vivi didn't have all the info in her own head; part of the directions she gave the egg, she read from notes. When they were aloft and presumably out of Frey's territory, riding at jet plane heights toward the southwest, from the left rear seat Deba Sayan said, "Tabor? Why do we abandon our own concerns to save this Changed person? What can such a move advantage us?"

Luke reached back to squeeze her shoulder. "This is—*was*—the guy we set out to find. And we found him—only now he's a her, don't ask me how. But if there's any better move to make just now than going along with these people, tell me what it is."

"No, I cannot." Then, plaintively, "When I escaped the dominion of Lord Frey, why did I expect life to be *better?*"

He squeezed once more. "Damifino, kid. Hang in there."

With Deba quieted, Tabor turned forward again. "Vivi, you want to tell me where we're going?"

"It's a sort of hospice. Derion endowed it when he

was here before—well, earlier in Hykeran—and it doesn't ask questions. It's the place she was trying to reach—but we didn't make it."

Luck, or foresight; who knew? "No report to your local Subcontroller, right?"

Looking to him, LaFleur grinned. "Close enough." She asked the egg something Luke didn't catch; the answer came in octal, so without the referent, it lost him.

Oh-kay: "How long 'til we get there?"

"Three–four hours."

"Fine." He was due for a snooze, and took one.

Vivi's nudge woke him. "You want anything to eat before I give the last of it to Derion? She still gets famish fits."

Last of it? "Hey, we started with—uh—a day's food, for four. And Deba and I only had a snack out of it. So—"

"I told you; sometimes Derion eats a *lot.*"

"Well, sure, go ahead. I imagine there'll be chow where we're going." And added, "He's awake then? *She,* I mean."

"I am." Slow and weak, the voice sounded familiar, yet different from what Luke remembered.

Well, it would: if *bone* could alter itself, so could the cartilage of a larynx. As Vivi passed rations back to Derion, Luke said, "How do you feel?"

"The sensations cannot be described. But I am improving; I can now sleep without sedation."

"That's good." *I guess.* Tabor wanted to ask more, but with Derion hurting he figured he'd better not. Later . . .

But Derion, after pausing to swallow, said, "I'm afraid I miscalculated. In the river of time, the landmarks . . . I dropped Jay and Carla, then you and Casey, and next the young couple I first met in the jail cell. No: before that, a person I don't know, who clutched at us as we left—"

Junior Yancey. "Yeah. He caused some trouble."

"He bore greatly unpleasant feelings; my concentration was disturbed and I overshot. Suddenly I was in a time barred to me by my own presence. I had accumulated too much momentum to reverse both my mass and Vivi's without leaving the river, but could hardly abandon her in a strange time alone. So I took her with me and beached us at Stopover, an Island of barely more than a year. Time enough, you see, to undergo chromosome regenesis—and a safe place to do so."

"But why do it?"

"I had dropped you all later than I intended; events would develop which needed my participation, yet I would be barred from them." In Luke's mind a question rose, but before he could ask it, the answer came. "A previous visit of mine to this time begins soon. If my current existence here should reach the beginning of that period, I would be ejected into time's river. Automatically: a natural reaction of the space-time continuum."

Derion chuckled. "But there are legends. Of a great lord whose bid for power failed, who reversed his sex and went back to before the beginnings of that bid, and *counseled* himself, so as to succeed."

"Changed his past? But isn't that an impossible paradox?"

Under the blanket, movement might have been a shrug. "It seemed worth trying." Then Derion commenced eating in earnest.

When the empty utensils were handed forward to Vivi, Derion said, "Luke, what has occurred with *you* in this time?"

"A lot." He began: solitary arrival, Casey's appearance, then Frey summoning an egg only to leave them aloft in it, the brush with the Subcontroller, and flight to the Lady Aliira's.

"Yes." Derion nodded. "Immediately after we arrived back here I queried several with regard to finding you— rather, others did this for me. Aliira was one such; I recall she said you had been to her headquarters and were gone. Before I could investigate further, our sanctuary was dis-

covered by agents of the Duke Mardeux, who will not be
known to you." Tabor recalled the name but saw no point
in saying so. "In my weakened condition I had no choice
but to flee." A pause. "But I interrupt. . . ."

Again Luke edited Aliira's comments regarding
Derion and Frey; instead, "We left because Frey had sent
us there and we wanted to get clear of him, and went to
what was supposed to be *your* HQ. But got picked off,
there, by a woman named Yrr who turned out to be one of
Frey's people. How do you suppose—?"

Another shrug. "Frey and I have played a grim hide-
and-seek throughout Hykeran Outjut until neither of us can
fully remember the where-and-whenabouts of the other,
here. Nor could Aliira. In my absence, presumably Frey
sent Yrr to scout my holding."

*If you say so.* "Okay. Then—" Frey's interim camp,
meeting there with others from Pullman jail, Junior
Yancey breaking all hell loose "—and then Frey took us
all to a more permanent camp, up near the Arctic Circle."

That name had been lost; before going on to describe
events, Tabor had to explain it. "So then—" and into the
workings of the camp. Including Lord Frey's genetic enhancement program.

"This, you see," said Derion, "touches on a major
crux of our dispute. We each have intention to add persons
from the far past to the gene pool available to the
Changed. But I wish them to be full citizens with concom-
itant rights and privileges. Frey, you will have observed,
views these as breeding stock, unpaid labor, to be kept in
restricted areas and used at his whim with no need of their
consent."

At Derion's pause Luke said, "That part came clear
enough." Then quickly told of Ahearn's attack and Frey's
counterstrategy. A thought came. "If Frey could put people
into berserker mode, why did he mess around with Hibit,
back at Pullman?"

Derion gave a low chuckle. "Mental inertia. His people at the northern camp already anticipated battle; inflam-
ing them further would not be difficult. But the much

larger crowd at the football match—aggressively partisan, yes, but not of a mood for physical combat on their own account."

Another point. "But why did he have the cans of Hibit with him, anyway? For that matter, what was he doing there?"

"I can only guess. He knew I was in the area, knew I was acting in some way and that the huge gathering might have something to do with it. So he equipped himself to disrupt any move I might make. When he saw me on the field . . ."

Derion shrugged. "My cuz-cousin thinks in devious ways and from obscure motives; leave it at that. Now then—after the battle, what befell?"

All right; what came next? Luke's capture, the boat ride, Ahearn's base, the march, the carrier ride to Resolve Village. "—so, given the chance we hijacked the egg and were heading for what was supposed to be a main base of *yours* when I saw Vivi flashing the S-O-S, and here we are."

"Yes." Derion leaned nearly upright to look out and down over the lightening terrain; dawn was almost but not quite ready to come onstage. "And now nearing destination." A careful look showed Tabor a sprawling lodge-type building set amid trees.

A few minutes later the carrier landed. Not long after, the four sat in a warm, dim-lit dining hall while two young attendants brought fresh bread, bowls of some spicy sort of goulash, and mugs of something very like a good lager beer.

Still muffled in a hooded cloak, Derion raised one such. "To our safe arrival." And then, "From what you tell me, Lucian, since yesterday morning you and your companion have had no more rest than Vivi and myself. When we are finished here I propose we bathe and sleep, in that priority. Later, at our convenience, we will confer."

The bathing area featured six showers along one side; after cleansing under those the four got into a hot tub about three feet deep and large enough for at least a dozen; in it two men and three women were already having a soak. Derion greeted each but grouped her own party at the opposite side. Once seated on the underwater benches, however, she made no effort toward conference, not even when the original five left.

Derion female, Luke decided, wasn't all that different from Derion male. Proportions had shifted, contours of muscle and so forth, but height and weight seemed not much altered: changes easily hidden by clothing.

The original facial features would have been heavy for a woman, yet Tabor was hard put to define what specific refinements had taken place. Just now the water-plastered hair dripped from somewhat below chin level. The only radical changes were the obvious lack of male genitals and the growing breasts, large in base area but youthfully conic and, as yet, not at all deep.

Derion seemed totally unself-conscious about her changed body. Well, that figured; what surprised Luke was that Vivi seemed equally nonchalant in the naked group, because that was no part of a girl's upbringing in Lewis Gap, and it wasn't so very long she'd been gone from there.

Showbiz, he guessed, could change such things in a hurry. Lacking that ambience himself, Luke was embarrassed to find that even after the coed living situations he'd experienced lately, he *was* embarrassed.

He hoped he wasn't showing it, in the tub or drying off or when, as they walked along a corridor, Derion offhandedly assigned Luke and Deba to a room next door to the one Derion apparently shared with Vivi. "There should be some spare clothing," she said. "Nothing well tailored, of course." Tabor nodded and followed Deba inside.

She touched the stand holding a dimly glowing light; it brightened to show a room containing a fair-sized comfortable-looking bed, a pair of large stools or perhaps backless chairs, an open closet with some clothing hanging in it, and the grade of plumbing Luke was getting used to.

Moving to squat on the ubiquitous saddle-toity, Deba

said, "Tabor? Twice I misgave your actions: first taking
the carrier and then landing it in dubious circumstances.
But you seem to choose fortunately." She gestured. "This
is considerable improvement over our prospects with
Ahearn." Before he could think of an alternative to aw-
shucks-tain't-nothin' she went on, "If I were not so tired,
I would offer quiting."

Huh? Oh; coiting, yes—or rather, no. "That's all
right." It wasn't that he had anything in particular against
healthy rawboned women with very little breast development, but he simply hadn't thought of her in that way.
"Let's get some sleep."

When he woke she was still sleeping. Hungry again,
Tabor dressed and went looking for the dining hall. He
found it empty and decided to search out a kitchen, but
was diverted by an open door at the end of a corridor and
went outside into warm breeze.

The day neared sunset; past an irregular grouping of
great trees a bank of cloud showed dark above and richly
red below. Stepping off a low porch Luke walked to his
right, toward and around a corner of the building wing he
had just left.

And nearly collided with Derion, coming the other
way.

Tabor stopped short. Derion's hair had been cut.
Derion moved differently. This was Derion *male*.

"Derion! How did you—?" Because Vivi had said the
changing process was a matter of months, not hours.

Stopping also, the man peered at him. "Why do you,
of the Unchanged, address me familiarly?"

The voice sharpened. "Who are you?"

# FOURTEEN

**"Who** am *I?* What's the matter with you? I don't know
how you changed back so fast, but did it scramble
your brains or something? You—"

"Hold! You who have not so much as divulged your
name—you claim to know me? So, then; where have we
met?"

"You know damn well. Back at Wazoo, in Pullman,
where—"

"If such a place exists, I have not been told of it."

"Not now; in the *past.* Before the Waste Times, even
the Genocides. You came back there, you and Frey,
and—"

"No, I did not. My arrival now, here at Hykeran Outjut, is the farthest uptime that I have yet ventured."

Oh bloody hell! All right: how to save the situation?
"Count Derion, I beg your pardon. I didn't realize; this is
you *before* you went back and brought us down the river
of time."

Derion's eyes widened. "I see there is more to this
than I had thought. Let us go inside."

For Tabor, even this late in the day it was breakfast.
After a few questions Derion nodded, then said, "Please
detail in rough the sequence of events as *you* have experienced them—from your first meeting with me, as distinct
from mine with you."

There was too much of it; repeatedly Luke got off
track and had to recap. At the end, Derion said, "Then
there is, in this time, a later, female version of myself?"

"Unless your coming bumped her out. Into the river."
Would the earlier presence supersede? Obviously the fe-

male Derion's hadn't kept this one out. "Why don't we go see for ourselves?"

"Soon, perhaps." Sipping coffee, Derion showed no intention of hurrying. "Tell me; what is my female self like?"

"At this point, weakened, following the change." Luke thought. "Not much different, temperament or personality, from the person I met in my own home time." And added, "Nor from yourself right now—except that I'm a stranger to you."

"What were your feelings toward my later selves?"

Were? "He was my friend; I expect she is, too."

Derion nodded. "Then so shall I be." He leaned forward. "I am most skilled at sensing the tensions which accompany deceit. I find none here."

He stood. "Come. Let us seek my counterpart."

When Luke located the right corridor, Deba Sayan was coming out the door of their room. She stared, confused; Luke said, "Don't worry about it. Are Vivi and Derion still next door?"

"They may be; I haven't checked to see."

Frowning, Derion said, "Would you do so, please? Pressure builds stronger; perhaps I should go no nearer, until . . ."

So Deba knocked. After a moment Vivi stuck her head out, did a double take, and pulled it back in, closing the door hard. Minutes passed; then she reappeared. "She felt you. Felt the push. She's holding on hard, not to go into the river of time."

"I feel it too," Derion said. "But until Lucian told me, I had no idea what it was. Yet in some paradoxical fashion it impelled me to thrust against it, to beach at this place rather than another." One corner of his mouth tightened briefly. "Go in—Vivi, is it? I shall attempt a calmness for us both, her and me, and then—slowly, and with care— approach, until we can essay embrace. The pressure, then, should vanish."

Again Vivi disappeared. Luke asked, "Nobody's ever

done this before, have they? What makes you think it'll work?"

"There is a legend. If true, this is how it was done."

Which was more than Derion female had told him about it . . .

Coming back out, Vivi gripped Luke's hand with a very cold one. To Derion, "She's ready; she'll try her best."

"Good." Derion's eyes half closed; his body settled into a stance that *said* relaxation. Then, one slow step after another he moved toward the door and pushed at it, still in increments, until it stood fully open. Once his measured pace took him inside, the closing was less deliberate.

Minutes, then, Tabor and Deba and Vivi stayed where they were. Luke found himself trying to keep his very breathing noiseless; a quick glance showed him he wasn't alone. He motioned to Vivi; she nodded, tiptoed over, put her ear to the door. Her brows lowered into a frown. Then it cleared; she soft-stepped away and past the other two well along the corridor.

As they joined her, Vivi grinned. "If I'm not mistaken, and I don't think I am, they're screwing each other silly."

When the three were called inside, into a room considerably better appointed than the one Luke and Deba shared, Vivi's guess looked to be on target. Side by side the two Derions lay, bare to the waist where the bedcovers were thrown back, both smiling, her head cradled on his arm.

All sign of weakness had left the woman. "Well," said Tabor, "it's good to see *you* healthy as a horse again." More than that; she looked younger than before the change. To the man Luke said, "That must be quite a legend."

"It does contain more truth than most." Then, "While true identity cannot coincide in duplicate, *near* identity, as here, exerts a lesser repelling force. Though still powerful."

He paused, gesturing in emphasis. "But as in atomic nuclei, opposing forces may vary differently with distance. When I made approach slowly, striving for calm and oneness, a point came at which attraction overcame repulsion, and—"

Derion female gave a nervous laugh. "Another few seconds, and either I would have left this time, or regurgitated!"

"It was needful, then," said Derion male, "to achieve empathic transfer in least time. Maximum sensory interplay was, of course, essential."

"Of course," said Luke. And fun, too.

Aside to Tabor, Vivi murmured, "That sounds like a line one of my directors used to try."

"Did it work?"

"Not after the first time."

Quietly yet with intensity, the two Derions had begun to argue. Or rather, it seemed, resumed a debate already in progress. At question was the name Derion; as the elder, she claimed it—but she, he pointed out, had changed identity by changing gender. Amused by these two high-powered individuals bickering like children, Luke asked, "What's the problem?"

They couldn't both use the same name, was what. But who had first dibs? Luke shrugged. "Vivi? What do you think?"

"Well, everyone's always known Derion as a male."

Derion female shook her head. "If I am not Derion, who am I? And how can I command the prerogatives of that name?"

"And I," said the other, "must take the same position."

Vivi snapped her fingers. "Twins." Silence. "Don't you get it? You're twins: Count Derion and Countess—uh—Deriana. Same rank, same authority. Like in *The Hidden Duchess*—that's a really hokey movie I did for holo, two–three years ago. The one twin's existence was a secret, you see, until—"

"Nonsense," said Derion female. "I am considerably the older, and—"

"Excuse me," Luke said, "but as I understand it you were born at the same time to the same parents."

After a few seconds the woman laughed. "Very well; I accept the logic of circumstance, and Deriana will do as well as any. Now, Derion, we must concoct for me a chronology of times and places which no one in this era of Hykeran could disprove."

She grimaced. "Including our estimable cuz-cousin, Lord Frey. For sooner or later he and we will find each other."

Immediately another quibble began; Derion wanted to know the outcome of this his first visit to the Outjut. "And how long do I stay? You must remember, I'm certain."

She shook her head. "Deri, you *know* we never reveal anyone's future, especially to that person."

"But, Derya—!" Nicknames, already? Well, why not? "This instance, two time frames of the same individual, has never before existed. Except in the legend, of course. So—"

Derya grimaced. "Insofar as possible, we must strive to conserve existent history. There will be change; on my first visit to the Outjut, this meeting did not occur. But—" She shook her head. "Change must be kept to a minimum; paradox generates chaos. Or so we are always told. I am beginning to develop a hypothesis—but this is no time for speculation."

She paused. "Let me see. I—you—came to scout Hykeran as a possible site for a genetic remediation project. But not until a later visit do you establish this hospice."

Brows aloft: "I do? Now *that* is something I had not planned on. How can I possibly divert my energies . . . ?"

Derya spread her hands. "You see? Had I not told

you, the event would have emerged naturally out of your own motivations."

Deri shrugged. "No harm done; if you did it, so will I."

"Not if our mutual actions take you on another path."

"So, then—how may such changes be avoided?"

Lips pursed, suddenly Derya made explosive exhalation. "Perhaps they cannot. And worrying about them could cripple our choosings." She looked around the room. "Would someone bring us coffee? I have not yet mind-registered the kitchen help, so I cannot request it from here. The way to the place is—"

"I know where it is," Luke said. *If I don't get lost.*

Vivi stood. "I'll go, too; then we'll both know."

Deba looked as though she wanted to make it three, but stayed seated as the two left.

". . . all well and good," Luke said as they walked along, "but what about our gang from Pullman? Look, it's been—" He thought back. "Why, it's only two days. Less. Since Casey and I—"

He made a face. "Seems at least a week. Anyway, I'm worried. Casey and Jay and Carla made it through the battle okay; I saw them, after. But Bruce and Alycia? And what's been happening there since I left? I've got to get Derion—Derya—to do something. Or try to, anyway."

"Maybe." Vivi looked skeptical. "Here's the kitchen. Let's do our errand; then you can make your pitch."

". . . into our far past," Derya was saying when they returned, "and finally my retreat at Stopover. Roughly four years, all told, between us." Her smile had a wry look to it. "A busy period—whether busy enough, time will tell. Is the crisis facing us all at Dietjen's reasonably clear to you?"

Cutting in, Tabor said, "What are you going to do about the rest of us you brought forward? The ones Frey holds. You're responsible, and—"

Deba looked stunned that he would interrupt a

Changed; Deri seemed only annoyed. Derya's brows lowered. "And yes, I feel that responsibility. There are, however, priorities—"

"How about the danger you've put them in? What's the priority on that?"

"Second only to devising an overall plan of action. Once I make a move noticeable to Frey there will be no time for further planning, only for execution. Do you understand?"

Luke guessed so; Derya continued. "To summarize, Deri. When court convenes at Dietjen's Hiatus, the Prime Peer will face a vote of confidence. Should he lose despite my support, I shall have his against any move from Frey—or worse yet, Mardeux."

Derion male nodded. "In none of these contests can we predict results. How have you planned your timing?"

"At the Hiatus I have left forward cusp at two days before the Plenum opens; it affords me little time for maneuver, but equally little for Frey to countermove, once I make appearance."

"And Frey's cusp?"

"Five days earlier, to my most recent knowledge."

"Forward cusp?" said Vivi. "What's that supposed to be?"

Again Deba looked horrified. Derya sighed. "We cannot swim past our most forward moment of experience; at that point the river ejects any swimmer into real-time existence."

Confused, Tabor said, "But all of us from Pullman—we're *centuries* downriver from any time we lived!"

"Cannot swim it, I said. Like yourselves, we may be *taken* farther. As all Great Lords are conducted, upon succession, to points in Dietjen's Hiatus when courts shall be convened. And note well, the Hiatus is just that: forward cusp for all Changed."

"I don't understand." For once, Luke found himself guilty of understatement.

"The Hiatus," said Deri, "is not named lightly. None

of us has been beyond it; from its own future, none have
visited. That Island is the limit of our known time."

*How? Why?* Tabor didn't ask aloud, but Derya said,
"We have no data. Perhaps some future event leads to a
ban on further timeswimming. Or there may *be* no Islands,
downtime, near enough that swimming upriver to Hiatus is
possible. Remember: until Frey and I succeeded, none
from our era had reached your own."

She made a sour-faced grin. "Though few care to admit it, one other possibility exists: that when the river of
time reaches whatever Island may exist next forward of
Dietjen's, there are no potants left alive to swim it."

To that, Luke found no comment; after a long moment he said, "What *are* these Islands? How are they
caused? Or do you know?"

Shrugging, Deri spoke. "Most speculations depend in
some way on the concept of probability resonance. The
Duke Terlihan—the elder duke—believes these resonances
interact to form nodes; Hykeran researchers contend that
Islands result from intrusions of one probability stream
into another. As to causes, the speculations invoke anything from planetary configurations to the proximate passage of objects so densified as to enfold themselves into
separate continua."

"Black holes," Luke muttered. "That was our term
for the phenomenon. But how could they—?"

"Who knows?" Derya chuckled. "Experimenters
working among small, closely adjacent Islands have tried
to establish differences in the specific physical constants
of space-time as measured both within and between those
Islands. To very little effect, I fear. But by persisting, perhaps they will someday discover something useful."

"Most useful, of course," said Deri, "would be the
means of *creating* an Island. As the Prime Peer's nephew
Greston is attempting to achieve. He claims to have produced short-lived, tiny Islets, but as yet nothing of useful
magnitude. And I should hate to postpone my next meal
until he does."

No one spoke until, first clearing her throat, Deba Sayan said, "Your pardons—but our own next meal is long overdue."

Luke's wasn't, nor Deri's, but they tagged along anyway.

One thing about the hospice, you couldn't knock the food. Tabor ate lightly, noting that Deri did also. Over dessert Luke reopened the question of rescuing Casey and the others.

Derya shook her head. "We must sleep now, and arise in accord with sun and dark." Luke didn't feel sleepy, but once he went to bed, sleep took him anyway.

He had time to think: Derya's probably *will*ing this. . . .

One way or another, early next morning he woke refreshed. Breakfast and council took place in the room occupied by Derya and Vivi—and maybe Deri, too; certainly there was space enough.

The Derions must have decided their political strategies; Derya began with, "Next item: how to retrieve my other protégés from our recalcitrant cuz-cousin. I welcome suggestions."

What she got were snags and obstacles: the distance to Frey's camp, his heap big firepower there—or maybe he'd already left. Et bloody cetera . . .

Seeking a handle on the problem, Luke asked, "This farsight thing: can you spot Frey from here?"

"I assume," said Derya, "he is maintaining shield against that faculty. As are we, currently. Without an accurate vector I could not focus well enough to identify him behind it."

"Casey, then, or Jay or the others. Can you—"

"If they are near him, he can easily hide them also."

Tabor scowled. "How good a vector do you need? I mean, how tight would the distance and direction have to be?"

Neither Derion could supply quantitative answers.

First asking which way was north, Luke took a guess and pointed.

Distance was another matter. But once he got it straight that latitude "arcpoints" were merely degrees expressed in octal notation, the two Changed prepared to make their try.

Extended farsight, it seemed, required great concentration and no distractions; watching, Luke and Vivi and Deba sat moveless and held silence. But although several Changed were sensed, none matched either Derion's mind-registrations of Lord Frey.

Luke shrugged his way to a dejected slump. "So much for that. Well, at least Frey can't spot us either."

Suddenly he sat straight again. "But what if he could?"

Both Derions frowned. The female said, "What advantage—?"

"He probably wants to find you as much as you want to find him," Luke pointed out. "And he might bring our people along."

Grinning, he added, "Either that or leave them there, unshielded from your farsight."

It wasn't quite so cut-and-dried; Frey could have other options. But so far, Luke's idea was the best card on the table. Possibly because it was almost the only one.

"Very well," said Derya. "Now we must plan carefully."

Frey could have no idea that *two* Derions were here, let alone that one was female. So it should be Deri who unshielded. The question was, how to make that unshielding plausible?

"It must be believable that I remain open for a considerable period," Deri said. "Because it could be a time before Frey next scans for me. So no momentary over-stress will do."

Silence answered him. Tentatively, Deba Sayan made a gesture. "Your pardon, Count Derion. But while you scanned for Lord Frey, were you not left open to farsight?

I have heard as much." Deri nodded, and Deba said, "Then supposing you search again—but for someone else, so as to avoid arousing Lord Frey's suspicion. Would that ruse not suffice?"

Derya clapped a hand to the woman's shoulder. "Of course! Good thought, Deba. Now then—who is it we would be seeking?"

"The Lady Aliira, maybe?" Luke suggested. Well, aside from Tlegg and Dennet in Frey's entourage, Subcontroller Svansek back at Enclave Whatever, and the woman Yrr, she was about the only Changed he knew.

Deri brightened. "Why not? We were at one time childhood sweethearts; I have often urged her to allow herself maturity. So it would seem reasonable that I make such an attempt."

Derya nodded. "She should be easy to locate; she travels seldom." She chuckled. "What you endeavor to communicate, if you do achieve contact, is your own concern."

Deri looked anxious. "Even now, she has made no change?"

Impatiently Derya said, "What does it matter? Any interaction you and she begin, now, commences an entire new chain of causation." *My* Derion, Tabor thought, has written Aliira's sexuality off as a lost cause.

Unheeding, Derion male smiled. "So it does. Very well; when our plans indicate, I will open all shielding and make the attempt. My sending, now, should be—"

Derion female cut in. "Do not dwell on that aspect; your objective is to draw Frey's attention. And when— *if*—he comes here, we need a very well prepared scheme to deal with him."

Deri's moonstruck air dropped away; he looked worried. In the matter of *will,* it seemed, Frey and Derion had always been a near match. And Derion had never been skilled at teaming, joining forces. "Now," said Derya, "it is time we learned."

First they tried jointly levitating Luke and Vivi and

Deba all together, a feat beyond the strength of either alone. Shaky at first, their coordination improved with practice.

Outside then, away from building and grove to where the land sloped off toward a distant ravine, the two set to manipulation of moving objects. Again, early results were erratic. What worked best was for either to initiate and guide an action while the other simply "helped push"—especially with projectiles.

The sun had climbed near noonpoint; Tabor had a sweat up, and thirst. He'd been doing no real work, just arranging props for various experiments, but in these latitudes a clear morning gave plenty of heat. Now he asked for a break, and got it.

Vivi followed him indoors. In the kitchen he poured glasses of a cold brownish liquid; it smelled like a cross between tea and cider. Vivi said, "Let's go where we can talk," and led him to the room she shared with one or more Derions.

He asked about that part. "Yes; Derya invited him to move in." Tabor intended to leave it at that, but she added, "We're not a *ménage à trois* or anything; I have the smaller bed to myself. Hey, if the two of *them* did anything last night, it wasn't loud enough to wake me up."

"I didn't ask—"

"But you wanted to, so I told you." She scowled. "You know what fries me? When Derion and I got to Stopover, I was really growing a case on him. But before I had any chance to work it up to anything, the lowlife started his damn chromosome regenesis. So in just a few days the opportunity was gone."

She giggled. "Visibly, in fact. Very frustrating. And as they say back in Lewis Gap, I'm still hankering."

"Now look, Vivi—!"

She laughed. "Not for *you*, Tabor." Then, with a rueful look, "I didn't mean that the way it sounds; it's just that I'm still pressurized for Derion. And right now, that means Deri. But I can't expect him to know it."

"No." Suddenly Luke chuckled. "You haven't met the Lady Aliira. The one Derion male has a crush on."

"You know I haven't. What's she like?"

"You wouldn't believe me if I told you."

"Try me." Then, "No; it doesn't matter. Never compete with anyone but yourself, is how I feel. Except that now I'm up against his own female self. That's hard knocks, Luke."

"Maybe not—unless you're after an exclusive. I get the impression the Changed are a bit free about such things. And—"

Puzzled, he paused; suddenly he had an impulse to go back outside. No reason for it, just the urge. "Hey, do you . . . ?"

They both came up standing. Vivi said, "We'd better get out there. We—"

A hunch triggered Luke's stubbornness. "What for? There's no reason." But reason or no, he had moved toward the door.

As Vivi started past him he grabbed her arm. "Hold it! You know what this is? They're practicing *will* on us."

"I don't feel anything."

"You're heading out, aren't you? Why?"

Another step; Luke forced himself to stop there, as Vivi's forehead wrinkled. "I don't know. I just feel . . ."

"Fight it." She looked bewildered. "If it's *will* they're trying, let's make it a contest." Yet while he talked they still moved. "Hold fast. There's no *reason* to go out now."

And then, immediately, there was. "Oh yeah, I wanted to ask Derya something."

But when they joined the others, not far from the building, he had no idea what his question might have been.

# FIFTEEN

※

Grinning like a kid with a new toy, Deri said, "Detected us, did you not? And resisted. That is good; it forced us to add a rationale buttressing the simple compulsion, as we should have thought to do initially. We—"

"Is that why you brought us out here? Just to see if you could do it?" Definitely peeved, LaFleur wasn't hiding it.

Derya waved a placating hand. "We need to test ourselves. And better with you, our friends who will understand that need, than upon staff members who would merely be confused, possibly even frightened."

"I guess so." Still pouting, Vivi added, "Okay. If there's more hoops, let's see you make us jump through 'em."

Her lower lip jutted. "If you can."

They could, all right. But even as their skills improved, Luke began to feel a difference between *willed* urges and his own. And then an internal reaction, a shadow of resistance, which after a time he could augment by volition. Not consistently, though. It was like a flabby muscle; overuse brought a kind of soreness. Not localized, but highly uncomfortable.

For now, he decided, this was something he'd keep private.

Shortly after the sun's position indicated noon, the two Changed focused on the kitchen staff to order by *will* a meal for five, to be delivered to the Derions' room. Derya said, "The concept must be kept simple: I cannot, for instance, select the menu, since I have not specified choices to be signaled."

This *will* stuff, Luke began to see, wasn't just a genetic magic trick; it was a skill needing intelligence and practice for best use. Yet no amount of effort could give *him,* or any other Unchanged, a real handle on it.

Oh, well . . .

After lunch Derya stated, "To deal with such as Frey we must improve greatly. But we have made a good beginning."

Luke nodded. "What's next? *Will*-wrestling between the two of you? Or are there any other Changed around here someplace who could make good sparring partners?"

Derion male gazed at him. "Tabor, you think well."

Using normal communication channels, Deri spoke with several nearby Changed. Later that day three arrived: Braun, his younger wife Olvia, and a large young man named Kern who at the age of three-six, octal, still remained prepubertal.

Apparently his kind and Aliira's were not rarities; Deba Sayan took Kern for granted. Vivi, though, kept sneaking looks at him; Luke had difficulty keeping a straight face. In a quiet aside he said, "That one has you interested?"

She leaned to his ear. "I don't understand him. He has the size and the muscles, but something's wrong; he's like a big kid, somehow. Not grown up at all. Do you know—?"

"Stick around. You'll figure it out." For next on the agendum came a hot tub session. Braun and Olvia appeared surprised that the three Unchanged were included; they—especially blond, plumpish Olvia—looked as if they wanted to say something and weren't sure what. But perhaps Count Derion carried too much clout to be challenged.

What Braun did question was "Deriana? Derion's twin? Why has there been no previous word of you?"

Luke missed an answer he really wanted to hear; Vivi's elbow poked his ribs as she whispered, "That poor Kern must've had the mumps. I have a cousin like that, up in Bonner's Ferry; mumps went down on him when he was thirteen, ruined him for life."

He shushed her. "Not the same. These Changed can stall puberty as long as they want, and some go overboard." Oh, why *not* tell her? "Like Deri's childhood flame. The Lady Aliira."

Loud and clear, Vivi LaFleur said, "No *shit?*"

Her outburst went ignored as Derya stood, abruptly crying out, "Deri! Put farsight to the location Tabor specified earlier. Someone of power moves there. What do you sense?"

Again the concentration, the total hush. Deri said, "This may be the one we seek; the strength is not only commensurate, but clearly in the designated area. And as you say, moving."

"But not directly toward us." Derya. "The vector is perhaps two parts in our direction to one off rightward."

Thirty degrees, about. Tabor spoke quietly: "If he stops across the strait from your tower stronghold, and just a bit upriver, that's Frey's staging area, with the impromptu huts."

Derya said, "But for Frey to reach there—if it *is* Frey we sense—would require several hours yet."

"I suppose you can't tell if any of our gang is with him?"

"Your supposition is correct."

So much for that. It was time for dinner, anyway.

After the meal, Derya led the way to a lounge. Talking among themselves now, the five Changed effectively ignored their less-abled companions. Quietly, Tabor left the room and kept going—out the front entrance, then to the edge of the grove.

Behind the hills at the ravine's far side the sun had set; streaked clouds carried bright pale reds, edged with more fiery tints, against a sky of paler blue. As the display began to fade, clouds greying first at their upper edges, Tabor perched on a stump and wished he had a drink along.

When only a faint band of deeper red hugged the horizon, he went back in, to his room.

Except that Deba Sayan was using it. She and another. She had found herself someone to quite with.

Spraddled supine, Deba waved over her partner's shoulder and invited Luke to stay. But caring neither to join in group sex nor watch the coupling, he got out of there.

To encounter Vivi LaFleur walking slowly and looking bemused. "Hi, Vivi. You know where I can find a spare room?"

She drew her brows down and squinted at him. "That's *my* line, buddy. The supertypes all moved in together; I took one look at available bed space and cut trail."

She shrugged. "The hell of it is, I doubt anyone noticed."

Luke nodded. "I guess they're like that. Before now, we hadn't seen a bunch of the Changed together, had we?"

As they walked together, she put a hand on his arm. "It's scary. Derion pulled us out of our own time; now they don't really give a damn." The hand clenched. "Luke—I'd been counting on Derya for help. But it looks like we're on our own." Her voice went shrill. "What are we going to *do?*"

They reached the entrance; Tabor opened the door and escorted her outside. "To begin with," he said, "maybe we—"

But then came a burst of *will.* An urgent summons.

Through clenched teeth, judging by the tone, Vivi said, "This is too muckin' futch, you know that?"

With conscious effort, Luke chose calm. "Turn the burner down, will you?" Even to his own ears, his voice sounded weary. "Or they'll just turn it down for you. I'm pissed too, but it won't pay to show it."

"And just what *will* pay?"

As they went back inside, "Calm and logic. They won't expect that, so it might get their attention."

She grinned. "What I like about you is your sneaky streak."

"Let's hope it works."

Luke wasn't sure what he'd expected, but among the five Changed he found an air of tension. Derya said, "Good; you're here. Why did you leave the building?"

She shook her head. "No, that's not important. We thought you might have been *drawn* forth—perhaps into grave danger. What we deal with, here . . ."

Grievances not exactly forgotten but certainly shelved, Luke said, "Do we have a bite from Frey?"

Brows aslant, Derya said, "No. He nears the temporary camp you mentioned. What we face now is unexpected—and deadly."

She paused; Deri said, "No sooner had I unshielded than I felt a scan of great force. But not Frey; this was no less than the Duke Mardeux himself. And his intent was clear."

His mouth twisted. "He will come here, and attack."

All five Changed seemed both impressed and subdued. Deriana summarized matters: "Frey can be a bitter antagonist: willful, daring, often heedless. To oppose him requires strength, forethought, and above all, caution."

She gave a brief smile. "But I neither hate Frey, fear him, nor seek his death. And I doubt he seeks mine—though in the heat of struggle, either could occur. Mardeux, though . . ."

Derya shuddered. "A man whose trademarks are cruelty and excess; his victims, living and dead, number in thousands." Thousands? Okay; Derion had learned decimal at Pullman WA.

Vivi said, "And all you *will*masters can't shut him down?"

Braun leaned forward. "To understand, you would have to know how the duke came to be what he is."

Derya spoke again. "Mardeux was reared under a regimen known as Primal Motivation; rewards and punishments were given freely and immediately but never explained. The child was to be motivated, by pain and pleasure, to generalize from specifics the principles by which it was expected to behave. Instead, the most usual result was a fragmented, insecure personality. But Mardeux was very strong of mind, and a superb potant. The principle he deduced was that power is its own excuse. And the motivations he developed were spite, vindictiveness, and sadistic hatred."

"To a Changed of average ability," commented Braun, "such behavior would have brought early death. But his family wielded great political power, and its genes carry utmost potancc. The first kept him alive through childhood."

And on the eve of legal adult status Mardeux unleashed his strengths to wreak a violent coup, usurping power over his father's realm and leaving only charred earth where the Primal Motivation center had stood.

"As to killing him," said Deri. "In person, he can keep one much too busy fighting *will*-induced pain—or as a variation, an overwhelming, paralyzing fear—to maintain such a purpose."

"Even you?" Vivi was wide-eyed.

He shrugged. "I can withstand that particular coercion. But the effort leaves precious little energy to do aught else."

Tabor couldn't resist asking one question. "What if people ganged up on him? *Wills* together, the way you're trying to do right here? Enough of you, I'd think you could outgun him."

Derya shook her head. "With much training, perhaps. As things are, my cuz-cousin Frey poses us formidable opposition. One such as Mardeux . . ."

"Also," said Braun, "Olvia and Kern and I are not potants of the caliber of these two, or Frey. Against such as Mardeux we would be helpless."

"What do we do, then?" Vivi's jaw was set. "Run for it?"

Slowly Braun nodded. "There are worse alternatives."

For the first time in some while, Deba Sayan spoke. "The Duke Mardeux: when you sensed him, Count Derion, did you ascertain his location? Or direction of movement?"

Derion male looked distinctly sheepish. "In the shock of recognition I did not remain open long enough to learn these things. He *felt* near—but that feeling may reflect only his abnormal potance."

Luke tried again. "I don't suppose any of you want to unshield and take another peep? Maybe find out for sure?"

Derya shrugged. "I will try. Setting myself to close, instantly, at any hint of the duke's attention. Please afford me total quiet." Eyes closed, breathing deeply, she began.

Long minutes later, she sat up. "I find no trace."

It was Deba who broke silence. "There is one we know, of potance to stand against the Duke, who has no love for him."

Derya spoke. "You mean Frey, of course." And as Deba nodded, "True. Brothers-in-law, they were for a time, when Mardeux fathered Ahearn on Frey's sister. Who, unfortunately for her, failed in that instance to transmit the Chi genes."

Derya's face carried a stern look. "When the boy was found to be Unchanged, Mardeux turned on the woman. Savagely. Young and vulnerable as she was, such treatment destroyed her. Had the duke a conscience, her ending should lie heavy on it."

Absorbing these facts, Tabor blinked. Still, the main point: "Even so—do you really think Frey would help *us?*"

"Under truce," said Derya, "we could set our differences aside long enough to unite against Mardeux. Of course those disputes would remain to be resolved at a later time."

"Well all right, people!" Nervously, Vivi stood, looking to one and then another. "Are you going to do something, or not?"

Deri shrugged tensions loose. "My task, I believe. I shall try, quite openly, to farsee my cuz-cousin and allow him to view me in turn. So that I may convey our need and its cause."

Again all held quiet; then Deri gave a start. "I found him, and he in turn located me. But then he—he vanished."

"Where was he?" asked Luke. "At your base, or . . . ?"

"Alighting from an opened carrier, apparently just landed at—I presume—the temporary camp you described."

"Who was with him?" Vivi sounded impatient. "Any of our people? And are they still there?"

"I had time only to sense Frey himself. But when he disappeared, the carrier was left empty."

And Deri didn't know them anyway. "Derya? Could you check, please? And also the sub-Arctic base we told you about? See if you can locate Casey, or any others of our group."

She tried for some time, but found no one they sought. At least, Luke thought, neither Derion had sensed Mardeux.

Or, with any luck, vice versa.

"It's past midnight," Derya said. "We should sleep."

*Here we go again.* Tabor opened his mouth to raise the question of "Where?" but Braun spoke first. "We wish to leave, Olvia and I. In our agreement, naught was said of joining you to oppose Lord Frey, much less the Duke Mardeux. So we—"

"Then go!" Derya's eyes narrowed; she turned toward Kern. "And you also, I would suppose?"

The overdue adolescent's plump face formed a grin. "I'll stay, if you don't mind." Before Derya could ask: "My effort may not add much. But I do not like anything I have heard about the duke. So if it's all right . . ."

It was. Helping Braun and Olvia carry their gear, Deri escorted them out. Luke moved over to where Deba, in self-effacing manner, hunkered. "You still have company in the room?"

"There was no company, only the one man, who left a time after you did." *Semantics*.

But as they made to leave, Vivi caught at his arm. "Can you spare me bunk space? Even with the chickens gone home to roost, four's a crowd in here."

"And three's going to be a jam in our place. But what the hell, come on. We can breathe by odds and evens."

Somewhere along the line Vivi had accumulated enough gear for two duffels; he took one from her and led the way out, back to the smaller room.

The long day had tired Luke thoroughly. He relieved himself, stripped and went to bed, taking the middle and lying on his right side. He fell asleep before anyone joined him.

Next day the Derions worked at teaming with Kern. Tabor couldn't be sure if the child-adult added much push, but he worked up a pretty good sweat. As Luke and Vivi and Deba played guinea pigs, again Tabor felt resistance "muscles" flex and gain in strength. Finally at lunch he said, "I'm noticing an odd thing." He told it and then asked, "Is it just me? Or why don't all Unchanged develop a sort of mental callus against *will?*"

Deri shook his head. "Two possible factors," said Derya. "Here, Unchanged are in normal course subjected to *will* from earliest days. By the time any thought of resistance is likely to arise, response patterns are firmed. And it may be that over centuries an original latent ability to resist has been lost."

Overall, that two-part theory could be tested. Low-voiced so that only Derya could hear, Luke said, "Deba, there. When I count three, push a simple *will* order at her. Something unusual."

Derya nodded; Luke counted; in a moment Deba stood, put her hands above her head, turned around twice, lowered her hands and sat again. Tabor said, "Deba, why did you do all that? What made you do it?"

Anger showed. "Nobody made me do anything! I *felt* like getting up, and . . ." Her face twisted; tears came, and her hands raised to cover them. "I don't *know.*"

He went to her and hugged. "Hey, it's all right." He turned back to Derya. "Now me. Not the same thing, though."

Nothing happened; he began to get tired of waiting. For one thing, he was getting thirsty. Hell with this; he started to get up and pour himself some cold water. Then "Oh no!" and he sat again. Pointing a finger, "I had a drink of water not five minutes ago." He shook his head. "Damn; you're good, Derya."

Her eyes widened. "And you, Luke Tabor, are something new in our world. You, and possibly others from your time."

Her one-sided smile hinted of irony. "As you said yourself, Lucian, at the Apple Cup when your Cougars scored their second touchdown, this could be a whole new ball game."

But the threat of Mardeux held priority; research into *will*-resistance would have to wait. The goal now was full three-way coordination of *wills,* and by late afternoon the three Changed showed obvious fatigue. Well before dinnertime the group adjourned to soak their tensions loose in the large hot tub.

For a time conversation idled; then Derya cleared her throat. "Kern? Your capability of *will* should be at or near that of your mother." Kern's father, Luke deduced, must be a Chi-carrying Unchanged. "But they are not even of the same magnitude. This lack seriously hampers our work here."

Kern looked embarrassed. "Yes, but I—"

"You remain, hormonally, a child. And *will* reaches full range only in the mature adult." Maybe so, Luke thought, but Aliira had shown a fair amount of clout. Well, people differ. . . .

Deri leaned forward. "Why is it that you hold yourself back from manhood?"

Kern's hands moved indecisively. "I—I wait until I find a woman I truly desire. Then . . ."

Tabor laughed; he couldn't help it. "Stay as you are, and you never will. Look, Kern; your mind can like and admire a woman—but it takes the good ol' glands to light the fire. You're cheating yourself, buddy." Deba looked scandalized: where did he get off, talking that way to one of the Changed?

Kern didn't seem to mind. "Perhaps you are right. But development requires days, weeks. . . ."

Her change of gender took none of the edge from Derion's hell-for-leather grin. "When it proceeds at natural pace, yes. But with two other strong *wills* pushing, how long?"

She stood, dripping. "Kern, Deri—after hunger is appeased, shall we adjourn to our room and find out?"

Dinner wasn't much for repartee. Not lingering, the three Changed took a pot of coffee with them. Draining his own cup, Tabor poured a glass of wine from the half-full carafe, then one for Vivi. Deba shook her head; frowning, she asked, "Can they truly, in such brief time, bring that outsize child to manhood?"

"Wouldn't surprise me," Luke said. "Not sure how, though."

Vivi smirked. "Ten to one he gets lots of direct physical encouragement." Then, "Well, look how the two Derions fixed *their* problem. Sex, the universal flu shot."

Puzzled, Tabor said, "Anything wrong with that? Whatever works, vote with it."

Pouting, she shrugged. "Lately, I wouldn't know."

He wasn't going to touch *that* line; in the pause, Deba said, "I will return at early morning." She turned and walked out.

Luke asked, "Where you suppose she's off to?"

"To the man she had in the room last night. Only at his place this time." Looking at Tabor, her gaze didn't move at all.

Well. Vivi's aims were clear enough; the trouble was,

Tabor's weren't. He tried a defensive sortie: "If they get Frey here, I sure hope Casey's with him." Then added hastily, "And the others, of course."

"Of course." Her headshake showed irritation. "Ease it, Luke. I know you're taken, over the long haul. But I'm here and she's not. Or are you too good for *leftovers?*"

Low blow! He started to say so, then changed his mind. "Casey and I, we've stayed just with each other, nobody else."

"While you were together. For all she knows, you could be dead." Leaving the horrid obverse unsaid, she added, "And by now she could be pregnant by Frey or somebody."

By now. How long had it been? Felt like a month, but couldn't be more than a few days. "It wouldn't be her fault."

"Who's talking blame? I—" Her lips tightened to silence; then she drained her glass and stood. "Good-night."

In moments he was up and following, then overtaking to walk alongside. In the room he turned her to face him and softly kissed her until her rigid lips relaxed. Which was more than he could do. All he knew of women's reactions came from Casey and no other; how could he possibly anticipate Vivi's? Tentatively he initiated a bit of erotic action. . . .

He wasn't sure what he expected: something sophisticated and exotic? Vivi was tender and giving, quiet and gentle. At climax she didn't dramatize; only her body's spasms told him the depth of her responses. In ways Tabor could not define she was exactly the same as Casey—and at the same time totally different.

Voicing only a few low murmurs, she lay against him fully relaxed, a picture of utter trust. It came to him that sex as such had been only a part of her need. As he began to doze off she roused and said, lazy-voiced, "You can tell Casey I raped you; I'll plead guilty."

"No. I'll just say you were very nice."

Before sleep one more thought came: he'd been wrong, when they first met at Jay's loft, about the silicone.

\* \* \*

No question of a morning encore; Deba came in while the two were barely waking. She looked chipper enough, bustling about as Tabor got slowly out of bed. Better than half-dressed he felt a great surge of *will* impelling him toward the dining hall. Nothing polite; this push had spikes on it.

As all three moved toward the door, Luke said, "Hold it! We get dressed first!" Already clad, Deba kept going. Vivi's face tightened; somehow, she and Tabor got most of their clothes on. Then, carrying the rest, they gave in to the summons.

That compulsion was general; the halls teemed with hurrying staffpersons. Plus a number of dazed-looking stragglers, in various stages of dress and undress, coming the other way.

Momentarily a clot of people blocked the dining hall entrance; Luke got his shoes on, and Vivi her skirt. Inside, among the disarranged tables a changing crowd of employees milled about; as some entered, others left. A sorting process, it seemed—and by the beleagured look of the two Derions and Kern, grouped at one side of the room, it was none of their doing.

Well, the commands hadn't felt like his friends' touches, either. Nor did the sick, paralyzing dread growing within him.

To the other side stood a tall, muscular man; dark coloring, pointed beard and saturnine features gave him a look of menace as he bent and spoke to a smaller companion. That man bore a mild face, crowned by a fluffy halo of short, wispy blond hair.

Luke wanted to go to the Derions, but the imperative of *will* swept him and Vivi and Deba into the circling mob. At random intervals one or more would stop abruptly, then make for an exit.

A sorting-out, yes. The herd was being cut, most likely by the big hunk of muscle, the Mephistopheles look-alike, who pretty much had to be the Duke Mardeux.

So far, at least, the man lived up to his advance billing.

# SIXTEEN

The slow, milling motion and dull, amorphous fear had Luke half-dazed when a new and violent *will* probe struck: a wordless attack on his very self, it triggered a flood of thought, a desperate effort to defend. He staggered, trying to find . . . what? *A place to stand,* he thought. *Like Archimedes.*

The pressure vanished; again, outside compulsion moved him, this time out of the group. Out of the room, too, he expected—but no, his steps took him across toward the Derions and Kern. And after a moment he found Vivi and Deba flanking him.

Either the *will*-imposed fear had been eased or Tabor's resistance was building; now he felt only a strong anxiety, natural enough in these dicey circumstances. A side glance showed Vivi obviously wired to the hot line but hardly panicked; by way of contrast, Deba stumped along with eyes locked straight ahead and face frozen rigid. He reached and squeezed her arm lightly; "Easy does it," then did the same to Vivi, who mumbled something through a shaky grin.

At close range Luke saw changes in Kern: nothing obvious, but a leaner look to his face, a tautness in both expression and carriage. How much the difference owed to force-fed puberty and how much to the young man's reactions in the situation here, Tabor couldn't guess; Deri appeared equally tense.

Only Derya seemed near to normal; only she took her gaze from the interlopers to greet the approaching three. "Good morning. I trust you had no difficulty finding your way here."

"Not much. When did Mardeux get here? That *is* Mardeux?"

"The duke and his symbiote Gonart landed a carrier at our door only a short time ago. We three were intent on breakfast when we felt their thrust of *will,* and all the hospice staff began to converge here. So we stayed, of course."

The sorting, it seemed, was over; no sooner did the last of the employees stumble from the room than Luke felt a renewed thrust of mind force stagger him. Derya's face tightened; she raised it to stare across at Mardeux and his helper. "What is it you want here?"

The big man's voice rumbled. "We will have your service. Your allegiance, your full loyalty. Here *and* at the Hiatus."

With only a hint of tight-lipped smile, Derya shook her head. "I think not. My loyalties follow my beliefs."

Fingers at his beard, the big man smirked. "Yet you will give them freely and in short order; you have no other choice."

"You think that?" Deri's question came as a challenge. "You two—Mardeux and pawn of Mardeux—you cannot kill us. Even should you possess the ability, which I doubt, the acts would outlaw you irrevocably, end forever your dream of high office. So by what threat do you coerce us?"

"These three Unchanged," the big man said, "are directly associated with you. That is why we have kept them here." He pointed a finger; beside Luke, Deba Sayan screamed and sank writhing to the floor. Derya knelt, hands to Deba's head.

For moments the woman shrieked and convulsed; then she went limp. "He varied his attack," said Derya, "too swiftly for me to counter it. I had to render her unconscious."

Glaring across the large room, she stood. "If I had a cat, I suppose you'd torture it as well?"

Both men shrugged; after a pause the smaller said, "If need be." The words belied his gentle, precise tone. "And please note: shielding the woman from pain does not ensure she will remain alive."

Had Deri been furred he would have bristled. "Pretend, at least, to some shadow of honor. Inflicting pain on the defenseless by *will* is a vile act."

Yeah. *Pick on somebody your own size, ya big bully!* But that's not the way bullies work. Migraine agony tore through Tabor's head and drove him to his knees. Blinding lights obscured his vision; nausea doubled him over. Slowly the seizure ebbed, leaving him weak and apprehensive, drenched with sweat.

Briefly Derya's hand, cool on his forehead, eased the worst of it. Standing again, she said, "Defense is futile." And shouted, "Have at them!"

All at once, *everything* hit the fan.

Still on one knee, Luke felt buffeted, yet unable to identify what hit him or where it came from. Waves of pressure, heat, sound, cold, grief, light, anger, and more—striking and changing, all mixed together. None of this onslaught seemed aimed specifically at him; it was the backwash—sideflash, what have you—of five battling *wills*. And so high-powered that any effort to resist was a bad joke.

For seconds the attacks were purely mental. Then came objects rising from floor and tables to accelerate, swerving and dodging under the force of opposing *wills:* everything from cutlery to saltshakers zoomed and caromed. Not hitting much of anybody, Tabor noticed as a ladle grazed his neck; could the Changed mount some kind of overall repelling shield along with their own bombardments?

*Will* or no *will*, here was a game Tabor could play too. He'd always had a good wing on him: what his pitching lacked in accuracy it made up in steam. A cruet rolled within reach; rearing up, he made the home plate peg, straight at the big man.

And hit him, opening a cut over the right eye! Snarling, the bearded one blinked as other missiles struck before he could regain concentration. Luke shrank under the savage stare, but at the moment his hands held nothing; the gaze moved on. As, visibly and unmistakably, the cut healed itself.

All right; if defense relied on detecting the *will* propelling a moving object, Tabor still had an advantage. He put all the steam he had on a pepper grinder; a shoulder twinge told him the thing was too heavy for that treatment. Also, he missed.

He was winding up with a metal candle holder when between him and the enemy duo the air began to shimmer; the painful impact of *will* forces ebbed, and a last few flung objects clattered against walls and floor. Then, as when Casey first arrived in this time, the shimmer darkened and swirled.

After moments it cleared; to Luke's surprise, Casey appeared again. She and Jay and Carla and Alicia, all hanging onto Lord Frey. As the group had clung to Derion that first time.

Facing the Derions and Kern, the Viking laughed. "So I was right. It was you, cuz-cousin, farspying me." He peered at Derya. "And who are *you,* who looks familiar though your name eludes me?"

"Behind you!"

Luke's yell spun Frey, scattering the others from him in time to deflect the big man's lunge; on the floor a heavy, cross-hilted knife slid away. As the attacker scrambled up again, Frey danced backward and stopped alongside Deri. "Now I understand your fleeting call, Derion. Truce between us, then, to deal with this . . ." He spat toward Mardeux and Gonart.

"What do we wait for?" Derya demanded. "Attack!"

Single-mindedly heading for Casey, Tabor felt *will* assaults slash out, as again objects whistled past with deadly speed. Sprawling, he soft-tackled her to the floor. "Stay down!" While he himself looked for something to throw.

He heard a cry and turned to see one of the heavy handguns, the bolters, wrench away from Jay Rozak's hand. No point in Luke's going after the thing; he wouldn't be let to hold it either, long enough to use it. He grabbed a metal tray and flung it backhand, sailing like a discus, hoping the edge would do some damage; inches away from the smaller man it lifted enough to miss. For moments that one glared at him, then obviously dismissed the suspicion. As a small metal pitcher, whipped sidearm by Vivi, caught him over the ear. *Good throw!*

Too damn much confusion! Tabor couldn't think; he turned to see Casey looking slit-eyed at their enemies. She said "Who—?"

"Mardeux. Ahearn's father." Would that make sense to her? Never mind. He was going to ask if she were all right, but a *will* surge struck; they both went flat.

The wave passed. Luke struggled to his knees as shrieks sounded; he saw Carla Duvai, mouth squared to a rictus, tearing at her head with both clawed hands as the big man, roaring, his beard disheveled and bushing out, aimed a forefinger that shook with tension.

"Ha-*yeee!*" From behind Tabor came Jay Rozak, up and charging. A buffet of *will* staggered him; his face contorted. But high and chilling, a second warscream came before another burst of *will* stopped Rozak a pace short of contact. His arm, though, came forward in a full roundhouse throw: suddenly the big man's mouth was plugged by the heavy cross-hilt of his own knife.

As he swayed and fell, around the smaller man air curdled to an opaque mass; the next instant, both it and he were gone.

Sudden absence of *will* force left a roaring in Tabor's ears. He looked down. The crosspiece of the knife's hilt stretched the dead man's mouth open to the jaw hinge; behind, through black curls at his nape the point emerged.

Shaking, Rozak looked ready to keel over. Luke put a steadying arm around him. "Well, buddy, you got Mardeux."

"No." Frey's voice. "It is Gonart dead, Mardeux who escaped."

* * *

Shaking her head and obviously getting her breath back, Carla came to embrace Rozak; together they slumped down, sitting. Hesitantly Tabor asked, "Jay? How could you beat all that *will?* And kill the big guy? I mean, a plain ordinary Unchanged—or do you have something the rest of us don't?"

Coughing a little, Rozak said, "Training, m'boy. We were taught, when attack comes to all or nothing, put *all* of yourself to the one goal; no other thing exists. No pain, no distraction, no other risk or danger—nothing at all except getting to the target." He grinned. "Seems it works against *will*, too. For long enough, anyway."

"Just what outfit were you in, Jay? You've never said."

"Twenty-seventh Messkit Repair Unit, what else?"

It had to be an in-group joke; Tabor left it alone.

He turned to Derya. "Is it true, what Frey said? The big one wasn't Mardeux? I thought . . ."

"Most people do. The duke is reclusive; in public the two always appear—appeared—together, with Gonart making an impressive show while Mardeux stood in the background. In their team of *wills,* Mardeux led; Gonart simply added raw physical energy to the duke's already impressive powers. But the general populace, and even many Changed not privy to secrets of the inner circle, mistook man for master."

"But why . . . ?" Casey looked as puzzled as Luke felt.

"Why not?" Carla gestured toward the dead man. "It worked, didn't it?"

Like a bubble, tension collapsed. Hanging onto Casey as to a life raft, finally Luke broke their kiss. "Hey. You all right? And what's happened, where you've been?"

"Too much; tell you later. Mostly okay. And with you?"

"A lot, yeah. Nothing that can't wait. Except—" and

he told her who Derya was, as distinct from Deri. And why.

Surprising him, Karen Cecile laughed. Then turned, as Vivi tapped her shoulder and said, "Blondie over there: she's one of ours, isn't she? From in the slammer at Pullman? Anyway, what's wrong with her?"

Tabor looked, to see Alycia Frazier huddled in fetal position. "Was it the *will* attacks?"

"No." Casey shook her head. Then, "Well, sort of, maybe. Anything out of the way, particularly any kind of violence, sends her into a world all her own. One in which she didn't see Bruce Garner dead after the battle." Her eyes teared. "We look after her." Suiting action to word, Casey went to Alycia and drew her up sitting.

Under his breath Tabor took stock: "One down, five of us functional." Then, realizing he'd forgotten Deba Sayan, he looked and found her standing back a little way, hands folded and no expression on her face.

"Are you all right, Deba?"

Solemnly she nodded. "Those great buffets of *will*, they shocked me. Like being struck with clubs; I never knew such force. I am yet somewhat dazed, Tabor. But I recover."

He patted her shoulder. "That's good. Take your time."

Behind him the four Changed broke their low-voiced huddle. Derya spoke. "Lucian. You and your group eat here, while we confer in our room. When we need you, we'll call." And they left.

Well. The dining hall was a mess: chairs and tables upended all over the place and no staff to give help. Exasperated, Luke said to no one in particular, "Our facilities are out of order for your convenience . . . !"

To begin with, not too far off the room's center lay a large body, very dead. "Jay? Help me drag this out of here."

But before they could get it past the door its sphincters let loose. Mess and stink and all.

Eat here? Forget it! And cleanup could wait until later.

Seven people crowded the little bedroom. In the kitchen Carla and Casey had rounded up food and drink and utensils; everyone except Alycia helped carry it here, and she did follow along without needing to be told.

There were only the two stools; Vivi took one. Deba and Alycia and Carla sat along one side of the bed, Jay and Casey at its end. The configuration didn't lend itself to conference, but setting the remaining stool out from the bed's corner so he could face nearly everyone, Luke tried.

First he introduced Deba all around; she responded in her usual guarded way. Then, "Let's compare notes, get everyone filled in. Vivi, how about telling yours first?"

She did: from overshooting the Outjut with Derion and their sojourn at Stopover, his genetic reshuffle, the return here, and on up to date. Tabor related his capture by Ahearn, subsequent experiences culminating in escape via the rebel's own carrier, and meeting with Vivi and Derya. From that point Vivi had covered matters pretty well; he added only a few details. "Now then; what happened at Frey's base and after?"

He was looking at Casey, but she said, "Jay? You know more about what Lord Frey was doing, before he pulled up stakes and brought us here. Tell it?"

"Sure." All right: Frey's people sustained perhaps half as many battle losses as Ahearn's, ". . . and very few from our time."

"Bruce, you said." Tabor glanced at Alycia, but she sat staring blankly. "I saw Junior Yancey lying dead."

"Yeah." Jay's mouth tightened. "The bastard gunned Garner down from behind; I saw him do it. So I took time out and broke Yancey's neck for him."

Tabor could see it. Guns were faster, but a man like Jay would want to *feel* it happen. Given the circumstances, maybe even a man like Luke . . .

"The only other one you'd know," Rozak continued,

"was the tall kid, James Wilson. The Phi Delt pledge; remember? Helped us get Yancey's badge that time. Not that it did us any good, with Frey turning up, but still . . ."

Yes. "Yes. A good kid. But then what *happened?*"

Rozak couldn't know all of it, only what he'd seen and heard. "Frey had most of the mess cleaned up, burials and all that, by late the next day. He sent scouts out on Ahearn's trail, but fat chance, so he concentrated on the genetic program. Sperm deposits, inseminations where the timing was right. Tlegg starred in the stud role, plus a few others Frey brought in to help out. In a few cases, Frey did the honors himself."

Jay continued. "Anyway—next day after the battle, I heard Frey mention to Tlegg that he'd had a farsighting on *you*, Luke, and fairly accurate as such things go. But then he lost it."

Luke thought back. "When Udeen—Ahearn's girl Friday—took Deba and me in the carrier? Has to be."

"Whatever." Jay shrugged. "But where you *had* been, Frey mind-registered. He knew it was Ahearn's people so he kept tabs, waiting for the man himself to show up."

"Any luck?"

"Nope. He had a fix on some gadget Ahearn uses to shield from farsight, but couldn't be sure the boss outlaw was really there. Then word came, Ahearn and some woman had escaped in a damaged carrier; his troops dispersed like good little guerrillas, just vanished."

"Udeen, the woman would be." Had he told them about her?

Rozak shrugged. "Then Frey got a bug in his ear. He turned the show over to Tlegg and told us—us here—to get our stuff into a carrier. And we took off and flew down to land at the temporary camp on the river island."

"But we'd no sooner climbed out," said Casey, "than Frey froze in place looking googly-eyed, and said 'Derion?' Then he told us to come hold on to him, and quick as how's-your-uncle we had another quick dip in the river of time and popped up *here.*"

"And that's it?" What more he'd expected, Tabor wasn't sure.

"All you need for now," she said. Whatever that meant . . .

Except for Alycia being coaxed by Carla to finish cleaning her plate, everyone was done eating. Looking around the place Luke said, "We need at least two more rooms, maybe three." He stood. "I'll go ask one of the Derions to fix us up."

"Mind if I come along?" Not waiting for any answer, Casey followed him. In the hallway she said, "I might as well learn my way around here a little." To next door? Oh well . . .

He stopped to hug her. "I've missed you, kid." And wished she'd arrived a day earlier; making love with Vivi had been a joy—but now it nagged at his conscience.

"Me too. You, I mean."

Should he tell her? And how? He prepared to speak, but she beat him to it. "I wish we'd pulled my implant and got me pregnant while we had the chance. I was going to suggest it, but I was too embarrassed."

"*I* thought of that, too, but I was afraid you'd get mad. Anyway, what does 'while we had the chance' mean?" Then with belated comprehension, "*Oh*-oh!"

Her hand squeezed his; when had she taken it? "That's right, the program. Frey made the donation himself, in person—and the same with Carla. I don't know who impregnated Alycia; she doesn't remember. Maybe she didn't even notice."

Tabor put his hands on her shoulders. "Did he give you a choice? Or just *will* you to agree?"

"We were all *brought* here to be fertilized; I had no choice and I knew it. That arrogant hawk-faced sonofabitch! I argued, of course, but . . ." Casey shrugged. "Anyway—he'd picked several of us for his own seed; my one option was insemination by syringe or naturally. Well, hell; if I'm getting knocked up against my will, the least the guy can do is look at me while he's at it!"

Something in Luke's expression brought a look of relief to hers. "He did use *will* as a stand-in for foreplay. I don't think he even knows about that; he's never needed to."

Back at Pullman, Derion had started to feel Luke up. But nothing said there couldn't be differences among the Changed. . . .

"Aren't you going to ask how it was?" No, he wasn't. "Well, physically, terrific. *Will*'s great for orgasms."

"I bet." But it wasn't *her* fault, and look what she was stuck with. He said, "When I get us a room we can see how the old-fashioned way stacks up. If you want to."

Just outside the Derions' room she squeezed his hand again.

His knock brought a *willed* summons to enter, along with total cessation of lively talk heard dimly through the door. Inside, Tabor deliberately gave Frey several seconds of deadpan stare before saying, "Derya, could you get somebody to assign us two or three more rooms, please? Preferably close together. With seven of us, mine's a little crowded."

She nodded. "I'll call someone. To here, or there?"

Luke couldn't see what real difference it made, but he said, "Uh—won't you have to give the instructions personally?"

"As a member of our party you are entitled to request services on your own account." Closed eyes, the now-familiar look of concentration. "A supervisor goes to your room."

"Thanks, Deriana. I guess we'd better leave, too."

"No. One of you be there to arrange matters; the other must stay for briefing, information to be relayed to the rest."

"I'll go," said Casey. What did it mean, her sidelong look at Frey? Saying nothing more, she left.

Ignoring any lack of invitation, Tabor poured a glass of deep red wine, then pulled a light, low-backed chair around to face the group, and sat. "All right. What do we need to learn?"

Where or when the Duke Mardeux had gone, no one knew. Anywhere in the Outjut's remaining future—or forward to the Hiatus, to lie in wait. "The worst possibility," said Frey, "is that he might bring back a Black Scarves squad." The duke's personal thugs, those: highly skilled potants, comprising a combined force this group could never withstand. Though not, luckily, timeswimmers themselves.

An idea sparked Luke; maybe the wine did it. "What if you waylaid Mardeux and his goons *in* the river of time? Would that give you a better chance?" He wasn't sure such a move was even possible—but it sounded so good, he spoke before he thought.

Frey's scowl looked intent. "Three against one, and that one burdened by nonswimmers unused to the stream—even Mardeux would be overmatched." His brows angled. "We could kill him!"

"Softly, cuz-cousin." Derya's tone was mild. "First catch your rabbit. Chances of intercepting Mardeux, *if* he comes, are slim except near his destination, presumably here. But here he could simply eject the lot of them from the river. And engage us not only unencumbered but with their aid. We must—"

"One of us floating a bit downstream as lookout," Deri cut in. "You're not a swimmer, Kern; I mean, even if you are, the ability takes time and training. But in the stream any Changed can be taught to hold position. Is your farsight adequate?"

"*In* the river? I have no idea."

"We will test; if it is, I will place you downtime, a day or less." He gestured toward Frey and Derya. "*We* hang uptime a way, showing no activity of *will*, waiting for your farsight signal. Then when you detect Mardeux and his group—" His fist banged on a table. "Moving downstream at full bore we catch them off guard, to scatter the Black Scarves past Outjut's end."

He rubbed his hands together. "And then we destroy them."

Derya spoke Tabor's thought. "It's worth trying."

The others nodded. Kern said, "Just so long as someone remembers to retrieve me from the timestream."

Coming out, in the hallway Luke met Jay and Carla with Alycia Frazier behind them. He said, "Derya was sending somebody to fix us up with extra rooms. Any luck?"

Carla shrugged. "We have one across from you, down a couple of doors; it has a bed and a cot. You get a spare cot, too."

"For seven, that's not too good."

"Six," said Jay. "Your local colleague—Deba?—says she'll bunk with her boyfriend. We'll keep Alycia with us; we're used to her. So that leaves you with Casey and Vivi."

*Shit oh dear!* "Oh, great."

"Something wrong?" Wide-eyed innocent stare.

"No, Jay. See you, folks," and Luke moved on.

In the room, Casey and Vivi were finishing off the coffee. Casey offered him part of hers but he shook his head. What to do about this situation . . . ?

In the bathing cubby he showered, feeling puzzled and getting nowhere. Dressed again, he rejoined the two women.

The only way was just do it. "Vivi? Could you please take this stuff to the kitchen? And come back in about an hour?"

Her brows lifted; she said, "You sure that's long enough?"

"For now, I think."

With a smile half-resigned and half-impish, she picked up the tray and left.

"That wasn't very polite, Luke."

"Best I could think of. Look, Casey—"

"I didn't say I don't appreciate it." She began undressing. "You haven't had your hormones jiggled in much too long, so let's not wait." Her smile suited the words.

But "I'm afraid I have, actually," and he told her. About to say he wished it hadn't happened, he swallowed the ungracious lie; Vivi deserved better. Instead, "I'm not sure just what agreement we had, you and I. But if I broke it, I'm sorry."

She paused, one thumb hooked into a bra strap half-off her shoulder; then she shook her head. "It doesn't *matter*. Except that maybe Vivi feels she has a share of you now, and you're the one who'll have to decide about that. One way or the other."

He must have looked as confused as he felt; she said, "Back home, the game was one-on-one; here, the Changed seem to make their own rules. Did I mention, Frey had me in twice? To be sure, he said, but possibly he just likes redheads. The second time he *willed* me so orgasmic I damn near dislocated both big toes. I'd read of that happening, but never believed it before."

She stood naked now, and he wasn't. "Luke?"

He felt about as sexy as skim milk. "I can't compete with that."

She laughed. "Who asked you to? Listen to me: when it comes to intensity, a vibrator beats any man who ever lived. But I've never been in love with one."

Then it was all right.

Whatever absence did to hearts—or didn't—Luke and Casey were not quite disentangled from their second round when Vivi walked in. "Come *on!* You said an hour; it's nearly two."

She started to turn away, but Casey said, "Stick around; we're in shape for socializing." Getting up, she put on a robe as Tabor shucked into his own clothes. "Anyway, I need to know what our rules are going to be."

"Rules?" Vivi's tone sounded cautious.

Casey nodded. "You knew Luke and I are lovers; now you and he gave yourselves a tryout." Under Vivi's look, Tabor tried not to be there at all. It didn't work; she still glared.

Casey was peeved and showed it. "Oh, be real, Vivi! We can't afford secrets, not in this situation. All I'm asking is, was it just a one-shot or are we going to be *à trois* here?"

"Triad?" Partly frowning, Vivi said, "I thought *I* was the show biz sophisticate around here, but I've never tried that."

Casey's eyes widened. "Me either; all I meant was sharing." She tilted her head. "I could, though, I expect."

Yes. Tabor remembered: she'd enjoyed her lady-love summer well enough in itself; what she didn't like was the labeled and limited life-compartment it put her in.

Under both gazes he fidgeted, unsure. Well, you can only start from where you are; he said, "This kind of thing, it's way beyond me. Vivi—you and I being together caught me off base; it wasn't right, probably, but thank you anyway." Then, all in a rush, "Casey you're number one in my life, the questions are is there room for a number two and Vivi would you settle for that, you two decide, I'll be back in a little while."

He was out the door before anyone could answer.

Tabor wanted a drink; he was heading for the lounge when he felt a *willed* summons, a call to the Derions' room. The touch was a strange one, more abrupt than his friends' yet nothing like the harshness Mardeux or his cohort had shown. Was this Frey, or maybe Kern? Whoever; obediently Luke turned and followed it.

He arrived to find a full quorum: all four Changed plus his five compatriots from the past. The group had run out of seats; Tabor hunkered down beside Casey's chair.

Frey nodded to him. "Good; we are all here." Deba wasn't, but the big Viking's thinking wouldn't include her. "You will need to know our planning, and time shortens."

"We prepare," said Derya, "to enter the river, to ambush Mardeux and any he brings. No matter the outcome, afterward we leave this place and possibly this time. Regarding yourselves, two matters are important."

She looked most serious; Luke paid close heed. "We must choose a location for you to wait for us in safety. And so we may find you without delay, you do not leave that place."

It made sense.

# SEVENTEEN

H igh atop Derion's offshore tower, the suite commanded a view of sea to one side and delta-accented shoreline at the other. Behind the well-furnished common room lay several bedrooms, plus kitchen and the normal facilities of this age. Not much, though, if anything, in the way of entertainment. Rozak, after a quick scout, announced that they were well fixed for food and booze. Just as well; no exit stood unlocked.

Stashing his and Casey's bags in a bedroom, Luke returned to the main group and sat down. The plunge into time's river had wrung him out. The roiling dark in which amorphous shapes flickered dimly, the buffeting, his lungs straining against thick, viscous air—it all felt like an eternity. Yet Derya said they had come hundreds of miles in only seconds of true duration, to materialize here. "Thus," Derya explained, "I did not have to neutralize the normal defenses before we could enter."

What that said about the worth of those defenses against timeswimmers, Luke wasn't sure; maybe he was missing something.

Derya had conveyed him and Casey, while Deri brought Kern and Jay and Carla. Arriving with Vivi and Alycia, Frey frowned at the latter's blank expression. "I had not noticed, earlier, the severity of her fugue. This will not do."

Closing his eyes he set his forehead against the blond young woman's, and to each side of her head placed one great hand. For moments neither breathed; then he released her and stepped back. "Heed me, girl. Freezing your mind to the point before you saw young Garner dead

243

has not returned him to life." And more loudly, "Own your
rightful grief and have done with it!"

Softly, then with greater force, Alycia began sobbing.
Carla moved to hold and comfort her. Almost apologeti-
cally, Frey turned to Derya. "I detest waste."

To intercept Mardeux, Tabor assumed the Changed
would need to hurry; after a while he said so. Derya
laughed. "We speak here of a moment in time. How can
one person arrive at that moment before another?"

"But . . ." He tried to state the problem. If Mardeux
left for Time B before Derya did . . . ? Then it all fell apart
on him. In this, what did "before" *mean?*

"Within the river," said Deri, "time is experienced
differently. Yet each of its moments corresponds to one of
ours here. You think of river-time as distance, and it is
not."

Luke shrugged; everyone was ready to eat, anyway.
Hungry as always, Jay had hassled Deri to show him how
to operate the unfamiliar cooking devices; looking wary,
Carla joined in to help. By chow time the results looked
good and smelled better.

As everyone dug in, Frey said, "Derion, from the past
I believe you brought only seven. Of whom six survive
here. On what basis did you make your choices?"

He was talking to Deri, who hadn't even been there.
Luke saw the man's blank look as Derya said, "And what
of yours, Frey? Opportunity and intuition; how otherwise?" She leaned toward her younger self. "Am I correct,
Derion?"

Tabor marveled that Frey didn't cop to Deri's obvious
relief as the latter said, "You know me too well."

Frey had more to say. "Of your seven, Derion, I
rounded up six for my own genetic program, and all do-
nated sperm or were impregnated, as applicable." Vivi
looked startled; hadn't she heard of those developments?
Her movement drew Frey's stare. "And this one? Have
you seen to her, Derion, or shall I?"

Again Deri had no answer. Vivi did: "Nobody takes

*me* to bed unless I want to. And anyway, I have an implant."

The familiar look of concentration came to Frey's face; Luke saw Vivi's eyes widen and her lips go slack as her breathing quickened. On her upper arm the skin stretched, then parted; a small capsule slid out and fell to the floor. One drop of blood trickled from the puncture. So much for implants . . .

Her dismay was obvious. Biting her lip she clutched her chair, white-knuckled, trying to control the small sensual motions of legs and hips; even so, her torso flexed and quivered. She bared her teeth: "*Stop* it, you goddamned stud horse!"

And Derya, voice rough-edged, "I think you'd better."

"Oh, all right." Frey laughed; his face relaxed. "But my dear young woman," smiling at Vivi, "you *were* timestreamed here in order to add new vigor to the Changed gene pool. So—"

Forgetting who was supposed to be who, Vivi turned on Derya. "Is that right, what he says? Did you—"

"I helped initiate such a project, yes," Derya cut in. "My version, however, included the matter of choice."

Vivi's exasperated look told Luke what she was thinking: why hadn't Derion made a pitch before changing sexes? Not that Vivi LaFleur would have gone for the pregnancy part . . .

But now she said, "If I *have* to do this—well, I was drawn to Derion from the first moment I saw him."

It was Derya she looked to, not Deri, but Frey didn't seem to notice and neither Derion betrayed their certain knowledge. Deri cleared his throat. "We can discuss the matter amicably."

And, Luke hoped, privately. All this war-of-the-sexes jockeying embarrassed him.

"You're so powerful, you people; you push us around, make us do things, drag us here out of our own *time,* even. But you know what? I think you're kind of dumb."

Reddened eyelids, tear-streaked puffy face and all, Alycia Frazier pitched her voice high and harsh. "All this work to haul us up here—and you let Bruce get *killed,* damn you—because you're too stupid to collect your sperm first and just bring it. How many of you does it take to change a light bulb, anyway?"

Blank-faced and stunned the four Changed sat. Luke choked back laughter. It was Frey who said, "But—but the cells would not survive such a journey. That is why—"

"You freeze the stuff, melonhead. Back home they do it all the time; all you had to do was ask. Ova, too: they extract those for test tube babies, put the zygote back in the uterus, or maybe a host mother. But oh no!—you're too busy pumping *will,* to learn anything." Elbows out and small fists clenched, Alycia stood. "Know what I think of you? You ooze scrunk!"

She stalked away; a bedroom door slammed. Tabor looked at a nonplussed Frey and said, "I have to hand it to you; you do one great job of therapy." A low blow, but what the hell.

He mused over her final barb. Scrunk he didn't know; it had to be teen slang, but since his time. Ooze, of course, superseded leak, as leak had long ago replaced suck. *Plus ça change* . . .

Subdued, the Changed spoke among themselves, low-toned. Until Frey's voice rose. "You take him into the stream, Derion; I will play Mardeux, and we shall see what Kern can do."

Around the three men, air darkened and swirled; when it cleared they were gone.

Given the river's nature, they could return any moment. And right now, Luke had a bellyful of the Changed and all their doings. He nudged Casey. "Let's get out of here for a while."

Once in their room, Tabor decanted two glasses of wine as Casey hovered over a small cabinet. Sound began:

music in a minor key, backing a lilting, androgynous voice. He couldn't peg the language. Not French, anyway; this one had real consonants.

She tried another control; atop the device appeared an iridescent hologram: abstract shapes moving to accent the song. *"Voilà!"* She came to accept her glass and sit beside him.

"When did you learn how to work that gadget?"

"Frey showed me. He had one in his quarters, where we . . ."

Anything Tabor said would have been wrong; he only nodded.

Tune succeeded tune. "Not a bit like shake rock, is it?" said Casey. "Back home lately, all the hits seemed to sound pretty much alike. And most of the groups, too."

"Mmm."

"Hey, wake up. You're the one said let's go; what you got in mind there, tiger?" Her hand dropped to his knee.

"Pooped and peopled-out, that's me. Too much happened. Mardeux, and you getting here, Jay kills that big guy and he's the wrong one. . . ." Out of gas, he ran down.

The hand moved away. "And I'm pregnant by Frey and you don't know how to handle it. Oh, Luke!"

"That's not it. I'm *sorry* you're stuck this way, but it doesn't change how I feel. Really not."

Casey nodded. "But tonight you'd rather not try to light up the skies with burning passion. True?"

Tabor grinned. "Very. What sounds good is some sleep."

She tipped her glass up. "That's a thought I can live with." She stood, then paused—no knock sounded, but Luke sensed someone outside, and knew Casey did also.

Raising his voice he said, "Come in!"

As Casey turned off the holo and music, Derya entered. "It is begun!" Excitement lit her eyes; her look held a hardness Tabor hadn't seen before. "Kern farsees the Duke Mardeux, and that one brings his Black Scarves *bandoleros.* Deri and Frey wait for me to join them; then we attack."

She glanced around; mind-registering the place? "I have already advised the others: if we have not returned for you by midmorning, you must assume us lost. Against such contingency, I will set the exits to unlock at that time."

She must have been in a real hurry. The cloudy, iridescent swirl of air had barely time to cloak her before she vanished.


Brought wide awake by Derya's urgency, Tabor found himself feeling amorous after all. But now Casey was quietly readying herself for bed; he decided he'd better let it pass.

Lying beside her in darkness a few minutes later, he wavered on the edge of sleep. A sound startled him, like a rush of wind though he felt no such thing; his eyes opened to see a glowing swirl loom beside the bed. It moved to engulf him; he felt an arm around his chest, jerking him against someone and lifting him. His next breath came hard, straining at thickened air, and now again he saw in dimness the frightening swells and surges of the river of time!


It felt different now; as his disorientation cleared slightly but not fully, Luke decided they were moving *up*stream. With whom? He discerned two presences; one was Casey but the other exuded a feeling of cold malevolent power. *Mardeux,* he guessed, and was surprised to sense a gloating affirmation.

Desperately he tried to struggle free, but with hardly any sense of his own physical body the effort brought no result. He made effort to focus a question: *Why?* What came was an impression of battle raging in this timestream, of men tossed free, ejected into normal existence or hurled downtime, helpless to control their paths. Then of one—*this* one—escaping the ambush, pressing uptime, backtracking one of his assailants (how could that be?) to make reprisal.

As to that reprisal's targets, Tabor held no doubts at all.

He felt a change in the surround; his half-thought question brought the knowledge that they had passed Hykeran Outjut's uptime limit and now swam an Islandless interval. Was this crazy sumbidge taking them all the way back to Pullman, before the Genocides? Fat chance—but it was worth the hope . . .

How long was this going to take? How long had it already taken? The questions had no meaning; in the river, time was distance and distance time—subjectively, of course. If he'd had the means to laugh, Tabor would have tried.

A slowing came, easing the subliminal force of time's current; now Luke could recognize the sensation of moving beside an Island. Almost immediately he felt Casey leaving—or more accurately, no longer detected her presence. Seconds later, or so it seemed, he sensed a pause, a stopping, then jarring impact as he hit rough ground and rolled. Thick air rushed from his lungs; rising to stand, thankfully he drew deeper breath.

And nearly strangled, trying to cough it out again.

Low and red behind heavy, smoky haze, the sun hung opposite the hillside where he stood. All around lay remnants of burned and shattered dwellings, a stark vista extending down and across the valley before him to an area of more massive ruins. A chilly, intermittent breeze made him shiver. After his first deep gasp he inhaled more gingerly, and found the air breathable though harshly irritating. About like a bad day in L.A. . . .

Where was Casey? Dropped away first while heading uptime, she could appear at any second or not for hours. Nearby? Tabor hoped so.

Looking around, for long moments he saw no one; nothing moved. Then far down the hill, muffled by distance, sounded shouts and cries; from behind a ruined house, largely collapsed, emerged several ragged figures striking with fists and clubs at one they dragged along in their midst. Incredibly the victim broke free and ran: a short man, and stocky. Before the pursuers caught up again, Luke saw they numbered five. Then, as the fugitive's kick struck home under a raised chin, only four still in action.

Ganging up was one of Tabor's pet hates. Before he thought, he let out an enraged yell and started running. The melee was at least two hundred yards away, over broken ground, and four to two was bad odds in anybody's book; belated discretion told him how stupid he was being, but he couldn't seem to stop himself.

Another yell seemed like good tactics; the war cry hurt his throat but he saw the attackers hesitate. He slowed; it made no sense to arrive winded. One man and one woman held the quarry; the woman, crop-haired and gaunt, seemed to be giving the orders as the other two spread out to come at Luke from opposite sides.

Not good. He grabbed up a rock and threw his fast ball at the larger attacker, missed his dodging target's head but registered a solid thunk on a shoulder. Briefly the man clutched it with his other hand, then grimaced, wiggled the arm and nodded. A good bruise, maybe, but no real disablement.

Two rocks thrown at the second man gave one miss and a glancing strike to the ribs. Picking up two more, Luke scanned the ground for something to use as a weapon, a club or staff, but the few items he saw looked either too heavy or too flimsy.

*Damn.* Circling to his left toward Mr. Sore Shoulder and trying to ignore the men's foulmouthed threats, Tabor tripped on something and looked to see a short loop of half-inch rope protruding from a mound of dirt and ash. Reaching, he jerked and pulled free a four-foot length threaded through the hole in a broken gearwheel and knotted around the damaged side. He hefted the jagged lump: heavier than a baseball, but not by much.

The construct had to be a weapon because it was no good for anything else. Who made it, Tabor couldn't know. The problem was, could he learn to use it in a hurry? Four feet was too much line to suit him; wrapping part of the rope around his hand he cut the free play down to about a yard and swung the gear forward, underhand. In moments he had it whizzing in a flattened ellipse, not unlike maneuvering a yo-yo. *Now then . . .*

The smaller man yelled, "Get him!" but the other hesitated. Timing his swing, Luke stepped within range of the nearer one. Whistling with speed the gear hit full on a cheekbone; the man went down. Charging from one side the bigger one walked squarely into Tabor's desperate, orbit-tilting backhand swing. Spitting blood and teeth he staggered but didn't fall. And now the other, right eye bulging above a ghastly raw concavity, came up standing. Resting his arm, Luke waited.

"Use it, you fool! *Use* it." The struggling captive did the yelling. "There's no point trying to hide it; they know what we are."

They do? Thoughts flashed: *the guy's a Changed, he thinks I am too, why the hell doesn't he use* his *goddamn whammy?*

None of this byplay was stopping Tabor's immediate opponents; damaged though they were, and slowed, still they came on. Stepping gingerly backward, Luke reassessed his options.

He didn't have to duke it out with these savages; from what he'd seen so far, he knew he could outrun them uphill. And hold the high ground by simply throwing rocks, the way he'd done one time when the Hagen brothers were after him. In the fifth grade.

But that choice left a man helpless to his captors' mercies. And might imperil Casey when she appeared. Also, Luke's stubborn streak was acting up. So he stood his ground and tried to spot some weaknesses.

The big man's club looked dangerous, but the other's knife scared Tabor worse. Now both men kept their arms held higher, shielding heads at the risk of body hits and bettering either's chance to grab the rope. All right; Luke revved up his weapon, making a few quick changes of path as he got the knack of it.

The little man was the quicker: watch him at all times. Start with him, in fact. As the knifeman lunged, Tabor ducked his head enough to tilt his swing away from vertical without hitting himself, then leaned low and forward to scythe the gear at a kneecap. Crunch and scream: the knife skittered across hard soil. Luke let it go; he had no skills with edged weapons, and his own central position denied the second man the blade.

That one rushed him; Tabor had to backpedal and pivot to get the whirling gear on a useful path. Its plane twisted; its upward arc evaded the club's swing to smash solidly into the big man's crotch.

*Two down.* Knee wasn't going anywhere; Balls lay in fetal position, eyes closed, bleating open-throated.

Reconsidering, Luke retrieved the knife. He had no real use for it but the two remaining predators couldn't know that. Still scuffling, trying to drag the captive away, they looked back often enough to keep track of Tabor.

Breathing deeply, he started after them.

When he was about twenty feet away the woman jumped back and yelled, "We gotta give it up, Flage. Kill him!"

Give what up? Never mind; Luke shouted, "Let him go and I'll let *you* go." Even to him it sounded grandiose, but on the other hand he was ahead on points. "Leave while you can."

Flage wasn't doing all that well. He was using some kind of garrote, but the victim wouldn't cooperate; he had one arm up, so that the wire circled neck and arm as a unit. Straining back and forth, the two men danced a sort of reeling waltz.

All right, the woman first. Raising an odd, crudely made gun, she edged away. "Get back or I'll shoot."

Luke didn't believe her; if she had any confidence in the weapon she'd have used it already. Deliberately blank-faced, twirling the gear leisurely and twitching the knife just often enough to divide her attention, he stalked her. While with peripheral vision he kept tabs on Flage's efforts. Hoping . . .

His hope paid off. The woman's line of movement took his own approach nearer to the two men, and a lunge by the victim swung them around to expose Flage's back. With two quick steps and a leap, Tabor brought the gear overhand to smash a shocking dent in Flage's skull.

The gun *did* fire! Luke hadn't smelled black powder since childhood, when local aficionados held shooting matches with antique rifles. He recognized it, though, and also the whine of a bullet passing closer than he liked.

Reflex, not thought, had him down flat. He looked for cover, then saw the woman wasn't aiming again but had turned to run. She made only about ten feet before a sharp *thunk* came. Her arms went up; she staggered, fell forward, and lay still.

With only a brief stare at the man he'd saved, Luke went to look at the woman. At the nape of her neck sat a thumbnail-sized pebble, imbedded well past its own diameter.

Unready to face the beneficiary of his efforts, Tabor picked up the gun. Crude indeed—definitely homemade. A muzzle loader, therefore single shot, its unrifled tube strapped to a wooden handle and primitive firing mechanism. He didn't recognize the igniting system; all sorts of variations were possible.

At any rate the weapon was useless to him; he dropped it and turned to inspect the other survivor. A man of apparent middle age, ruddy-faced, with dark hair greying slightly around a balding crown. In a mild tone Luke asked, "Why did you do that?"

Not burdening his answer with any semblance of thanks, the man said, "She was going for the rest of them; she's one of the leaders. And speaking of whys, why didn't you use some *will* on those Unchanged beasts?"

Suppressing a residual bias toward honesty, Luke said, "I had my reasons. For that matter, why didn't you?"

The man seemed embarrassed; after a moment he put out his hand. "Yes. Exactly. Thanks for helping." Helping? Oh well.

"My name is Inson. I'd been in the area three years, arousing no suspicions, and managed to seed a number of their females. It is of course too soon to determine if any were Chis and produce true Changed. Certainly, though, there will be more Chi-carriers available should one of us sojourn here a couple of decades hence." Decades, huh? No octal counting yet . . . "But this morning, being in a hurry, I was careless. Someone saw me catch a rabbit without using my hands."

He shrugged. "Reliability of farsight is not one of my greater strengths; they were on me almost before I sensed their nearness. Well, now it's a *real* hurry, to leave this charming place with none of my cherished belongings, and get away far enough that word won't catch up with me in recognizable form. Would you care to travel together for a time? It is pleasant to be with someone who will not try to kill me for what I am. We shouldn't settle in the same village, of course."

Of course? Tabor let it pass. "Luke Tabor here. And you were saying? Why you didn't use *will*, I mean . . ."

"Oh, that. I've always found my skills more effective at manipulation of physical objects than of persons. And I'm used to having time and quiet for concentration. Those animals caught me by surprise; they were *beating* me. They—"

"Right; you couldn't get your act together."

"Uh—" Inson looked puzzled, then brightened. "It is time to leave. Are you coming? Where do you hail from? Did you relocate under pursuit also, or simply to avoid adverse reaction to lack of aging? We do have our problems, don't we?"

Luke wasn't listening closely. "How far would the woman have to go, to find the others you mentioned?"

"About five miles."

Miles, not rambs: this Island was some way back from Hykeran, all right. "There won't be anybody come looking for her right away; you don't have to be in a rush."

"Perhaps not." They were walking uphill, toward Tabor's point of emergence. As they came to the two downed Unchanged, Inson drew a small dagger. Pausing beside each in turn, he cut their throats so quickly and deftly that only the second managed a syllable of protest. Wiping the blade on that one's jacket, he smiled. "Four fewer *will*less beasts. Not a bad day's work."

It was nice, Luke supposed, for a man to have a hobby. And was thankful he'd been less than frank about his own status.

He wasn't looking uphill, so until he heard Inson's gasp he didn't see the opaque, sparkling vortex that signaled Casey's arrival.

Rubbing a hip as she stood, Karen Cecile grimaced. She had, Tabor gathered, landed a bit roughly. Beside him Inson spoke in hushed tones. "Incredible. Such a potant. How—?"

"Hey, Casey!" Luke ran toward her. "Great timing. You missed a nasty fight."

She met him with a hug. "Where are we? When, I mean. Do you have any ideas?"

"Genocides, or maybe Waste Times; not a very nice neighborhood." Inson pulled at his sleeve. "Oh yeah— Casey, this is Inson. I ran into a bunch of Unchanged trying to kill him." He gave her what he hoped was a warning look. "You know how *they* are."

"Huh?" Then, "Oh yes; sure." She frowned. "Luke, when you get the chance, tell me just what the hell is going on here."

"When I find out, you mean."

Inson couldn't wait to get his oar in. "Madame Casey. How do you achieve that phenomenon, appearing from nowhere? No potant known to me could accomplish such a feat. Have you—?"

She squinted at him. "If, as a member of the Great

Lodge, you are privy to that information, let's hear the password."

*Oh, beautiful!* Luke stifled laughter as Inson gaped. The man said, "Pardon, please. I did not mean . . ."

"That's all right. Everything in good time." Turning to Luke, she rolled her eyes. "F'Chris'sakes, take over."

"Okay. First, we need to haul ass out of here before more locals show up; they're pretty lethal. Second . . ."

"Never mind," said Casey. "I'll settle for first."

Fine. But which way to go? Inson might know, but before asking, Tabor made a quick scan. Facing across the valley he saw the sun standing higher than before, so that was somewhere near east. To his left, where the hillside sloped down to a valley filled with mist (or smog, more likely) allowing only glimpses of a sluggish river, the landscape was less cluttered with ruins.

He pointed. "Let's go that way." Inson did not dissent.

They had covered nearly half a mile when a few yards to their right a muddy, lightning-shot vortex appeared and slowly dissipated.

*Mardeux,* thought Luke.

Guessing right was no thrill at all.

Tabor hadn't remembered the little man's looks clearly, but one glance clinched recognition. Knowledge identified the cruelty behind that mild face; its pallid aspect, heightened by the wispy halo of colorless hair, held no hint of innocence, nor the bland smile any amiable quality—behind them lurked only implacable lust for something Tabor could not understand.

Heedless of caution he said, "Where the hell have you brought us?"

"That is a matter of definition." The placid, precise voice was just as Luke remembered it. "Late in the Genocides or early in the Waste Years, I would say. Or perhaps they can be said to overlap." He shrugged. "Does it truly matter?"

Casey was asking "Why?" but Tabor overrode her. "I thought there was no Islands in these times."

"We knew of none. But when my agent reported that Frey planned to venture far uptime, well before the Genocides, and seek Islands there, I entered the river myself and followed his residual wake therein. When to my surprise I sensed Derion coming downstream I retreated to the—well, shoals is a fitting word—and waited, drifting, for him to pass. Which he did, and Frey soon behind. Meanwhile this Island, quite small and obscured from the main current by an eddy, came to my attention. So I noted it for possible utility."

His smile radiated false benevolence. "And I have found that use. Now we conduct an experiment, you and I. This Island ends soon. I shall leave it, and forsake you also. Before the day is over you will be trapped inextricably, to live your lives in this time and place. Your friends Frey and Derion will know where you are and yet be wholly unable to reach you without themselves becoming trapped. This is the beginning of my revenge for Gonart." His laugh was icicles shattering on cement.

Stuck *here?* Tabor's gut went cold with nausea. He couldn't speak. It wasn't that he was too proud to beg; simply, he knew it would have no effect except to add to the duke's pleasure.

While he tried to think of words, something that might at least sting the sonofabitch, Inson burst out, "It is *time,* then, great potant, in which you and these two move? But you say they are not of our kind," looking reproachfully at Luke. "I had thought they were. Else I—" Falling silent, he fingered his little knife. Then, "Take me with you! I am skilled at controlling objects, and I learn well. Please—!"

Mild blue eyes narrowed; Mardeux half whispered, "Why not? Come, brother; you might well be of use to me." He held out his arms. "Hurry; I have my fill of savoring these creatures' doom."

Hesitantly, as the air began its change, Inson went to embrace the duke. Opacity was near completion when

Luke's mind exploded with insight. "Come on, Casey!" As he lunged he heard her shout him the same urging; together they drove into the vortex and grabbed hold of those within.

Though lacking normal physical senses, Tabor knew without doubt that he and Casey clung to each other and also to Mardeux and/or Inson, while the duke tried his best to throw them clear; that dimly felt struggle made breathing even more difficult than usual in this continuum. Clutching grimly with his mind, Luke knew by the feel of Casey's presence that she too was holding on.

It couldn't last. Suddenly in close succession Tabor felt two things happen: the change in surround which meant they were no longer proximate to an Island, and a sundering of his grip on Mardeux. Luckily they occurred in that order.

Luke sensed Casey still with him. He couldn't actually see or feel or hear or talk with her, but she was there. Whenever *that* might be; only Mardeux could possibly know for certain. Were they drifting, perhaps? And if so, how fast?

In the river of time, Tabor wondered, how long could you go without eating?

# EIGHTEEN

> ✳

**A**gain Luke endured timeless eternity, the nonphysical bumpings and turnings of time's river. Some part of his mind choked back a silent scream. Determinedly he focused on the idea of Casey, the sense of her presence with him, the effort to reach her beingness with reassurance. Maybe something did get through; he felt a surge of some kind from her but could not define it. Content for the moment, Tabor tried to relax.

A moment came when he realized that only seconds earlier he *hadn't* been aware. Could he have slept, here? His burst of panic subsided when he sensed Casey still with him; again he sought to convey his feelings to her, but could find no response.

Something else, though; unmistakably the surround assumed the feel that meant an Island lay nearby. If they were drifting downtime—and why shouldn't they?—then perhaps . . .

What had Aliira said? Between the Waste Times and Hykeran Outjut a few small Islands, none over a year in span . . .

He wished there were some way to gauge "objective" time, see how long it took to traverse the length of this Island and thus estimate their downtime rate of progress. To what purpose, Luke had no idea; he'd just like to *know*.

As he reached that conclusion the last of the Island was passed and gone; once again they drifted through no-exit country.

Whether he'd dozed or merely daydreamed, Tabor found himself jarred to full cognizance as a new presence impinged; now there were three, grouped together. And no longer merely drifting in time's current, but being moved by volition.

*Who?* Not Mardeux, for damn sure; this one, very near recognition, felt unmistakably warm.

Downtime speed accelerated; Luke wasn't sure how he knew, but he did. Another Island's uptime headland loomed; abruptly their course turned. Within seconds Tabor plunked down, still in a double embrace, onto a grassy slope bathed in sunshine that slanted through scattered drops of light spring rain.

After the slagheap look of the Waste Times, the contrast brought tears to Tabor's eyes.

His first thought, while he tried to work loose from the general sprawl: "Casey! You all right?"

"I guess so." Sitting up, while his legs still held hers pinned, she looked definitely mussed but nothing worse. "Oh, Luke! So *lucky* we grabbed that sonofabitch Mardeux, before he could strand us in those bloody Waste Times. I—"

Her voice rose near hysteria; hugging her, he silenced it with a kiss driven to fierceness by his overwhelming relief. Then "Lucky, yeah. We *both* yelled go get him, and went. If either of us had to prime the other first, we couldn't have." Surprising himself, he laughed. "It wasn't luck, Casey. We've learned to think good together, that's what."

"All quite interesting," a third voice said. "Which is why I have held pause until now." Luke looked around. Partway risen, one hand and one knee still to ground, Derya gazed at him and Casey with a quirked smile. Now she stood. "I would hear, later, more of your experiences. Existence of an Island in the Waste Times does surprise me. Quickly, now, here is the gist of what you don't know and may need to."

When Kern as downtime lookout alerted the Derions and Frey that Mardeux and his Black Scarves approached, all three sped downstream to attack. "Like hawks looming out of the sun's glare, we caught them by complete surprise."

Derya wasn't certain how many rogue potants Mardeux brought along. "At least four we ejected into normal time, too near the Outjut's downtime rim for Mardeux to retrieve. The same fate the duke meant for you—though in less dire times." She frowned. "What with all else, it may seem strange that I find that one malevolence so uniquely unforgivable. The fact remains, I do."

She shrugged. "Mardeux fled uptime, then. Two of his minions chose to manifest for physical attack; since they knew little of the river's deceptive ways, we killed them easily. The rest—not many—we pushed off downtime and good riddance. They will beach where their fates decide. Or perhaps, never."

Casey said, "You don't play around, do you?"

Deriana's answer came quickly. "Why should I wish to?" Then, "Leaving my younger self to retrieve Kern, I undertook pursuit of Mardeux. But when farsight showed several persons nearing at speed, that group immediately split apart. On such brief view I could not distinguish identities; by that uncertainty, the duke made past me and escaped. Only then did I detect who you were, and gather you to this place."

Feeling very glad she'd done so, Luke said as much.

The way he remembered the land contours, this could be the same valley he'd seen scarred by ruins. Now it was largely meadow, with occasional clumps of trees. Along a central creek clustered a few smallish buildings; among them wandered a few lazy goats, the only movement in the entire vista.

Derya unslung a knapsack, revealing—to Luke's joy—*food*. "Unless you have eaten your fill of fried rat or some other Waste Times delicacy . . ." she said, bringing out a tray.

Tabor grinned. "No such luck." Beneath the tray short legs unfolded, making a small table which Derya proceeded to stock. Sitting around it the three dined, largely on bread and cheese with various greens, plus a flask of nalcwine.

The brief spatter of rain had left the grass barely dampened. "Y'know," Luke said, "back where Mardeux took us, things are really nasty. That man Inson: I saved his life, but if he'd realized I wasn't a Changed he'd've killed me. And *he* was attacked because after living there three years and getting along just fine, somebody discovered he was one."

"The Genocides . . ." Derya shook her head.

"We're out of that now," said Casey. "What happens next? Is the alliance still holding up with Frey?"

"Very well, considering his tendencies to greed and impulse. Why, his own genetic program is but a means toward his aim of becoming Prime Peer." Derya chuckled. "It's the *position,* you see; the details of that job would bore him stiff within a week."

Luke frowned. "So how does this cooperative effort fit in?"

"Now, all else gives place to the vendetta brought by Mardeux. Once that imperative is past . . ." She shrugged. "The experience of collaboration may temper Frey's urges. We next meet early in the Node of Terlihan, where we each have unused time. Not immediately; our struggles were very draining. And Frey wishes to gather a number of his supporters in our cause. Deri will bring only our own existing group, and do his recruiting at the Node itself before our joint final move."

Luke asked, "That would be to Dietjen's Hiatus?"

"You remember well." Eating was done, and all surplus foods repacked. The look of *willed* effort came to Derya's face as soiled utensils rose from the tray and proceeded sedately to the nearby stream. A considerable amount of splashing ensued, and the entire batch, cleansed and dripping, returned.

"Now that's what I call a neat trick!" said Casey.

Right. The light dishes hadn't moved with any great speed; energy drain was minimal. Good enough . . .

Derya spoke. "None of this venture has gone as

planned. Distracted by the ragings of my unwanted passenger . . ." Yancey, yes. ". . . I deposited you all at the wrong times. Forcing me to avoid preemptive presence by chromosome regenesis—which nullified my intent to seed you, Casey. And the others. Given your consents, of course—though I assure you I should have been most persuasive." *I'll just bet you would.*

"Now Frey has seen to that aim. With the exception of Vivi, who appears to look with favor on my younger self." *You should only know,* thought Tabor. "But I can still bear a child myself."

He saw it coming, braced for it. "Lucian, I want you in my child's heritage. You rejected Derion; will you accept Deriana?"

Casey stood. "I think I'll take me a little walk, folks. Up over the hill there. When you want me, just whistle."

At least she didn't conclude the line.

At the hilltop Casey passed from sight. "Why did she go off half-cocked?" Luke asked. "I hadn't even said yes yet. Maybe she figures I don't have a choice." He squinted. "Do I?"

"I am not using *will,* nor shall I. Except perhaps for enhancement, given that you do wish to proceed."

As Tabor looked at her, the special intensity and vigor of this most superb potant struck him anew. His nervous laugh came unmeant. "You don't need *will,* Derya. All you need is you."

*Will* or no, Tabor's erotic sensations came every bit as intense as those earliest, totally unexpected convulsive responses that had scared him, forced him to fight for control, to bring sensory impact within limits he could bear.

Now Derya expanded those limits, and here was another effect he'd known: total inability to ignore any part of sensory input.

That time it was the synthetic cannabis in the Rho Delt punch. This was different. For one thing, his head

was tracking; throughout, he missed no slightest nuance.
They didn't do anything exotic; straight was great.

As they sat, Tabor stewed. Was this the start of something, or a one-shot? He'd never been good at signals.

Derya seemed unconcerned. "Deri worries: that in changing his present, my past, I imperil my own existence."

"Paradoxes," said Luke. "What do *you* think?"

"That in all timeswimming, discrepancies result—minor ones, difficult to ascertain. Deri's and my action, to circumvent exclusion by preemptive presence, should answer the question."

"Either you disappear or you don't?" The idea shook him.

She swung her hair back. "To me these lapses indicate a new principle, undiscoverable *until* someone challenged causality."

"And this would be . . . ?"

"Discontinuity of causation." Derya leaned forward. "Minor changes do repair themselves somehow; later times show little or no evidence of alteration. Instead of 'conservation of reality' I postulate a break in the causative process. Existent event sequences remain, yet new progressions also come into being."

Luke gestured a branching. "You mean creation of an alternate timestream. Both happen, but separately."

"Not entirely so. Disparate events may exist in the same continuum, but no longer casually *connected.*"

Stumped, Tabor decided he truly hated hypotheses which could neither be proved nor disproved. You could argue all night. . . .

"I find lovemaking quite invigorating," Derya said next. "I feel ready, now, for downtime reconnaissance." Briefly, the look of concentration. "I have called Casey; she should be here soon. I will stay to bid her good-bye."

Some things were none of Tabor's business but he asked anyway. "Do you like being female better than male? And do you intend to stay this way? Or do you have any choice?"

She looked surprised. *"Better?* Either guise holds advantages." She shook her head. "Our child—I must of course maintain gender until weaning. After that . . ." She shrugged. "Regenesis opens much time heretofore barred by preemptive presence, not a benefit to be lightly discarded. Yet at some point I might well opt for my original state."

The impish, sidelong smile. "Of my own person I could not again become male. In regenesis, my X-chromosome formed the basis of viruslike constructs, to insinuate and replace the Y. Which is now gone; I would need to retrieve it from tissues extracted before regenesis, to recapitulate the overall process."

"Then you do know ways to preserve viable cells." Behind Luke, Casey's voice startled him. "Alycia had it right. You and Frey just bulled ahead—where with a little thought you could have collected gametes *without* all this hassle."

"For that matter," Tabor put in, "why not slip Chigenes into that handy-dandy virus and produce Changed by regenesis?" Not too different, he thought, from gene surgery of his own time.

"The Chi grouping," Derya answered, "lacks stability. Volunteer subjects suffered pain and illness to no benefit." Then, "You, Casey, are correct, as was Alycia Frazier. At the Hiatus I shall present your joint suggestion to the Plenum."

Standing, Derya stretched. "Now I go to Terlihan's, to report Mardeux's escape and your safety here. And to learn what preparations my colleagues are making. Once briefed, I will come for you. I could return almost at once—or would you prefer a time to rest, and recoup your own energies?"

Casey spoke. "How about sunset?"

Derya nodded. Around her the air opaqued, then cleared to reveal her absence.

* * *

"Now," said Casey, "we've both had experience in servicing the Changed. Though I doubt you minded your part all that much."

"But I *like* Derion. Always have, more than not."

As Casey echoed "Always?" Luke knew he'd said— and meant—more than he intended. Yes; even against the society's rigid conditioning, Tabor had at some level been drawn to Derion's extraordinary vitality. The unexpected pass had panicked him, because for moments he'd almost responded. And that was something his acculturated belief system could not accept.

He said only, "The Changed do pull a lot of whammy. Frey's carries threat, even when he's being friendly. But with Derion, there's all that charismatic attraction."

Casey peered sidelong. "Yes. Before, though, I wouldn't think you'd notice. Anyway—with Derya, what's it like? And are you a permanent item?"

"I don't know; she didn't say. As to how it was—" He shrugged. "I don't know how to describe it."

"Did she monkey with your nervous system?"

Accuracy now; Luke paused. "Not directly, like Frey or Aliira. But she opened all my awareness, parts we blank off a lot. I felt *everything* that happened. It was like—"

"Like smoking black hash? The five-hundred-minute hour?"

"Maybe." He cited the THC. "Frightening, when you don't know what's causing it."

"I'll bet." She squeezed his ankle. "Suppose you could gear up again? Once we rejoin the Crusades, private moments might be few and far between."

Tabor grinned. "Plenty of time before sunset."

"Just so we don't leave it until too late."

"We won't."

Derya's tinkering still prevailed. Now with Casey it was almost like being fourteen again—except that now his heightened senses didn't scare him; he could go with it, and did.

Derya's return, with the sun at half-mast, caught them at a washoff in the clear, chilly creek. Splashing ashore, they let the breeze dry them, carrying their clothing upslope.

In speaking range, Tabor said, "How's it going, down at the Node? Everybody get there okay?" And marveled at his matter-of-fact acceptance, now, of these flights through time itself. It's all in what you get used to. . . .

Nodding once, Derya said, "It is much as we had planned. Except that Frey has recruited none other than Ahearn and his aide." Her frown was quizzical. "A rather odd little person."

"Udeen?" Luke chuckled. "You could say that. But how did Frey nail Ahearn? By sheer *will?*"

"Only to compel a hearing, as he offered passage to the Hiatus and a chance to oppose Mardeux. Though Ahearn claims to hate all Changed alike, Mardeux is truly his *bête noire*. Alliance must be a bitter pill, but my cuz-cousin says his nephew is sworn to it."

Luke said, "Maybe a way out of exile had something to do with it." And thinking back, "Ahearn struck me as a man who'd stand by his word."

"Let's hope," Casey put in. "He looks like Frey, you said?"

"Except younger. His bad luck, not turning out full-Chi."

"That Mardeux—*punishing* the boy and his mother for the way Mendel's dice fell! Pure probability, no fault of theirs. He—"

"No one denies," said Derya, "his retroactive contraception would bless the cosmos. May we take the fact as given?" Abashed, Karen Cecile closed her mouth and kept it so. "Now, I think, it is time we leave this Island."

"Where are we going? I mean, to when?" Noting how near the end of Derya's patience seemed, Luke spoke softly. "The Node?"

"No. Directly to Dietjen's Hiatus, near and prior to the Plenum assembly. In that place, stay near me; its parameters lie outside your experience."

She spread her arms. "Come."

Hugging together with the two women, Tabor felt air thicken as the familiar disorientation struck. He thought: *Don't stop me now; I've got to where I like it!*

He was kidding himself and knew it. But not by much.

Between the relative ease of downtime flow, confidence in Derya's intentions, and simple familiarity, Luke found this timeswim almost relaxing—until speculation began: at the Hiatus, what awaited? *No,* he thought. *Lie back and enjoy the ride.*

Subjective duration ended; without a jar they came to rest on sleek, iridescent fabric; Tabor looked around to see a domed, oval chamber outlined all in gently glowing surfaces.

Illumination changed and shifted, its basic or median color close to peach. He said to Derya, "You know where we are?"

"My reserved quarters. I see they are moded for social entertainment, large group." The *willed* look came. Walls and ceiling flickered; the surface underneath changed to coarser, rust-colored carpet as a smaller, rectangular room came into being, its white ceiling offset by walls of pale blue-green. In some fashion not clear to Luke, various items of furniture emerged: chairs and three small tables, one including a bar with food service. Okay—much of the decor might be materialized force, but meals and booze had to be the real thing.

Deriana's expression said *"Voilà!"* Feeling contrary, Luke maintained full deadpan as he said, "Your force field equipment is almost as versatile as the Lady Aliira's."

"It suffices."

So much for getting a rise out of *her.* Grinning at him, Casey didn't say a word.

Never mind local time; next came dinner, dispensed by Derya from the machine. Feeling oddly detached, Tabor ate without paying much heed. Then, unable to ignore the vaguely disturbing music provided by one of the room's amenities, he asked, "Derya, could you show us sleeping quarters?"

"Of course." She fiddled with controls; in one wall a door appeared. "Your bedroom. I trust you will find it adequate."

"Thanks. And good-night." He went in and Casey followed. The room was straightforward enough: pastel walls, soft lights, closets for which they had no current need, and a sizable bed.

After soaking out in a long, warm shower, they bedded down. For a moment Luke thought Casey's kiss hinted at something more, but then it relaxed and they lay back, bodies barely touching.

He wasn't awake long enough to get introspective about it.

Sleep vanquished Tabor's malaise; waking, he felt great! Casey still slept; making a brief washup, then dressing quickly, he decided not to wake her yet.

If anything in the room concealed food, he couldn't spot it. Okay, let's go looking.

Nobody had moved the door; on the other side, though, things had changed. A conference room: one large table and one smaller, numerous chairs, sundry items of purposes not clear to him, walls of burnt orange below a nacreous-speckled ceiling.

Not a soul in the place; the food-and-drink console, beside the lesser table, he had all to himself. He tried the controls. With any luck he could take Casey her breakfast in bed. . . .

The problem was, no labels; he had to guess. Utensils were easy, and he had fair luck with beverages, but food was something else. His first effort produced a bowl of crisp, colorful salad that smelled like a skunk with terminal glandular dysfunction.

If the unit had a disposal mechanism, that facility was

well hidden. Hell with it; he could get rid of this mess in the bedroom's saddle-crapper. Now let's see. . . .

Four more tries gave three inedibles and finally a steaming tray that could have been chicken curry mixed with chili but probably wasn't. Quietly, not to wake Casey, he dumped the rejects. And then brought the tray, with juice and coffee.

"Rise and shine! You wanna die in bed?"

"Humh?" Blinking and stretching, she got out of bed. "If that's food, I forgive you whatever you yelled, there."

The chicken chili curry wasn't bad at all. Not until Luke went for more coffee did he find that it was no longer party time. The conference room was full of conference.

Frey and both Derions sat with five others, some bearing the indefinable air of top-notch potants. Also among them sat Kern, and from behind, Luke recognized the blond mane of Lady Aliira.

At and around the smaller table Luke spotted his fellow exiles from the past. But it was Udeen, standing alongside Ahearn, who first looked around and saw him.

She pulled at the rebel's sleeve. "Ahearn! Here is the one who stole our carrier. Now he will answer for it."

Peering past her, Frey's nephew shook his head. "The thing has been scrap, Udeen, for centuries. Yet still I would know how he managed the theft." Waving a hand he gave hail. "Ho, Tabor!"

Luke rather enjoyed the startled looks from his friends as this younger, scarred Viking, grinning though his brows frowned, gave greeting with a backslap that made him catch his breath.

Everyone wanted to talk, and all at once. Answering Ahearn (". . . carrier left open to orders, so I tried a few . . .") gave Tabor the floor; he took advantage to tell of his time at the Genocides ". . . or maybe Waste Times; nobody's sure which." Eras are seldom named until afterward. . . .

Deliberately he focused on the grim, ruined aspect of the place he'd seen. He did tell of intervening in a gang assault on a lone victim, but not its cause. Nor Mardeux's presence; Derya would inform all who needed to know, and this bunch likely didn't. Well, his own people, of course, but that could wait.

Oops; not all of it. "Jay; Casey needs to be in on this. Excuse me outa here a minute." But going into the bedroom, the Pullman group followed. Karen Cecile had dressed, so that was okay. And now, away from the others, they could trade some info.

# NINETEEN

At the Node of Terlihan, Jay related, they'd spent over a week cooped up in a high-rise suite. Toward the end of their stay, even the view down the bay lost its charm.

On the third day Lord Frey arrived with a group of his own recruitment, taking a pair of suites nearby. "That bunch kept to itself," Carla said, "and Deri and Frey were out a lot. So what we had for amusement was the local version of holo."

"They must have it here, too," said Rozak. "Being later in time, and all. Yeah, here's the control unit."

Beside him suddenly appeared a tall, willowy blond woman wearing a sheer robe. Turning to face Luke, in a flagrantly sultry drawl she said, "Come to me."

This far downtime they had the Playboy Channel? As the woman's hand reached out, Tabor waited for the illusion to break, for the image to be interrupted by his own flesh.

But the thing *touched* him. "Shit oh dear!" Laughing at Luke's startled reaction, Jay operated a control; the image vanished.

Casey gasped. "You *felt* that? Like a real person?"

"No; not exactly. More like a force field wall. Sort of smooth and cool and somehow vibrating. Touchable but not real."

Quite an achievement, though. How could the gadget sense its viewers, to have the projected image interact with them?

Back to business. Tabor asked, "Have you seen much of Ahearn? What do you think of him?"

"As fanatics go," Vivi said, "I guess he's not so bad.

But any time Deri or Frey showed up, you could feel him bristle."

Rozak grinned. "I thought he kept it under wraps pretty well. But hey, I like the guy."

"Sure; you're two of a kind," said Carla Duvai. "Not the bitter part. But the attack mentality you do share."

"Ahearn, though," Luke persisted. "What's he here for? More to the point, what does he *think* he's here for?"

"Depends," Carla said. "Deri sees him as a symbol, on parade to shame Mardeux. Frey wants him for a decoy, to distract the duke's attention. Derya's strictly hands off. But my guess is, Ahearn has his own plans. Grim ones."

"Still and all," said Vivi, "the man *is* a weapon. In Frey's arsenal. Targeted on the Duke Mardeux."

"And what's *our* part in the big plan?" Tabor asked.

Rozak snorted. "Sniff some fresh air, Luke! To Frey we're pawns. Sure, the Derions treat us like people, when they have the time. But comes to shove, buddy, we're on our own!"

He stood. "Wouldn't be smart to let on, o'course. But that's how I see it. You ask me, Ahearn's our best bet. He—"

Casey interrupted. "But you said he's just a tool."

"What I said," Jay answered, "doesn't mean things have to go the way Frey wants. I think Ahearn and I need to talk."

As he left, Vivi said, "Tell me, Carla. Are that guy's instincts worth trusting?"

Duvai shrugged. "He survived Caracas—and Operation Weedout. Plus a few little nasties his agency kept the lid on."

Casey said, "He told you that much?"

"Course not; it could get him shot. I made it all up."

Luke sighed. "Come on; we'd better keep tabs on him."

In the larger room Rozak was already with Ahearn and Udeen, saying, "Now look; all I'm asking is, how could we *help?*"

The scarred Viking face twitched. "No need. One night you sang a song. From one of your old wars, I would think."

"What song?"

"It began, your eyes had seen the glory of some event. I could not follow the next phrase. But the one after it . . ."

Ahearn drew deep breath. "Rozak, *I* am the fateful lightning, the terrible swift sword. I am all of that."

Turning away, Jay shook his head. Luke heard him mumble, "A loose cannon; just what we need."

As Tabor paused, indecisive, from behind a hand gripped his shoulder; he turned to meet a fierce hug and fiercer kiss. Too near to see who it was, after a few seconds he pulled back.

To look into the widened blue eyes of the Lady Aliira.

"Lucian! You have done much, I hear, since departing my enclave." And stepping back a pace, added, "As have I."

She certainly had. For one thing, she'd done puberty.

"I see you took my advice." Luke hadn't heard Casey approach. "It looks good on you."

It certainly did. Not lush but definitely well accented, Aliira's new figure had grace and beauty. And now she bore the unmistakable aura of a high potant. On a hunch Luke said, "You did it for the greater capabilities?"

Aliira nodded. "In especial, to swim time, far-seeking as my father did. Marvelous to achieve." Pushing her hair back she said, "Other benefits, Casey, are much as you predicted; I had *not* had full enjoyment of my body. But how could I know?"

"How indeed?" said Luke. Then, "Who are you siding with, here? Derion, or Frey?"

Briefly she frowned. "Since they are now allied, I venture to hope the matter will not arise."

*Dream on.* "And what's your personal interest?"

"A debt I had thought beyond redemption. A death

long mourned, its counterpart owed me by the Duke Mardeux."

Well. Talk about adolescent rebellion . . . ! First Ahearn and now Aliira. *Change the subject.* "How's your fusion research coming along? Any useful results yet?"

Her lips compressed. "I had hoped to defer maturation until our work was completed, but Frey insisted I come here at full potance. Still, I can report excellent progress to the Plenum. But until the Prime Peer has been informed, I may say no more."

"Sure." Abruptly Tabor felt a summons of *will* and looked around to meet Frey's stare. "Oops, excuse me."

He moved across the room to face the tall man. "Now what?"

"You've spent time with Ahearn, and that eerie little woman of his. How far can I trust them?"

*Or* me, *for that matter.* "You know Ahearn hates all Changed. But Mardeux most of all." The fateful lightning and terrible swift sword, Luke decided, were none of Frey's business. "And Udeen seems to mirror his attitudes."

"Talk to her," said Frey. "See what you can find out."

Luke was a little tired of being everyone's errand boy, but what the hell. Across the room he located the small woman. She spoke first. "Consulting with your master, were you?"

"He's not, you know."

"No, of course not." Her tone dripped sarcasm. "You come from his camp, steal one of our carriers, and now we find you in his company. Obviously you have nothing to do with Lord Frey."

"Frey and Ahearn both captured me, and each time I got away. Deba and I found Countess Deriana with a friend from my own time." He didn't let Udeen cut in. "Later we met with Count Derion; if any Changed is my friend, Derion's the one." Well, two—but keep it simple. "Mardeux attacked us. Frey came, with some of my friends. One of them killed Mardeux's man Gonart; the duke escaped. Eventually we all wound up here. And that's it."

"You swear you do not serve Lord Frey?"

"All we have in common, you and I and Ahearn and Derion and even Frey, is the deadly enmity of the Duke Mardeux. That's quite a lot, come to think of it. Maybe even enough."

From the small face her great, wideset eyes stared at him. "I will speak with Ahearn. He decides where trust is merited."

"Tell him not to take too long about it."

Now standing with Kern and the Derions, Frey beckoned. As Luke obeyed the gesture, Jay and the other pasttimers followed. Somehow it didn't seem quite the time to report on Udeen.

As Luke poured himself coffee, Frey said, "Kern offers a possibility I had not dreamed of." And to Kern, "Tell it."

The new adult began: "It is an old man's ramblings. My aged tutor, now pensioned, formerly served the household of Mardeux. One night during Ahearn's infancy, the duke and another Changed had a frightful clash of *will*, a terrible struggle. They—"

"Get to it!" Frey looked thunders.

"I beg pardon." Sweat showed at Kern's brow. "Mardeux literally destroyed the other's powers, and to some degree his blasts of *will* affected the abilities of every Changed in the area. But the most dreadful part . . ."

"*I'll* tell it." Frey's voice grated. "To then, the babe Ahearn showed every sign of latent *will*. But the duke saw too little of him to notice one way or the other, and he's not a man to whom information is lightly volunteered. After that night, though, the child displayed no hint of potance. The duke drove his potential capabilities to hiding; they never again emerged."

Derya spoke. "Wouldn't his mother have known?"

"How could she?" said Frey. "Only a potant can detect an infant's *will*. Unless some Changed associate told her . . ."

A moment's silence shattered with Jay's harsh laugh. "Bad enough, punishing his kid for not being a Changed. But Ahearn *was* one, and Mardeux his own rotten self put the stifle to him."

Jay's right fist beat first into his palm, then on the table. "You see what that means?"

Frey's great hand pinned Rozak's. "Yes. And much more than you might think."

Drawing a glass of spirits from the bar console, he made a tiger's grin. "This may be what we have needed."

The Viking's calm did not endure; soon again he was fuming. Low and harsh, his voice trembled. *"For his own misdeed,* he destroyed my sister. I shall . . ." A blast of *will*, unfocused but feral, shook Tabor; he missed the next few words. ". . . hanging by the genitals; gut him, keeping him alive . . ."

Luke was edging out of earshot when Frey's voice stopped, then came clear and light. "No. I have a better idea. Much better." Suddenly he came aware again of others' presence. "Fetch me Ahearn. He should have a voice in this matter."

As Tabor left the room, Derya caught up with him. "Come with me a moment." With a sigh he followed her along a corridor of flickering translucent crystal, possibly a force field simulation, then into a room with walls of a delicate apricot and furniture in black-trimmed teal. From the luminous ceiling, illumination followed wherever he or Derya moved.

Silently she poured him a drink, almost-bourbon dark over ice, then coffee for herself. "Cheers, I believe the word is." Luke sipped. He could really get used to this stuff. . . .

"I must thank you for helping me conceive," she said. "Shortly after our engagement I achieved ovulation; the resulting zygote has implanted most securely."

"Huh?" Oh, yes: engagement as in contact, not betrothal. Then, "Inside yourself, you can sense these happenings?"

"To some extent, even the Unchanged can do so."

*Whatever you say.* "I'm glad we succeeded."

"As am I." He waited; would she say now, whether she expected encores? Instead, "Tell me of Frey and of Ahearn's woman, what they say to you. I need to know these things."

As best he remembered, Luke told it. She said, "Frey and Ahearn share impulsive tendencies—which left to themselves, are all too apt to reinforce. And Udeen offers no promising avenue." She stared without blinking. "Do you have a suggestion?"

He thought back. "To me, Ahearn was never hostile. He only captured me to make his escape, and then even tried to recruit me. It was Udeen who always saw me as Frey's man, an enemy."

"Does she still?"

"Who knows what that little witch thinks? She said she'd confer with her boss."

"And so, also, should you. As I have said, Frey must not be the only one privy to Ahearn's confidence."

So now he was to be queen's pawn? Oh, well. "I'll try."

In the conference room Luke found only a woman tidying up. Best move, he decided, was to locate Ahearn's quarters. The woman didn't know the man by name, but ". . . two tall, fair men. The younger, with the scar . . ." brought results.

A few minutes later he knocked on a door, true matter by the sound of it. Inside he heard voices, but no one came. Turning to walk away, then he decided to try again. A minute or so later the door opened; towel around his middle, hair mussed and sweating, Ahearn said, "You visit inconveniently, but enter."

Edging past the big man, Tabor saw no sign of Frey—only Udeen lying in a rumpled bed, covers thrown back to her waist. Small, Luke noted, could be beautiful.

Embarrassed, he said, "I'm sorry. You shouldn't have let me interrupt."

"I did no such thing, of course." The wait—right. If they'd finished faster than intended, it was none of Luke's business here. Which Ahearn now addressed: "What do you want?"

Actually it was what Derya wanted, but Tabor said, "Has Frey talked to you within the past hour?"

"He summoned me. I sent word I would join him after a bit."

Well, then. "The question is, are you still hell-bent on getting Mardeux all by yourself, or will you help with a joint effort?" Seeing the man's ire rising, Luke spoke fast. "On your own raids, is it every man for himself? Or do you work to a common plan? This crisis isn't all that different."

Ahearn's explosion came as harsh laughter. "You have caught me out." His expression sobered. "To work together with the Changed outrages a deep conviction: that their abilities should be mine by right. Logic or no, this feeling lies deep. Taking my hate beyond the swine who sired me, to all like him. I . . ."

As Ahearn ran on, Luke pondered. *What if I told him?* And in moments, the urge triumphed over common sense.

When he finished, the rebel shook his head. "This explains much; strengths I cannot otherwise account for, and how I have to some extent resisted *will* when others cannot."

His stare became fiercer. "I can regain my heritage!" Then, in calmer tone, "This knowledge aids me. Now I can center my hatred onto its rightful target—and join effort, partially at least, with all whose aims coincide with mine."

His smile evoked a lion beside its kill. "To my uncle, say that I have reconsidered. Sharing intention, we may also share its planning and achievement."

For the first time, Udeen spoke. Sitting up, she said,

"I hope you will not regret this, Ahearn. And mark you, Tabor—if he does, so also shall you."

Small though she was, her words sent ice down Luke's spine. He said, "If Mardeux has his way, there'll be enough regret for all of us. Those who live, anyway."

*That* seemed to set her clock back a few ticks.

"Look," Tabor repeated. "I took a chance and it worked."

Frey's glare dissented; maybe he'd been set on delivering the bombshell himself. Derya said, "What would you expect? We give someone a mission; must he pause at each juncture and return for further direction?"

The sulky expression broke. "So, perhaps now I can speak with Ahearn without weighing each word for possible offense."

Deri laughed. Well, the idea of Lord Frey worrying about tact with an Unchanged struck Luke as funny too. Frey said, "Still I must seek further accommodation with my nephew. He wants only Mardeux dead; for me that is not enough."

Frey, Tabor decided, would make a much more dire enemy than Ahearn. And *will* was only the half of it.

Whatever the clocks might say, Luke's belly felt like lunchtime. Signaling Casey, he headed for the conference room and its food dispenser. This time he did better; his loaded tray carried only one truly inedible choice.

Entering their own room, Casey said, "Thanks for making the first move out of there. I was drowning in tension."

"I wish you'd let me know; we could've cut out sooner."

She sat. "I didn't want to be the one to break it up. Self-consciousness is a curse."

"I never would have noticed."

Casey snickered. "Shut up and eat."

\* \* \*

A time later, someone knocked. "Come in!" But no one did, so Luke opened the door.

Clothing piled over one arm and a shopping-type bag on the other, Derya moved to dump both loads on the bed. "What I tell you now, please heed carefully. Tomorrow when the Plenum meets, it is agreed that you and your people attend. As well as others, chosen by Frey. For your own safety in that place, you must learn and observe some rather arbitrary customs."

"Let's sit down, then." Luke set the example.

"Very well." Seated, Deriana faced the two. "The kinds of relationships which have evolved among ourselves are not usual here between Changed and Unchanged; most members of the Plenum would neither understand nor countenance our informalities. Here is the way it must be. . . ."

Briefly, Tabor and the rest could only be present as uniformed attendants to one or another of the Changed: he and Casey with Derya, for instance, and Vivi with Derion. "Frey wishes Jay Rozak and Ahearn as his side-men, so Aliira will take Carla and Udeen, while Alycia Frazier accompanies Kern."

"And they all get briefed?" Casey asked.

"Of course. All those are meeting together. But I wished to speak with you, both of you, privately."

Shrugging, Luke said, "Here we are; let's do it."

"First, then, the protocol you must observe tomorrow."

For instance, the blue-and-white Subcontrollers' uniforms, and how to arrange them properly. And while the traditional bald look was no longer required, on ceremonial occasions snug hoods concealed that lapse from orthodoxy.

Keeping one's place: walk less than fully abreast of one's sponsor, do not sit until the sponsor does—and be alert to rise first. Speak only to answer direct questions.

"Or so it should appear," Derya added. "Some dialogue will be necessary—but must not be obviously noticeable."

There was more; Luke hoped he could remember all of it.

Now she said, "Whatever may happen tomorrow, know that I repent of having brought you to the perils of these times. I had no right; my act is the fault of my station, with its tacit assumption that Changed and Unchanged are almost different species. That only *our* rights and purposes hold importance." She made a deprecating gesture. "I was not callous by design, only by circumstance. Which I now regret."

"What made you change your mind?" said Casey Collins.

"You two, and others of your time. To you we weren't masters, to rely on or rebel against. We were, as Jay put it, just some guys with a lot of extra clout. Facing powers you could not understand, you went ahead *anyway*—and sometimes won."

She shook her head. "In the long run you cannot. Any more than American tribesmen could prevail against European invaders."

"The technology gap." Luke nodded.

"Worse," said Derya. "Those natives could obtain rifles and learn to shoot them. You cannot buy *will.*"

"I'm learning to resist it, a little," Tabor said.

"But our crisis will not wait for that learning." She reached out both hands. "If possible, I shall return you to your own time. If we live, and I retain sufficient influence."

She frowned. "Understand—not even the Prime Peer himself could act to deprive this time period of the children some of you bear. Our need is too great. But later . . ."

The slight tightening of Casey's jaw might have escaped Derya, but Luke read it. "One crisis at a time," he said. "Okay?"

"Yes." Derya stood. "I wanted you to know, I will help you as much as circumstance allows."

She grinned. "Given the desire, circumstance may stretch."

Then she left.

Next day as the group assembled in the conference room to wait for orders, Tabor felt reasonably loose; he'd give it his best and see what happened. His uniform's broad, dressy belt with its large metal buckle was dragging down a bit; he cinched it in a notch and it rode better.

Hooded and gloved, showing faces only from brows to chins, his friends looked alien. Blessedly the fabric was porous enough to "breathe." The coil of hair bulging the top of Casey's hood could hardly feel cool or comfortable, but she didn't complain.

The wait ended when Frey looked in. "Follow me."

As they walked behind, along a dully shimmering corridor Luke hadn't seen before, Casey nudged him. "Notice Alycia?"

He looked and saw a new intensity, part apprehension and part secret glee. "You know what it's about?"

"She's miscarried; Vivi told me."

He nodded. "Feeling relieved, then. A whole lot. But scared of Frey finding out."

"That's about it. So we mustn't say anything."

"Course not." Then, "Oops. I think we're on now."

Ahead, near a pair of huge entrance doors, the other Changed were grouping. Vivi, Luke noticed, went straight to Deri. If anything was up, between them, they'd kept it private. Though she *had* admitted, semipublicly, that she had steam up for him.

Well, either they'd get her pregnant or they wouldn't. . . .

After less muddling around than Luke expected, Frey led off, flanked by Jay and Ahearn. Deri and Vivi went next, then Kern and Alycia. Carla and Udeen followed the Lady Aliira, who seemed excited but said nothing. Derya, Luke, and Casey took rear guard; as they entered, Derya said, "Look around, absorb the feeling of this place. But do not let it impress you too much."

Tabor needed that advice; first look brought an involuntary gasp. It wasn't the size; normal seating would have accommodated perhaps eight hundred. But beneath a domed and ornamented ceiling at least a hundred feet high he saw richly appointed luxury loges, grouped in bowl-shaped array to face a larger and more lavish box. And the lot supported in midair by a network of connecting ramps, translucent and sparkling in ever-changing, muted colors. Force fields, of course, but still . . .

*Don't let it impress you. Sure not!*

# TWENTY

><

They stood on a solid, material ledge projecting a few feet inside the door at about twenty feet above floor level, facing a choice of four translucent walkways. Those looked dangerously fragile, but by now Luke was used to force fields.

Nearly half the opera-type boxes, he noticed, sat empty. Some of the rest bore diaphanous shimmering domes, like soap bubbles; others, open to view, contained groups varying from two or three to nearly a dozen. At the larger central construct, seated or standing around a speakers' table and podium, were gathered almost twenty. "The Prime Peer," Derya explained, "and his immediate council."

Pointing to the nearer left-side ramp, Frey said, "The two loges over there, side by side. Since none of us held assigned seating for this occasion, I've registered our group for those."

Again he led the way. Trailing with Derya and Casey, Luke spoke quietly. "Anybody spot Mardeux?"

"He will arrive not quite insultingly late," said Derya. "He always does."

"You've been to these shindigs before, then."

"Lesser ones; nothing of quite this significance. The Prime Peer," she said quickly, "has held office longer than I have lived. To have his station questioned is disquieting."

"You're sure someone's going to?" Casey whispered.

"Frey's bloc planned as much," Derya said. "Mardeux's aggressions may have changed his mind. But he's too stubborn and tight-lipped to ease tensions by declaring his stand. And the duke's actions can never be predicted."

As they walked the immaterial ramp, which—as Luke had bet himself mentally—gave not a millimeter under their combined weights, Tabor eyed the boxes at either side. Behind the iridescent films vague movement showed, but figures could not be discerned. Only a few occupied loges stood open to view; from those, men and women looked at the Unchanged contingent with languid but unmistakable disdain.

*Take a good look, Lord and Lady Upsnoot; we're the kids from the wrong side of the tracks.* Or maybe the Genocides . . .

Derya's and Frey's groups entered the leftward of the two boxes the tall man had specified; the rest took the other. As everyone settled down quietly, Frey waved a hand toward someone farside of the hall; looking, Tabor recognized Tlegg among a group of Changed. Some of their attendants might also have been brought from the Arctic camp—but at this distance the hoods blocked identifications.

Within the large box, the hall's focus, several men and three women conferred closely. When one of the women stood to speak, Luke expected the blare of a PA system. Instead her voice came at normal level and as though spoken a mere five or six feet away. "I am Dhukaira, moderator pro tem. This Plenum is opened, its authority confirmed. We shall now . . ."

Throughout the hall, filmy obscuring bubbles either vanished or peeled back enough to give the boxes' occupants a frontal view.

Anticipating immediate conflict, Tabor was confused as the assemblage made tedious progress through a succession of apparently routine matters he understood not at all, each settled by a vote which made no sound or other manifestation he could detect. Direct perception of voters' *wills?* Lapsing into boredom, he almost missed the advent of the Duke Mardeux, strutting down an adjacent walkway and followed by more than a dozen Black Scarves.

Plus, Tabor noticed suddenly, the man Inson from the Waste Times. Looking as appropriate as a pimp in Sunday School, that one peered nervously from side to side and fingered the knife hilt at his belt. Catching sight of Luke and Casey, he sneered.

*Well, same to you, fella.* But Tabor kept his expression blank—or hoped he did.

What Mardeux saw or didn't was not so obvious. He led his entourage to a loge two tiers to the right and one forward of Derya's group, and sat facing the speakers' position. Looking slightly downward, Luke had a three-quarter rear view as the duke spoke first to one of his Black Scarves and then to Inson. Both turned to give flat stares at the Derions-Frey contingent, then faced forward again. Tabor looked to Derya, but she made no sign of having noticed.

A change in the speaker's voice, rising to announcement mode, signaled finis to her opening agenda. ". . . all stand; the Prime Peer now consents to address us."

Not even the entire audience, rising simultaneously, caused any slightest tremor of the force field support web. Then, as a tall, spare figure stood and moved to stand front and center behind the large table, everyone sat again.

Wearing a short, spotless white jacket with breeches and knee-high boots to match, the man somehow displayed more energy than his overall appearance justified. This was an old person, very old. But also very assured, as he began, "I add my welcome to that of our moderator. We have several vital matters to consider here. There is no time to waste on trivialities." He paused. "I am advised that a number of complaints have been entered. Those who bring them are well aware that I am available for such discussions on my normal schedule. Therefore—"

"Trivialities?" For a small man the Duke Mardeux, now standing, produced a creditable roar. "Do you consider a vote of confidence, seeking an end to your inept leadership, a triviality?"

"Out of order!" On his feet in one swift motion, Lord

Frey thundered the words. Further to Luke's surprise, the
Viking added, "Matters already before this body must be
addressed first. As you most certainly know."

Tabor's confusion must have shown; to him and
Casey, Derya whispered, "Whoso compels such a vote
gains unspoken advantage, a primacy in the race to become successor. Frey will not give Mardeux that edge if
he can help it."

Whatever, the Prime Peer took it from there. "We
proceed. First are proposals from Lord Frey and Count
Derion, similarly aimed but differing, for revitalization of
our genetic heritage. You seem in good voice, Frey; you
may speak first."

So the situation was urgent enough that illegal kid-
napping by both timeswimmers was being swept under the
rug. And Frey's unexpected defense of the Prime Peer *had*
scored him some brownie points.

The man told it quickly: bring Unchanged from before the Genocides, for breeding stock. Keep them separate from the general population, that their matings be
properly monitored. "For we know not what long-
eliminated defects we might again introduce to our collec-
tive genome; full supervision is essential. The same, of
course, is true of old diseases—and of new ones we might
unwittingly transmit to *them.*"

Those last two caveats struck Tabor as pure bullshit;
past-timers had been here for quite a while now, and so far
as Luke knew, no cross-time contagions had come to light.

Frey went on outlining his plans, rosier versions of
his sub-Arctic encampment. Which hadn't been all that
bad, really—except, of course, that its inmates were
brought and held there by compulsion, whether they liked
it or not! Ignoring that aspect, Frey wound up, "I have arranged and managed a test enclave, achieving a number of
pregnancies which are now in progress. My records will
be available for your study."

As the only Count Derion who looked the part, Deri
had to make the pitch for Derya. Deciding that the ficti-

tious twinship could not be made plausible in this more sophisticated milieu, she herself was present in the *persona* of a near relative of Derion's, born in inaccessible time and maturing just prior to the uptime end of the Node of Terlihan. Various records, Luke gathered, had been cooked to fit.

So it was Deri who now opened fire.

"We are dealing here with human beings, not herd animals. Together we and they can act responsibly, ensuring that neither defects nor disease are spread. Those persons brought downtime, who remain in our era, must become fellow citizens, not the property of breeding farms."

He paused to let crowd murmur subside. *"But—"*

Now he paraphrased from the Book of Alycia Frazier as annotated by Casey Collins. Why transport entire live human bodies down time's river when only gametes were needed? All necessary means and procedures already existed in pre-Genocidal times. So, "by means of this alternative we can produce thousands of cross-matches, rather than the meager few we now have. To achieve any significant improvement in our genetic potential, this course of action is imperative." Sweating visibly, Deri shut up and sat down. He had not, Luke noted, made any real commitment toward returning anybody to home time. . . .

The Prime Peer nodded. "I thank you both; the Council will consider your proposals and advise you regarding implementation." Brows lowered, he gazed around the hall. "So. Although we may now have an answer to one of our major problems, two others are equally dire. The increase in timeswimming activity, seeding new sequences of causation, threatens to fragment reality itself. And in ways we cannot imagine, much less predict. Secondly, it has long been known that beyond this Island, well-named Hiatus, we have no true assurance of continued survival."

"Because you take no action!" Again Mardeux stood, and with him his coterie of Black Scarves. "Resign *now,* while you may do so with full honors. Avoid the shame of a vote to strip you of them."

He paused. "For if you do not . . ."

*If you don't!* Unthinking, Luke grabbed Derya's arm. "He's bluffing! The Prime Peer should tell him go to hell. He has to. The bastard's bluffing!"

Because Tabor knew that routine: tell 'em they have to do it, no other options, and maybe the threat will work. But ". . . if you don't . . ." gives away the whole scam. He didn't know just what the loophole was, here, but there had to be one.

He'd been only sixteen when Lewis Gap's Principal Klemper blew an O-ring over the class numerals Luke and two friends painted, after a frightening midnight climb, high on the high school's brick chimney. At next day's assembly meeting, ranting about "shame and dishonor to this entire school," Klemper scared all three boys pretty badly. "Make no mistake; I know who did this. And if they will stand up and admit it, like men, perhaps I can find some leniency for them." Luke Tabor shivered.

Then in dire tones, "But if they *don't* . . ." And suddenly, like reading the man's mind, Luke knew the entire pitch was bait. Bait for a trap. To Pinky on one side and Ace at the other he whispered, "He's bluffing! Keep steady."

They did. Klemper went on, working the more gullible students into baseless anger at the "outrage." But after a while, when nobody bit on the hook, he ran out of steam and that was it.

A few years later, seeing the army pull the same trick ("If you *don't* extend your enlistments . . ."), Luke was grateful to Mr. Principal Klemper. Again he passed the word to a few good buddies: "The lieutenant's bluffing. Stand fast."

Here was the same old game. Except, the stakes were bigger.

All across the hall sounded the muted growl of excited mutterings. Afrown at Luke, Derya was mouthing "How—?" when from the next box Deri spoke. "Threats have no place here. And again the duke's petition is out of order. Not only one but two matters have been presented for consideration. These interruptions are unseemly." He nodded to the speaker. "If you would continue, Your Primacy ..."

The place quieted. At the podium the Prime Peer said, "Thank you, Count Derion. Whoever may sit presiding when this Plenum adjourns—and I assure you all, including our colleague Mardeux, that I have no aversion to a vote on that matter—these questions first need our attention. Since I have studied them, and commissioned the pertinent research, I feel best equipped to present the results to this assembly."

Giving the duke a "Try *that* on for size!" look, the old man continued. "In the matter of our future survival I call upon the investigative scholar Greston, my nephew, to explain what he has learned."

Tall and pale, with rebellious black hair retreating from his forehead, Greston struck Tabor as perfectly typecast. His voice, though, broke the stereotype; crisply he began, "For some years I have studied the parameters of Islands and tried to duplicate them. I can now announce a limited degree of success."

Much of the technical description went over Luke's head (how long *is* a ramb?), but the gist seemed clear enough. In a sense Greston had lengthened the extent of Dietjen's Hiatus; he had produced a restricted form of artificial Island which, unlike those existing naturally, manifested itself solely in the space enclosed by its generated field: namely, one smallish building. Its duration continued so long as its generators supplied it power. Due to an unfortunate interaction between its own field and that of Earth's gravity, its demands were extremely high; to optimize the research, Greston and his backers had opened their Island only a few months from the Hiatus's downtime end. By obligating all available project funding they had ensured a duration of four years, well past Hiatus limits.

So much for background. "Inside this construct," Greston now explained, "I have swum the river over three years past our Island's ending, emerged temporarily into normal time within the field's limits, and returned safely."

He smiled. "As you can see."

No, he had not attempted to leave his small Island's spatial confines; he wasn't sure he could reenter the river. "The Islands of time as we have known them have only chronological boundaries; so far as we know their properties extend over the Earth's entire surface, perhaps throughout the universe. The mathematics of a *spatial* interface are not wholly clear. Though entering or leaving my construct here in the Hiatus presents no difficulty." He had, however, extended a pickup arm out through the building's door and retrieved a few small stones which he had brought back with him. "So my extreme caution may have been unnecessary."

"Being *brought* into the field," Derya said, "and entering it of one's own volition, might prove to be somewhat different."

"As may be," said the Prime Peer. "Tell the Plenum, nephew, what else you learned of that time."

"As expected," Greston responded, "my data terminal in the building maintained access to all continuing records systems. So I made inquiry. And discovered surprising information."

At either side of the small dais the man's long fingers flexed open, then reclasped its overhanging edges. "It was not unexpected to find that no timeswimmers had gone passively into inaccessible time. But those future records showed no living persons known to carry timeswimming *potential.*"

The Prime Peer leaned forward. "We are something less than one-tri-zero, are we not, we potants and Chi-carriers of descent from Ulf Cragnor the first effective timeswimmer? And now you say that so shortly past the Hiatus, *none* of these still live?" Roughly five hundred of them, Luke made it. . . .

"Not only that. The last known appearances of each of us—such as could be determined—all occurred within a relatively small area. Yet over a considerable part of this

Island's duration." Greston cleared his throat. "I do not understand the significance of these findings, but for the present I feel it best not to disclose that location."

Widespread muttering showed how little the crowd liked the scholar's reticence. But before he or anyone else could speak, the Lady Aliira stood. "Your Primacy, I request a recess! And permission to address the Council privately. For I believe I know the meaning of what your nephew found."

Leaning toward Frey and Derya she said, "Greston has solved *our* group's major problem—one he could not have known we had!"

First hesitating, slowly the Prime Peer nodded and began to speak. But only a breathless grunt emerged, as suddenly and without warning came a great, numbing blast of *will*.

Driven to hands and knees by its sheer force, Tabor struggled to his feet. Throughout the hall, Unchanged persons did the same—or tried to. Casey came up fast, looking ready to chew nails if only she could find some.

The place was wall-to-wall uproar. Down forward, the Prime Peer himself was being helped to his feet. Too fast to be seen clearly, small projectiles screamed and whistled. Only nuisance to the Changed but deadly to others; seeing a man's face vanish behind a great spray of blood, involuntarily Luke crouched beside the railing. Struck by no physical object but battered suddenly by cold pangs of terror, he remembered Deri's telling: how the duke projected fear as a weapon. Well, he'd felt it before . . .

Memory gave impetus; fighting the alien force he achieved a stubborn, active resistance that quickened his pulse. He reached to hug Casey and shouted, "The panic's from Mardeux. Don't let the sumbidge throw you." As Derya gripped them both, saw they had themselves in control, and turned to help others.

The duke also shouted, about *his* right of primacy and he'd waited long enough for the courtesy of a vote; if he couldn't have one, he'd take command by right of potance. Deliberately, Luke set his concentration to ignore the words. Taut-faced and silent, leaning on two others for support, the Prime Peer gestured to those around him; Tabor saw each take on a look of sameness, of joined *will.*

Abruptly the waves of terror ceased. Mardeux went rigid, then turned upon his Black Scarves with obvious rage. Tabor couldn't make out the gravel-voiced diatribe but their faces, also, blanked with the intensity of *will.*

Missiles still streaked, but fewer, and now Luke saw that Inson the Genocides barbarian, panting with effort, flexed and bent in aid of each trajectory. *Body English!* That and the man's sudden vindictive look gave Luke warning; he ducked a projectile he barely saw. Behind him sounded a meaty thump; he turned to see Ahearn, gasping, clutch his left shoulder.

Across the floor rolled a lump of metal; Tabor picked it up. A little light for throwing, but what the hell; at the hospice the Changed hadn't detected un*willed* projectiles. Inson had turned aside; rearing back, without a windup Luke delivered his smoke ball and saw his target jerk and drop. Not for keeps; with one hand clapped to the side of his neck the vicious little man struggled to his knees and glared wildly. Facing aslant, Luke watched sidelong; Inson's searching scan passed by him.

A new thrust of *will* staggered Tabor; the Changed among his split group crouched now, facing Mardeux's enclosure, faces intent on immaterial conflict. What he'd felt, then, was only the side blast from their combined push!

Blaspheming methodically in a low voice, Ahearn worked at loosening up his left arm and shoulder. Abruptly he nodded. "Rozak! Tabor! Time we take our part. Be it only a feint, in aid of these cursed *will* attacks, we need do such as our abilities allow. Come!"

Well enough for the young Viking to say: his knife hilt first showed only a laminated stub protruding, but with a whipcrack shake he snapped out a telescoped blade. Near onto two feet long, and solid-looking as ever was.

Luke's hands flexed as eyes and mind sought for

something—*anything*—he might wield. Getting a nudge from Rozak he saw Jay wrap a few turns of his uniform's belt around one hand, leaving the heavy ornamental buckle with a free half-meter swing. "The old barracks belt, Tabor."

Once, on leave in Fairbanks, Luke had seen three gyrenes clear a bar using no other weapons—but had never so much as hefted a belt that way himself. Still, though: what about the broken gear and length of rope he used, going to Inson's defense? An act he found himself regretting . . .

But those were side thoughts. Once his own belt was primed for mayhem he made a few practice swings and moved to Ahearn's left flank; Jay had the right.

As he matched their leaps, first to the group's other box and then to the one remaining between it and the duke's, their sudden war screech caught him unready; Tabor's own yell came a full breath late. The storm of *will* blurred his thought; movement came hard, like nightmares' futile efforts.

Right about then, he lost track of who did what to whom.

If he'd allowed himself to think before the final jump to Mardeux's box, he never could have done it. But thought froze; muscles carried out his original intent, launching him squarely into and through a suddenly appearing burst of searing flame.

Panic shook him. No time to guess how *will* might do such a thing, but the fire came from near the duke. As it swirled across Luke and Ahearn and Jay, he felt his clothing heat and smelled it charring; then he dodged to one side and was past, grappling with someone his tear-blurred vision failed to name. Getting his hand free he chopped down with the edge of the belt buckle; it drew a grunt of pain. *Will* numbed his senses but he struck again, and once more, before the other lost grip.

Then with both hands he gripped a throat, beating the head against the box's floor; in his own skull a dull roar muffled all the shouts and screams and crashings outside himself.

A huge hand on his shoulder pulled him up. "He's done." Tabor looked down to see Inson dead, then into Ahearn's soot-streaked face. "But we're not. Come *on*, Tabor!" Pushing Luke forward and to the side, Ahearn swung his blood-dark blade against a Black Scarf.

The hall rivaled bedlam. Some stood rigid, locked in silent combat of *will*. Others, fended away from the stilled potants by no visible force, raged in bloody melee. Across in the speakers' loge the Prime Peer's council struggled to shield their stricken leader from attacking Black Scarves; only a few of those remained here with the duke.

In the boxes he'd recently left, Luke saw turmoil: no sign of Frey, but Deri threw someone over the side to crash on the hall's floor below. Moments later a tussling group, Changed and Unchanged interlocked in combat, obscured Luke's field of view. While others stood motionless, transfixed and staring.

Recovering from Ahearn's shove, Luke caught his balance to find himself behind Mardeux; impulse sent his heavy buckle flying at the duke's head. Perhaps *will* shielded the man somehow; inches away, the swing deflected and missed. The duke didn't so much as look around; Tabor retained enough sense to feel relief.

Attacking, a Black Scarf tried to freeze him by *will*. But like Inson, this man was no Derion or Frey. Fear and rage powered Luke's resistance; his cannonball swing landed the belt buckle just under the Scarf's ear and dropped him limp.

Without warning the buffeting of *will* slackened. Mardeux and his Black Scarves stood quiet, looks of concentration deepening as their shieldings seemed to hold off all attacks. Seeing Frey approach, his savage grin frozen like a gargoyle's, Luke exclaimed, "What's happened? What are they doing?"

"Don't know. Something all together. Nothing good, you may wager." Looking to his left, the big man waved. "Derion! Over here, before—"

The crashing hiss of energy guns—bolters—cut his words short. On an entrance ledge across from the one Luke's group had used stood a squad of armed guards. Now, with no orders given aloud, they began to gun down those opposing the Duke Mardeux.

"No!" Singed and bleeding, Ahearn charged the duke. From his hand the weapon twisted and fell away; an unseen blow staggered him. Yet his legs pumped forward until he gripped his father's arm. Mardeux's face tensed; Ahearn's convulsed and purpled. And again, projected terror crashed through Luke's defenses. But didn't stop the leap he'd made, crunching his heel down on the duke's instep.

Pure *will*, no physical touch, slammed Tabor flat. Only his own fixed purpose got him up again, swaying and dizzy, a punch-drunk fighter without the sense to quit.

Like the grandfather of all curses came Frey's spitting snarl. He made three stalking paces; one flailing arm knocked a Black Scarf away and over the railing before the Viking's impetus slammed him against Mardeux and Ahearn. As his arms locked onto them, their lungs emptied explosively.

Around all three the air thickened, curdled, became opaque; surging force drove Tabor back. With a sound approaching detonation, the blurred mass vanished.

Blinking, Luke fought to recover his own breath.

By distracting Mardeux's commanding *will*, Ahearn's onslaught had stopped the shooting; apparently bewildered, the guards showed no intent to renew it. And without that same driving force the Black Scarves—those who survived—began to falter. Some died trying to call truce, but as battle frenzy ebbed, others managed safe surrender.

Limping and bruised but looking more pleased than not, Jay Rozak came over to Luke. "Mardeux took Frey and Ahearn into the river, did he? Shouldn't somebody go after them?"

"Maybe. Who, though? Anyway it was Frey did the taking."

"Yeah?" Rozak frowned. "Never thought I'd catch myself worrying over that big pirate, but I still think . . ."

He shrugged. "Let's go round people up, see how everybody is. And what we're supposed to do next."

". . . medicians have treated the Prime Peer," Deriana continued, "so that he may now preside at emergency session, where Aliira insists the Council hear her solution to Greston's puzzle." Last time Tabor had seen the Lady Aliira, she hadn't even unbloodied the matted hair at a scalp wound. But whatever was on her mind, she was hell-bent that the Prime Peer share it.

Here in Derya's quarters the group from Hykeran, what was left of it, took stock and tended wounds. Except for a long, ragged gash in Udeen's arm, which Kern stitched with surprising dexterity while the small woman's expression changed not at all, most of the damage responded to healpads wielded by the two Derions. Remembering how Ahearn's had helped his battered face, Tabor was grateful when his own turn came.

They'd been lucky, this bunch: no fatalities or cripplings. Casey had sore ribs—but only bruised, said Derya, not cracked. A semirigid sleeve encased Carla's broken wrist, and Alycia Frazier wore a shiner rivaling the one she'd had from Junior Yancey. She was grinning, though; when the duke's man tried to follow up, grabbing at her face with one hand, she'd bitten his thumb nearly through. No doubt about it; this crippled bird was back to flying trim.

As usual, Jay was first to cry hunger; his plaint triggered a roomful of sudden appetites. But the riot, though confined to the Plenum hall itself, had monkey-wrenched operations throughout the establishment: lunch arrived late, raggedly served and not especially close to what was ordered.

Tabor didn't care; he ate what came and enjoyed it. The coffee urn had emptied. Derya's frown of *will,* seeking that another be brought, was becoming downright malevolent before Aliira came in carrying one. Somewhere along the line she'd managed to neaten up a bit; damp now, her hair was no longer bloodsoaked. She said, "So much *will* being tossed around, and very little control, the staff's selectivity suffers. When I sensed your call it seemed simplest to comply personally."

"And I thank you." Then, dropping formality, Deriana said, "Now will you kindly tell us what's going *on?*"

Aliira had told Luke and Casey truth about her fusion project and its starship goal—but not *all* of it. She'd left out both its state of progress and its full purpose. Now, having fully informed the Prime Peer—who, she said, was still shaken but recovering well—she was free to speak here.

Timeswimming was a fairly recent development. Ulf Cragnor's birth came midway of the Node of Terlihan. His death occurred much earlier; at a fairly advanced age, even for a high potant, he was "lost" by inadvertently living past the downtime end of Hykeran Outjut. Roaming the Islands his descendants created many anomalies; their cumulation, change upon change, already played hob with continuity of causation. At major Islands the stressed continuum had become unnervingly discrepant. Since Hiatus marked the end of swimmer-accessible time, these same time spans would also suffer the impact of any further time-tamperings. Therefore, the Prime Peer felt, such acts must cease.

Yet how could this decision be mandated? How enforced?

Aliira told it.

Makes sense, Tabor decided: get all swimmers *off* Earth.

"In principle the Prime Peer supported this solution. And my research team has achieved a level of *will*-aided fusion that could power interstellar travel. But we are years—octades—short of building a ship to carry all with timeswim potential, plus supplies for the resultant colony. Let alone, enough accompanying Unchanged to form a stable gene pool."

But when it's Steamboat Time . . .

"Casey and Alycia, your proposal to substitute gametes for breeders drops the requirement by three magnitudes at least." Octal, Tabor reminded himself: about five hundred, then. Okay . . .

"Still it was far too great for our capability." Smiling, Aliira threw her arms wide. "But Greston's Island! Build it to encompass the *ship;* once away from Earth's gravity the long-term power demands will be well within our abilities to provide. And do you see what we will have? How we can reach new worlds? Instead of living aboard for octades we can enter at launchsite, swim time's river, debark at destination." She paused. "There would of course be some aboard at all times, each serving for a period to operate and maintain the vessel."

"Wait a minute," said Luke. "What about forward cusp? I mean, if you haven't been there, you can't swim there; right?"

Aliira nodded. "It will be what you call a bootstrap operation. As each crewing team completes its service, one or more returns to bring the next relief group to existing forward cusp. Only when this continuing process has established cusp at destination will the main body be taken forward, in groups as large as the ship's size will allow. You realize, of course, that the real duration of passage, divided among many small teams, has no effect on the timing of embarkations here."

The concept took a little time to grasp—but it *would* work. Aliira continued, "So now the project has full approval, subject only to confirmative vote by full council."

"And—" Sudden insight made Luke catch his breath. "That's why everybody vanishes from the same area!"

"*Yes!* Greston's finding proves we are to succeed. Give to all timeswimmers a new world. Profiting from our mistakes, perhaps there we may plan and act with greater caution. And in any case, endanger this earth no further."

Still something wrong with that picture, but Luke couldn't pin it down. Another thorn pricked the concept. "How does everybody get to launch time? Won't it be barred to some? Preemptive presence?"

Before she could answer he smacked palm to forehead. "Oh hell yes! Greston runs another limited-space Island, spread long enough to give all your swimmers an access slot, and connects it with the one in the ship. So—"

As several talked at once, absorbing and elaborating on the possibilities, Luke spotted the crack in the picture. "Just a minute! You say you know it all comes up roses. But you don't. All you can know is, probably all the swimmers get off Earth. Not whether they find a decent place to land."

Aliira's mouth opened, found nothing to do, and closed again. As she sat wide-eyed, Rozak cleared his throat. "You *are* picking destination stars with the best chance of habitable planets?" She nodded. "But from here you can't tell for sure."

"That's what I said, wasn't it?" Luke put in.

"You're both missing something." Jay's eagerness showed. "Before you launch your ship, colonists and supplies and all, send probes." His hand chopped off interruptions. "Little ships, to support one or two observers in place while they make their checks. Let *them* swim downtime leapfrog, evaluate, and bring back reports. Then you send the big ship where the gravy is."

Rozak certainly knew how to patch a picture.

The talk wound down. Luke wondered aloud how anyone was going to keep all those headstrong potants in step, get them to go on the ship instead of following their own whims. Aliira said only that the Prime Peer was planning for that necessity and knew what he was about.

Maybe so. Anyway, the party was breaking up. Deri and Vivi left first, then Jay and Carla. As Derya stood and exchanged a few last words with Aliira, Luke nudged Casey and they slipped out quietly.

As usual in this place, they missed a turn somewhere. Standing at a juncture of corridors Tabor sought to find familiarity in any branch but had to shake his head.

He chose at random. Two turns later they had the luck to meet Kern, who directed them to the proper corridor, where they found the conference room and thus their own.

Inside it they stripped and showered, then lay down and relaxed. Tabor dozed; a knock woke him. Pulling on his pants, he went to the door and opened to Deriana.

He tried to blink sleep away. "What's up?"

"The jig, I believe you would call it."

# TWENTY-ONE
※

"**W**hat—?" Or rather, *now* what? "Have a seat?"

"Thank you. During recess of the council session I spoke with the Prime Peer. In passing he showed me a report which at first meant little to him, but which I found most disturbing."

"You mean, compared to what happened at the Plenum?"

"Listen first, then decide. The consort of Lord Moyton, who is one of Frey's cronies, has unearthed a major historical find on the third nearest of the small Islands above Hykeran Outjut. A quake had opened a rift which subsequent slides reburied within days; she chanced upon the brief period of accessibility."

His brows said "And?"

"What she found were pre-Genocidal records: journals and reports encapsulated against deterioration in a way we have only recently learned to decipher. And from these, for the first time we know the true origin of the Changed."

"What's bad about that?"

Her index finger pressed where his clavicles met. "All history lies delicately balanced on what might seem trivial turns of chance. That of the Changed, even more so. The discoveries leading to our emergence stemmed from the persistence of one man, a genetic engineer whose early work was ridiculed. Yet without his partial successes, no other would have followed the seemingly fruitless line of research which eventually produced us."

"So, one was all it took. What's the problem?"

"That man made his crucial discovery at the age of fifty. He lies dead, not yet twenty, at Hykeran Outjut."

She grimaced. "He was Bruce Garner."

After a brief involuntary whistle, Luke tried to think. "But wait a minute. How about your discontinuous causation? Or the other idea, of reality healing itself? Either way . . ."

"Those are speculations, only! And this is a *known* singularity of cause, now erased. Our entire existence rests on the shoulders of a man who will never himself exist."

"Then how come you haven't simply vanished?"

"I don't know. Inertia of change is one hypothesis. Finite rate of propagation is another. In any such, confirmation by experiment is elusive and perhaps impossible. Many have tried to devise tests, but the logic is slippery; almost inevitably, theoretical flaws can be cited. And this peril is too great for reliance on guesswork."

"So?" He wasn't being very helpful—but then, how could he?

"It is imperative that we buttress reality as we know it. Several, at least, of your women who are pregnant must return to deliver their Chi-carrying offspring during the era, a generation or so past your own, when our own scanty records indicate the Changed *did* appear. We—"

"Like hell we must!" Unnoticed, Casey had left their bed to sit and listen. "You'll take us to our own time or not at all!"

Her surprised look, then, said she hadn't meant to put it quite that way. But after a frowning pause, Derya nodded. "You are right. Our knowledge is too little to justify displacing you again in time. Possibly to no advantage, since generations might pass before carriers mate to produce truly Changed offspring. And—I did promise to try to get you home."

She shook her head; Tabor said, "Now what's wrong?"

"There are so few of you," Derya answered. "The needs of genetic survival . . ." And that much was true. Derion had brought four women downtime and Frey a greater number, though Luke had no clear idea how many.

Nor if most were successfully impregnated; Alycia might not be the only one to miscarry. Further, the limited selection of sires could hardly produce much of a gene pool. . . .

Casey made a snort. "Don't you people ever listen? It's the same as I said before: don't send just us few preggies back. Take along some frozen sperm; we can sneak it into sperm banks. Or do it yourselves, using *will* on the folks in charge."

She paused. "I'm not sure why I even want to help, on this. Except that it could get us home. But what is it we're out to save? The Changed, the Genocides, the Waste Years—why *not* let it all collapse to nothing? Leaving just plain old Unchanged humans." If she saw Derya's stricken look she gave no sign.

Luke saw—and winced—but something else needed saying. "How many billions of us? Unable to stop the overbreeding. Killing the only world we have." His thoughts gave no mercy. "Maybe the Genocides were the only way we could survive at all."

Her face contorted, then relaxed. As she looked at Tabor, tears overflowed; she didn't wipe them away. "That's a horrible thing to say. What I really hate is, you're probably right."

With one hand to Luke's shoulder and the other at Casey's, Derya gave each a token shake; regenesis to female structure might have lessened Derion's original strength, but not by much. She said, "I have some ideas on this matter. At the beginning, we Changed were only one new variant among many. A number of those were predatory, maleficent; it was their doings that unleashed the fury of the Unchanged."

One hand gestured to halt Tabor's protest. "I know; some of *us* may well have been among the malefics."

"And might again," said Casey. "Think of Mardeux."

"Hear me," Derya said. "The earliest Changed grew up in ignorance, not knowing what they were and with no guidance suited to their capabilities. In a new line of causation the case might be quite otherwise; emerging

Changed could be taught and guided. To be a force for stability, for moderation."

"One snag," Luke put in. "We'd have to run our own sperm bank. The women who draw Changed sperm need to be part of the overall support group, or we'll have the same old wildcat situation all over again."

"Well thought, Lucian." Deriana squeezed his shoulder. "But now, you realize, the Prime Peer and I face the problem of convincing the Plenum to approve your return."

"Horse puckie!" Karen Cecile's dander was up again. "You and Frey sure didn't have any Seal of Approval when you went back and put the grab on *us*."

"True." Derya cleared her throat. "In that matter, each of us conducted a clandestine operation. But what the Plenum knew nothing of, it couldn't forbid. It does know you are here now, and why. Its members would take considerable offense if—"

"And so what?" Tabor said. "What are they going to do about it? Come back to our century and spank us? Except for you and Frey, how many can even *get* there? Mardeux, maybe." If that devil-ridden man still lived . . .

"Deri, of course. And Aliira, I would think. Her father could have done, had he chose; developed, she shows indication of equaling his potance." Deriana frowned. "Even so, a mere four of us would be hard put to ferry the entire lot of you—including the greater number brought forward by Lord Frey—against time's current all that way. If only it were not so *far!*"

"Doesn't have to be." Casey looked smug. "You could make a rest stop. Remember, back in the Genocides, the Island where Mardeux took us?"

"But—" Derya shook her head. "I have passed by it twice, obviously. And without sensing its presence."

"Hang on a minute," and Luke told what he could recall of what the duke had said. ". . . normally hidden by an eddy. But now you know it's there, and approximately how far back."

"Perhaps one of us should scout first, to locate it precisely. Then, possibly . . ." And after mentioning that Frey's group of abductees needed enumerating, Derya dropped the subject.

Luke didn't, though; with the thought that hit him now, he couldn't. "Dammit, you're missing something here."

"And what might that be?"

"You're moving all timeswimmers off Earth, right? And all *potential* for the ability. But now you're fixing to take back, all the way to our time, viable embryos with swimmer genes."

Casey looked stricken. After a moment's blankness, Derya said, "A point needing address. I thank you." She frowned in concentration, then her expression cleared. "Ulf Cragnor was not the first to swim time's river—only the first to display that talent in great potance. Although some such may have lived their entire lives between Islands, their gifts never realized. But Cragnor saw the potentialities; his descendants submitted to inbreeding until the ability bred true. Only later was the strain spread more widely."

Still puzzled, Tabor asked, "So how does that help us?"

"Small populations conserve genetic changes; in larger ones they fail to find reinforcement and are lost. By positing all donors who carry the Tau complex—swimmer genes—as being closely akin, we can invoke your culture's incest taboos, to make certain the configuration does not reproduce and persist."

Her smile showed strain. "The more severe problem," she said, "may be arranging a sufficient degree of inbreeding to ensure the survival of the basic Chi configuration itself."

As Luke wrestled with uncertainty, Deriana stood. "Deri and I will confer, and advise you of our decisions."

She left. After a moment Casey said, "She's nice, you know. Was before, too, as a he. But I wish to hell these Changed could get it through their heads that we'd like a vote, too."

"At least they take suggestions, sometimes."

* * *

What this day needed, Luke felt, was a positive note. Casey seemed to agree; their kiss was working up to something really constructive when a knock interrupted.

Jay Rozak, this time. "Come on, folks. We have to talk."

"If you say so." And *sotto voce* to Casey, "Just when we were getting into potatoes au gropin'!"

They followed Jay to a fairly large room. Tabor had no idea whose it was, but for once there were enough chairs to go around and some left over. Carla and Alycia sat—with Udeen, looking strangely out of place, between them. Giving a head jerk toward the Hykeran woman Rozak said, "What's she doing here?"

"I brought her." Alycia's tone made no concessions. "She doesn't know anyone else; I told her Luke would be here."

In a small fierce voice Udeen said, "Where is Ahearn? He came to *help*—and Frey and Mardeux took him!"

Without the hood's partial disguise she looked fragile and vulnerable. "That's not how it was," Luke said. "Ahearn tackled the duke, but it looked like Mardeux was killing him. What Frey did was take them all into the river of time." He saw his words held no comfort. "I don't know what's happened; I wish I did." And to his surprise, found that no matter Frey's arrogance and excesses, more than not he'd come to like the outsized corsair.

At the small bar console Vivi LaFleur finished preparing a tall, wickedly dark drink. "Let's cut the amenities; we're here to figure where we all stand."

"About what?" Quiet but challenging, Casey asked.

Carla Duvai took it up. "There's some talk you may or may not know of; we could get back home." And just how, Luke wondered, had *that* circulated so fast? "Best I know, it's purely up for grabs. Question before the house is, how do we help make it happen?"

"And do we want to?"

Jay's flat query brought silence, until Casey said, "*I* do. Luke . . . ?"

"Affirmative!" Until he'd said it, Tabor hadn't known how he felt. But—this difference-torn society, its best hope a further fragmenting, siphoning its strongest potants to another world to keep them from destroying this one? A time and place where people like himself and Casey might influence by suggestion but had no voice in their own right? "Affirmative as all hell!"

Again Rozak spoke. "Voting time, then. Who's for home?"

Casey's hand went up. Luke's, Carla's, Alycia's.

"And who isn't?"

"I don't know," Vivi said. "Color me doubtful."

"But why?" Alycia sounded bewildered. "You're in movies; you double in holovid. You're a star. Why would you . . ."

Vivi shrugged. "Count Derion." Seeing how everyone looked at her, she glared straight back. "Yeah, sure; in this culture the Changed are King Shit and I'd be some kind of concubine. If that. But all my life I've never known such a man."

Her defiance melted. "Hey, it's not like working the studios was pure heaven. And being pregnant's not my image; I couldn't work again for a while anyway." So she *had* conceived.

Ruefully she touched her cheek. "Not until I get the leather out of my complexion, for another thing. So actually I could do worse than stay downtime."

"I hear you," said Jay Rozak in an ironic singsong. "Funny thing; I feel the same way for different reasons."

"Like what, Tarzan?" Carla's lips seemed poised to spit. "You run out of wars back home? I thought you'd kicked that."

"Right, I did. But weren't you listening, a while ago? They're fixing to send off a *starship*. Onc that time-swimmers can use to take people to the far end the same way we were brought here. I can't help thinking, here's a chance I never dreamed of. A guy from our time, when the

space program's been eaten by weevils, to maybe go see
a new star system, a whole different world." Jay shook his
head. "Carla—I can't pass that up, not without some real
hard thought."

Her face had gone wooden; he said, "Hey, I was
gonna pitch it better, get you sold on going with me, before I sprung it. You don't think I want to go by myself,
do you?"

Briefly Carla pursed her lips; then she said, "It's up
to me, you mean?"

"Pretty much. Yeah, I guess it is."

"Then that's all right. And Jay—I *will* think about it."

"So. Three for home, three undecided," Casey said.
Tabor decided not to mention the effect of Jay's words on
his own intentions. Another *star*, for Pete'sakes? She
added, "We can count on you mugwumps, can't we, to
help us homing pigeons?"

Vivi nodded. "For what it's worth, sure. Because you
never know: *I* might want to get back, later. But I doubt
the lot of us carry much influence either way." Luke's own
thought, exactly.

Before any other could speak, Udeen burst out, "All
of you—you may not be where or when you wish, but you
*have* a place." On the small, uncompromising face, tears
looked incongruous. "I have none. I was of Hykeran Outjut. Now, even were I returned there, I would not belong.
I fled my own liegedom for Ahearn; now *he* is taken. By
Lord Frey, whom you, Tabor, cozened him into trusting. I
should kill you for it, but I have no heart to do so. Or anything else. For me, nothing remains."

She stood. "Belonging nowhere, I do what is necessary."

Alycia caught her at the door. "Wait. We're all of us
screwed up, with this time-jerking. Stay with me; we'll
work something out." With a gesture to the others she
eased herself and Udeen out of the room and closed the
door behind them.

* * *

Sobered by the small liegewoman's anguish, the remaining group had little to say. Luke reached to Casey. "I'm stretched too far, can't take any more. Let's get out of this morgue."

They left, but if Tabor expected a lull he guessed wrong. Reaching the conference room he and Casey were just in time to encounter Lord Frey entering from the room's opposite side.

No need to ask if he'd been in a fight; his torn clothing, smudged and bleeding face, and dogged, weary gait told the story. His gaze held to the floor ahead of him; only when Luke spoke did he look up, stopping in his tracks. "Frey. Are you all right? What happened? Where's Ahearn? And Mardeux—"

Frey's stare brought silence. "Mardeux's gone. He won't be coming back." Shockingly, the big man giggled. "He can't. No matter what he does. And I hope he bursts an artery trying."

"I don't understand," Casey said. "What did you do?"

"His own plan," Frey said, flat-toned, "with necessary embellishments. First, struggling in time's river and hampered by entanglement with Ahearn, I was hard put to survive. When the rebel somehow fell free I was able to force the duke back into normal time, and there I made short work of him." He grinned. "Cut his consciousness off at the carotids, you might say. Then, entering the river again, I took him downtime toward this Island's end, intending that he awaken beyond the Hiatus, tied to universal entropy for so much of his life as might remain."

Another giggle. "I *told* you my revenge would beggar any physical torture. My regret is that I shall not see his face when he comprehends it." He raised a hand against comment. "But soon I realized my plan had flaws. Three of them, in fact."

Luke waited; Casey said, "Three?"

"Yes. We are not certain—we *can't* be—of the exact lower bound of the Hiatus. If I left him just short of my own established preemptive presence he might wake in time to outtime into the river and save himself. If I beached just beyond it, which would occur if I swam to my own forward cusp, I could find myself trapped also. And even were I to avoid those two pitfalls and strand Mardeux successfully, he would still retain his holdings, his power."

"So?" *Get to it, man.*

"Then," said Frey, "I remembered his intentions for the pair of you. Once more into the river I swam us far uptime, to the Genocides period. And after painstaking search located an Island, very likely the same you experienced. *There,* at its lower reach, I left the duke to a fate worthy even of him."

Something felt wrong, but Tabor couldn't pin it down.

"And Ahearn?" Casey asked. "Where's he?" *Or when.*

"Yeah," said Luke. "Udeen's going through hell; she thinks he's gone forever. If we could tell her . . ."

One hand made surrogate for a shrug. "In the river Ahearn drifts safely enough; you may reassure his small companion of that. When I regain strength I shall retrieve him."

"Won't *he* be frightened? Terrified? Someone else could—"

For the first time Frey's smile looked genuine. "I will join him only instants after he separated from us. He will barely have time to wonder what is happening."

"Wait a minute." In Luke's head, complexities were tying knots. "Won't you meet yourself? I thought—"

"In the river one cannot do so. Don't ask why; none of us knows. Think now: did *you* see yourself when passing the same time period a second time, or a third?"

"Well, no." Which didn't prove much; hell, in the river Luke could barely sense who was holding on to him or vice versa. But no point in arguing . . .

Now, though, his earlier misgiving crystallized. "Look, Frey; you left Mardeux uptime from your entire post-Rebirth civilization. Who knows what he'll do to causation, to your history? He could beget a whole new dynasty of timeswimmers—and when one of its generations hits an Island . . ."

Frey's grin came wholly savage. "I neglected to mention our stop at Hykeran Outjut. Since I did not allow Mardeux to regain consciousness, he will not know his genitals received sufficient radiation to scramble his genome. His sperm may seem viable, but he is no longer interfertile with our species."

Casey's horrified look contrasted with her sputter of laughter. Then, "You left him in the Genocides, unconscious?"

"Though I wish the duke the utmost in fatal misfortune, it is first essential that he know and relish his predicament. To that end, before departing I cleared the immediate area of human predators. For several, who distressed me esthetically beyond endurance, the removal was permanent."

He laughed. "I hung their scalps on Mardeux's belt. That act should gain him a lively welcome to the community." With a nod the Viking stalked away, stamina deadlocked with fatigue.

To Casey Luke muttered, "Life of the party, that's good ol' Frey." It was a cheap shot, but sometimes you have to.

In their room again, Tabor shucked his outerclothes and flopped onto the bed. "Anybody else knocks, I don't care who, can go jump."

"I'll sign for that." She lay down also; it couldn't have been long before they both slept. Waking first, Luke dressed and went out to the larger room, found coffee available from the machine, and filled two cups just in case.

Going back he closed the door quietly. Casey was awake, though. "Hey, coffee. Good idea; thanks." But as they sat, sipping away, neither found much to speak about.

Finally, stepping around a footstool, Luke went over to the panel Jay had used to evoke the holowoman. He had no real idea how the controls worked so he punched the center stud and waited to see what happened. When a figure appeared, facing and almost touching him, he moved back hurriedly. Well, according to Deri, none of the group were really comfortable with these forcefield holos. Not even Frey.

This holoperson was a man, medium height with rather generic good looks. "What is your selection?"

"What's available? News, sports, weather?" Soap operas? Where there's a *will* there's a way, maybe?

"Most of our usual selections, of course." Which told Luke exactly nothing. "One special event: an emergency Council meeting is in session. From these quarters one is authorized to attend by proxy. Do you so choose?"

Why not? But, "We'll be seen as well as seeing?" The image nodded. "Position us inconspicuously, then."

Luke and Casey placed two chairs side by side as the image indicated, and sat. The air took on a subliminal glow. Around them the room seemed to fade; its outlines became mere shadows across the new scene that appeared. To all intents, Luke found himself seated in the back row of a smallish auditorium.

Small, but not quiet.

"—*not* resigning!" declared the Prime Peer. "It is no successor I appoint, but a deputy authorized to act on my behalf. And I choose to name Count Derion."

Lord Frey, now cleaned up and neatly dressed, didn't like it. "I claim equal status by birth, and equal or higher rank by potance. So if there is to be no voting, then we must contest! My *will* against his, and the winner ..." Some of the background murmurs seemed to agree.

"We have only your word," said the leader, "that the Duke Mardeux did not die of your doing. Yes, I know—" He raised a hand. "If so, you had provocation, perhaps enough to justify. Still there must be a finding, a legal settlement of all salient issues. Until these things are done you cannot be eligible, and at this point we have no time for them."

"For myself," said Derion male, "I am willing to waive such obstacles to my cuz-cousin's candidacy. Yet this assembly, not any sort of contest, should decide between us."

Tabor heard a few grumbles; no one, however, spoke to demand place on the slate. The Prime Peer said, "I table this question for later consideration. More urgent is . . ." He outlined Aliira's proposal much as Luke had already heard it. "For us to implement this course of action we must at the Plenum display a unity of agreement. For it is necessary that *all* timeswimming potential be removed from this world's continuum. So I ask now: do we have that unity?"

"Leave Earth, all our holdings? Begin afresh, with only what can be laded to one small starship, or river-carried downtime within it?" The woman, handsome and statuesque, looked to be in late middle age and well accustomed to luxury.

"Begin small, yes," said Derya. "But among us we shall possess an entire world. The possibilities have no limit."

A younger man spoke. "Is it only swimmers who may emigrate? My genome does not carry that trait. Yet—a new world? I should like the chance to help establish ourselves there."

The Prime Peer's smile betrayed his fatigue. "While our paramount goal is removal of all timeswimmers from Earth, there are by no means enough potants of that ability to form a viable society. We shall need many others, Changed and Unchanged both. Your desire is noted. Favorably."

There seemed no end to the raising of caveats, but finally, after much more discussion than seemed necessary, the group agreed to agree.

On that one matter, at least.

In a nasal, twangy voice, a tall man two seats ahead began complaining about something Tabor didn't understand at all; the Prime Peer's obvious impatience indicated the issue to be trivial. Bored, Luke stretched his legs straight—and toppled the empty chair directly in front of him. Surprised that he and it were solid to each other, quickly he reached to set it upright, and again was startled. For his tactile sense told only that he was touching something, and the weight of it—nothing at all about texture, temperature, or the like.

So this was what being a force field image was about. Yet his real body had to be going through the same motions—and looking pretty foolish, likely. And suddenly he was reminded that maybe force fields didn't have to pee but he certainly did.

Now how was this going to work? He had to get his real body to a real toity, and here in public he certainly couldn't put this image through the motions. (If he did, would it make the illusion of a stream? He didn't want to know!)

Maybe if he walked this one out into the hallway, he'd snap back from here. Standing, he took two steps before his real shin hit the footstool in the bedroom; here at the auditorium he tripped over nothing to land on hands and knees, real and imaged impacts mingling in decidedly odd fashion.

"Damn!" It came out an explosive mutter; in desperation he whispered, "Get me out of here" and found himself back in the room. Beside him, oblivious to this reality, Casey looked in the direction where her image self had seen him vanish.

While he thought it over he took his leak, then returned to the real chair. "Put me back there."

As the auditorium materialized again, only Casey noticed his advent. Standing two rows forward, the twangy man had most of the attention. With his gun aimed at the Prime Peer.

No one moved; on every face Tabor saw the set look of *will*. No single person could withstand such numbers; there had to be two sides here. Suddenly Luke realized: all this *will* being thrown around, and he himself felt no slightest effect.

Because he wasn't really here! He was solid, though. . . .

His body made up its own mind. Hoping to hell he wouldn't run into something back in the room, he took two leaping paces. One hand knocked the gun up off its aim; the other chopped a murderous rabbit punch to its holder's nape. Tabor braced against pain—but of course his real hand hadn't hit anything . . .

The twangy man went limp. Off balance, Luke's real body fell, taking his holoself down also. Getting to his feet again, careful not to trip on another unseen obstacle, he started back toward his chair.

To be stopped by Frey's hand on his arm. "Man! I heard you'd been developing resistance, but *this* . . ." Then the hand moved on the imaged arm and the big man grinned. "Clever. Very clever. If *I'd* thought of this trick, for the Plenum session . . ."

He blinked. "Where are you, really?" Abruptly he shook his head. "It doesn't matter. Don't flick back just yet, though." The big hand squeezed once, then Frey stalked to his seat at the forefront of the assemblage.

Sitting down, seeing the question in Casey's face, Luke said only, *"Will* doesn't work on holos; haven't you noticed?"

For answer she kicked him on the ankle. Not very hard, but back in the room it did hurt a little.

Guards, summoned by the Prime Peer, carried away his recent attacker. Also they escorted several persons pointed out by that leader as the downed man's supporters. Outnumbered and now lacking any advantage of surprise, these latter submitted to manacles without further resistance.

The Peer rapped for order. "When we finish here I wish to speak with the man who subdued Fenian, heir apparent to the Duke Mardeux. Sir, you have my thanks. But first there is another matter, in which we shall need to persuade the full Plenum to a radical change of announced plan." And, much the same as Derya had told it to Luke and Casey, he explained the threat Bruce Garner's death posed to the very existence of the Changed, and her proposed solution.

It wasn't selling; these people didn't want to believe, so they weren't. Derya, Tabor decided, had made one big mistake: had Frey been informed privately, included as one of the insiders, he might have gone along. But having it sprung in open meeting as a done deal, the Viking got his back up.

"We are here; we live!" Pounding one fist into his other palm, Frey paced. "I have begun a valid program of genetic resurgence; I will not have it destroyed by timid theorists."

"Oh sit down," Derya snapped. "Try using logic rather than offended arrogance. I also essayed a program, and with high hopes. But the loss of Bruce Garner, in one of *your* battles, renders both our attempts futile. We must return the seeds of Change to that time when they need emerge, or imperil the very existence of our kind."

Frey sneered. "You would climb into your stargoing pillbox and run away? Entrust all our destinies, or so you see it, to the mercies of pre-Genocides Unchanged? Well, I shall not. Once we finish here, then at Hykeran I resume my own project."

"You must not!" Aliira's voice, as she stood, was pleading. "What is your difficulty? Do you not comprehend the danger?"

"Certainly. But put simply, I don't believe it."

"Belief or no belief," came Derya's edged voice, "the whole of us can't risk our all for your whim."

"It is hardly your choice." Frey's tone mocked her. "Do you propose to stop me? Exert your *will* then, acolyte of my cuz-cousin. Subdue mine, and I'll conform to your wish."

He laughed. "Mardeux might have done it. And my old friend and enemy, Count Derion your somehow-relative, could always give me a good run. But you, novice from the fringe of inaccessible time? Whatever force you think you can mount, Deriana, proceed!"

*Take your best shot.*

She turned to the Prime Peer. "Your permission, sire?"

"Contest it, if you must. The two of you."

Seeing Deri's shoulders move as if bracing for combat, Tabor knew better. "Two on one is chicken fun," the old playground saying went. But the urgency of this matter allowed no room for fairness.


"I—I don't understand!" Bleary-eyed with exhaustion, Frey dripped sweat; neither of the Derions showed to much better advantage. But after long struggle, clashing *wills* impartially battering everyone physically present, together they had forced the Viking's surrender. For Casey's and his own proxy/image vantage Luke felt profoundly grateful; just watching the three had put him through the grinder.

"You're *both* Derion." Frey shook his head. "You can't be, yet to my mind you register identically. How . . . ?"

*Trade secret.* But surprisingly, Derya said, "I needed to circumvent preemptive presence. By means of regenesis I did so. Thus, both my current and earlier selves can be here."

Mutterings swept the hall. Leaning forward, the Prime Peer said, "And which are you?"

"The later. And no, my memories of *his* stage of my life do not include meeting *me;* I have, I fear, produced yet another causative discontinuity. I regret the necessity, and fully support Aliira's plan to avoid further breaches."

She added, "Returning our pre-Genocidal guests to their own time will inevitably create a major one. As will, for that matter, the removal of timeswimmers from Earth. But to ensure the beginning of our subspecies, and put a stop to the random addings of strain to the continuum, these risks must be taken."

"And you've tricked me into helping incur them."

Oddly cheerful, Frey seemed better recovered than Luke would have expected. "Well, another visit or so to our far past might yield me some amusement, come to that."

He looked around. "Someone there must be, here, desiring to return me a favor. Ah yes: Sarise?"

With a start the pampered-looking woman, the one who had fretted over leaving her possessions, turned to face Frey as he said, "I need an errand run, having exhausted the energy required to do it myself. Pop into the river, would you, like the good and grateful person I know you to be? And fetch Ahearn. You'll find him downtime a bit, but still within your reach."

Looking perplexed, after a moment she nodded. "Where and when do you wish him brought?"

The big man smiled. "Here and now would suffice."

The familiar whorling blur took her. Two breaths later, another formed, then dissipated. Shucking loose from the woman with no waste of time on thanks or other such formalities, a gasping Ahearn glared around him. "Where's Mardeux?"

He didn't calm easily, but Frey managed it. Word of the duke's fate brought a war whoop; for a moment Luke wasn't sure whether the man would hug his uncle or strike him. In the end he did neither, but shook his head and demanded, "All right, what's happened to Udeen? Where is she?"

Aliira told him; without a word he was out the door.

"Frey and Derion and—uh, *and* Derion," said the Prime Peer, "I will speak with your further." And raising his voice, "For the rest, we stand adjourned here."

He'd forgotten about wanting to talk with Tabor, but Luke didn't mind at all.

# TWENTY-TWO

### ※

**P**ullman or elsewhere, late November wasn't Luke's favorite time of year. But splicing back into time, near as possible to where he and Casey had left off, he didn't have the option.

Deeming a Plenum vote too risky, the Prime Peer had bypassed the larger body and apparently was braced to take the rap for it. Further, to ferry the abducted far-pasters uptime he assigned additional high potants to assist Frey, Aliira, and the Derions. All in all, Tabor wished him well.

Aided by a young man named Jorr, Derya and Aliira first brought their group to the hospice at Hykeran Outjut, not long after Luke and Casey had last seen it. Vivi, Jay, and Carla had decided that even if they did settle downtime, they needed to say a few good-byes. "Call me sentimental," Carla explained.

"Not really," Alycia said, "or you wouldn't leave again. And then offworld, leaving *everything* behind."

Suddenly quiet, Carla only shook her head.

Deri was off helping Frey coordinate the other timeswimmer assistants, to shepherd the Viking's own abductees. "That's our good luck," said Deriana. "He can keep an eye on Frey, just in case." The big Viking hadn't disclosed his own stopover agendum; likely his party wouldn't be seen again this side of Pullman.

After Hykeran came Genocides Island; being there again depressed Luke. From behind scraggly brush they watched a grinning Frey implicate the unconscious Mardeux in outrageous massacre. Then, safely uptime from the Island's perilous lower end, they took some needed rest. In summer's warmth.

For that refuge Derya chose a wooded Islet inhabited only by noisy birds and a few bumptious gophers. Violence had been here: a half-burned shanty lay amid shattered trees. All was overgrown with grass and weeds; the debacle had not been recent.

Time in the river defied measure, but the hospice breakfast seemed ages ago. A spectacular sunset found the nine of them around a fire of scraps, the shanty's leavings, dining on rations from the hospice; the blaze served to heat them well enough.

Not for the first time, Derya opened discussion on the matter of reentry: into the world of studies and labs and ball games. And of course, police and jails and felony charges . . .

Where and when? How to reconnoiter? Who first to approach, who to *make* first recons? Too many possibilities, too many opinions; roused from his fugue by good company and a full stomach, Tabor shook his head.

"Look. We can't tell the truth, any of it. We have to rig this so that little—preferably nothing—needs explaining. Then we play by ear and take our chances. Here's how I see it. . . ."

Close beside them in the jail's holding room, an opaque, swirling air mass dissipated. *There we went.* Tabor looked around; whatever else, the special effects had quieted the house. He hoped it would stay that way. Then relaxed; Derya could cope.

For what had anyone seen? Air murking up around a group of people, apparently moving slightly, then clearing. Not an event susceptible to explanation; not easy to blame on anyone, either. So far, so good.

No plan could hold against conspicuous discrepancies. Clothing had been chosen to match what each last wore in home time, including a dress resembling the robe in which Casey had been hauled downtown. Deriana's unbelted coat disguised her contours; her hair was trimmed to match the style she had worn here as Derion male. Jay's beard was gone. As nearly as possible, visible changes had been minimized.

Not all, though. Moments before, Junior Yancey and Bruce Garner had been here; now they weren't. But in all the to-do, could anyone keep count? And if they did, so what? People just disappearing: who could explain such a thing? Or believe it . . .

A police sergeant came, peering in through the barred door. Derya's face took on the look of *will*.

"I don't know how you got us out of there," Casey said, ignoring the light cold rain as they walked. "All I'm wondering is why you didn't do it the first time."

It was still Tuesday, Tabor told himself in wonder, and barely past nine-thirty. Here in chilly Pullman, WA 99163 only about an hour had passed since the end of his session with Franson's tutorial group. While far in this era's future . . .

". . . take you downtime anyway, and there you all were, nicely gathered for me," Derya was saying. "Well, I did have two more in mind. But given the situation it seemed simpler to leave immediately than try to deal with procedural complexities I didn't fully understand. Now, however . . ."

"Oh, good!" Casey cut in. "There's a cab at the stand." They had walked only a few blocks, but not all, when arrested, were dressed for this weather. Shivering, Casey rapped at the window; old Ludie the night man looked up and came outside.

"Where to, folks?" Seven plus Ludie made a tight fit, but with Casey on Luke's lap and Carla on Jay's, everyone managed.

Caught off guard, Tabor couldn't remember his own street number. All right: "Sarge's Select Foods. Up the hill on Oak."

Ludie put the cab into motion before saying, "Ain't likely open, this late of a weeknight."

"That's okay." Something else wasn't, though: did anybody have any *money?* "Casey? Maybe we'd better stop by and see Maylene first." He whispered, "Borrow some cash so we can pay!"

"Oh. Yes." To Ludie, "We need to make a side trip," and gave her address across the hill, at the bottom of Monroe.

There, after a surprisingly brief visit indoors, she climbed back onto Tabor's lap. "Here. Maylene could only spare a twenty, but Cliff was there and came up with fifty more."

"I'll keep track. Okay, on to Sarge's." So Ludie nursed his cab back across the hill, to the darkened store.

"Told you he'd be closed."

"That's all right; here you go." These days the old Norwegian drove only part-time, to stretch his Social Security pension; Tabor overtipped.

Upstairs at his apartment door, he realized he hadn't the faintest idea when the hell his keys were. "Excuse me," said Derya, and knocked. After a few seconds the door opened.

"So you have succeeded," said the Lady Aliira.

All right; simple enough for Derya to drop Jorr and Aliira off here. Could have said something, though.

Leading the way inside, Luke turned up the thermostat—Casey wasn't the only one shivering—and said, "Get comfortable, folks; I'll see what's to eat." Well, there sat the bag from Sarge's: buttermilk, bread, Swiss cheese. By now, of course . . .

By *now?* Downtime he'd lost track of the days and weeks, but here—ninety minutes, tops, since he'd set this bag down. Tabor shook his head. "Jay? See if there's beer; I forget. I could make coffee, though. Yeah, I'll just—"

Casey gripped his arm. "Sit down, Luke. I think you need to." She was right, of course, so he did.

". . . that your group had been detained at my agency's request," said Derya. "Specifying none, but relying on implicit assumption of authority." She could make that stick, all right. "No record remains; I confiscated the arrest warrants, and . . ."

"The guy believed you?" Casey sounded incredulous.

"I *willed* him to believe."

"Right," said Jay. "But whoever authorized the arrests still has a bug up his tail. What happens when he catches on and sends out the next round?"

Derya spoke patiently. "Until we find and neutralize the source of this persecution, you five require oversight. Deri and Frey can help, since none of Frey's lot were implicated in—"

"Hey!" Jay cut in. "What about the rest of the Brigade? Maybe they're getting collared right now."

Patience ended. "We cannot shield all who demonstrated! For a time, some may indeed suffer inconvenience." She looked at Rozak a moment longer, but her comment had put a cork in him.

From the bathroom Aliira called. "This device does not operate properly!" Derya went to explain that unlike the units of their own time, this toilet did not function as a bidet.

When, Carla asked, would Deri and Frey appear? Alycia said Frey had to drop people off over several years, so it would take him longer. No, said Tabor, that didn't apply to swimmers. Frey *had* left here after the others, though, "so preemptive presence holds him away now. But Deri hasn't been here before, so—"

"Ah, but he has," Derya put in. "*I* was here, still of his same identity, to the very moment we entered the river."

Well, yes . . .

Bed and sofa, plus one beat-up sleeping bag, weren't going to sleep nine very well—let alone any latercomers. Rozak cleared his throat. "Our place; we have room. And there's a stack of mattresses, bunk bed size. Left over from the frat days, but clean. So whoever wants . . ."

Frey and thus Deri would come here to Tabor's. "And when Frey arrives," Derya stated, "I wish to greet him."

For quite different reasons, Vivi felt the same way concerning Derion male.

"That just about fills you up here," Carla said. "We can handle everybody else."

The walk was only six blocks or so, but largely uphill, and *cold*. Belatedly Tabor found his spare keys, and detached the Tesla's. "Here, Jay. My car holds five if you breathe by odds and evens, so I can't drive you up. Get it back tomorrow?"

"Sure. Thanks."

Young Jorr spoke. "Now that my job is done, I would seem to be superfluous. My return to Hiatus would ease the crowding."

Derya's brows lowered. "I thought you wanted to look around here, get the feel of the era, pre-Genocides."

"I had so intended, yes. But . . ."

"Well, then," said Jay. "Like I said, we have plenty of space." Jorr's misgivings allayed, the five took leave.

"I've wondered, Derya," Casey began, "why you and Frey both wound up *here,* before. I mean, with all of time and space . . . ?"

Deriana smiled. "The same needs: a time before the Changed appeared, yet technologically advanced, so those we took might adapt to our era. And well clear of the Island's downtime end. Fatigue, I fear, governed my own beaching. Near a city: Seattle. Its major university seemed a prime source for my project; later circumstance, of course, changed those plans."

"You didn't know Frey was here too?" Casey asked.

"I knew he had similar goals, but in the river I saw neither him nor sign of any exit. When I came to this town, by physical transport, he sensed my presence and veiled his own. I did not detect him until he stood to disrupt the demonstration."

She shrugged. "There was more, but that is the most of it."

The river's equivalent of jet lag had tired everyone.

As soon as enough beds were improvised, Luke and Casey retired to the bedroom. "See you tomorrow, folks."

In bed he stayed awake long enough to kiss her good-night.

Voices brought Tabor awake. Rolling out of bed, he put on pants and shoes; leaving Casey undisturbed he went to see what was happening. On the sofa, holding a beer, sprawled Lord Frey, flanked by several women including Seena Haymes.

"Hi," said Luke. "As always, your timing's perfect. Where's Derion?" And why was Seena here, ten years displaced?

"I emerged as far uptime as my earlier presence allowed. Derion essays a task, but asks me not to speak of its nature. Our current need, I would think, is provision for these females who are to reproduce my subspecies." Emptying his beer flask he let it drop; first pausing, it arched its way to the wastebasket. And in a brief swirl of darkened air, the big Viking made exit.

Of Frey's captures, nineteen had survived and been brought back uptime. Each of the eight men chose return to his own departure time. Five of those were near the current date, and all eight agreed to keep contact with the group, now and later.

The women, though. Nine carried child, eight by Lord Frey's contriving. Some could at least blend into previous routines relatively unnoticed; others faced unexplained time lapses of two to ten years. None, however, wished to be cast loose, alone and pregnant. Even Carol Harper, the blond woman who had conceived before taken by Frey, felt she needed the group's support.

"If we're going to organize, work together," said Shelley Lenoir, "we'll need facilities. Residential, for starters."

"As soon as possible," said Derya, "I shall locate a suitable property. Meanwhile I trust that some of you can utilize current abodes, and perhaps make room for others: those absent too long for easy explanation."

Around her, then, a hum of discussion grew. But apart from the rest sat Seena Haymes: neither pregnant nor, apparently, interested in group planning. And looking somehow older.

Luke sat to face her. "Well, Seena. How come you didn't go back and pick up your career where it left off?"

"Because I had a better idea. Much better. I was kidnapped, you see—by humanoid, English-speaking aliens. Talk about publicity . . ."

A grin restored her youth. "Tabor, it's perfect! Every word of my story will be exact truth. I don't know where I was taken—and if anyone happens to think of *when*, that's all right too, because how would *I* know? But I saw thus and so, this and that happened. There were other captives, of course," and she reeled off names of timenapped persons killed in Ahearn's attack. They'd strengthen her case, all right, but . . .

Tabor's face must have betrayed his reaction; eyes narrowed, she said, "You think I'm callous? Look, it's not as if I could bring them back to life."

True enough. "Skip it. What else do you have in mind?"

"A routine physical will prove I haven't aged any ten years; right? And get this! When Frey took me I had a new temporary filling. Good for six months, maybe; in ten years it'd be shot to hell. That dentist wasn't much over thirty so he's probably still healthy. And he'll know his own work; they all do."

A deep breath. "They can't catch me on what's happened since then; I don't know and don't intend to find out. Current slang or politics or fashions or *one damn thing* that could trip me." She spread her hands. "You see any holes in it?"

Luke couldn't. "You'll have to begin from scratch, though. Any money you had, before . . ."

"Bingo! My will has it all in trust for my niece. She's an orphan, gets the money in three more years, when she's eighteen. For now it pays her support; that's all she knows about it."

She waved off any objection. "Proving I'm alive, legally, may take a little time. But it's a sure thing."

Suddenly she looked very earnest. "It's not as though I was stealing from anybody. I mean, it practically *is* true."

Just as suddenly, Luke's own reservations collapsed. "Hell yes, kid. You've got the cards; go play 'em."

Discussion over, they rejoined the main group. Derya was saying ". . . good diamonds, as I brought before, and brokered in Seattle. So, financing should be available early next week."

"Sooner," said Vivi LaFleur. "I make big bucks and keep half my portfolio liquid, like anybody who grew up poor. Find your property; I'll spring for the down payment." Her sudden grin made her an urchin. "Hey, if I go downtime to stay, you can have the whole schmear. Whoever runs the place, I mean." She paused. "Well, except something for my family. They don't deserve it, but what the hell—you have to, don't you?"

"I can help too," Seena put in. Odd looks came her way. "Okay, so I'm not part of it. But at Hykeran I sure as hell was, and things being different I'd carry the same load you all are. So take it the way it's meant and don't give me any crap."

Wow. Luke guessed he'd got to her more than he'd thought.

Alycia Frazier did not disabuse anyone of the belief that she too was still pregnant. As Jay had put it, "If Frey found out she'd miscarried, he might want to give her a jump start."

Deliberate or not, Luke felt the pun was best ignored.

Half-past last night was no time for a hike, but these women needed places to sleep and Tabor wasn't pregnant. Bundled up, he plodded overhill to the former fraternity. At the parking lot behind it he remembered the key he'd taped, two years ago, under a fender. Kneeling down, he found the tape had petrified, but clawed it loose with fingernails intact. If he didn't want the Tesla reported stolen, he'd better call Jay early.

He didn't have to, though. Shelley to the Thetas, Carol to the dorm, three doubled into the apartments of another three, but still a final trio with no place to go. So, leading that group he climbed the stairs to Jay and Carla's loft after all.

At a quarter to five. Jay was no happier to be wakened than Luke had been.


Back to labs and classes: teaching or taught, Tabor figured to be rusty. To others he was here today the same as yesterday. But for maybe three months he'd struggled with problems and events these people couldn't so much as dream of, not system equations or the vagaries of lab instruments. Entering his first class he truly sweat the coming day. Lack of sleep didn't help.

Somehow, though, familiar surroundings helped him pick up pretty much where he'd left off. There came moments of disorientation, incongruity, but mostly he coped well. Until midafternoon when fatigue began collecting its dues, and by that time he had enough confidence to coast a little.

Tabor wasn't much of an actor but Alycia Frazier was even worse. Luke coached her: "Remember, you'd just begun dating Bruce; you're only a little surprised he's disappeared. And curious." Luke saw her performance as transparent, but no one else seemed to notice. As Garner's lab instructor he was entitled to more visible concern; still he knew a guilty relief when interest in the mystery died away.

By the end of the week he was able to quit worrying, and even make some progress on his long-neglected thesis.


Rozak had been right; the second day home, more Flag Brigade members were arrested. Jay wasn't happy about waiting until Ray Higgins the lawyer returned, but Deriana insisted.

It was Aliira, though, who accompanied the pudgy little man on his rescue mission. The way it worked was that he spoke the legalities and she *willed* the magistrate to agree with them; all cases were summarily dismissed. "Actually," she said afterward, "Counselor Higgins seemed quite surprised that his arguments resolved matters so easily."

With the new batch of arrests, down from Spokane came Channel Four's Sybil Shumway. Her main interest was another interview with Vivi LaFleur. Watching "State of the State," Luke and Casey could sympathize with Ms. Shumway's frustration.

For Vivi stayed largely with the Misery Tax issue, finally giving Shumway one newsbreak carrot: her possible retirement. "I'm considering a major break, to a different arena. Far, far different. I doubt that it will draw much media coverage."

Casey whooped. "Would you look at that *deadpan?*"

Whether or not Vivi's words *or* the Apple Cup demonstration had any great effect, the state legislature caved in to voter resentment. Headlined AXELSON AXED, the story reported a rush to disavow the tax package, even by its original sponsors.

"I'm springing for a keg tonight," said Jay Rozak, "and getting the whole Flag Brigade fried."

Returning from her Seattle jaunt, Derya gave assurance that finances were well in hand. Meanwhile, aided by a consummate hacker from Rozak's Brigade, Aliira enriched major data nets with solid backgrounds for the visiting Changed. So if Derya liked the property recommended by Jay and Carla, she was free to dicker on it.

Kamiaken Clinic, a few miles out from Pullman, was deep in hock. Inept management, apparently—its professional reputation was sound. Boning up enough to pass as a medical administrator acting for financial backers, Derya bought heavily into Kamiaken and began expansion plans.

"The fertility clinic," she announced, "can be cover

for our sperm bank. I'll breathe easier when our downtime gamete supply is stored in currently standard containers." With that task accomplished, actual operation could begin.

Vivi financed a cluster of fast-build housing adjacent to the clinic and its existing staff residences. Derya purchased three vans, for commutes from Kamiaken to jobs and classes.

On Military Hill, across the valley from Wazoo, Seena Haymes bought a large, rundown house, paying double shifts to ready it for occupancy. Soon only Luke and Casey and Jay and Carla remained in their original digs. "I have to hang around," said Tabor, "for Frey and Deri to home in on."

When Deri did turn up, Luke came close to fainting.

*"Bruce!* How—?" *I don't believe it.*

Dirty and sweaty, bruised and scratched, Bruce Garner stood on shaky legs between Frey and Deri, as Frey addressed him: "If you wish to bathe, perhaps Tabor can oblige you."

The tall man's glare emphasized his words. Swallowing hard, Luke said, "Yeah, sure; right in here, Bruce."

Shepherding the younger man toward the bathroom, he heard Deri's stage whisper: "He has not been told."

From the bath came sounds of water running and splashing. "All right," Luke demanded. "How can this be?"

"Frey was barred from that time," said Deri, "but I was not. He shared with me his mind-registering of young Garner, the timing, and the locale. Thus prepared I went to the point of Ahearn's attack and found the boy. Another man, following him, raised his gun to shoot. By *will* I threw that one to the ground, then outtimed Garner and myself into the river, meeting with Frey at an agreed moment earlier in Hykeran. Then we came here."

This guy, thought Tabor, could make a pretty fair reporter. "And Bruce doesn't know, you say? That he was killed, I mean?"

"Such knowledge," said Lord Frey, "may have distressing consequences to the mind."

"Before he meets the others," Luke said, "we'd better brief them." Come to that, he could have used some briefing himself.

At the loft next day everyone played the reunion coolly—except Alycia, whose loss of control seemed to strike Bruce as natural enough. Tabor laid no odds against her unbagging the cat sometime in future, but later certainly beat sooner.

Equally shaken, Jay Rozak didn't reveal his own shock until he had Luke and Casey and Carla together in private. "This is fucking impossible! I saw him killed; hell, I broke Junior Yancey's goddamn neck for it." He shuddered. "So what's true now? Is Yanccy dead, or isn't he?"

"Wrong tense," said Carla. "Will be, you mean."

"Everybody will be. Eventually." Jay's voice rose. "And I *know* what I mean—did I kill him or didn't I?"

Carefully Tabor said, "You know what you did and what you saw. Timeswimming can't change what happened; it just slaps a patch on the results, sometimes." Luke shrugged.

And hoped he knew what the hell he was talking about.

". . . need to bring us all back here at all," Vivi said next day. "Not with Bruce rescued. Better hope *they* don't figure it out, or you all might get yanked downtime again." She hadn't said much lately, Tabor mused, about returning there herself.

Her conclusions, though, turned out to be wrong. Even though Garner knew nothing of the discontinuity in his own existence, somehow he learned of his crucial future role in the genesis of the Changed.

Luke came in at the middle of Bruce's surprising reaction. "Like hell I will! Look—I don't hate these people, not even Frey. But my whole life's work, damn it, is *not* going into producing that arrogant pack of overlords. Grab us, take us downtime, stick us in some kind of concentration camp ..."

"Changing your major, are you?" said Jay.

"No such thing. Just my specialty."

Luke squinted at him. "Like how?"

"Food crops. Soy beans never kidnapped anybody."

# TWENTY–THREE

✳

**C**hristmas vacation, Casey said, was probably the best time to get married. Well, sure, Tabor agreed. "Okay by me."

"Gee, Luke; don't get *too* romantic. I don't think I could stand it."

If they hadn't been well into the last minute or so before actual quiting, he might have taken the rebuke seriously.

First order of vacation business was moving to one of the new duplexes at Kamiaken Clinic; Jay and Carla had the other unit. The wedding was festive enough, Tabor guessed—although to his mind it merely rubber-stamped what already existed. Both his parents sent gifts but neither attended. Casey's folks did show up, though not long enough for Luke to get any real feel of them. Karen Cecile obviously enjoyed their visit. . . .

The Rose Bowl came as a welcome distraction, especially when the Cougs aced it with a field goal in overtime.

"I'd been a little worried, Carla," Vivi was saying as Luke joined them. "But my doctor says it's okay."

"What's okay?" he asked.

"The baby." For a moment she seemed embarrassed. "Hell, Tabor, you remember me as a kid. Downright deformed. But what it was—" Suddenly her tone changed to "country," straight childhood Lewis Gap. "We wuz dirtpore, us Lefebres. And some y'ars the crops done porely." Then switching back, "Vitamin deficiencies, while my mother carried me. Congenital flaws, not genetic. I was lucky not to have a harelip, maybe a cleft palate." She smiled. "But the baby's going to be fine."

Seena Haymes became every bit the nine days' wonder she'd hoped to be: major talk shows, newspaper features (as well as the inevitable scandal rags), a veritable flurry of magazine covers. As she'd predicted, nobody could shake her story. Eventually her notoriety faded into the comforting glow of lucrative film contracts and a holovid series. She played a young woman kidnapped by interstellar aliens.

Tabor wished her purely the best of luck.

At breakfast one damp March morning, Jay aired his disquiet. ". . . don't *know* what to do. I want to see that new world so bad I can taste it, but Carla . . ." He shrugged. "Yeah, you said you'd go if I really need to. But years of seeing you unhappy . . . !"

He shook his head. Frowning, Carla said, "And if we stay, *I* get that choice assignment? Not much of an option."

The Lady Aliira spoke. "Must you travel there yourself, Jay Rozak? Or would it suffice, partially at least, to know that your descendants could see that world? That they can—"

"I don't have any." Jay's tone came bitter. "And if I did: the way I hear it, after the Waste Times there's maybe a million or two alive, out of eight billion right now. Even if some of my genes beat those odds, kinship would be so diluted, by then, that it hardly counts. Sorry; the prospect doesn't appeal."

"I had not finished. I did not mean progeny so far removed. My proposal refers to your own child."

"Didn't you hear me? I don't *have* any. And Carla's . . ."

Is by Frey; right.

Aliira's patience showed ready to split at the seams. "*I* wish a child, bearing pre-Genocide Unchanged genes, to carry to the Hiatus and—and beyond. Your genome is

eminently suitable and your vigor of spirit attracts me."
She smiled. "So . . . ?"

His mouth moved without sound. Carla said, "Jealousy doesn't apply here. If she's right, if you'd feel better . . ."

"Yeah. My very own kid out there, and a Chi, to boot!" Then to Aliira, "Not from a cold start, though; we need to do this right." And, "Luke? Borrow your car?"

"Uh—yes, sure." Huh . . . ?

"Aliira," said Jay, "you and I are going out. Dinner in town, dancing, the works. Then we'll see what goes on, or doesn't." He stood. "Dress for it. Six o'clock okay?"

"Yes. Oh—one question: do you prefer a daughter or a son?"

Along in April, spring shifting from windy to warmer and shoots of winter wheat brightening the contour-plowed brown hills, Deriana held a board meeting. Of the Changed, only she and Deri and Aliira attended. Jorr was off happily researching life in pre-Genocidal times; Frey hadn't been seen since New Year's. Timenapped returnees present numbered nearly two dozen, lacking only Seena Haymes and two men of Frey's group.

Kamiaken Clinic, Derya announced, was now into operating mode. As a co-op corporation, herself chairing the Jailhouse Six as directors, the setup encouraged flexible governance. But now was the proper time, she said, to set policies for future aims. "As you know, not all of us will remain here much longer."

True, Jay muttered; nobody expected all those potants to hang around forever. "After all, they have to shag ass down to the Hiatus, push Greston's Island ship through space with Zen fusion. Maybe they'll reach Alpha Satori. . . ."

"I," Derya continued, "will remain to help set this project a stable course. After that . . ." Toward the Six, she gestured. "You are the ones who must provide long-term guidance, a stable outlook. For perhaps three generations."

Luke snorted. "Your time scale's off; we'll be in

rocking chair country by the time the *grandkids* hit puberty."

Deriana blinked. Aside to him and Casey she said, "But Frey—did not you six receive the L-series injections? That is his custom, with those in positions of trust."

"L-series?" Oh yeah, the shots that made him sick because he caught them all at once. "Does that mean something?"

"Longevity, of course." Numbly Tabor shook his head. "A partial regenesis, via a tailored virus that throughout every cell affects only the small gene-complex associated with aging. I had thought you would know . . ."

"How—" Casey stammered, "how long are you talking about?"

"Genetic potential varies; L-regenesis may double or even triple remaining life span. More precise estimates rely on assessing individual metabolic changes over several years."

Intent now, Casey said, "Would this effect breed true? Because if it does, you're starting the same elite-group set-up that brought on the Genocides."

Unperturbed, Derya said, "To produce any Changed at all creates that risk. This is why *guidance* is essential. But the L-factor is relative, not dominant or recessive; as with height or skin coloring, the result is not a dichotomy but a gradient."

Maybe so. Stunned by the concept, Tabor lost track of the meeting; Derya's bombshell had him on the ropes. Afterward he went to her quarters—to find the other five ahead of him, and Carla asking, "What's this about living longer? Casey says—"

Deriana explained. After moments of silence, Vivi spoke. "Those shots you gave me, down at Stopover. Same thing?"

"Yes, of course. I'd intended to treat you all—but Frey took care of it, so . . ."

"Talk about smelling like a rose! Imagine being in show biz and staying *young*." Vivi beamed, then sobered.

"Later I'd have to fake *that* out with makeup, wouldn't I?" Then a shrug. "If I go with Deri, there's no problem. But it's hard to decide." So despite her holovid statement, she still wasn't certain. . . .

Frowning, Rozak said, "You realize, we'll *all* need ways to cover up? New identities, stuff like that?" Then he grinned. "Hey. We had some tricks at the agency, could come in handy."

Casey looked anxious. "What about the others? Seena Haymes, for instance? She *is* staying in the holo business. Is there any chance she—I mean, did Frey . . . ?"

Derya shook her head. "And before you ask, none of us here has the remotest idea of how the L-sera are produced. You must accept the fact that this boon cannot be shared with others."

A grimmer note, thought Tabor, was that in a world menaced by overbreeding, such sharing would speed disaster. And Rozak said, "Which means we'd sure as hell better keep clam about it."

And how long, Luke reflected, could secrecy be held?

After dinner Jay reconvened the group at his and Carla's place. "We need to talk about the long haul. I mean—Derya, you keep saying we have to guide these new Changed, so they don't repeat the history you had. But you don't spell it out."

She pursed her lips. "What is your own view?"

"Authority—or special powers—means responsibility. Those kids have to know, right from the cradle, that *will* carries obligations. To protect their own kind by keeping it hidden. And that taking advantage of unearned clout is chickenshit."

*"Noblesse oblige,"* said Casey.

Jay grinned. "So your French is tidier than mine."

Carla wore a brooding look. "You realize we have to feed those kids altruism up the kazoo? Long before any Changed could appear; right from the git-go, we have to push it."

"Which means," Luke said, "we'd better make sure

we've cleaned up our own acts. Somebody has to set a good example."

Breaking a sobered pause, Vivi raised the question of other major problems: environment, overpopulation . . . Could just a small group of potants influence whole nations?

"Wouldn't have to." Alycia. "Take our Supreme Court. Turn two or three fuggheads around, the whole country steers better."

"And that idea," Casey said, "holds in other areas, too."

From there, Luke thought, the talk went pie-in-the-sky. Except for Deriana, who listened more than she spoke.

Next day she left on what she said was a recreational trip. Returning a week later, she didn't mention where she'd been. Tabor watched the news, but couldn't be sure of anything.

Commencement ceremonies came and passed; somehow Luke's long-awaited master's gave him no lift. To his parents' separate gifts and greetings he wrote thank-you notes as if he meant them. But the M.S. did give his teaching stipend a healthy boost.

One evening Jorr returned with a veritable library of holodiscs he'd recorded. And also three newly pregnant women: quite a recruiter was young Jorr. Janet Akito, a registered nurse, particularly impressed Luke; the other two deferred to Jorr, but Akito held her own with him beautifully.

"All dressed up and no place to go," said Vivi. "I wish Frey would get his butt in gear." She'd made her decision, to return downtime, but now the big Viking's absence kept the entire party waiting. Still wary, Derya wanted to make certain of the man's intentions before relinquishing the support of three perfectly good backup *wills*.

Then, late on a warm June evening he did appear—

not in a swirl of turbid air but walking dusty from a neighboring field, nose and cheeks peeling sunburn, ears hidden by shaggy hair, and face bearing several weeks' growth of beard. He wore coarse, ill-made cloth and badly cured hides; his hands and bare feet showed grimy callus; his grin was wholly carefree.

"Hoy!" Everyone sitting around the group's common courtyard turned to stare as the big man approached, then sat across from Aliira and the Derions. "I would welcome a cold drink."

"Plenty in the pitcher," said Jay, and from the next table handed it across. "So where you been, big fella?"

The past, the far past: Islands scattered over centuries. In only months of his own time, Frey had explored more than a few. "Ere we abandon Earth," he said, "I wished to see more of the times my kind never knew, that will be forever barred to us."

Forever? Yes. Once all colonists and supplies debarked from the starship, the exodus would be rendered irreversible. "How, I do not know," said Derya. "But Greston insists he can do so."

". . . did *not* meddle with history," Frey protested. "For instance: the man who was likely the Arthur of British legend, though known at the time by another name entirely. I did get him rather drunk a time or two, but that was nothing unusual. And—"

Even considering that Islands weren't necessarily when you'd like them to be, Frey's taste in visits struck Tabor as odd; most seemed to lack all historical interest. Winter famine in central Europe, the year *before* Vesuvius erupted, an uneventful harvest in early Mesopotamia: not what you'd expect the Viking to seek out. He'd made a stop near the time of the Crucifixion—but spent it among Germanic tribesmen, learning to hunt wild swine.

"And have you now had enough?" Deri asked.

"No!" Vigorously Frey shook his head. "One more swim, far as I can manage, even with occasional rest pauses. But then I'll return, and join our hegira to a distant world. And yes," nodding to Derya, "I shall visit here before going onward." He thought, a moment. "That event will occur some years forward, so I may see your progress and report it to the Prime Peer."

Later over dinner, with Frey clean and barbered and wearing fresh clothing, Aliira rather hesitantly broached a query. "How is it that you have changed so? Which is to say . . ."

Lord Frey nodded. "I know. The creature of impulse; any who stood in my way, regretted it." He shrugged. "Two factors, Aliira. Mardeux: after our final struggle it came to me that although I never shared his venom, my worst excesses bore more than a little resemblance to some of his lesser ones. Also—"

Briefly he grasped the wrists of Tabor and Rozak. "Familiar contact with Unchanged of this time, so different from our own. Love us or hate us, those downtime cannot but view us as beings almost supernatural. And of course we do not disappoint them."

"But these?" He laughed. "To them we're merely people who can do things they can't. Which is how it *should* be." And Tabor realized: Derya had once said much the same thing.

Frey's grip left Luke's hand numb and tingly; he flexed its fingers. "But why did you shift gears so fast? When the two Derions ganged up on you, you took the loss so gracefully. . . ."

The big man grinned. "My bombast at that time was sheer habit; my previous plans had become irrelevant, but still I resisted admitting the fact. Being pummeled by their two *wills* in concert gave me the excuse to do so."

He gestured. "What other choice? Downtime of Hiatus, in normal time, I could become Prime Peer over all who remained. A hollow glory! Or I could hide until the starship took all competitors away, leaving me to juggle causation with their earlier selves—and possibly, though not by intent, disrupt our continuum's reality irrevocably." Frey leaned forward. "Mardeux might have done so. But I am not Mardeux."

He waited for comment, but none came. "Well, then—what's left?" He spread his hands. "Why, to savor all I can reasonably manage of pre-Genocidal times. Before we all go sheeplike into the more limited society emergent on our new world. Oh, I'm sure it won't be as boring as it sounds—but I'm in no hurry for it!"

Some days he rode in to Pullman, spending hours at Wazoo's library. One afternoon Luke found a message on his phonedisc—the newly assigned office wasn't much bigger than a broom closet but the door did carry his name—to pick Frey up at the vet barn.

He found the big man querying a veterinary student who hammered a red-hot iron horseshoe, slowly spreading it wider. On their way out, Luke said, "What was that all about?"

"Learning."

Next evening was good-byes: Jorr and Aliira and Deri and Vivi for downstream, Frey to wherever he had in mind. Unplanned, dinner developed into a sort of farewell party.

Jovial, his harsher edges barely noticeable, Frey conversed freely. Most of the women's pregnancies showed unmistakably; blithely ignoring his own causative roles he complimented each on health and appearance.

Chance movement opened an aisle of view to where Alycia stood, slim and straight. Frey stared; seemingly frozen, she gazed back. Luke saw no scowl of *will* but slowly Alycia walked over to the big man. "That's right, I'm not. I miscarried."

"It is well I learned," said Frey. "I can yet—"

"You can damn well *not!*" Fire in her eyes, acid on her tongue: "That baby was sired by a syringe. And you wouldn't be much better; whambam good-bye I'm off to the future, don't forget to write only there's no mail service."

She aimed a forefinger. "Oh sure, you can use *will* on

me and I can't stop you. But I—I'm *asking* you not to. Please."

Seeing that he still listened, she said, "Bruce and I, someday. And he'll be here with me. You see?"

Tabor saw the effort it cost Frey, but the Viking managed a grin. "The numbers are too few, but I suppose we can spare one more. You suffered much; I will not impose my wishes further."

As she walked away he turned to Derya. "Now, your earlier questions. I have seen only the latter fringe of the Bronze Age, and intend going far past, to times known only in myth and legend. To learn what truths might lie in such old tales." And added, "I am prepared to spend considerable time, seeking."

Maybe so, but he didn't seem to be in much of a hurry.

Kisses, hugs and handshakes; from the Lady Aliira, Jay Rozak had an especially fond embrace. One cloaking twist of air for Frey, then a larger one for Jorr and Aliira and Derion who held Vivi. In moments the crowded room felt paradoxically empty; over the next half hour it emptied in truth.

Back to quarters, Luke said, "All good-byes are a lot alike. But the hardest are like this, when nobody's ever coming back."

"Not exactly," said Karen Cecile. "Frey is."

"Yes. You know, I think he may have actually grown up."

Casey looked puzzled. "Grown up? Oh—you mean, finally realized he has to accept limitations like anybody else?"

Tabor paused to think it out. "Yes—but there's more. You can't let the limits shut you down; you have to go right ahead, taking your best shots *within* the rules."

"If you say so." She frowned. "You know, I didn't expect to feel so lonesome."

"Well, Derya's still here for a while yet."

"Long enough for you to see your firstborn."

"Yes, that's true." Though he felt little relation to that pregnancy. After all, just *once?* On a smallish Island downtime from the Genocides, a time and place he'd never see again ...

"Stop gloating and come to bed."

"Quite." He started for the bathroom.

"Only if you hurry. Otherwise I'll start without you."

He hurried, all right. Because judging by her girth, they were getting close to cutoff time for this sort of thing.

Swimmers excepted, time's juggernaut neither slows nor hastens. Casey came to term in the heat wave August brings to the Palouse. With air-conditioning either out of order or never ordered at all, University Hospital emulated a broiler oven.

Frey's genes showed to advantage; the boy's face had the Viking cast but not the harshness. The touch of red in the hair of young Lucian Jay Tabor came from Karen Cecile.

Not Lucian West Tabor: "I'd never saddle a kid with Junior. And that's from *before* that sumbidge Yancey." Rozak pretended indifference to being namesaked, but fooled no one.

Born two days later, Carla's son resembled the Viking more truly. Of course he wouldn't sunburn so easily. . . .

All the Hykeran cross-matches, Luke reminded himself, carried the Chi gene group. But only on one side.

Now that program hit stride; birth followed birth like final due bill notices. Last came Deriana's son; the Changed, it seemed, ran to longer gestation. She dubbed him Lucian, also.

To Luke, the baby looked almost entirely like Derya. Except maybe the outsized ears.

Not long after, mothers and children moved to Kamiaken's own care center, Janet Akito in charge. And by fall term one van was rigged as a mobile nursery. Jay's idea: women enrolled in the university could visit and tend infants at free periods or between classes, with one of

Akito's aides presiding full-time. Near as Luke could see, it all worked.

Between a teaching fellowship and his own graduate course, Tabor had little time or attention for clinic affairs. He knew the sperm bank project was moving well and that the co-op was running in clover, but in the main his interests focused on his own work, Casey, and little L. J.

After a time he barely remembered that the boy was anyone's but his and Casey's. Chi-carrier or no Chi-carrier.

L. J. was five and his sister nearly three when Deriana, in *ex officio* meeting with the board, announced she'd overstayed her intentions far too long. "The clinic is financially stable and your teaching programs are excellent. I am no longer needed." Tabor lacked her certainty, but she wasn't asking anybody.

"What about Frey?" Alycia asked.

"He will not come," said Derya. "Neither here, nor downtime at Dietjen's Hiatus to join the exodus from Earth. I have resisted that conclusion but it is inescapable." She smiled. "Further, I am now certain it is no disaster."

Rozak scowled. "You're not worried he's ramping around somewhere, back in the morning of the world, doing something to screw things up?"

"I *know* what he has done. Consider the old Norse myths. Their Aesir are credited with having certain powers. . . ."

Brows rising, Casey said, "You think Frey went *way* back and started breeding Changed descendants?"

Derya nodded. "What could better account for the Norsemen's legends? An early flowering of Changed development, yet doomed to the Ragnarok of genetic extinction."

"Too small a gene pool, you mean?" said Bruce Garner. "But he'd have known, wouldn't he, that he couldn't seed a new race all by himself?"

"He did know. Consider: he could have taken specimens of Changed sperm—they are not locked away securely—to augment his own genetic endowment. But for reasons of his own, he did not."

She shrugged the mystery away. "Also supporting my major hypothesis is other evidence, circumstantial yet indicative. . . ."

"The blacksmith," said Luke, "at the vet barn, that time. Frey was studying basic Iron Age know-how, so he could take it back to the Bronze era."

"Then what happened?" said Alycia. "Why hasn't he ever turned up again?"

Jay spoke. "What if he just wanted his own little Asgard, sired all by himself? All his very own, to play with. He'd know it couldn't last, couldn't endanger future reality—but why would he trade such a fucking great experiment, for a lousy coach seat on Greston's joyride?"

He paused. "Maybe he did plan to return someday, and just plain slipped up. Forgot to peg the end of his Island. Lived past it and wound up stuck there."

Or, Tabor mused, the big Viking could simply have gotten himself killed. Somehow he couldn't quite believe that. . . .

"No matter," he said. "Derya's right; he won't be back."

Carla shook her head. "I don't know. How can you be so sure?"

"Because it's all in the myths," said Jay. "Frey the father of gods, the thunder god, with his hammer Mardeux that returns to his hand. But none of it survived Ragnarok."

"There you are." Luke spread his hands. "And if anything doesn't fit, blame it on discontinuous causation."

Now why, he wondered, did Deriana quickly hide a smile?

**F. M. BUSBY** lives in Seattle with his wife Elinor and their two cherished cats, Ivan the Terrible and Molly Dodd. His science fiction novels include eight in the worlds of Rissa Kerguelen, *The Demu Trilogy* in Barton's, and—each in separate continua—*All These Earths*, *The Breeds of Man*, *Slow Freight*, and *The Singularity Project*. His forty-odd shorter works tend to defy classification.

Buz grew up in eastern Washington and schooled there. His major studies, physics and electrical engineering, help him keep his numbers straight. Between college terms and two Army hitches he held various incongruously assorted jobs, all prior to his first career: communications engineering. In the Army and later, he spent considerable time in Alaska and the Aleutians, and swears his tales of Amchitka weather are simple truth. His interests include aerospace, unusual gadgetry of any kind, dogs, cats and people, not necessarily in that order.

In addition to this present book he has completed a stand-alone sequel to *Slow Freight* (forthcoming from Avon Books), and has another in progress.